God's Gym

Leon de Winter

god's gym

TRANSLATED BY

Jeannette K. Ringold

· *The* Toby Press

God's Gym

First English Language Edition 2009

The Toby Press LLC
POB 8531, New Milford, CT 06776-8531, USA
& POB 2455, London WIA 5WY, England
www.tobypress.com

God's Gym by Leon de Winter © De Bezige Bij, 2002
Translation © Jeannette K. Ringold, 2009

The right of Leon de Winter to be identified as the author
of this work has been asserted by him in accordance
with the Copyright, Designs & Patents Act 1988.

Publication has been made possible with financial support from the
Foundation of the Production and Translation of Dutch Literature.

ISBN 978 1 59264 265 6, *paperback*

A CIP catalogue record for this title is
available from the British Library

Typeset in Garamond by Koren Publishing Services

Printed and bound in the United States

Prologue

The confluence of circumstances on December 22, 2000

Notes by God for Mr. Koopman

Circumstance One

Anyone who looked at the earth from space three hundred million years ago would have seen a different image of the surface of the earth from the one that has become familiar to us from maps and from the photos that satellites send to decoding computers. You and I recognize the continents: the two teardrop-shaped North and South American scraps of cloth that are connected to each other by the umbilical cord of Central America; the fat, upside-down African *L*; jagged Europe that reminds you of a misshapen hand with a Greek, an Italian, an Iberian, and a Scandinavian finger; the dripping paint spot that is Asia; and the lost pieces of Australia and Antarctica.

Three hundred million years ago there were no continents. Before they came into existence around two hundred and twenty-five million years ago, the earth was covered by a gigantic ocean and one colossal continent, Pangea, or the "whole land" in Greek. No one knows exactly what Pangea looked like, but it probably resembled an embryo, with Asia forming the head, Africa the body, and Australia and Antarctica its little legs.

The Dutch mapmaker Abraham Ortelius—one of your compatriots—was one of the first who noticed that the coastline of America fit so nicely into that of western Africa and Europe. He assumed that America had drifted off because of earthquakes and floods, but his ideas on this subject gained very little support. It was not until 1912 that the theory of continental drift achieved a scientific basis with the publication of two articles by the German meteorologist Alfred Wegener, who dated the breakup of Pangea to more than two hundred million years ago.

Wegener had not only noticed that the continents fit together very nicely, but also that there were striking fossil and geological similarities between the east coast of South America and the west coast of Africa. In addition, the discovery of fossilized tropical plants in Antarctica could only mean that the soil of Antarctica had in the past been located in a much milder climate.

In his day, Wegener was considered crazy, but recent research has shown that he was right. What follows is almost certainly the cause of continental drift: the earth's crust consists of "tectonic plates" that move independently from one another. On the ocean floor there are mountain ranges that meander over the whole earth like the seams of a soccer ball. Along these mountain ranges the earth's crust is relatively thin, and from the interior of the earth new rocks are pushed upwards, which causes the plates to move and to collide with one another.

That is called an earthquake.

Circumstance Two

The large fault line that runs through the earth's crust of California is called the San Andreas Fault. This fault line indicates exactly where the tectonic plates of the Pacific Ocean and of North America press against each other. Through the centuries these forces can increase and be released in destructive explosions. This was the case in the Northridge earthquake of January 17, 1994. At exactly four thirty in the early morning it struck the suburb of Northridge, northwest of Los Angeles. (Were you at home?) The epicenter of the earthquake was located at a depth of twelve miles, and its force was six point seven on the Richter scale.

The Northridge Earthquake is said to have killed sixty people and resulted in nine thousand wounded and thirty billion dollars worth of damage. The earthquake took place along the Santa Monica Thrust Fault, a side branch of the San Andreas Fault. It lasted only fifteen seconds.

Circumstance Three

In the fall of 1945, in Ridgefield, Washington, Leonard S. Shoen built his first trailer in the stable of his wife Anna Mary Carty's family farm. He had set aside five thousand dollars in savings. He envisioned offering movers the convenience of a *do-it-yourself* and a *one-way* move. Shoen painted the trailer bright orange. Within four years it was possible to rent one of his trailers in any American city and to turn it in elsewhere. On each trailer it said in large letters: *U-Haul Co.—Rental Trailers—$2 Per Day.*

Nowadays a U-Haul trailer or truck can be rented at more than fourteen hundred franchise rental centers. U-Haul is the largest American renter of moving vans and also one of the largest storage space renters. Anyone who is planning to move without the help of a professional moving company looks in the Yellow Pages, where U-Haul is the largest advertiser, for the nearest U-Haul office—often around the corner—to rent a truck. Every day thousands of these trucks drive through the residential areas of every American city (the office nearest you is on Lincoln).

Shoen was a special class of visionary. His idea about the use of rental trucks for moves was exactly what postwar, mobile America needed. U-Haul also did trailblazing work in the area of adapting truck models for movers.

U-Haul trucks are part of the US street scene and are real American icons. In the seventies, the Ford F-350 was the famous workhorse of U-Haul. Behind an angular front that reveals the van's early-seventies design, the F-350 has a detachable cab that has space for three adults. The cargo space, with the well-known extension above the passenger cab, has an enormous capacity. As much as twenty-one hundred cubic feet of household goods can be moved with it, sufficient for the possessions of an average family with two children.

The prototype of this truck was developed by the company technicians of U-Haul in Tempe, Arizona, and was based on the relatively lightweight F-350. Ford was skeptical about the wishes of U-Haul, but the prototype convinced the automaker that a sturdy cab could be placed on the light base. Between 1976 and 1979 Ford successfully built the modified U-Haul version. Even today many F-350s are still being driven through America. They can be bought second-hand either through U-Haul or through third parties, at prices starting at two thousand dollars.

Circumstance Four

During the night of January 16 to 17, 1994, the night of the Northridge earthquake, a sixteen-year-old Ford F-350, which had functioned trouble-free until that time, was in the service bay for routine maintenance at a used truck dealer in Northridge in the San Fernando Valley.

The well-known U-Haul logo figured on the worn sides of the boxy body, even though the truck had not been the property of the L. S. Shoen company for several years.

Because of the earthquake, the Ford slid partially off the rack, outwardly sustaining no damage (the reinforcements that had been designed for this model by the U-Haul technicians seemed to have absorbed the blow). Yet during the months that followed, traces of oil were noticed under the engine block. Mechanics replaced the oil pan gaskets twice. The leak turned out to be a stubborn one.

Circumstance Five

Lille is the capital of the French administrative district Nord; the city is one hundred and thirty-seven miles from Paris and only nine miles from the border with Belgium. Lille—the name comes from *l'île*, the island—was established between two arms of the Deûle river and obtained city walls in the eleventh century. Despite the destructions it suffered in the course of the centuries, the city flourished economically because of its location at the crossroads between the Netherlands and France. Just as in the Flemish cities of Bruges and Ypres, there was a busy commerce in wool and cotton.

The decline of the textile industry after the Second World War plunged the city into a deep crisis, and in the nineteen-seventies unemployment was so high that it looked as if the city would never be able to struggle out of its economic quagmire (this did not happen—since the opening of the high-speed rail link between Paris and London, the city has completely recovered). Anyone with ambition left.

Yves Pascal was the best bread and pastry baker in the city, but he had difficulty keeping his head above water financially. The middle class was shrinking in size, and all of the northwest of France was suffering from the collapse of the traditional nineteenth-century industries.

In 1962, Jim Bailey, an American soldier stationed in Germany, had a short stopover in Lille on his way to Dieppe. In Yves Pascal's well-known bakery, he bought several *chaussons aux pommes*, that were handed to him wrapped in soft paper by the girl of his dreams. She was Valerie Pascal, the youngest sister of Yves. Later that year she followed Jim, her great love, to America, and they have lived in Los Angeles since 1963.

By 1974, Valerie's brother Yves had saved enough money to be able to visit her, and after two months in Los Angeles, he returned to Lille to arrange the sale of his house and his business. Since then he has been living and working in Marina del Rey, California.

In the fall of 1974, Yves Pascal started Progress Bakery. Within a year his bakery had fifteen employees, primarily unskilled Latinos who were available day and night for minimum wages. He added pastries to his bread products.

Nowadays, Pascal's products are available in delicatessen shops and in upscale supermarkets. Pascal has bought a house at one of the yacht-basins in Marina del Rey and currently heads a company with ninety employees.

Circumstance Six

In 1994, the manager of Yves Pascal's Progress Bakery purchased a used Ford F-350. The medium-heavy truck, which had a built-in cooling unit, was offered by a second-hand truck dealer in Northridge for only twenty-five hundred dollars. The truck was built in 1978 and had two hundred and fifty thousand miles on it.

The salesman neglected to point out to Pascal's manager that a time-consuming and therefore expensive replacement of the oil pan gaskets had been carried out twice on the Ford, still without fixing the oil leak. The truck was sold without a warranty.

When the leak was discovered by one of the Progress Bakery drivers, the dealer refused to take back the truck. The manager made sure that the oil of the truck was checked and topped up monthly. Eight months after the discovery of the oil leak, the manager took another job that allowed him a normal night's rest. He is now working at a travel agency in Studio City.

On December 22 of the year 2000, the day that keeps cropping up here, the former U-Haul truck was being used by Yves Pascal's Progress Bakery. The regular driver was Juan Armillo, the son of a former illegal immigrant who had received a green card during a general amnesty in 1986.

Circumstance Seven

In 1942, when he became a soldier, Frank Miller was a shy eighteen-year-old shopkeeper's son from a small town in Idaho. At the end of the Second World War, he had fought the Japanese in the Pacific Ocean; in 1946 he was decorated and returned as an adult to the village of his birth. The last year of the war he had been posted in the Philippines, and to his surprise he noticed that he preferred its warm climate to that of his home state.

In May 1947, he left by bus for Los Angeles. He had planned to continue traveling to Hawaii, but he stayed on in LA. In a cheap one-bedroom apartment on Beachwood Drive in Hollywood, he hung his only suit carefully on a hanger as he looked at the rustling palm trees right in front of his window. The war hero found work at a convenience store; he restocked shelves and delivered purchases as cheerfully as possible—since that yielded tips—to coquettish ladies in the neighborhood.

During the evening hours he studied bookkeeping. In September 1949, he obtained his diploma, and with his very first job application got the job that he wanted: he became manager of the First Hollywood Commerce Bank.

Margaret Boyle was two years older than Frank. She was born in Fresno, and at the age of ten she moved to Los Angeles with her mother, who had become pregnant by a good-for-nothing alcoholic. She was twenty-three when she became the assistant to the senior administrator of a warehouse at the corner of Wilshire and La Brea.

She went regularly to the First Hollywood Commerce Bank and became charmed by the young man who invariably spoke to her. One day he asked her for a Sunday walk and picnic in Griffith Park. On the sixth date there was a timid chaste kiss. On the twentieth date he carefully fingered her breasts, and after the thirty-sixth date Margaret became pregnant. (Mr. Koopman: I'm only imagining this, but I do think that it went approximately like that.)

Frank Miller and Margaret Boyle—four months pregnant—were married in 1951, in a small church on Franklin Avenue in Hollywood. They had twins, two boys who both became doctors and found jobs and wives on the east coast, both in Connecticut.

In 1961 Frank was named manager of the branch in Marina del Rey. Two years later they moved to a small house in Playa del Rey, a coastal town just south of Marina del Rey, where they experienced the happiest years of their marriage.

At the age of seventy-eight—to be exact, on October 3, 2000, at one thirty in the afternoon—Margaret suffered a severe stroke. From that day on, Frank visited the Pharmacy del Rey regularly in order to get medicines for her.

Until that time they had barely seen a pharmacy from the inside (except for a short period during the illness of one of their sons) and were under the impression that they would reach the age of one thousand together.

Sometimes Frank brought Margaret a croissant from the fancy Progress Bakery which was right next to the pharmacy. But he saw that she ate it without zest, and it pained him that it was only for him that she chewed the croissant with such difficulty.

Circumstance Eight

Progress Bakery and Pharmacy del Rey in Marina del Rey are both located in plain, rectangular box-like buildings without any embellishment; functional structures, built with wooden frames and wooden walls, plastered with a thin layer of stucco, like most buildings and private dwellings in California.

Most of the floor space of the pharmacy is taken up by a chaotic display of suitcases, racks with cheap knickknacks, drugstore articles, candy, hats and baseball caps, and random stuff, like dolls or briefcases, that the owners managed to snap up at bankruptcies or auctions. It is only in the back of the store that the customer discovers the professional counter of experts in medications. This is where serious people in white coats carefully decipher the strange scribbles of doctors' pens and impassively give out real pills as well as placebos.

Customers of the bakery and the pharmacy can use the parking lot that is located in back of the stores. It can be reached only through a narrow gap between the two buildings. A total of twenty-five free parking places are available, but the customers of the pharmacy and the bakery prefer to park on the street, even though it costs twenty-five cents for ten minutes.

Why is the parking area not in demand?

Because it is surrounded by the barred windows of a number of neighboring buildings and because half a dozen garbage containers give the place a dreary, rather dilapidated prospect. There are surveillance cameras that connect to monitors in the bakery and the pharmacy, but the feeling remains that criminals will attack here. This has never happened.

The only people who do use the parking lot are the pharmacy suppliers and the drivers of the Progress Bakery delivery vans.

Circumstance Nine

On that same December 22, 2000, Jeremy Swindon gave a party in his home in Malibu to celebrate his sixty-fifth birthday. He had asked Kelly Hendel, the party organizer who since time immemorial had organized his cocktails and parties, to spare no expense this time. In past years, a party had cost around fifteen thousand dollars, but this time it could go up to twenty-five thousand. At eight o'clock in the morning the first van drove up to the house. Young Latinos, moving noiselessly in snowy white T-shirts and black cut-off pants that left their calves bare, started placing tables, chairs, and parasols on the lawn in the garden and on the terrace near the pool.

Jeremy had ordered understated invitations on hand-made paper to be sent out: *Jeremy Swindon invites you to observe his sixty-fifth birthday with him on 12/22/2000 and to start your Christmas Break with a late lunch (or a very early dinner). You will be well taken care of starting at 1:30 PM. Dress: formal. RSVP Kelly Hendel.*

At parties of the truly rich, the guests are served caviar, but Jeremy, who together with his partner Jonathan had made a total of four million dollars profit from their films (an astronomical sum in the rest of the world, but one that makes little impression in Los Angeles), did not want to allow himself that extravagance. There were good causes to which he wanted to leave his money. Jeremy and Jonathan had always been satisfied with a modest producer's fee, and had let their income depend on the quality of the films. And because they had always bet on quality and had never run covetously after the trend of the times, their films had seldom made more than the production costs. Over the last ten years it had become practically impossible to raise money for the kind of movies that Jeremy wanted to make. Three times, just before shooting was due to start, he had received the unnerving phone call from a studio executive or bank officer that the involved parties were pulling out—meaning the collapse of the dreams of hundreds of people and months of wasted preparations. After the third time, he decided to hang up his boots. That was also at the time when Jonathan, who had been his lover, friend, and colleague for two decades (they were called The Two Js in the industry), had become seriously ill. Jonathan had died eighteen months ago, and since then, Jeremy had lived all alone in the big house in the hills of Malibu, looking out over the Colony and the sea.

Pointing, reprimanding, correcting, Kelly hurried from the kitchen to the pool house and back inside to the living room (a quote from her: "Are those the roses? I asked for a hundred roses with long stems, not medium-long ones!"), to the terrace on the lawn, to the front door to yell at a new supplier, meanwhile hissing viciously into her cell phone, because unfortunately she determined that no one had really kept to the smallest details of the agreement. ("It's always the same with you. If there were another decent cheese shop in the city, I would have gone there!")

Starting at noon, she called the Progress Bakery every five minutes; at a quarter to twelve they were supposed to have delivered large quantities of baguettes, French farm bread, and six tarts—one apple, one pear, one raspberry, one lemon, one peach, and one strawberry with custard cream.

Circumstance Ten

(not a real one, but it still belongs here)
Perhaps it is important here to call to mind the location of Malibu. Seen from Santa Monica, the Pacific Coast Highway follows the westernmost coast of America with a big curve to the left. The driver has the impression that he is driving north, but that is not the case—at this point the PCH runs due west. Malibu is not located northwest of Santa Monica but, connected by the Pacific Ocean, exactly to the west.

The long, rather narrow, always busy coastal highway, a four-lane road—the first part without median strip, crash barriers, or guards from oncoming traffic—is separated from the interior of Los Angeles County by the Santa Monica Mountains that stop abruptly at the coast and dive into the sea along steep inclines. There has been no building where the subsoil is insufficiently solid, but for the rest, these slopes boast hundreds of villas and cottages built on piles or on tall concrete foundations. From them one can enjoy breathtaking views over the narrow coastal strip and the turquoise ocean that often hits the rocks violently, and, as you know, is one of the favorite spots of surfers.

On the way to the west and the north, the PCH follows gentle curves along the sea which is often hidden from view by the houses on concrete piles on the strip of sand. Then the building density increases, stores appear, and the driver enters the center of Malibu. This center is located on a rather wide, flat area that forms somewhat of a bulge into the ocean. At this point, the mountainsides are at a distance of two miles from the water.

The center of Malibu doesn't amount to much. There is a covered shopping mall, designed around a sandbox with some climbing frames, located between nondescript low-rise buildings; there are some supermarkets and bank branches. The most striking aspect of the center is the Colony, a protected, secluded settlement of movie celebrities at the beach side of Malibu, a gated community of beach houses built close together where the inhabitants (without exception, multi-millionaires famous from film and gossip magazines) don't have to fear attacks from fans.

Jeremy Swindon's house is four miles beyond the Colony, on the PCH—hence even more western as seen from Santa Monica—while Elaine Jacobs, who will be mentioned in the next circumstance, lives in an apartment in one of the beach houses built on piles east of the center of Santa Monica, hence closer to Santa Monica.

Circumstance Eleven

On December 22, 2000, Elaine Jacobs, professor of experimental physics at UCLA, did not have to give classes, and she wanted to use the day to buy Christmas presents at the Promenade and at the Santa Monica Mall. Elaine's research focuses on "strings," the bizarre mathematical theory which states that more dimensions exist than the ones that are familiar to humankind, and that the existence of an infinitely great number of parallel universes is possible. Many of her colleagues were unable to summon much appreciation for the theory. She thought that it was little more than the next step in a lengthy process in which science banishes mankind in a convincing and implacable manner from the center of the cosmos. She was fascinated by the fact that it is clearly not enough to say that humankind is on a random planet of a random star in a random Milky Way of a random cluster, in short, in a random corner of the universe. Not "the" universe, but one of the very many possibilities. The more we understand about it, the more we get lost in an ever greater randomness. Living with this awareness was impossible for many, but for Elaine it was exactly the motivation for penetrating ever deeper into science. She didn't like belief in myths or tradition.

It took Elaine almost four very long minutes to merge her silver-gray Ford Explorer, a mid-weight four-wheel drive, safely into the stream of traffic on the PCH.

Sometimes the inhabitants of the houses on piles at the ocean need a lot of patience to back out onto the busy PCH. Often there is no more than a six foot distance between the garage doors of the houses—often small apartment buildings—and the asphalt of the PCH. Visibility is bad, the traffic too heavy and too fast. One time Elaine had to wait more than fifteen minutes before finding a driver who would allow her to enter the cruel stream of cars.

It was exactly twenty-seven minutes before one on Friday, December twenty-second, when Elaine's Explorer started to move.

Circumstance Twelve

(for the sake of completeness)
Bob Morris's Paradise Cove Beach Café is on a small bay called Paradise Cove, approximately six miles west of the village center of Malibu.

From the Pacific Coast Highway, a segment of the famous Highway 1 that runs along the west coast of the continental United States, a narrow winding road leads after one-tenth of a mile to the gate of a large parking lot. Initially, the place looks like one of the many ordinary eateries along the PCH, but as soon as you walk onto the beach, it suddenly becomes clear why this is called Paradise Cove. At the right a cliff rises almost straight out of the water, barely making room for a rocky passage to other beaches, and at the left, to the east, green hills slope from the blue-green water to the mountain ridge behind the coast.

At thirty feet from the sea there is a wooden building that houses a fish restaurant. In the summer months and during weekends, umbrellas and lounge chairs are set up on the narrow strip of beach between the restaurant and the Pacific Ocean. The young people who live in the area and have their weekend or vacation jobs there, run back and forth between the kitchen and the beach to fill the orders of the guests who are stretched out in the shade of the umbrellas and have decided not to move for several hours.

The portions are gigantic, the french fries big and tasty, the fish is fresh, and the rosé is like the sun itself. It is one of the rare spots on the California coast where you can drink alcohol while sitting on the beach in the open air. It is a favorite spot to celebrate birthdays.

A Confluence of Circumstances

I was the owner of God's Gym, a health club on Main Street in Venice, and I worked with Miriam for a whole year. Twice a week, Miriam, wearing tight-fitting shorts and shirt, would come in to perfect her body.

On December 22 of the year 2000, at exactly 12:19 in the afternoon, I got on my Harley Davidson in order to drive to Malibu, where I had to give a private lesson to an actor who had accepted a movie role as a body builder.

On that day Miriam was going to celebrate her birthday with her girlfriends at a lunch at the Paradise Cove Beach Café. With Miriam on the pillion seat of my motorcycle, I left for Malibu at 12:20 PM.

On that same day, Frank Miller was a man in a hurry. In the pharmacy next to Progress Bakery, he was waiting for medicines for Margaret—a nervous old man worried about his seriously ill wife.

If Frank had parked his car in the parking lot behind the pharmacy or simply in a metered parking place on the street, then the F-350 truck of Progress Bakery, which had been loaded on the parking place behind the bakery and was going to Jeremy Swindon's party, could have used the exit.

But Frank wanted to get home quickly. All the parking places in the street were taken, and he refused to let his car be exposed to theft or burglary in the deserted parking lot behind the pharmacy. Therefore, he parked his car exactly in front of the parking lot exit between the rectangular pharmacy and bakery buildings at three minutes before noon. He assumed that no one was using it and that he needed only a minute.

Juan Armillo, the driver of the Progress truck, was late loading and got no reaction to his impatient honking. After five and a half minutes, at two minutes past twelve, Armillo decided to drive the truck to the street over the sidewalk and its high curb. He felt the bottom of his truck hit the curb hard, but he continued driving. He had warm bread and fresh pastry in the cargo space. Customers were waiting.

Six years before, the bottom of the engine block had been structurally damaged during the Northridge earthquake, caused by the previously mentioned earth crust plates that had started to move hundreds of millions of years ago. Because of Armillo's maneuver, the engine block grazed the concrete curb and tore the vulnerable oil pan once again. Gouges in the concrete curb are the silent witnesses to the incident.

During the drive from Marina del Rey to Malibu, the leak increased.

At 12:38, in a bend of the Pacific Coast Highway, the wheels of my Harley lost their grip on the asphalt on the oil slick left behind by the delivery truck of Progress Bakery, and the motorcycle overturned.

Miriam slid across the slippery road surface underneath an oncoming Ford Explorer that was driven by Elaine Jacobs. Within eight minutes, an ambulance was on the scene and the paramedics determined that Miriam had serious injuries.

It took another eleven minutes before an emergency helicopter could land safely on an open area of the beach; Miriam was placed inside and was flown to Cedars-Sinai.

I didn't have a scratch.

Your daughter died in the early morning.

Part one

Chapter one

On Friday, December 22 of the year 2000, Los Angeles lay under a fog that varied in thickness during the course of the day. Around one o'clock in the afternoon, it thinned and seemed to dissolve, but three hours later it reappeared. From the coast, the skyscrapers in the center of Los Angeles and the snow-capped mountains in the distance remained invisible all day long. The average temperature was fifty-two degrees Fahrenheit; it was a cool day.

Joop Koopman had taken his Dutch bicycle out of the shed, greased the chain, pumped the tires, and had bicycled to the First Motor Inn, a motel on Santa Monica Boulevard. The big black trainer in Miriam's gym had advised him to move more. It had been harder than he had anticipated. He was half an hour late, and despite the unusually low temperature, he arrived at the motel, sweating. He wore one of Miriam's small backpacks—the least showy one, pink with yellow dots—to carry his wallet, cell phone, pocket calendar, and notebook. He sweated most under the backpack.

Philip had said that he didn't need to check in at the screened-off area that served as the reception desk. The rooms of the two-story

3

motel could be reached from a parking lot, and Philip's room was on the top floor.

Joop dragged the bicycle up the stairs. He had left his house without the heavy padlock that was somewhere in the shed, and had bicycled for an hour, steering close to the curb, constantly casting glances at the car traffic that was not used to bicyclists. His muscles tingled and the bands of his briefs cut into his groin, but he felt as fit as a fiddle. As he approached the room number on the open walkway with his bicycle, a door opened and he saw Philip appear. Grinning, Philip lifted a hand and saluted him in greeting. Evidently he had been watching at the window.

"The Dutch are really incorrigible," said Philip, "finally you're in a country where you never have to bike, and what do you do?"

He pulled Joop to him and shook him boyishly. Philip's white hair was cut short and lay on his skull like a tight swimming cap; his skin looked tough as leather, and his hands had a powerful grip.

"How are you, you're looking good, how is the writing, everything okay with Miriam?—yes, I've done some checking; you're divorced. I know everything about you, everything is perfect for me too, just got divorced for the second time, everything could be much worse. I've only got some juice here, all right?"

Philip spoke Dutch with an exotic accent. At the end of his sentences his words danced in the direction of a question mark the way the Israelis do, as if Hebrew were a language that consisted of nothing but questions. Certain sounds were nasal, but his *g* had remained hard and growling because the rasping throat *g* also occurred in modern Hebrew.

The last time Joop had seen him was right before his departure for America, eighteen years ago. Philip's father had died, and Joop came to the Jewish cemetery in Vught for the *levaya*, the traditional Jewish funeral. They had never been really friendly, but in the small Jewish community you bade a personal farewell to every one of the deceased. Next to Philip, he had walked past the graves. Old Jewish names on weather-beaten stones, underneath the rustling branches of springtime. After his studies, Philip had gone to live in Israel, where he had fulfilled his military service. Philip had been muscular, his skin tanned, and he had looked grim-faced at the names chiseled into the stones.

When he was young, Philip accompanied his father to the synagogue every Saturday. He had finished high school before Joop, who had to repeat the fourth year. Philip wanted to become a dentist, just like his father.

"It's about the names, Joop," he had said at the cemetery, "as long as the names are there, there is hope."

Joop had not understood what he meant by that, just as he didn't understand now what Philip wanted.

Philip was wearing a simple Swatch watch, but he wore expensive loafers; the motel was low-end and favored by budget tourists, but a leather Gucci suitcase stood next to the bed in Philip's modest room.

Their bond consisted of the simple fact that they had grown up as Jewish boys in the Catholic town of Den Bosch. Joop had been a quiet student who would sit near the teachers; Philip was a noisy kid in the back of the class, quick with ideas, always talking back, pushy in his gestures; he was always touching people and would grab your arm or your shoulder when he'd start a tall tale.

"I always like being in LA," said Philip, while he unscrewed the cap from a hefty family-size bottle of cranberry juice. "If I weren't living in Israel, I would have come here. You've made a good choice. You don't have our tsuris."

"Other tsuris," Joop answered. "Don't forget what just happened in Florida with the elections."

"For whom did you vote?"

"Gore."

"Makes no difference. Bush will be as good for us as Gore."

"Us?"

"Us—you and I—the Jews."

"I belong to nothing."

"Makes no difference to me. For Jews and for anti-Semites you remain a Jew. Here." He handed Joop a plastic cup with juice.

Philip lifted his cup and said, "L'chaim."

"L'chaim," Joop imitated him. He poured the contents of the cup down his throat in a long gulp.

Philip asked, "More?"

"Please."

"You can take a shower if you want.

"It's okay, thank you."

The sound of sirens traveled from the street into the room. Philip filled the cup and passed it with a steady hand.

"That's quite a distance you covered. Did you come on Lincoln?"

Joop gestured that he would answer after finishing his cup. Panting, he placed the empty cup next to his backpack on the floor and said, "I should have taken the rollerbladers' path on the beach. I'll do it on the way back."

Philip sat down on the bed and tapped on Joop's knee. "Good to see you. It's been eighteen years. You've changed, but not really."

"You've changed," said Joop. He didn't know this man. Not in the past, and not now. But Philip had remained the same person who always touched others.

"I know. I remember who I was in Den Bosch. I've been through a lot. I was in the middle of the war in Lebanon, had six children with two women, and I have learned. But you pay when you learn. You exchange illusions for facts."

Philip had called the day before and arranged the meeting. They had talked for a few minutes, and Philip had mentioned that he worked for the Israeli government. But Joop didn't believe that. He was convinced that Philip would ask him for money; Philip had called because he was broke. The expensive suitcase in the cheap motel room meant that he had done well at one time, but now he had got himself involved in a game where he didn't know the rules and he had lost his winning cards.

"What do you do for the government?"

Philip glanced at the door, and the window with the view of the parking lot and Santa Monica Boulevard. "I do jobs for the government. Ministry of Defense. Things that they ask of me. And you?"

"Struggling. A difficult field. I've had good times, these last years it's been tougher."

The truth was that he hadn't sold anything in six years. The scripts he had written lacked the pace that the studios and TV stations demanded. He had earned some money with a few rather unspectacular rewrites and there was the inheritance from his mother. With that he had played the market and had provided for himself and Miriam. For some years that had gone well, but his latest purchase was likely to end in disaster.

Philip asked, "Do you have time to write a script?"

Something was wrong here. The Israeli Ministry of Defense had no need for a Dutch-speaking screenwriter in LA. Philip was no bureaucrat. Was it a money laundering operation in which Joop was to become the key figure? Israeli drug money that was going to run via Joop and would result in years of prison? He could not afford to do that. He had a daughter to take care of. He lived in a world of small worries and exact rules. At one time Philip's loftiest ambition had been to drill holes and fill cavities, and now he gave the impression that he had turned into a shady fixer. Joop began to feel uneasy. He had been there for only a few minutes.

Joop said, "Philip, I work only for producers with established track records. You never know what'll happen with people who don't know the business."

"Maybe I'm talking about people with lots of experience."

"Tell me more," said Joop, "but—I have time issues and I don't know if I'll get around to a new job."

"Perhaps you could write a script of *The Golem*, the book by Gustav Meyrink. Do you remember when we read it? It was terrific."

A smile spread across Joop's face. "Yes, I remember it."

"But I won't insist. Think about it. I haven't had breakfast yet. Do you want to come along and eat a sandwich? Put your bike inside, and we'll walk to the place; it's two blocks from here. I'll pay."

As they walked, Philip mentioned that he had stopped off in

the Netherlands two weeks ago and had visited Den Bosch. In Vught, he had said kaddish at his parents' graves. The city had changed.

"Everything is renovated. Cafés, restaurants, shops everywhere. It was almost disgusting—everyone looked so rich and carefree. I even sailed on the Dieze in a small boat, underneath the houses. Lovely."

Two years before, Joop had made the trip himself with Miriam, so he knew that the tours on the early medieval canals underneath the center of Den Bosch ran only in the summer. He said, "They do that in the winter?"

"They were willing to make an exception for me. They would do it for you too."

Philip pushed open the door of a simple diner. He spoke to a waitress and motioned Joop to a table against the back wall. They each slid onto a bench. A formica tabletop. Vinyl upholstery. A classic booth, smelling of deep-frying oil and stale coffee.

The waitress offered the menus, but Philip immediately ordered a pastrami sandwich.

"You can safely order that here," he said, as he refused the menu.

Joop ordered the same, even though he was on a diet.

"Iced tea, you too?"

Joop nodded. The waitress thanked them for their order and walked away.

"I know that you're used to fancy places; it doesn't look great here, but the sandwiches are perfect. By the way, how old is your daughter?"

"She turns seventeen today."

"The same age as my oldest. Also a girl. Everything good at school for her?"

"She is talented in mathematics. Gets it from my father. But she has more than he—"

"Hans," added Philip, making it clear that he still remembered.

"She sees through mathematical problems the way artists suddenly have an idea. Intuition."

"Will she pursue it?"

"She was offered a scholarship. MIT. My daughter. Next year she'll go there."

"Are you still in touch with Ellen?"

"Very little. Once in a while a telephone call."

"In Israel, children have to go into the army at eighteen. Rachel will have to in one year. Girls don't have to go to the front. David is two years younger; he'll have to. But even with Rachel—in a year I won't sleep a wink."

"Never thought about going back to Holland?"

"No. I've found my home there. My destiny. The Jews belong there. Not in Den Bosch. Not even here, even though the Jews are well off in America. But history will repeat itself. Different, unexpected, not understood at first, but history is an endless repetition of maneuvers."

"You were always more religious than I."

Philip smiled. "True. But I'm no longer religious."

"And yet you believe that all Jews belong in Israel?"

"Yes. But that has nothing to do with religion. It has to do with the urge to survive. The only place where the Jews are masters of their fate is Israel."

"And you say that even now? The Second Intifada has turned the Occupied Territories upside down!"

"The Intifada isn't the problem. That's Palestinian folklore, something like pole jumping in Friesland—do they still do that?"

"No idea," said Joop.

"If we wanted to, we'd break the Palestinians as though they were matchsticks. Our military might is colossal. If they really provoke us, we'll wipe them away and flush them down the toilet of history. Yet we don't do it. Why? Appearances? Afraid of the looks of the goyim? What do you think the Syrians would do with stone throwers? What do you think Saddam Hussein does with the Kurds?"

"You want to act in the same way as Arab dictators?"

"The world wants us to make peace with Arab dictators! Arafat is an Arab dictator! His clique consists of corrupt profiteers! But that's their problem. And I want it to remain their problem."

"That will happen when Israel gives up the Territories."

"If that were the solution, we would have done it a long time ago. No one enjoys keeping three million Palestinians on a tight rein.

The problem is that we can't be sure that Arafat or someone who will take his place won't change a free Palestine overnight into a terrorist state. It is one already, but it's not yet an independent state. How do you think that the left-leaning world press would react if we were to invade a free Palestine when that scum has committed attacks on us?"

"Has launched," corrected Joop.

"Launched, thank you," Philip answered, annoyed. He continued, "What do you think the newspapers will write? And what will the politicians say? What we have to do now is not pretty, but at the moment any alternative is even worse."

"How long can this continue?"

"Until we're fed up with it. Or they. I think the second."

They had sent each other Chanukah cards for several years, and Joop had always signed his with only his name. And he was sure that he had gone to Philip's father's funeral without Ellen. Philip couldn't know about Ellen's existence. Nor about Miriam. Had he made inquiries? Why? Joop wasn't much in the mood for shady affairs or intrigues. He was a writer who urgently needed to sell something.

Their order was placed on the table.

Joop asked, "Will you stay long in the city?"

Philip shook his head. He took a bite and, eating noisily, said that he was staying for a few days.

Joop asked, "Are you here for business or for a family visit?"

"Business."

"For the Israeli government?"

"Yes."

Joop had not yet taken a bite and stared at the thick sandwich in his hands. "What else do you do—in addition to being a bureaucrat?"

"I had an interest in a company that was going to develop networks of fiber optic cables. GlobSol. Global Solutions. Messy business."

Joop had put his money in GlobSol. Did Philip want to let him know that he knew that?

"GlobSol," repeated Philip. "Ever heard of it?"

He took another bite while Joop averted his eyes in order

to hide his embarrassment from Philip. Philip was playing a game. Games belonged in the fictional world of scripts, not in reality.

"Philip," he said, "I've got to go. It was nice to see you again."

"You haven't eaten anything yet!"

Joop picked up his backpack and slid to the edge of the bench. "I have to go home. My daughter, it's her birthday and—"

"Joop…stay."

"Philip, I…er…I'm going. It was nice. But we've become strangers. Good luck and—"

Philip grabbed Joop's arm right above his wrist and bent toward him. "Joop, you can trust me. Don't run away from me. What I know remains between us. There is nothing wrong. I am the boy who you used to sit with in synagogue. And I don't need money from you. So wait a moment."

Motionless, Joop sat on the edge of the bench, one moment away from the step that could free him from Philip's manipulations. But then he remembered—his bicycle was still in Philip's room.

"Eat your sandwich, your *broodje*. Nice thing in our language, those cute diminutives. Relax, you don't have to worry. Very soon you'll be able to go home and you'll never have to hear from me again. I promise."

He looked at Joop with a penetrating gaze. He gave Joop's arm a friendly squeeze and let go.

Joop swallowed.

"Take a bite and I'll explain," said Philip, as if he read his thoughts. "If I were you, I would also find all this weird. Normally things go as follows: I make contact, we meet each other several times, we have drinks, we become friendly and a bond is created. That takes weeks, even months. Until I say: do you know that you can earn money with what you know? And then it dawns on them what is going on. But you I've known since I was born."

Joop had no idea what Philip meant. He sat back again and tried to be patient.

He asked, "The Israeli government?"

"The government, yes," affirmed Philip. "I need your help. We would pay for it. Enough to be able to live for several years. I've had to delve into your past, into your present life. I know details. That feels threatening to you, but it's the procedure. My bosses know everything about me. I've chosen that; it's the life that I have chosen freely. You haven't. You haven't declared that we are allowed to check your background. We brushed away your privacy."

"Brushed aside."

"Brushed aside," repeated Philip, pleasant this time. "Yet we did it. Because the issue is worth it."

"The issue?"

"Yes. The future of Israel."

Joop looked at him incredulously. Pointing at himself, he said ironically, "You need *me* for the future of Israel?"

"Yes. That's why I'm here. That's why I called you. That's why I went to Den Bosch. That's why I collected everything that could be collected about you. That's why I'm making you an offer. If you say no, I'll regret it, but I won't insist. One 'no' is enough. But you have to hear me out first. I think that I'll convince you."

Joop looked away, at the orderly human world outside in the street, where the rules were known and clear. Why did this have to concern him? He needed tranquility and regularity to do his work. He needed safety and security for his daughter.

Joop looked at him again and asked, "You work for…"—now he whispered without breathing, speaking only with his lips—"the Mossad?"

Philip didn't seem to hear him. He answered, "I work for Defense. We are preparing an operation. We've identified a possible terrorist. We need someone who speaks Dutch and lives in Los Angeles. Someone we can trust blindly."

"Nice that you thought of me," said Joop. "I feel special."

Either the dentist had become a secret agent, or a brilliant con man. It might be material for a script, so he needed to stay near him. It was out of the question that Philip was telling the truth.

"How can I verify what you're telling me?"

"By listening to me. Bring your sandwich. We're going back to that beautiful hotel and I'll explain it to you. Anyway, your bicycle is in my room."

Chapter two

After Philip had opened the door for him and then left for another room on the walkway, Joop sat down on the only chair in the motel room. He opened the paper bag and bit into the now cold pastrami sandwich.

Joop had been an impulsive pacifist who wanted to avoid the army when there was still compulsory military service in Holland. After rubbing his body with oil from his moped and smoking joints all night long, he had gone by train to a barracks in Breda for a test. In the examination hall he ended up in a regiment of farmers' sons from the province of Brabant who had come for a written intelligence test. Around him he saw contemporaries plunged in dogged concentration, who were clearly choosing the uniform with dedication. Joop, dizzy from lack of sleep and sick to his stomach from smoking, desperately looking to create an incident, had started to scream that they were all going to be cannon fodder and that they were crazy to be part of this and should use him as an example. Surprised at his courage, he flung the papers from his table with trembling hands, and with a dry mouth waited for whatever would happen next. Two of the professional soldiers who were supervising intervened and expelled him from the room amidst approving applause. He was held in isolation for several hours, glowing with pride because of his incredible conduct. He was the boy who used to whisper when he had to talk in class, had never been on the stage in the auditorium, and yet suddenly had dared to disturb the order in a room full of a hundred hog farmers. In the afternoon he received a document which stated that he had been declared unfit to serve because of s-5. In those years s-5 was a mark of honor. His mental stability was completely at the bottom of a scale where number one indicated perfection. At the station he telephoned his mother: "Mom, I've been declared unfit!"

"Come home quickly—I'll get a treat at Van Berkel!"

Van Berkel was a famous patisserie in Den Bosch, specializing in small cakes. Joop had been too young for the generation of '68, but he had studied their ideas, both on the jungle of the Vietnam war and the history of old Europe that had betrayed his mother's family, and he had developed an aversion to the army. That was why he let himself be declared unfit. And also because of his mother, who couldn't bear the thought of her only child wearing a uniform and being exposed to danger.

This had been several months before the outbreak of the Yom Kippur war. When Egypt and Syria started their attack on Israel, Joop reported as a volunteer at the Israeli embassy—without telling his mother—out of an impulse of burning solidarity, convinced that all Jews were threatened.

While he was waiting in line—all young Jewish Dutchmen, all descendants of survivors—he saw that Philip van Gelder had also made the trip to The Hague. At school Philip had been the uncontested leader. Not just a bigmouth, but also a star in mathematics, physics, and chemistry. A good soccer player and a strong swimmer. And during synagogue services he could recite parts of the service in Hebrew by heart. Many boys at school hated him.

Joop could read the Hebrew texts, but he didn't understand a word, just as he could read mathematical equations without any understanding. Only his mother was Jewish; because of that he was still considered Jewish according to the rules of Judaism, and on his thirteenth birthday his bar mitzvah was thrown into his lap because the small Jewish community urgently needed to be enlarged by a boy who could assure the continuity of the services. Ten men had to gather on Saturday mornings—which was often not possible—and the request of the Jews of Den Bosch to proclaim Joop officially a Jew had led to bitter fights between his parents. His father was a strict atheist for whom any religion was an expression of backwardness, but Joop's mother had won. In 1945, she determined that she was the only survivor of her family. Her father had been a prosperous tea merchant, and in the thirties she had grown up with wealth, but the entire family fortune had disappeared during the war. It took her eight years to decide to bring forth a new generation with the man with whom she had fallen in love. She had one child, Joop, and her involvement with Judaism consisted solely of sentiment. Before the war, her father had gone to the synagogue on Saturdays, and she would be able to restore this interrupted tradition when her son took the same route, on foot, holding a dark blue velvet bag with a tallit and a prayer book dangling off a gold-colored cord, a yarmulke in his pants pocket, in polished shoes that were worn only on Saturday morning.

"Life doesn't consist only of matter or of hunger or passions. There is also something called tradition. Things that you do to mark life. Days when you celebrate or when you mourn. For me it's not about belief; it's about tradition."

Joop had listened to these words of his mother, but he hadn't understood them until years later. His father had countered that one thing leads to another, but she had rejected that. "We're right here! He doesn't have to become an Orthodox Jew because he helps these people by once in a while sitting in a pew on Saturday morning! It may be only once a month."

"That's what they say. Watch out, it will be every week—give a Jew a finger, he'll take the whole hand."

"That is an insensitive remark."

"Anneke, sweetheart—it's a joke."

"It's not a funny joke," his mother said fiercely. "Anyway, he doesn't understand Hebrew, so he doesn't understand what it's about."

"In those prayer books the translation is on the left and the Hebrew text is on the right," his father pointed out.

"Good for his general education."

"Bad for his world view."

"Hans, I like it when he goes. I don't have a real reason for it. It's a feeling. That's an impossible category for you, but that's what it is. It's about people who are no longer here, something like that."

"They won't come back when Joop goes there."

"I know that. But I have the feeling that it consoles."

He got to know Philip at synagogue and in school. Saw him for the last time in 1982 and now again here in Los Angeles.

Philip entered the room with a second chair, identical to the one that Joop sat on, and looked approvingly at the sandwich in Joop's hand.

"Good, isn't it? A nothing place, but excellent sandwiches. They also have perfect chopped liver. More to drink?"

With a full mouth, Joop nodded yes.

Philip bent down to the plastic cup next to Joop's chair. The pink backpack with the yellow dots lay between the chair legs.

Philip poured the cranberry juice and handed Joop the cup.

"I've looked at what has been recorded about you. Even though you went to synagogue almost every week, you never actually became a member, and your mother never became a member either. Why not?"

"My father didn't want to pay for it, so we didn't become members. He was a frugal man."

"Just like your father, your mother was buried in a nonsectarian cemetery, and you've never been interested in anything Jewish or written about it."

"She wanted to be buried next to my father. And my father was a hardcore unbeliever," explained Joop.

"For the outside world you are therefore someone who won't be associated with Jews or Judaism. Your name is an advantage; for that matter your mother's name, De Vries, is neutral too, and that means that you could be a perfect fellow-worker. If they checked you, they couldn't conclude anything but that you're a non-religious Dutchman. Often we devise a whole new identity, or we use an identity that we've prepared beforehand, but there is nothing better than the truth, here too. You don't have to fake that your name is Joop Koopman—it's your real name. And if someone wants to check who Joop Koopman is, you have the perfect background: a normal guy from Den Bosch, no crazy details, nothing to worry about."

"And those months when I was in Israel?"

"It's recorded nowhere, impossible to verify, therefore doesn't exist. What is important now, and that's why I'm here, and that's why I called you: We've looked for someone who can do this work for us. It has to be a Dutchman, that's essential, and he has to be absolutely loyal. We looked for someone here—and then we happened on you."

Philip paused and poured himself some juice. Joop observed him intently, as if even the way that Philip poured the cranberry juice was part of the unreal affair in which he was about to become involved, and with his eyes he followed the cup to Philip's mouth and saw the Adam's apple in his throat bounce up and down as he drank.

Philip said, "That pastrami makes you thirsty." With the back of his hand he wiped his mouth and set the cup down on the floor with a sigh. "I'm sorry to catch you unawares with all this. You have your life; you have your own problems, your own certainties, your own things that bother you, and then I suddenly appear and try to pull you into a world that you don't care for at all. A world of deception. A world that also involves danger, even though the chance that something will happen to you is just as small as you being robbed here at the door, and yet—I call on your solidarity with the Jews in Israel. I know that you have that. I still remember how you were, that time in Israel."

"I cleaned chicken coops for four whole months," said Joop.

"What did *I* do? Did dishes, scrubbed bathrooms, made beds! But it was necessary, everyone was at the front, the country shouldn't be allowed to fall down, therefore we did those chores."

"Collapse," said Joop, "not fall down but collapse. The country shouldn't be allowed to collapse."

Philip smiled. "If this continues, I'll soon speak better Dutch than before."

"The details have to correspond."

"My work exists thanks to details," said Philip. "A detail can never not be right. Of vital importance. Of national importance. I want to have a cigarette—you too?"

Joop shook his head. Philip leaned toward the nightstand at the head of the bed, took the telephone off the hook, and entered a short number. At the other end someone picked up immediately and Philip said something in Hebrew.

When he put down the phone, he said, "I'm not here by myself. A few of my people have come along. Our American friends don't know that we're here. What I tell you now could cause a diplomatic uproar. Our friends in Virginia always like to know what happens in their own backyard, and they are furious when we enter without knocking. I tell you this to make it clear that I'm putting all my cards on the table. I'm holding back nothing, because I know that is always counterproductive. You have just now been informed about something that would make our friends rather angry. But we take that risk because our interests are not always synchronous. We are more sensitive to some things as them."

"Than they."

"Than they," repeated Philip. "They are invulnerable. We, on the other hand, can in principle be toppled by the least little push if we're not prepared."

There was a knock at the door. Philip called out something and the door opened. A short dark man entered, with piercing eyes under thick eyebrows that formed an uninterrupted line above his nose and eyes; he was at most thirty years old. Like Philip, he had his hair cut short, which emphasized his angular skull. He wore a dark green Adidas track suit, and the way he moved showed that he made daily visits to a health club.

He gave Philip a plastic bag and a lighter, offered his hand to Joop in greeting, and said, "I'm Danny, great to meet you."

There wasn't a trace of an accent in his American pronunciation.

"Hi, Joop Koopman."

Philip said something else to him, and Danny disappeared.

He slid out a full carton of Marlboros from the plastic bag, which was from a duty-free shop at Charles de Gaulle Airport, and worked open the packaging. Evidently he had flown via Paris.

"Okay," said Philip while opening a box, "so what is all this about?" He broke the filter off the rest of the cigarette. "Crazy habit," he said, "I do it for the taste."

He lit his cigarette and inhaled deeply.

"You too?"

"No, thank you," answered Joop.

Philip started to talk about a man whose name was Omar van Lieshout. For the first two years of his life his last name had been Bajoumi, but when his parents divorced he got his mother's name. Omar van Lieshout was born in 1968 in Beverwijk. His father was one of the first guest workers from Morocco in Holland.

"Ahmed Bajoumi could barely write his name and could not earn enough to keep body and soul together in his village in the northeast of Morocco. Therefore he did not have a chance to save · for a dowry, and he went to Holland because there was a shortage of workers in a company near the coast where they operate blast-furnaces. Heavy, dangerous, hot work. The Dutch no longer felt like doing it, but North Africans stood in line for it. Literally. Recruiters would set up a table in the village square, sit down behind it, and the young men would come running from the hills, away from the goats and the sheep, because they all wanted to leave. The recruiters chose the strongest ones, and not exactly subtly; they were treated like horses on the livestock market, and Ahmed Bajoumi was one of the lucky ones. The factory rented an old school building in Beverwijk where the young men were supposed to live in dormitories with bunk beds. Their food was cooked for them until it became clear that the men were losing weight because they didn't like Dutch fare; then they were allowed to cook for themselves."

He took a puff and looked at the smoke. He had come to LA to tell Joop about a pathetic guest worker. People traveled to California for all sorts of reasons.

"Jannie van Lieshout worked in a grocery store. Jannie was a real Beverwijk girl. Her father worked as a street cleaner, her mother earned extra at home as a seamstress. Ahmed did his shopping where Jannie worked. A good-looking boy with short black curls. A fine full-figured blonde. The cultural hole was—"

"Cultural gap."

"The cultural gap was as wide as an elephant's behind, but they were young; she was hot for his black hair and his fine circumcised schlong, and she let him mount that full-figured Dutch body of hers. In the evenings they would meet next to the North Sea Canal, and, with a view of the smoke plumes above the blast furnaces, they screwed themselves silly. Her parents were unaware of it at first, but Beverwijk was in an uproar in no time. A respectable Catholic girl made pregnant by a horny Moroccan guest worker. Catholic, so she didn't want to do anything about it. That's why we now have to deal with Omar van Lieshout. Jannie's parents broke ties with her, but she refused to listen and married the man with whom she had fallen in love—until he almost knocked her out cold. Ahmed may have been in Holland, but his customs and traditions derived from what was normal in the villages and hamlets in the Riff mountains. She had the child, but her life was miserable. I'm not telling you anything new; you must have heard this before about this kind of marriage in Holland between guest workers and Dutch women. He wanted her to go to Morocco to live with his family; he made her wear a head scarf; he really went all the way. Jannie decided that she could no longer stand it. Omar was two years old at the time. Jannie actually had to go into hiding, and she stayed in hiding for three years until Ahmed had an accident. He was hit by a 660 pound piece of iron that fell and hit his back. It broke two vertebrae and put him in the hospital for several weeks; and when he was discharged, he had to undergo a physical examination, and he was declared unfit to work. wao—Disability Insurance. The winning ticket of the Dutch social lottery."

Philip chuckled. "I love that country." He stubbed out his cigarette, stood up and silently paced back and forth, then leaned against the wall next to the nightstand. He bent down to reach the cigarette pack and immediately lit another cigarette.

Joop thought: a great actor, a perfect manipulator. Maybe I

should be taking notes. A melodrama about a guest worker in Holland. But he doubted that there would be any interest for it in LA.

Philip continued, said that Ahmed returned to his village, married an obedient Moroccan girl, and received a monthly check from the GAK, the Industrial Insurance Administration Office. Ahmed was considered a successful guest worker. His son Omar van Lieshout grew up in Emmen. He was a good-looking boy just like his father, with skin a fraction of a shade lighter. During the day his mother worked at an assembly line while Omar was cared for by a neighbor. Omar said his first words when he was four. Initially it was feared that he had brain damage since there had been an oxygen deficiency during his delivery, but Omar's language problem had nothing to do with his intellect. Even though Omar could barely spell and did not finish high school, he was quite intelligent. Omar was fourteen when he had his first run-in with the police.

"That had no consequences because he was a minor," said Philip with distaste. "Community workers and welfare counselors were involved. But Omar just continued doing what he had done before—small robberies, break-ins, and, above all, dealing. He threw money around, always had something nice for the girls who liked to be screwed by him, but he didn't have a steady job. They were never able to catch him. They watched him, but he was too clever for them. He was twenty-two when he went to Morocco for the first time. At that time his father was seriously ill, something with his intestines which had nothing to do with the accident in Holland, and Omar wanted to visit him. But Omar didn't speak a word of Arabic. Well, he speaks a few words, but he is a Dutchman, curses like a stevedore, and sees windmills and polders in his dreams."

Obviously Philip had read Omar's file several times—he didn't have a scrap of paper to refer to. At school Philip had been known for his infallible memory for formulas, facts, and exceptions in Latin and Greek declensions.

"Omar goes to Morocco, visits Dad, who is dying, meets five half-sisters, and finds his vocation. He encounters people who need him, for whom he is a hero from Holland. And for the first time in his life he visits a mosque. He doesn't understand a word of the service, but his genes kick out—"

"In, kick in," Joop corrected.

"And he finds his roots. Back in Holland he reads the Koran—in a Dutch translation. He does his best to learn Arabic, and over the course of the years he does pick up some and can make himself understood. But the language is not comfortable in his mouth, nor is it in the language center under his skull. Even though Omar can't read the Koran in Arabic, apparently the Dutch translation is so good that he becomes religious. Within a year his life changes. He grows a beard, prays five times a day—don't ask me in which language—and the following year he makes the hajj, the pilgrimage to Mecca; that was in ninety-two. He was twenty-four. A Muslim in full swing."

"And his dealing?" asked Joop, curious about the combination of crime and religion. He waited patiently. Still no point that could give meaning to the story.

"He continues it. After all, he has to live off something. But he moves. He looks for like-minded people, and he finds them in Amsterdam-West. There he rents a room from a Moroccan slumlord. In Amsterdam someone gives Omar an idea. At least, we assume that he was inspired by someone, for we have no indications that he had radical ideas before that time. We think that he visited a training camp in Yemen sometime in ninety-seven. With Islamic Jew-haters. But there are only indirect indications. At a certain point he was again walking around in Amsterdam, without a beard and dressed as a playboy, and in May of this year he had a meeting with an Iraqi diplomat in London. This Iraqi is a big fish. One of Saddam Hussein's top boys. We had already been keeping an eye on him for a year because he is a colonel in one of their secret services that carry out operations—think of assaults and such—and damn: an unknown Dutch Moroccan suddenly turns up with him! Omar! A meeting that looks accidental but was planned; we know the habits of our Iraqi friends. It's in the past few months that we collected the facts that I've just recounted."

This was the point. Beautiful. Silently and calmly Joop had anticipated it, but now he realized that Philip's story far exceeded fiction—Joop's domain. Joop was someone who imagined things, who, since Ellen had left him (and since those two shameful, irresponsible years afterwards), had lived for his daughter, not for the protection of Israel against Moroccan Dutchmen. He wasn't eager to be involved with people who spied on Iraqi bombers. Unless it involved a fictitious story or a historical fact. What Philip told him wasn't in either category. It was about a future secret action.

Philip lit another cigarette. With his aliyah to Israel, he had found the surroundings that did justice to the cynical look in his eyes. "And now Omar is here. In the San Fernando Valley. Just as you have Jewish neighborhoods on this side of the Hollywood Hills, you have Islamic ones there. And what makes us so nervous is the unpleasant feeling that Omar is not on vacation here. We're keeping an eye on him, but we have to get closer. With someone who is above suspicion and harmless. A nice Dutchman who has been living here for years."

Joop was a careful driver; he didn't smoke and drank little. He was a born coward who abhorred risks. That he of all people should be approached by Philip—Philip! This man who had been a stranger to him even as a child—for an undercover job. He was a writer, a reasonably good, pretty talented writer who'd had bad luck the past few years. Not a daredevil hooked on adrenalin.

Philip continued, "We decided to make a list of who in Los Angeles…"

He stopped in the middle of his sentence when Joop's cell phone started singing. His ring was the first bars of the *Wilhelmus*, the Dutch national anthem, a sentimental sign of solidarity with his native country, found on the Internet by Miriam.

"Sorry," said Joop, even though he wanted to answer the call, "I'll turn it off."

"Go ahead and take it, you never know if it will lead to earning some money."

Joop leaned forward and pulled the small pink backpack toward him. On the lit screen of the telephone he saw his daughter's name. He pushed the speaker button.

"Hi, sweetheart," he said.

But an unknown voice came from the telephone. "You are

speaking with Dr. Hemmings, Cedars-Sinai Medical Center. Am I speaking with Mr. Koopman?"

He pronounced it as Koopm'n, with a drawn-out *oo* and a swallowed *a*, as everyone did.

"Speaking," answered Joop, surprised. "I thought that my daughter was calling me. Are you using her telephone?"

"I'm sorry to have to bother you," said the voice, "you are the father of Miriam Helen Koopm'n?"

"Yes, I am—why are you asking? What was your name again?"

"Dr. Hemmings. I'm the emergency room supervisor here in the hospital. Your daughter was brought in half an hour ago. She is now in intensive care. I have to ask you—can you come to the hospital right away?"

The man was talking gibberish. A crazy man who called a random number and scared people stiff.

"What are you talking about? It's not clear to me what you are talking about."

"I understand how you feel, but unfortunately this is not an error. Your daughter Miriam Koopm'n was brought in here after a serious accident. It is really important that you come here."

"How can that be, my daughter? How do you know that it is my daughter? I have no idea who you are; I must say this is a strange conversation."

"My name is Robert Hemmings; I am an internist, and I urge you to come immediately to Cedars-Sinai."

"Why do I have to come?"

"Because things look very bad for your daughter."

Strange that everything stood still. The traffic in the street, the particles in the air, the smoke that rose from Philip's cigarette. And his heart froze in his body; the blood in his veins came to a standstill. And then everything started moving again, and in his head it started to storm.

"What is very bad?" he asked in a flat voice, while he leaned forward wanting to hide within himself, to flee the threat, the upcoming blow inside his head.

"We don't know if she will make it through this coming night," said the voice, the voice of this Dr. Hemmings who didn't know what he was talking about.

"It's not possible," said Joop, louder now, as if he could convince the doctor this way and drown out the noise in his head. "My daughter is in Malibu having lunch with her girlfriends! Today is her birthday! That's where she is, I can call her cell phone!"

"This is her cell phone; I'm calling with her cell phone. You were listed as Dad. I think it's awful, Mr. Koopm'n, what happened to your daughter."

"What exactly happened?!" he roared.

"A traffic accident."

Suddenly Joop became furious, enraged with hate at this voice and at the telephone in his hand.

"Where?" he screamed.

"Pacific Coast Highway. Twenty-five minutes ago she was brought in by an emergency helicopter. Are you coming?"

Joop saw his knees move up and down as if they were electrically charged. And Philip appeared in his field of vision, squatting next to him. Philip, next to whom he had prayed in the past in an unfamiliar language and who had turned into a fighter. And Philip said something, but Joop didn't hear him.

"This can't be true, Dr. Hemm...Hemm..."

"Hemmings."

"Dr. Hemmings, listen, my daughter, it can't be; she went to Malibu. You can't say that—it's my daughter's birthday today! I saw her this morning! She has a eh...ponytail and she turned seventeen today! For that matter, how do I know that you're telling the truth? Any lunatic can dial my number! How can you prove that you really are a doctor? At what hospital are you? Why are you saying all this?"

But when he felt Philip's arms and heard his voice that tried to calm him, he could no longer talk because a frantic fear obstructed his voice.

Imploring, he looked at Philip and stammered, "Philip, here, can you...can you talk with that man, that man is...he says that he's a doctor, maybe he'll listen to you..."

Chapter three

That morning, Joop had been up as usual at a quarter to seven in order to put out the ingredients for Miriam's breakfast. Normally he only placed the bowl with fruit next to her plate, and Miriam herself would peel an apple, a kiwi, an orange, and half a banana. That morning he did it for her. Today his daughter was turning seventeen. Her present, in the delightful wrapping of Saks Fifth Avenue in Beverly Hills, was waiting on his desk. He cut the fruit into pieces and stirred them into the yogurt.

Then he put the water on for her tea and made cappuccino for himself. Two years ago he had bought an Aquaviva, an Italian espresso machine which since that time determined his morning beverages. Ever since he had given up breakfast, he limited himself to cappuccino. Last week, after months of Miriam's insistence, he had finally gone to the gym where she was a member. Before that, the last time he had stepped on a scale was years ago; he discovered that he had gained twenty-two pounds.

After she left for school, he would drink an espresso while reading the paper. Around ten thirty he drank a second espresso, and the third one would follow at noon.

The Aquaviva stood on the counter of the square kitchen, in front of the window that looked out over the small garden behind the house. A fence overgrown with ivy that he had put up himself a dozen years ago separated his garden from his neighbor's, but over the fence you could see their bedrooms. Diagonally above the espresso machine, a small television set stood on a swivel base; it was tuned to the morning program on Channel Five.

As he did every morning, Joop listened to the local news. Reports about murders, kidnappings, traffic accidents, and fires that had occurred in the region during the night. In between the news reports, the newscasters in the studio, laughing and in high spirits, traded remarks about their spouses, their pets, their plans for the weekend—all this on a level that was accessible for beings with the intelligence of moths. Channel Five had its own helicopter that flew over the freeways in order to shoot videos of the traffic flow. From the helicopter a female newscaster would report on traffic bottlenecks on the freeways and advise the viewer about alternate routes. The local news and the inane studio talk were part of their early morning ritual, just like Miriam's complaints about her school schedule, about her hair, about the clothes that no longer looked good on her or suddenly didn't fit her because she had gained ten pounds overnight, about his refusal to let her get a driver's license before she was eighteen.

A light hissing passed through the water pipes; this meant that Miriam had opened the shower faucet. Joop left the kitchen and walked around the house to the front yard. There, on the front lawn, lay the *Los Angeles Times*, protected by a plastic bag against the morning dew. He picked up the paper and, with shoulders hunched in the chilly December air, he returned to the warm kitchen. He could hear that Miriam was still in the shower and thought that this was the right moment to get her present from his study so that, when she came into the kitchen, she would immediately find it next to her plate. He went upstairs and passed by the bathroom.

Today Miriam hadn't pushed the door shut. She usually did so, with a short, forceful swing of her elbow which made the door fall into its frame with a metallic bang. He could have turned back or he could have passed the bathroom door with his head averted, but he couldn't keep his eyes from the chink. In the fraction of a second that he glanced at the mirror, he saw the naked body of his daughter.

It was years since he had seen her undressed; since she got pubic hair and it dawned on him that it was no longer possible to lift her onto his lap, to press her against him, and to cover her face and neck with kisses. Since Ellen's return to the Netherlands he had year in and year out cared for and cleaned her body, had wiped her bottom when she called his name—like a psalm, singing, whining, wheedling—and pointed proudly to the turd in the potty. He had kissed her knees, fingers, shoulders, and cheeks when she fell, had stroked her tummy when she had a stomach ache, and when she had a rash he had rubbed her little pussy with cream, until the moment when touching her body had become taboo.

What he saw of her was mainly her shape. But a number of details did not escape him. Before she could discover him, he turned back and went downstairs quietly and hurriedly, horrified by the strength of his curiosity. And by the weakness of his respect for her privacy.

He pulled the newspaper out of the plastic bag and on the kitchen counter turned the pages very quickly, looking for something that could bury the images in his head. His daughter was an adult woman. No boy or man could pass her without undressing her with his eyes, and Joop assumed that it was more than just her looks, it must be instant chemistry caused by her pheromones that changed men into unresisting victims. From the time she turned twelve, she had been approached in the street by talent scouts almost every month: do you want to become a model, an actress, a star? Would you on such and such a day come to audition for such and such a film? You are the new Sophia Loren, you have a great future ahead of you. She was less Mediterranean than Loren, but just as feminine.

Today she turned seventeen, and he firmly resolved to protect her for at least a few more years against the sharks, snakes, rats, and crocodiles of Los Angeles. Until she was twenty-one he would impose limits, restrain her with prohibitions. Although they spoke Dutch at home, their lives were in America. In respectable Holland the attraction of the entertainment industry was only a weak reflection of the temptations of Hollywood and therefore barely threatening for young women like Miriam. But in Los Angeles, physical beauty was of greater consequence than intelligence. Since she was thirteen, there had been plenty of admirers. It was impossible to keep her behind the dikes of a Dutch polder, hidden from the outside world, even if he wanted to.

The bathroom door had stood open, and without ever before feeling any inclination to do so, he had looked at her body. He was not guilty of carrying out a forbidden act, but still, on noticing the open bathroom door he should have turned around immediately with lowered eyes. Instead he had turned his head, and for a quarter or a third of a second he had let his eyes slide over her body. His seed that had become a woman. His daughter who met the standards of beauty of this time: she was slim; she had big breasts, a narrow waist, long legs. A perfect creature that one day would love a young man who at this moment was still squeezing his pimples. It seemed obvious that for the sake of the so-called bikini line she had to depilate certain areas, but he had seen that she had shaved her pubic hair into a pencil-thin line. She had paid attention to that part of her body for the sake of a visual effect. Or perhaps it was more than visual, perhaps she had done it for someone who was allowed to touch her with his fingers.

Joop couldn't judge. He had been sixteen when he was allowed to finger Linda, his distant cousin. In exchange she whacked him off. For a year Linda had lived with them, and every day after school he had hurried home with her; his parents, hard at work, wouldn't show up until after five o'clock. Sometimes she whispered to him on the way, stroking her skirt as if trying to beat bits of fluff from it: "Joop, you know, I'm not wearing panties today. What do you think of that?"

Within twenty-four hours after his father caught them—he had come home early from the school where he taught math—Linda was staring at the gray waves of the North Sea on a ferry that was sailing to Harwich. His father was friendly with British mathematicians and after telephoning for three hours, he had arranged a boarding school for her. Joop's mother had kept in touch with her. Linda de Vries, the daughter of one of his mother's cousins.

Early in December he had received a letter from her. She wrote that she had lived in America and in India for the last fifteen years and that she had been in the Netherlands again for the first time since she was a teenager, and had visited Den Bosch. After the Netherlands she would continue her travels, and in several months she would also visit LA. She would like to see him again. After thirty years.

Miriam was now as old as Linda had been at that time.

Joop leafed through all the sections of the *Times* and put the paper back down, with the front page on top. Bush had appointed Condoleezza Rice as national security advisor, the most powerful position ever held by a black woman. Other articles referred to the discussion about the decision of the Supreme Court to dismiss the request for a recount of the votes in Florida. He also read an article about the disasters at dot-coms, and because a few years ago he had invested his savings in a promising—success assured—but now faltering fiberglass company, reading the article caused the memory of his daughter's body to be driven to the remote corners of his consciousness.

He deviated from his morning routine and made an espresso right away.

"Hi, Dad," he heard.

He turned around and saw his daughter standing next to the breakfast table. She was wearing a denim miniskirt, black tights, a tight black T-shirt, and a denim jacket. Sea-green Puma running shoes. Her hair was bunched in a ponytail, which gave her bared neck and ears an intimate air.

He turned off the coffeemaker and kissed her on the cheek. She smelled of soap, of youth and of femininity.

"Good morning, Miriam. Congratulations." He kissed her once more.

She beamed at him with her lightly made-up eyes, clear, expectant.

"Are you making a cappuccino?"

"Espresso. Headache," he said.

"You know what, Dad? I feel like having a cappuccino today."

"No yogurt?"

"Oh yes, also. But coffee too. It's time that I start behaving like a caffeine-addicted adult. Starting today, everything is downhill. Have you already made the tea?"

"Yes, but I'll make coffee," he answered. "Deterioration doesn't exist. You don't believe me, but the odd thing is that you'll always remain as you are now."

"Except that in ten years I'll wake up wrinkled and with my breasts on my knees. Terrific prospect."

"I'm glad that you're so positive about it."

"Still, a handful of illusions can be quite a relief at my age, Dad."

"The illusion of today," he said, trusting that she knew what he meant. "Now or later?"

"Now, of course!"

"Will you watch the milk?"

He ran upstairs and grabbed the present from his work table. When he came downstairs, he saw her standing at the stove in the morning light, the short, tight skirt around her buttocks, the slim calves, the graceful ankles. The long, brown ponytail fell between her shoulder blades. He felt like kissing her neck, the way he had done when she was a toddler and every day he would lift her into the bath with a high swing. At the top of the swing her neck would appear in front of his mouth and his lips would taste the soft child's skin. For years that had been part of the bath ritual—he lifted her up and kissed her.

"Miriam," he said, and she turned halfway toward him, throwing him a glance over her shoulder with her black eyes. And he realized what havoc she would soon cause in the world with that look and posture.

She recognized the wrapping paper in his hand.

"Dad, you did it after all?"

"First open it," he answered, sick with love. "Congratulations."

She accepted the package and in passing planted a kiss on his cheek. In passing. Joop was dizzy with emotion, with despair that time had torn her away from him, and that he would never again be able put her in her bath with a swing (whereby they both made a cartoon-like noise—*zooff*) and would never again experience how she lowered her chubby bottom into the warm water. Now she had a woman's buttocks. Woman's thighs. Woman's genitals. Her body and all thoughts about it were forbidden.

Miriam pushed the yogurt aside, put the shiny white Saks Fifth Avenue shopping bag on the table, and took out the present wrapped in black tissue paper. Carefully she unwrapped it with her red-tipped fingernails and, smiling, took out the leather organizer that she had wanted. Sturdy black leather, with edges stitched with beige linen, simple but expensive, because it was a design by Kate Spade. Joop was indifferent to the logomania of the city, and he had tried to protect Miriam against the psychosis of brand advertising, but he had lost the fight against the manufacturers.

"Wow, Dad, even the contents are exactly what I wanted. Thank you so much, darling."

She flung an arm around his neck, the other arm around his shoulder, and pressed herself against him while she kissed him on his unshaven cheek near his ear. Carefully he placed his hands on her hips and took care not to push hard in order to shut out any ulterior thoughts, but he felt what had attracted him in the past in Ellen, the same sturdy softness, the same feminine strength.

He let go of her hips.

"It's awfully expensive, Daddy. You should know that I think it's terrific that you did this, but it really wasn't necessary. I very much wanted a leather organizer, but you could also have bought it at Staples, they have lovely ones there too; I mean it."

"Then give it back to me," he said.

"Too late," she answered.

"Do you really want cappuccino?"

"Yes, strange isn't it? Perhaps it was because you were just making that espresso when I came downstairs. That organizer is really beautiful. Sometimes the coffee smells so good. I'm starting to resemble you more and more."

"Don't do that to me," he answered.

She didn't resemble him at all. Joop was a forty-seven-year-old Dutchman with too much fat around his shoulders and chest, hairy arms and hands, flat feet, and light brown hair that was starting to turn gray at the sideburns. His eyes were always clear and curious, sometimes cynical and ironic, but never bored or narrow-minded. Some of his girlfriends had told him that he had gentle, boyishly innocent hands, even though they were hairy like a man's, by which they liked to be caressed. He had the genes of his non-Jewish father, Johannes Koopman from Eindhoven, who had wanted to become a great inventor at Philips Electronics but had instead served as a math teacher at a high school. His father had graded tests, had sarcastically called uninterested classes to order with his biting voice, had corresponded with foreign colleagues during weekends, and had hoped in vain for a university-level job that could have given him respect and time for scientific research. He died when Joop was twenty-five. On his bicycle on the way home, his father had had a heart attack and lay gasping for breath under the bicycle panniers filled with tests, until he was transported by ambulance to the local hospital, Grootziekengast-huis. There he was declared DOA, dead on arrival, a term that Joop had used in a script a few times. He had been five weeks from retirement.

In Miriam's looks, the almost gypsy-like features of Anneke, Joop's mother, had been continued. Anneke, in turn, had inherited her exotic features from her father. Herman de Vries, Joop's grand-father, had been murdered in a Polish village in 1943, and the only thing that he had left behind was a handful of photos of a dark ladies' man: a pencil-thin moustache that followed the curve of his upper lip; thick, black hair; the half-closed eyes of a born seducer; a self-assured chin—a Jewish noble who ran a wholesale business in tea. Miriam was from that side of the family. Ellen, Joop's ex, was a blonde who seemed to have added little to the appearance of her daughter, as if during her pregnancy she had acted only as a temporary carrier for the family features of Joop's mother.

He heard the milk creep up against the side of the pan and reached straight for the handle in order to place the pan on the counter.

She was silent as she leafed intently through the organizer.

"You do know that I'll be gone later?" he asked as he was beating the milk.

"What time will you be back?"

"No idea. Maybe we'll go out for lunch. And you won't ride with Caroline."

"No-o," she sang.

"It doesn't matter who you ride with, as long as it isn't with that daredevil. A child of seventeen in a Porsche, ridiculous."

"In a regular car she drives very safely."

"*No.*"

"I'll ride with Pat."

"Pat is okay. She has a sense of responsibility."

She asked, "You've arranged everything, haven't you?"

"I stopped by yesterday. Everything is in order. You can eat and drink whatever you want, but no alcohol. And don't let anyone else order it either. Eight pretty young women together can get any young man to order anything at all."

"No wine, no beer," she said, to humor him.

He looked back at her quickly and saw that she was still engrossed in the organizer. She looked up and smiled contritely.

She said, "We'll all get plastered and dance on the tables. Dad, what do you think I am?"

"Someone who knows her limits," he said. "Here."

He set a hefty mug of cappuccino down in front of her and sat down next to her.

"A bathtub with coffee," she said.

"You don't have to finish it. I'll take what you leave."

"You've already had a cappuccino and an espresso; that much coffee isn't good for you," she said.

"I'll watch it."

She folded the black tissue paper around the organizer and put the package back into the Saks Fifth Avenue bag. Then she took the mug between both hands and sipped the coffee with a half-opened mouth, with pursed lips that one day would give someone a blow-job. No, Joop looked away, nauseated by his own imagination.

"Is something wrong?"

"Nothing. A bit of a headache," he answered.

"Is it a producer?"

She was referring to the meeting he was going to have later. While Miriam was lunching with seven friends at Paradise Cove in Malibu, he would see Philip van Gelder again, after almost two decades. Van Gelder, who yesterday morning had turned up unexpectedly, was nowadays called Uri Gelder.

"I don't know what he wants. Just an hour of old men's talk."

"You won't be too late for this evening, will you?" she asked.

"Sweetheart, it starts at eight thirty; I'll be back no later than two thirty."

That evening they were going to a special screening of a new movie in the theater of the Directors Guild. There were going to be film stars, and Joop had managed to get three tickets so that Caroline, Miriam's best-friend-with-Porsche who was the child of rich toy manufacturers, could share her excitement. For days she'd been in telephone discussions with Caroline about their choice of clothes.

"Dad, Caroline is coming with the Porsche this evening."

"Fine, but you're riding with me."

"You can drive the Porsche; I've already told her."

"What's wrong with our car?"

"Nothing. It drives and it brakes. But it's not cool."

Joop drove a Jaguar xjs that he had bought new in 1984. The body was dented and damaged on all sides, but the motor was indestructible, and the electrically operated windows kept on buzzing.

"A smooth, new Jaguar is bourgeois," he said, "but an ancient Jag that is practically falling apart is mega-cool."

She put down the mug and looked at him pityingly.

"Dad..." She paused for a moment to give her words more emphasis. "Dad, never say cool. Someone who is older than twenty-five should never—*never*—say cool!"

"Why not?"

"Because you don't know what's cool, but you think that it's cool to say cool. And, Dad, that's really uncool."

She had looked at him with a superior, ironic glance, her irises so dark that they could hardly be distinguished from her pupils under the graceful arches of her eyebrows, with lashes that were so long that a bird could use them to fly. When she said cool, she rounded her sensual lips, as if for a kiss.

Despairing, he stared at her untouchable face. And she assumed that she'd hurt him with her words, for her face clouded over and she looked at him guiltily.

She spoke, "Dad, sorry, I don't want to hurt you."

"You're not, my dear."

"Then why do you suddenly look so miserable?"

"I'm not looking miserable. But…it's starting to sink in that you're now seventeen—and that means that one day you'll leave, with a sigh of relief, to start your own life."

"Oh Daddy…"

She stood up, placed her head on his, while she stood half-bent over him. He grabbed her hands and pressed them against him.

He whispered, "Would you like me to sing for you?"

"For God's sake," his child whispered back, "don't do that to me."

Before breaking away from him, chuckling, she kissed him on the top of his head. She snatched the present and the yogurt dish from the table and whirled out of the kitchen. He watched her go, even though she had already left his sight. The telephone started to ring, but he continued to listen to her quick steps up the stairs while he kept his arm stretched out to her in the air that she had just left, as if he could in this way tempt her to stay with him.

She called out, "If that's Mom, tell her to call back in five minutes. I really have to go!"

When the bathroom door slammed closed, he got up to answer the telephone.

"Congratulations, Joop," he heard Ellen say.

"You too," he said.

"Did you sing for her?"

"That doesn't make her happy anymore."

"She is too tough on you. Everything all right with you?"

"Everything's fine. And you?" he asked.

"Busy, fortunately many commissions. It's going well here in Holland because of those fiscal subsidies. I don't know exactly how it works, but there's a lot to do. And your work?"

"It's going fine too," he lied. He heard busy background noises, a loud voice announcing something.

"Are you at the station?" he asked.

"Heathrow. I'm flying on to Capetown. Will do a few commercials there and then take a week's vacation."

"I feel sorry for you," he said.

"May I speak to the lady?"

"She's just on the john. Can you call back in a moment?"

"I'll call back in...exactly eight minutes. Tell her to be ready. Okay, Joop, Make a nice day of it!"

"Always," he said. "Watch out over there. Have a good vacation!"

"Absolutely! Kisses!"

"Kisses," he answered before hanging up.

Chapter four

Had she driven with Caroline after all? He had forbidden it explicitly, but she had ignored his warning. Despite the low temperature, Caroline had lowered the top, pressed on the gas and steered the Porsche between other cars, passed on the right, accelerating like a bullet, had taken risks, laughing because she was young and frivolous. With one hand, busily chattering, she had driven the brand-new Porsche on the Pacific Coast Highway, the famous PCH, a busy four-lane road without a median strip, with lots of turns, sudden vistas, side-roads that leaped out of the mountains, and numerous garages that were right next to the road and forced those parked in them to make lightning-quick maneuvers.

Caroline might be frivolous, but Miriam was not. She was a serious person with a touch of brilliance. His child, just like his father, was endowed with insight into the bizarre order that human beings share with nature: math. She was voluptuously feminine, seductive, and aware of her power to attract men, but it was only one of the roles she could play. In the evening she would often, without make-up, curl up next to him on the couch—if it was chilly, dressed in sweatpants and a shapeless heavy sweater; if it was warm, in a large

T-shirt and shorts—to read together in silence or to watch a classic movie that he wanted to show her. The last two years she would go out on weekends. In the beginning he had anxiously accompanied her and had driven her to a girlfriend's and waited in the street until it was ten thirty. Initially he'd listen to radio talk shows, but when that got boring, he got himself a reading lamp that ran off the battery and read a book until it was time to pick her up. One time he was confronted by patrolling policemen. Suddenly a bright light shone into his face and he heard a voice asking for identification. Behind his car stood a patrol car. He showed his driver's license and explained that he was waiting for his daughter. "And where is she, sir?" they wanted to know. They checked whether he was telling the truth, came back to say that everything was in order and wished him a good evening. But Miriam was furious. "Just drive around a little if you're dying to wait, explore the neighborhood, but don't just stay and wait in the car like a rapist. You really make me look like a fool." He realized that this waiting until she reappeared was his very personal way of attending church, his once-a-week moment of contemplation in the silence of his old Jaguar, listening to the crickets, a crying baby, the slamming of a door, the starting of a car, the growling of a dog, the sounds of television programs (laughter at a sitcom, ricocheting bullets in an action film, slow meandering music for a love story). Distant sounds of worlds in which he had no part. He was here to watch over his child. Time passed and had a purpose: the appearance of his daughter. At the agreed time, exactly to the minute, the front door of the house where the girlfriend lived or where the party took place swung open, and there she'd appear, smiling, swaying as she danced down the steps to the sidewalk and looked around. She waved when he started the car and switched on the lights. He'd drive the car to right before the spot where she waited, and the light of his headlights would sweep over her body. She opened the door, sank down into the low car, and her short skirt crept up and revealed the entire beauty of her legs. She never pulled her skirt down; she was safe next to him on the beige leather of the old British car. The air conditioning provided a cooling-off after the sweaty hours at the party, which she talked about excitedly on the way home until he brought her to the door of their house on Superba Avenue. Go inside, sweet child, breathe, dream, live.

Philip had to support him when he staggered down the stairs of the motel and walked to Danny's car. Strange how emotion affects your body. Joop could have taken a taxi, but in Santa Monica you often had to wait for them for a long time. Cedars-Sinai was past Beverly Hills, in West Hollywood, next to the colossal gray bunker of the Beverly Center. Cedars was an extensive complex of buildings where the best doctors in the city worked. Via the Santa Monica Freeway and the Robertson exit they drove there in twenty minutes. Danny drove like a professional racecar driver. Joop had never reached West Hollywood in such a short time. There were good movie theaters, restaurants, stores, cafés in the area, where Miriam knew the way better than he. It was strange that Joop had a cigarette in his hand, sucked sharp, hot smoke into his lungs, and didn't even remember that he had lit it.

Suddenly the car came to a stop, and he looked up at Philip who stood outside next to the opened car door and extended his hand to help him get out, as if he were an old woman. He now saw that the car was blue, an Infiniti. They walked in, checked in at a desk and were sent to another department. Long halls here, many nurses and patients, and he really felt like an old woman, his legs seemed to be made of jelly, but Philip held him upright.

"Emergency," it was called here. He lowered himself onto a seat between other people who had to wait until the nightmare was past and the loved one suddenly appeared, laughing and singing. Just a joke! Nothing wrong!

Someone caught his eye and strangely enough pointed at his hand, until Joop, after staring for many seconds, understood that the man meant that he was holding a cigarette, which was forbidden here. He stubbed out the cigarette.

Why had the sight of Miriam this morning brought about so much melancholy? A premonition? He didn't believe in premonitions. Premonitions were for people who lived in magic worlds. People who believed in signs of the zodiac, iridology, and aromatherapy. Their world was filled with omens, supernatural connections, and divine phenomena. But even though he was a nonbeliever, he could not deny that this morning he had looked at his daughter in a different way than in the past seventeen years.

Someone who believed in premonitions also believed in mythic punishments after a violation of taboos. A father may not observe his unclothed daughter. He had not desired her, at least not with a sexual intention. But maybe, in the world of the person with premonitions, any form of observation was punished regardless of the intent. In that case he was guilty—but why should Miriam be punished through his fault? If anyone was to be reproached for anything, it was he, and if a punishment had to be meted out, he was the one who should be stricken. Or is this reverse, unfair punishment precisely the hallmark of magic worlds? Does the sword hit the innocent of all people, which causes the sinner, convinced of his sin, to be doubly punished? No, he didn't want to exist in a world that was that blind and cruel. But perhaps this world, the world of chance, was at least as horrible.

In front of him Philip and a white-coated man appeared.

"Joop, this is Dr. Hemmings."

"Mr. Koopm'n…"

Joop stood up and looked into the thoughtful face of the doctor, the magician who could reverse chance. He shook the doctor's hand, the hand that could prevent a final parting. Around forty years old, but already completely gray. Glasses with thick lenses. Hemmings had read a lot. Small, tired eyes.

"Where is she, doctor?"

"We're still doing some tests. We are sure about some things. Would you come with me for a moment?"

They walked onto the shiny floor of the hall and entered a side room.

"I'll wait for you here," Philip said at the door.

"No, no, come along," Joop insisted. "That's okay, isn't it Doctor?"

"If you want him to."

"Yes. Come along, Philip."

Philip came inside with them; the doctor darkened the room. A light box fastened to the wall started to glow. There were x-rays.

"Your daughter was sitting on the back of a motorcycle. The motorcycle toppled over, and she was flung to the side. She fell under an oncoming car. This caused grave traumas."

On hearing the word "motorcycle," Joop had a sudden burning, liberating, heartening insight: It wasn't Miriam! They had mixed her up with someone else! Of course, her cell phone had been stolen that morning without her noticing it, and now they thought that someone else was Miriam!

Joop interrupted the doctor: "You're making a mistake. A motorcycle? She knows no one with a motorcycle. It can't be. It's impossible. It can't be her! No one we know has a motorcycle! There must have been an identity switch."

Hemmings said, "It is understandable that you are grasping at every straw, but the driver of the motorcycle gave her name. These are x-rays of your daughter's spine. And her cervical vertebrae. Here is her skull."

"I want to see her."

"We'll go to her in a minute. I first want to explain to you what the situation is."

Joop nodded, but he didn't acknowledge defeat. He didn't know who lay in that emergency bed, but it couldn't be Miriam. He was going to call her immediately after this. The restaurant was called Bob Morris's Paradise Cove Beach Café, the only business in this part of California that was actually located on the sand of the beach and served fresh fish and crustaceans. Yesterday he had driven there to have them make an impression of his credit card and to put his signature on the bill so that all Miriam needed to do was fill in the amount. That past summer they had twice a month on Sundays sat under an umbrella at Bob Morris's, pushing their toes into the sand, shelling peanuts that lay ready for the taking in an old wine barrel at the entrance, and sometimes he misled the ever-changing servers—surfing, sunburned boys and girls from the area who earned a little extra income here—about Miriam's age and poured her a glass of cool white wine. She was probably sitting there now, chatting with her girlfriends, seven other daughters at her table, all around seventeen, smart beautiful girls next to his princess.

Well, this was a misunderstanding.

Hemmings said, "The spinal chord has been seriously damaged, irreversibly damaged. Injuries like these cause permanent damage. If she would ever come to, and unfortunately that chance is virtually zero, she would never again be able to walk. These traumas lead to permanent paralysis."

Joop could not control himself: "I've told you already, this is not Miriam! She couldn't have been on the back of someone's motorcycle because she doesn't know anyone with a motorcycle! I think this must be unpleasant for you, but I have nothing to do with this! Right now my daughter is in a restaurant at Paradise Cove... Malibu...Bob Morris's Beach Café, of course you know it too...she's having lunch there with her girlfriends! That's where she was going! Therefore that's where she is now!"

Looking worried, Hemmings waited until he finished speaking.

Joop continued, "I, I understand quite well that her cell phone has led to this confusion, but it should stop. This is too horrible. I don't want to link my daughter to such misery. She is the only one I have. If that sounds like a melodramatic cliché, so be it. She is my life. That's why...I'm going to call her now, then you can continue with your work, and I too..."

As if someone had directed it, Joop's telephone sounded the *Wilhelmus* again. Philip was holding the pink backpack in his hand and looked at him questioning, uncertain if he should hand him the phone. Without a trace of impatience, the physician crossed his arms and waited for Joop to act.

Joop smiled. "This is she. Want to bet? This is she."

He motioned, and Philip opened the bag and handed him the telephone.

With a hopelessly trembling finger that he tried to control because he didn't want the physician to see that he was on the point of collapse, Joop pressed the button.

"Yes," he said.

"Mr. Koopman? This is Caroline."

"Caroline, it's good that you're calling. May I speak to Miriam? She has lost her telephone."

"I've already tried calling her, but she doesn't pick up. She is forty-five minutes late and we're a little worried."

"Isn't she there with you? Didn't she ride with you? What's the matter, Caroline?" He became livid and shouted, "I don't want any jokes! No adolescent pranks! Where is she! Hand her the telephone so that I can talk to her!"

The girl started to cry.

"She isn't here, Mr. Koopman. She didn't ride with me or with Pat..."

He barked, "And with whom did she ride!"

"With God..."

"With God? What in heaven's name are you talking about? God? GOD? My girl, I want to tell you that I'll inform your parents about this, and I assure you that..."

Crying loudly, Caroline said, "The man from God's Gym, the health club, you were there yourself last week! Everyone calls him God. Short for Godzilla. Because he's so big."

He had been to God's Gym. He had himself weighed there. By a black man who was six and a half feet tall, weighing at least three hundred pounds, a giant. When the business opened several years ago, religious people in the neighborhood protested. They demanded in court that the neon letters be removed from the façade, but the demand was rejected.

"What—what was she doing at his place?" he asked, now softer, but still overcome by an intense hatred.

"We had only an hour of school this morning. The last day before Christmas. We went to the gym and then we were going to come here. God had to go to Malibu too. And he has a beautiful Harley. A classic. He was glad to take her."

Joop knew the moments from films, films that colored the imagination of people in the twentieth century, and he wondered if the generations that lived before the movie generation had known the same experience: the world slowed down, it was as if he looked through water at the light box and at the x-rays, and then he slowly turned his head in the direction of Hemmings and Philip, who came toward him with arms outstretched as if they too were moving in water, slowed down by impossibly heavy air, and oddly enough he saw the telephone slip from his fingers, the expensive Motorola, while thinking: fortunately I'm insured for damage to the telephone. And suddenly he fell through the floor of the room, at least he felt that he moved downward, and he also felt that his heart was burning, was simply on fire, and he really wanted to get out of there and go home to cook something for Miriam, a delicious pasta with seafood, or a quiche with real Swiss Gruyere, or a real Dutch meatball that he had taught her to eat, a simple round succulent Dutch meatball with onions; he saw her cutting the onions, tap the cutting board with the knife, and by cutting the onions tears welled up in her eyes; she looked up at him smiling: "Look, Dad, I'm crying."

Chapter five

In the early morning of Saturday, December twenty-third, in the silence of forty minutes past three, the depth of the night, Miriam died. She lay in a room filled with high-tech apparatus, surroundings that would have sparked her enthusiasm. Outwardly she was just as perfect as the last time that he had seen her, on that intangibly distant Friday at ten to eight in the morning—about twenty hours ago—when she went to school for a short assembly to close the year and to celebrate the start of the Christmas vacation. She had waved to him when she walked by the house with her white Koga Miyata in order to bicycle the three miles to the school at the corner of Seventh and California. Perhaps her legs had become so beautiful because she biked every day like all Dutch girls. Bent over the handlebars of her racing bike that he had bought second-hand, she bicycled over the ribbon of concrete on the beach with sand on her lips. If she took Lincoln, with her rear moving back and forth on the narrow saddle, her short skirt riding up, her beautiful hair blowing behind her head like a black flag, she would be accompanied by an uninterrupted horn concert from hopeful motorists. Therefore she chose to bicycle over the beach, navigating between rollerbladers and joggers.

A dozen tubes and wires connected her body to a wall of computers and screens where her "vital functions," as the nurses and physicians call them, could be read in graphs. For hours on end he held her hand. He whispered to her that everything would turn out all right and that she would recover and that he would not leave her side, and he talked about the past, a small journey through the filled treasury of his memory. He talked about what he found there, caressed her fingers and her wrist, waited for a sign of recognition.

At sunset on that Friday, not even ten hours after Joop had watched her bicycle away, a physician asked if he could speak with him. Joop read his name on the nametag: Dr. Benjamin Pollock. In the hall Pollock explained what he wanted to discuss. Joop had come to know the members of the team, and he had been informed that the team no longer had any hope. Pollock emphasized that they were doing everything to save his daughter, but they had to be realistic, and unfortunately there were limits to their chances for success. Perhaps Joop should start considering the inevitable. Pollock explained that he belonged to another team. It was set up like that legally in order to keep the responsibilities and interests separated. He had to broach the subject because his daughter could save a life. The chance that she would survive was in fact no longer present, but one organ had survived the accident. Her heart was in perfect condition. She herself had no future, but she could offer a future to someone else.

"Will you think about it, Mr. Koopm'n?" he asked. "Take your time and ask yourself what your daughter would have wanted."

There followed half an evening and a night. Joop stayed with her. Philip and Danny refused to leave the waiting area and relieved him when he needed a cup of coffee or a cigarette, which he had to smoke outside. Danny kept the small pink backpack with him, an innocent cotton thing with leather straps that had pressed on her shoulders for days; the backpack was a sign that everything could again be as it was yesterday. Miriam had a life ahead of her. She had been born to discover an elegant and shockingly simple mathematical equation that could predict all the prime numbers.

He called Ellen. Her voice on the answering machine said that she was out of the country and would not call back until after

January seventh, but in the meantime she wished the caller a merry Christmas and a happy New Year.

He left a message: "Ellen, when you hear this, call me back right away. Something has happened to Miriam. Something terrible. Call immediately, please."

Around midnight something happened that he could not explain. He held her hand, talked about the vacation to Holland they took several years ago, and tried to get her to laugh with reminiscence about a quarrel he'd had in the train with a conductor. He placed his head on her hand and remained lying down with his eyes closed, his cheek on her skin. Admittedly, he was tired, and what he experienced then couldn't be anything but an intense dream, but it was strange that he saw himself, half leaning over the bed, sleeping next to Miriam.

He was somewhere high in the corner of the room and looked down at himself and the bed and saw how Miriam got up, even though she remained lying down at the same time—something broke away from her, and although he could see, even though he had no eyes, he could not describe what exactly separated itself from her, but it was something real that he called Miriam. She came toward him, this disembodied being, and he realized that she consisted of the same material—insofar as it was material—and that she had the same sensation as he. He felt how his body, even though he didn't have it, was penetrated by boundless happiness. He had no mouth but yet he called her name, and she heard him without ears. There was no longer any pain, no longing, everything was fulfilled. And without words she told him that he should have her body cremated and scatter her ashes in the sea near Catalina Island now that she had left the world of the four dimensions. "Four dimensions?" he asked without voice. "Aren't there three?" She answered, "You're forgetting the time dimension, Dad."

He was awakened by a male nurse who responded to a code. Six others appeared and he was asked to wait in the hall; her bodily functions were failing one after the other; she was put on the heart-lung machine and lost a lot of fluid, which indicated that her brain was dying.

Under the light of fluorescent tubes, pacing in the hall and the waiting area, his eyes raw with exhaustion, Joop knew what he had to do when she died. She wanted to be cremated; her ashes had to be scattered in front of the coast of Catalina.

They had once spent a week there, on the island across from Long Beach. In the shade of a giant eucalyptus she had for hours read *The Man Who Loved Only Numbers*, a biography of Paul Erdös, one of the greatest mathematicians of the twentieth century, and taken notes in a notebook with a heavy black cover. She had wandered over the island while he was at work in their rented house, and in the evening they had stared across the ocean and talked about his life with Ellen. She asked, he answered.

He knew that she wanted it. In the dream she had made it clear to him, although he didn't know how it had happened. He would do what she wanted, and he had no doubt about it; he should let his daughter be cremated, he would let her unite with the water around Catalina.

Hours later the team finally let her go. Machines and computers insufflated her and circulated blood to protect the organ that was suitable for donation until the recipient was made ready. The recipient was somewhere in the United States. If he wished, and if the recipient agreed as well, he could later get in touch with him or her. That was not necessary, he declared when filling in the questionnaire. Was he authorized to make this decision alone? He answered yes, even though he realized that he should inform Ellen.

At the first light of day he was taken home by Philip and Danny. Her heart had already been taken out of her body. The thought was enough to drive him crazy—the image of the beating heart that was being taken out of her chest. Science had made irrational fears real. In almost all languages the heart corresponded to love, honesty, humanity, but ever since heart transplants had become possible, the heart had also become a pump that could be replaced. A pound and a half in weight, flesh of his child.

Never before had he lived in this house alone. First Ellen had been there, then Miriam, and when they were physically absent, the delightful expectation of their return floated between the walls.

It took hours before he had the courage to go upstairs and to open the door of her room. When he did it, he saw the half empty yogurt container on her nightstand and the bag from Saks on her bed, the organizer on the unfolded black tissue paper.

Chapter six

The first time he saw Ellen was on a film set. She worked in wardrobe. After high school she had completed a two-year course in fashion design and found work as a wardrobe assistant for television programs. The short film was her first solo job. She was barely paid anything but had taken the work because she got a credit: costume design—Ellen Meerman.

The first production set was behind the Central Station in Amsterdam. At eight o'clock in the morning Joop ducked into the hall under the train platforms, walked to the IJ-side, and the first crew member that he saw, next to a Volkswagen bus filled with clothes, was a young woman who defied the cold in tight short pants. They were called hot pants, and that year they were part of an already bygone fashion. But Ellen hung onto it stubbornly, knowing what effect the sight of her frivolous shorts produced. She had dazzlingly beautiful legs, and the hot pants were so tight around her bottom that the form of her buttocks was sharply defined. In addition she wore a tight jacket with a fur collar, net stockings on her legs, and off-white sneakers on her feet.

"Do you know where the set of *The End of the Line* is?" he asked.

"Come with me," she said. A pleasant, low voice. An elastic step, as if she were walking on air pillows.

"Are you an extra?" she asked.

"No," Joop chuckled with difficulty, disappointed at the way she classified him, "I'm the writer of the script."

"Joop Koopman?"

"And you?" he asked.

"I do wardrobe. I'm Ellen."

As they walked she shook his hand, smiling.

"Clever, the way you tell that story. Tremendously clever. I admire that tremendously."

Twice "tremendously," he thought. She was stunning. With those lips it didn't matter how often she said "tremendously."

Although he hadn't planned to visit the set often, he returned every morning. For her. He got coffee when she wanted it, kept her company when she had to wait, helped her when she stood with an armful of clothes in her rented van.

The modest budget of the film allowed no more than six days of filming, but even a short film had to conclude with a party. He went because the party marked the completion of his first real film and because he wanted to make a date with Ellen.

With four dinners, spread over four consecutive weeks, he courted her in an almost old-fashioned way. He invited her, he paid, he accompanied her home properly and took leave with a formal handshake. Meanwhile he devoured her with his eyes. Ellen was different from the women he knew. She had not gone to college, never read a newspaper, had worked since she was nineteen, was not interested in the abstractions that obsessed him as a young writer—form and content, reality and fiction—and was more spontaneous, intuitive, and direct than he. He'd had several girlfriends but hadn't plunged into the bachelor's life of Amsterdam. He had read and studied, searching for answers to the big questions about life and the world. But he couldn't deny—even though he had tried during his earnest pursuit of knowledge—that he also longed for swishing skirts, a slender woman's hand that brushed back a lock of dyed blond hair, the delicate manner of sliding a ring on a finger, how a pantyhose was rolled up before a foot slipped into it. Ellen was the female body that could hold his floating spirit on earth. She stood in the middle of the world while he looked at it from behind a frosted glass window.

The fifth time, he saw her by chance in front of the dairy case of Albert Heijn. She was holding a jar of yogurt in her hand and was reading the label. She wore jeans, a bulky nylon jacket, and was pushing a shopping cart. She had an athletic build, and at a distance seemed taller than she was. Her face reminded him of Egyptian statues, a long neck, an oval face with a rather large nose, large green eyes, and hungry lips. She was earthy. A priestess of nature.

What had he said to her in front of the dairy case? Gee, what a coincidence, I was just in the area, are you in a hurry, do you want to have a drink? Ostensibly casually she had looked in his shopping cart and saw that he was going to take home canned tuna, eggs, mayonnaise, and red wine. She said: "I have lettuce, tomatoes, beans—you know what? If we combine our purchases we can make a niçoise together. At your place or mine?"

Her shopping bag was waiting next to the front door when she pulled the jeans down her legs in his tiny bathroom and, even though he had just lit the gas heater and the rooms exhaled cold, she stood stark naked on the threshold of his bedroom. Was it the cold or the excitement that made her nipples so hard?

Solid, virginal breasts, a gentle slope of her belly, magnificent legs, graceful fingers, and thick blond hair that she had loosened in the bathroom and which now covered her shoulders. He desired her body and Ellen enjoyed his desire, which gave her power and hence the chance to give herself to him.

"Do you think I'm very ugly?" she asked. As if posing for a nude magazine, she placed her hands on the doorframe to the left and the right of her shoulders and unafraid, she let him look at her breasts and at the small triangle below her belly.

"Hideous," he joked bravely. He motioned to the pillow next to him. She came toward him and he saw her breasts undulate slightly. She turned back the blanket, looked approvingly at what she had caused in him and crawled on top of him, covered him with her soft body while she slid over him until her breasts reached his lips.

It was 1979. In the late afternoon sun of a clear blue November day they went at it unashamedly for an hour. He didn't know that he dared to do all that. Afterwards, with animated gestures, Ellen made a niçoise salad for which she had prepared a simple but perfect dressing of oil, vinegar, garlic, salt, and pepper. Because she was cold, she drank tea with it. In the small Volkswagen bus everything hung neatly and perfectly arranged, but after her departure it took him forty-five minutes to clear off the kitchen counter.

What would have become of him without Ellen? A shy, spectral poet who, chain smoking and running up debts, would see his life fly by until he would one day be found dead in his bed by an annoyed landlord.

When Ellen danced into her small place in the Jordaan quarter, the curtains fluttered with exuberance, the kitchen counter became gleefully buried under pots and pans, and the neighbors prepared themselves expectantly for another episode of the noisy drama that preceded Ellen's orgasms. Everything she did was charged with eroticism. All her senses were in direct contact with her sexuality. Joop didn't know why she had chosen him—the first few months they let each other be "free"; he knew that she did it with others and was sick with jealousy—but he had resolved not to think about it too much. She reminded him of Linda, his distant cousin who had lost her parents in a car accident. Linda was seventeen when she was taken in by his parents, he a year younger, and for ten months he was initiated by her into acts that held him day and night in a feverish intoxication which led to a disastrous school year. His later girlfriends lacked the intense physicality that he had found in Linda. Until Ellen turned up. Intelligent but not intellectual. Earthy and sexy. Elusive and inscrutable.

Despite his intentions, Joop had to admit that he was obsessed with Ellen. He could hardly bear the fact that she still had a life outside one with him. He kept an eye on her constantly—even if it was only in his imagination—when she talked with his friends in a bar, when she did her work during the day without his supervision and caused the imagination of the men around her to run wild, when she lay in bed alone and probably did it with herself. For during that first period he was convinced that she thought of nothing but sex all day long.

A lot changed when they decided to become serious. He kept his apartment in the Pijp quarter and actually moved in with Ellen. In her apartment in the Jordaan, he would write, trying to satisfy the requirements of the commission for film subsidies. Sometimes she burst into the room and appeared in all her glory, her cheeks red from the cold, her hair framing her face wildly, pulled him with one hand against her to kiss him fiercely and grabbed his crotch with the other.

Immediately after completing his training at the Film Academy, Joop had written *The End of the Line*. The film was directed by Bert Hulscher, a filmmaker who had left the academy two years before Joop. Bert had approached him after Joop had published a short story in a literary magazine; according to Bert, the story had a movie in it.

After his first film, Bert was immediately embraced by the small elite that divided subsidy money in the Netherlands, and he was allowed to prove his potential with a longer movie. Joop Koopman submitted one application after another to the film commission to write screenplays. One after another they were rejected because they were judged to be "too literary" and "insufficiently visual."

While Bert worked on his first full-length movie, Joop turned one of his screenplays into a novel, and the second publisher he approached decided to publish it. The critics confirmed what he already knew: he could write, even something as complex as a novel, which was praised sympathetically by the critics as the work of a "prominent new talent." But the frustration of being unable to find support for his movie projects increased his obstinacy, even though he was successful with the novel and his bank account conveyed a comforting balance.

In two years he submitted nine projects. While a project was under consideration, he asked invariably to be allowed to elucidate his submission orally. The committee praised his effort and talent and, carefully expressed because of his sudden literary reputation, explained each time that in their eyes he was more of a literary narrator than a screenwriter. When he called a day later to hear the committee's decision, he invariably received a veiled "no." Joop didn't even have a chance when Bert Hulscher was invited to be a member of the committee. And he knew what it meant when Bert no longer answered his messages on the answering machine. For some time he suspected an evil plot to keep him outside the movie world, but when he couldn't find a sound reason for it, he assumed bad luck and fate.

After *The End of the Line*, Ellen made a career for herself. She had an exhibitionist taste which went well with the style of the commercials of that time, which is why within several months she was offered more commissions than she could accept. And from costume design she broadened her field to art direction.

In the early summer of 1982 Ellen received a telephone call from a Dutch cameraman with whom she had worked on some advertising spots. The cameraman had left for Los Angeles in the spring and was preparing a big feature film. He had told the producer about her exuberant work and asked if she could send a tape. Three weeks later she received a ticket with the request to come and have a talk.

A day after her departure she called.

"It's called the Sunset Marquis. Everyone sits around the swimming pool here. I've seen Robert Duvall and I think Clint Eastwood also."

A stab of jealousy. "Do you think so or are you sure?"

"It must have been him! It looked just like him!"

"And the weather?"

"Wonderful. Very warm, but really nice. And listen to this..."

"Listen to what?"

"They want me to do it!"

"Really?"

"Really. Eight weeks' preparation. Eight weeks to shoot. And guess for how much per week?"

"Tell me."

"Two thousand dollars per week!"

"That much?"

"But...I'm doing it only if you come along."

"What will I do there?"

"You're going to write there. Fuck those subsidies! One day you'll sell something. Mark my words."

"It's even more difficult there than here," he said. But he didn't really want to argue about it with her. It was exactly what he wanted.

In the summer of 1982 they left with four suitcases. Since Ellen had an income, they could rent a studio—a living room-bedroom with an open kitchen—in a Hollywood neighborhood inhabited by addicts, maintain a used old Chevrolet, and feed themselves with cheap Chinese take-out meals.

The movie was postponed one month, and then another month before being canceled once and for all. Ellen had been paid, but she now experienced what was the order of the day in Hollywood: many movies, even if they were prepared and the whole crew was working, were never filmed. With the money that Ellen had put aside they could hold out for a while.

Joop wrote scripts, translated them, and made the rounds to those agencies that didn't refuse unsolicited work as a matter of policy. After five months he found an agent who believed in him. On his advice he acquired a pen name. According to his agent, scripts by foreigners were often returned unread because experience had shown that foreigners were not used to the Hollywood system and did not apply the rules of the game consistently. And without taking into account his feelings, the agent took a red felt tip pen to Joop's work.

From then on Joop Koopman called himself Joe Merchant, a name like that of a vaudeville artist, and a year after his arrival in Los Angeles the miracle happened: his agent sold one of his screenplays. For as much as fifty thousand dollars. Real dollars. A check from a real Hollywood producer. A fortune.

In Venice, the part of Los Angeles that was still under the spell of flower power and therefore attracted hippies, dealers, junkies, artists, writers, and film people—and where Joop and Ellen often strolled on the beach on weekends—they found an affordable house. Venice was relatively cheap compared to other parts of West Los Angeles.

The house had been on the market for eight months and had obviously been waiting for their bid. It was a detached wooden house in a quiet, middle-class neighborhood where gentrification had not yet hit and which had not yet been infected by gangs. The house was on Superba Avenue, halfway between Lincoln Boulevard and the beach. A five-minute walk to the west, past well-tended small gardens with palms and ferns, led to the famous boardwalk of Venice Beach, and to the east to the supermarkets, snack bars, dry cleaners, and car washes on Lincoln. The house was not yet a wreck but showed signs of serious overdue maintenance. "Just a coat of paint, and it will be good for years," the realtor had lied.

After they had gotten out of the Chevrolet and were looking at the house, Ellen said, "Joe Merchant in Venice. *The Merchant of Venice.* Isn't that a play? By whom?"

"By Shakespeare," he said.

After the first visit they walked through the neighborhood to the beach.

"It's ideally located," said Ellen. "But a lot needs to be done to it."

"Almost everything," he said. "New kitchen. Bathroom. Toilet. Gutters. Roof."

"If we pile on even more expenses, it will get too expensive."

"Oh well, those are the expenses," he answered.

She repeated, "There could be other expenses."

"You mean: hidden defects, or something like that?"

"I mean something different, something very different."

"What else?" He stood still as he clasped her hand. He asked, "What do you mean?"

"Do you remember—that I forgot the pill?"

Ever since he knew her, she had frequently skipped a day because she had forgotten or because she couldn't find the strip, but his sperm had never found its target.

He repeated: "What do you mean?"

"What should I mean? I'm pregnant. This morning I got the result. I didn't know either...perhaps it's tremendously stupid, but... what do you think?"

They bought the house. They had no money for a contractor and did everything themselves. They slept in sleeping bags, bought their food in Mexican fast food restaurants, showered without curtains, painted the walls, sanded and varnished the floors, repaired the baseboards, installed new kitchen cabinets, and Joop discovered that he was able to walk on the roof like a tight-rope walker and to replace rotting shingles.

On September 18, 1983, they got married. Ellen was six months pregnant. Their mothers flew to Los Angeles and shared a room in a motel on Lincoln Boulevard. The ceremony at city hall took three minutes. Their mothers were witnesses. Ellen felt the baby move wildly all day, as if it wanted to share in the rush of happiness.

Chapter seven

Joop woke up at one o'clock in the morning, the start of the twenty-fifth of December of the year 2000. Christmas day. He remained lying down for a minute and wondered why he was on the sofa in the living room at this hour. For a moment there was peace, as he assumed that Miriam was in her bed. Until suddenly, in fiery fragments that shot to his heart from the farthest corners of his memory (oddly enough it was a physical realization that dominated the innermost part of his chest), the events of the past few days joined to form a coherent whole, and he was overcome by the unacceptable notion that Miriam's bed had not been slept in and that she would never again come downstairs. He jumped up, made sick by the images in his head, rushed upstairs, and threw open the door of her room.

He lowered himself onto the threshold and sat with his head hidden behind his hands, moving back and forth like an Orthodox Jew in prayer, while calling out her name incessantly. Then he lapsed for minutes into a silence that was accompanied only by his breathing. At times he imagined that this was a nightmare from which he would awaken, but just as often he knew that Miriam's death was an irrevocable fact and that her voice would never again sound through the telephone, that she would never again run her fingers through his hair. But if he concentrated, squeezed his eyes shut and gnashed his teeth, clenched his hands into fists and tensed every fiber of his body, then he saw her, heard her voice, and could caress the smooth skin of her neck.

After an hour the pain seemed to ebb and he went soberly to the kitchen. He lit a cigarette from one of the cigarette packs lying next to the small pink backpack that Philip—Philip? Oh yes, Philip had faithfully kept him company during the afternoon and the night of the catastrophe—had left behind. He walked into the nighttime garden and smoked the cigarette. It was calm, the outside thermometer indicated fifty degrees, and from far away the sound of airplanes landing at LAX fanned out. He saw no stars; mist hung above the city. No lights burned in the homes that he could see from his garden. Later that day, all the families would gather to eat turkey. They had been invited by Caroline's parents. Nouveaux riches, but warm-hearted. Lived in an enormous house on Main Street in Santa Monica, above a private underground parking garage where about ten valuable cars were parked. Wealth in this city was often slightly degenerate. Around forty guests were supposed to come, their lawyers, business associates, almost all Jews who let Chanukah and Christmas coincide this year. Miriam knew that Joop was going through a difficult period financially, and after a tentative attempt—she didn't know what she should wear at the dinner—she had no longer insisted, for she could live with the limitations imposed by his financial situation. But he knew that she wanted to wear something new, even though she would appear dazzling at the table in any of the dresses that she owned—two closets full, he thought, but apparently not enough, or not exactly right, or not quite right, or not suitable for certain days (as a man he would never be able to fathom the delicate balance of choice of clothes and female mood). He had given her his credit card, and Miriam had come home with a dress that cost only forty dollars. On Sunday of last week she had taken the bus, had rummaged through the stores on Melrose, and at the flea market on the corner of Fairfax she had found a second-hand dress. Scarlet velvet trimmed with black frills, ruches they were called, falling fairly decently halfway down her thighs but with a dangerously low neckline. She had inherited the jewels from Joop's mother; anyway, he had given them to her, a few rings and necklaces, and after the purchase of the dress she had come into his study in the evening and had asked if she could appear in public like that. Hair pinned up, earrings with corals, jewelry, stiletto heels, her legs in shiny black pantyhose. He nodded.

"Really, Dad? You really can't tell that it's an old dress?"

"No, absolutely not."

"You don't think that the jewelry is too much?"

"No. Nothing is too much on you."

"That's a dangerous answer. You're not being honest."

"I'm always honest. At least to you."

"You're getting yourself into hot water! Really?"

"Miriam, you've seen yourself in the mirror. You've evidently decided—and it's taken you more than an hour—that you look good enough to ask your poor father for his opinion, and do you really think that I'm going to say that you can't present yourself like that?"

"You're saying terrible things. You're making me tremendously insecure. I just want to know exactly what you think; there will be real heavy hitters there."

"Since when are you interested in heavy hitters?"

"I don't want them to think that we are white trash."

"You've got more royalty in your pinkie than they…"

"A cliché, Daddy, the exterior counts too."

"Your exterior is hors concours."

"Hors concours? So that means something like outside competition? And that means?"

"That you're so beautiful that you're excluded from the competition out of pity for the other competitors."

"Well, you're a sweet dad."

"A kiss?"

"All right." She pressed her full painted lips on his forehead. "An extra mouth on your forehead is always useful," she said as she walked away.

Involuntarily his hand moved to his forehead and touched it as if he could find the impress of her lips there. She was going to wear that dress today. With his mother's glittering jewels. Gleaming pumps. Glistening pantyhose. On the threshold of his consciousness lay the terrifying thought that everything was different, that she would not appear, and that his life was suddenly dominated by something catastrophic; but he didn't want to think about it, refused to find the words that gave shape to that reality. Soon everything would be normal when this bizarre night had dissolved in the light of a normal morning.

He lay down on the sofa, a coat pulled over him, realizing that he should not go upstairs anymore, should avoid the doors and the rooms up there, and turn his mind to the images that he encountered in his memory, that rich, roomy ballroom of his mind that offered what he longed for.

Chapter eight

Sitting on a small stool, he had supported Ellen when, groaning and cursing, she tensed the muscles of her body to liberate it from the child. Looking over her sweaty shoulders, her blond ponytail in his face, his hands under her armpits, Joop started to push along with her, not only in his imagination but also physically, as if he could help by taking over the rhythm of her breathing. He too gnashed his teeth, braced himself when she plunged with all her strength into a contraction. In between the contractions he breathed, just like Ellen, with short, fast breaths, like a dog after running. Because he held onto her and was carried along by the tensions in her body, Joop had contributed symbolically to Ellen's struggle on the birthing stool.

To make space, Joop had pushed the kitchen table against the wall an hour earlier, and then placed a piece of building plastic on the just varnished wooden floor. The windows behind the kitchen counter overlooked the garden. It was the first winter in this house, and he had noticed that during this season the sunlight didn't come in until late, but under the clear blue sky this day sparkled with light and life.

With her howling in his ears and her raging body against his chest and between his arms, he saw something appear between her thighs.

"Yes, one more!" the midwife encouraged.

Ellen nodded and looked for strength that seemed to lie far beyond her capacities, but suddenly her body hardened, and with Ellen's primal scream a small, shriveled human parcel appeared. The midwife caught it, and the child started to scream immediately. Was it beautiful? No, it was animal-like and atrocious, but of course it was also the way that National Geographic documentaries illustrated nature: with an immoral aesthetic order that lay beyond all human norms. His sperm had penetrated Ellen's ovum, and now it was time for a human being to enter the world.

Even before she had caught her breath, Ellen murmured, "May I hold her?"

"Just one second," answered the midwife.

She cut the umbilical cord, placed the little creature on a scale, did some quick tests that Joop didn't understand. Then, with a hoarse, ruined voice Ellen whispered in his ear, "Joop, we have a baby, a real baby."

For a moment she placed her sweaty, tired head on his shoulder, and he kissed her ear. After ten seconds she sat up again and said, "My baby."

The creature was wrapped in a blanket and Ellen accepted it eagerly, with the care, meticulousness, and experience that she seemed to possess naturally. It was December 22, 1983, ten minutes past noon.

"My baby," whispered Ellen, while the little creature, that kept her big eyes focused on the world, shivering in her arms, searched for warmth. It had dark hair, pale red skin, a wide mouth.

"She's going to be beautiful," said the midwife. "I've done thousands of deliveries and I see immediately how the baby will turn out. She'll be a knockout."

Over his wife's shoulder Joop looked at his daughter. He tried to recognize something in her gaze and the shape of her face, but she was a stranger, or rather: she belonged to no one; she had her own, independent character, an individual with her own source of strength, her own destiny that she would unravel over dozens of years. They gave her his mother's middle name.

"Miriam," whispered Ellen. "Hello, Miriam. Welcome to our family."

Six weeks after Miriam's birth he sold another script. Again, fifty thousand dollars. The difficult first year in Los Angeles had ended in a period of prosperity. That evening, after the end of Johnny Carson, Ellen rubbed her bottom against him in the typical way that traditionally meant: I want to, I'm ready, caress me. When she was pregnant, she had, in order to protect her full belly, always leaned on her hands, bent forward on her knees, her rear up toward him when they made love.

It had been three months since they had made love the last time. Afterwards she lay in his arms with her back toward him. Silently they listened to the breathing of their child. Ellen held onto his hands between her breasts, pressed them forcefully against her and said, "I'm afraid."

This took him by surprise, and he asked, "Afraid?"

"Yes," he heard, "afraid—that this will pass."

"This will not pass," he answered.

"Are you sure?" she asked.

"Never," he said.

But suddenly a paradox struck him: the fact that happiness was something that could only be grasped when it had dissolved. He moved even closer to her. When happiness glittered in his eyes, he couldn't see anything. Happiness existed only in memory. But it was frightening to think of that, as if words could damage feelings. Ellen had expressed something that should have remained unsaid.

He pressed her against him and said as a prayer, "This will never pass. This may never pass."

Chapter nine

I t was the front door bell that dragged him from a deep sleep. He didn't want to, but the bell kept jangling. He opened his eyes and listened. Someone was now pressing the button in a steady rhythm, and the electric bell buzzed off and on, like drops from a leaky faucet.

Past the small pink backpack that he had hung on a coat hook, he walked to the front door and looked through the window. Philip. Philip saw him, lowered his hand, and smiled wistfully.

Joop unlocked the door.

"You're not answering the phone," said Philip. "I didn't want to disturb you, but I was starting to get worried."

"That's nice. Do you have any cigarettes with you? Mine are finished."

"Let me in, or are we going to stand here?"

"Come in."

Joop stepped aside and made room for Philip. In front of the door stood the blue Infiniti in which they had driven him to the hospital. Danny leaned against the side of the car and lit a cigarette.

Philip asked, "Do you know that someone is sitting in a car in front of your house?"

"Danny," said Joop as he closed the door.

"No. A big black man. I think that it's him."

Joop walked back immediately and looked outside through the small window in the door. Partially behind the Infiniti stood a shiny, new black Jeep Cherokee. The windows were tinted, but it was clear that a big dark man was sitting behind the wheel.

"What's he doing here?" asked Joop.

"Call the police if you want him to leave."

"Yes."

"And plug the phone back into the wall. No one can reach you."

"Will do."

But he could not keep his eyes off the man in the Jeep, the man who had transported his child to her death. If the man remained waiting there, Joop would kill him. He could imagine that the man had come of his free will to die for the evil that he had committed.

Philip said, "You're staying here. Leave him alone. The police will take care of it."

Joop didn't answer. He felt Philip's hand on his shoulder.

"Enough peeking. Look at me. How are you? You don't have to shave; a Jewish man doesn't have to shave after something like this, but go and wash yourself. You stink. You were wearing that shirt on Friday. That was three days ago."

"Do you have a cigarette for me?"

"Of course. Is the kitchen there? Come along."

They entered the kitchen. On the counter stood eight empty wine bottles. Joop drank nothing stronger, and the eight bottles were witnesses to the way he had sought sleep. Tylenol with wine. The pills were in the living room. He had two more boxes with six bottles each. A big supply, but they were a Trader Joe's special.

"Have you eaten?"

"Not hungry."

They sat down at the kitchen table. Philip pushed a pack of Marlboros toward him.

"I want you to go outside for a while. Come and eat something with me. Everyone here is Jewish, but at Christmas all of them are goys for a day. We're going to eat turkey somewhere."

"That's nice of you," answered Joop, who could barely speak because the roof of his mouth and his throat hurt, "but I don't need anything. I'll make something in a while."

"You mean you have stuff in the house?"

"Yes."

Of course he had food in the house. A seventeen-year-old daughter who could descend on him with two or three girlfriends. Always enough Diet Coke, chips, chocolate chip cookies, marshmallows. And in the freezer: salmon, tuna, whitefish, bought every month at that expensive fish store on Colorado. Every month he calculated carefully what he could spend.

"Do you have friends here? You shouldn't stay alone. When something like this has happened there should be people in the house. It's for a good reason that the old Jews invented sitting shiva."

"Sitting shiva," mumbled Joop. That's what he did. Devoting himself to a standstill. Not on a chair but on a pillow right near the floor, on the couch. He said, "I don't need to see anyone."

Philip looked at him, worried. He pulled a business card from the chest pocket of his jacket and said, "Call me. Doesn't matter what time it is. I'm here two more days. After that I disappear again. My numbers in Tel Aviv are on it too."

Joop nodded, tried to read the letters and numbers on the card, but his eyes couldn't decipher the trembling signs.

"What are you going to do with her?"

Joop stared straight ahead, searching in his head for the decision that he had made. He swallowed with difficulty and said: "Cremation. And after that…Catalina Island, right off the coast here. A few months ago we were there for a week; she wanted to live there, she said, and after her studies buy a small summer home there when she had become rich and famous."

"Good," said Philip. "Good that you know that."

"Yes," agreed Joop, and remembered that she had revealed the message to him in a dream.

Philip said, "Come along and take a short walk with me. It's nice weather now."

"No, no—I have to do things here."

"Good," said Philip and stood up. "Call me. But first make sure that you can be reached. There are people who want that, you know, especially now."

"Will do."

He followed Philip to the front door—that man who liked physical contact, who had wanted to become a dentist but who in Israel had trained to be a spy. Perhaps he should also have gone to Israel with Miriam. Perhaps he should have let her have her driver's license. My God, if she had driven herself, nothing would have happened.

"Take care, my friend," said Philip, turning to him.

"Yes," said Joop.

"And watch that Jeep over there."

He gave Joop's arm a strong squeeze, affectionately and encouraging, and walked through the front yard back to the car.

Joop remained standing in the doorway. He could not recognize the features through the reflective glass, but he knew who it was, as if he could smell him.

Chapter ten

Again he was awakened by the doorbell. He sat up but remained sitting, rubbing his eyes with the backs of his fists, waiting until the bell would fade away, but this time, too, someone continued to push the button stubbornly, not pulsing but continuous. The bell sounded like a long howl. Until the noise suddenly stopped.

Joop leaned back and waited until he had enough breath to walk to the bathroom. There was tapping on the window. He opened his eyes and saw two uniformed policemen standing, their faces pressed against the window. They drummed once again and he sat up. One of them pointed to the front door.

Groaning, Joop pushed himself up from the couch and walked with small steps to the door. His body was weak and vulnerable. He felt like he had slept for years. He was an old man and would die soon.

He opened the door.

"Mr. Koopm'n?"

"Yes. That's me."

He saw that his bare feet, his dirty shirt, his unshaven face and bloodshot eyes depicted him at a glance on their identification list: alcoholic, not dangerous, unkempt but not yet eligible for immediate admission. Two broadly built men in tight shirts with short sleeves, heavy belts with weapons and all sorts of objects packed in leather, walking communications centers. They had smooth cheeks, crew cuts, hands that could strike straight through a wall. The older one, who fostered a bushy moustache on his upper lip, a grumpy officer, a real "Bromsnor," was around thirty years old. Miriam had never seen *Swiebertje*, the Dutch TV series that in his youth had kept every child glued to the tube, but the name had become part of her stereotypes.

Bromsnor said, "We have received telephone calls from your daughter's school. From parents of your...daughter's girlfriends. First of all, our sympathies. What has happened is tragic. We just wanted to check if everything is okay. Can we do something for you?"

"No, no, I can manage."

"It would be nice if you could be reached. The telephone makes a big difference. Can we call someone for you?"

"No, thank you."

"We also received a telephone call from Cedars-Sinai. They couldn't get a hold of you either. If you would please contact them."

"Yes, yes, I'll do that."

"You know that the Malibu police is working on the investigation?"

"I immediately had...that same Friday afternoon, there was a policeman in the hospital."

The other officer now joined the conversation. "We also want to point out to you that there are support groups for family members of traffic accident victims. We've brought you a packet. Do look through it. Many people find it very useful."

The policeman offered him a packet of brochures. Joop accepted it and he saw the dirt under his own nails. It hadn't escaped them either. He held the brochures behind his back and slipped the other hand into his trouser pocket.

Bromsnor asked, "Mr. Koopm'n, do you have relatives in the city?"

"No, no relatives."

"Friends?"

"Friends, of course."

The other officer said, "It is our experience that it helps when people, in these sorts of circumstances, go to other surroundings for a while. You can also read about it in the brochures. All sorts of tips that may be useful."

"I'll read it."

Bromsnor took over from his colleague. "The administrator of Cedars said that it was urgent. It would be nice if you would call them soon."

"I'll do it right away."

They looked at him silently for a while, uncertain about the result of their mission.

Joop had the impression that they were waiting for a reaction from him. To please them, he asked, "Do you know who called?"

The younger one answered, "No sir, we simply got the assignment to check on you."

"Good," said Joop, waiting for their departure.

Bromsnor said, "There is one more thing, sir. One of your neighbors told us that someone has been sitting in a car in front of your house for several days. A big African American man, thirty years old, heavy. Three hundred pounds. He isn't there today. Have you seen him?"

"No," said Joop.

"So you haven't been bothered?" asked Bromsnor.

"No."

"The license number of his car was passed on to us, and we checked it. It's the man who was involved in the accident. Have you met him before?"

"Yes, yes," said Joop, unwilling to think of moments that he had not carefully chosen himself. "One time, yes."

"Would you mind saying where?"

"I was in his gym for an hour—God's Gym."

"The health club on Main Street?" asked the younger one.

"Yes."

"Not apart from that?"

"No," said Joop.

"Do you think that he has any reason to threaten you?" asked Bromsnor.

"No."

"If you need it, we could ask a judge to order an injunction."

"I'm not bothered by him."

Bromsnor nodded. "Good," he said. "Once again, Mr. Koopm'n, our sincere sympathy. It must be very hard for you."

Joop bowed his head and couldn't say anything. He saw that each of their pants had a sharp crease. How many pants did they have? Five, so that they could wear a clean pair every workday? Every day four dollars for the dry cleaner. Twenty dollars per week. Perhaps they got a discount at a law enforcement dry cleaner.

"I'll read the brochures," he said.

"Excellent. Thank you," he heard them say in unison.

Joop nodded and closed the door once their heavy black shoes left his field of vision.

Chapter eleven

A week had passed. She had now been gone for a week. It was seven thirty in the morning. A week ago he had been talking with her in the kitchen, and she had opened the paper-thin tissue paper that had been carefully wrapped around the organizer. A week.

He held onto the furniture and the wall in order to reach the front door. He staggered because he had been keeping himself anesthetized with pills and wine, but the time had not escaped his notice. The shrill doorbell continued ringing, and he managed to reach the door, almost letting himself fall against it.

He looked through the small window. And had to let his eyes travel upward. The big black man looked at him from above. The almost round head, the bull's neck, the nose which had been battered flat in fights, the heavy eyebrows under a low forehead, the wide, predator-like lower jaw, the dark brown eyes with yellowish whites. Unshaven just like him. For long seconds they looked at each other, judged the havoc that had been wreaked on the other.

"What do you want?" said Joop. But he heard that his voice had barely any strength. He cleared his throat and yelled, "What are you doing here?"

The man had heard him. He nodded.

"She has to be buried!" he said with his resonant big man's voice.

Joop saw his lips and tongue move, strong African lips that had to process a lot of food every day in order to supply that big body with fuel. Bury his Miriam? He wanted nothing. Time had to congeal. Any change could cause the silence to tear.

"That's not your concern!" Joop shouted back. "Get away from here! Get out of my garden!"

The giant nodded. But remained standing stubbornly.

"It's for her," he said. "She is lying in a mortuary on Beverly. She had to leave Cedars. You didn't react. I let her be taken there. I did that in your name."

"You're not allowed to do anything!" roared Joop. "You're not allowed to meddle with anything. Butt out, you! Go away, you!"

Again the man nodded, with bowed head this time. But he was so tall that Joop could still see his face unobstructed.

"What are you waiting for! Out! Do you want me to call the police?"

"It can't stay like this," said the man as he looked at his hands. "When people die, they have the right to a ritual. Miriam has to have a grave. I don't mean to meddle with anything, but you don't react. You don't pick up the telephone. You don't get the mail from your mailbox. I had to do something. So I said that I was acting on your behalf. Please do it yourself. Do it for her. She has the right to it. Mr. Koopm'n, she still has rights!"

The big man's face was suddenly constricted in a spasm and his eyes filled with tears. While he squeezed his hands, he pressed his lips together and tried to swallow his tears. But the tears kept streaming down, and the man stood crying with deep howls in front of his door. His shoulders shook and he opened his mouth and took deep breaths to be able to resist the shooting pains of sorrow.

The sight of the man was unbearable. Joop took a step to the side and used the wall next to the coat hooks for support, his shoulder against the small backpack, and withdrew from the view through the window. He heard the muffled sobbing of the man. The man had driven the motorcycle. His daughter had died, but the man was unharmed, stood here blubbering as if she had been his own child. He had no right to pity. Not from Joop. Not here.

Joop waited until no more sobbing sounded through the door. After a few minutes, the man seemed to get his crying body under control. The sobbing stopped, and Joop heard the man blow his nose. "Mr. Koopm'n, sir?" Joop heard then. "Mr. Koopm'n. Would you listen to me for a moment? I know that you can hear me. Mr. Koopm'n, I sold my business yesterday! You were there, only recently! I have to continue giving lessons there, but I sold it, and I've got money left over from it! Real money! Mr. Koopm'n, I want to erect a memorial for her! A temple, sir! A statue in a Greek temple with pillars! Something like the temple of Artemis in Ephesus! Something that will stand eternally! I'll pay for everything, sir! Italian marble—it can't be beautiful enough! Ionic pillars with slender echinuses! With a decorated torus! And a frieze with figures! She will be embalmed just as the Egyptians did; there are still three people in Cairo who know how to do that—I've already worked it out! They are ready to do it, sir! One sign from you, and they're here tomorrow. The architect lives in Bologna, in Italy; he is working on a design! Money is no object! May I call you soon, sir? Will you answer the telephone? Something has to be done; it can't go on any longer. It was a week ago, sir. No one should be treated like this longer than a week. And certainly not she. Think about it, sir. I'll call you."

Chapter twelve

Three days before, Joop had ordered a carton of cigarettes to be delivered, and now he had only one pack left. He sat in the kitchen and smoked. Channel Five announced that it was going to be beautiful weather today. Joop watched—sound and image wallpaper for his wandering thoughts. He had taken in the newspapers that had lain in the front yard in their transparent bags, old news for eyes that couldn't read. The telephone rang.

He stood up, walked to the kitchen counter, and turned off the TV. The yellow telephone hung next to the shiny Aquaviva espresso machine.

He lifted the receiver from the hook and said, "Yes."

"It's me, sir, Erroll Washington. Godzilla."

"Listen, Erroll Washington or Godzilla or whatever they call you. She doesn't want a mausoleum. Miriam is not a girl for a mausoleum, was not a girl…"

He took a deep breath and closed his eyes, leaned against the counter, overcome by fatigue, reluctance, and the need for silence.

Joop mumbled, "You are responsible for the death of my daughter. You caused it. I'll never forgive you. I don't know why I'm speaking with you. Therefore I must say: I appreciate it that you came by, thanks for your offer, but I prefer no more contact."

"I understand, sir, and I will respect that. But I want to tell you: my life is yours. I have taken a life, and I want to give back life. My life. The life that I've led is finished. I have to compensate for the death of your daughter, even though compensation is impossible. I would love to change places with your daughter, but that's not possible. I've considered putting an end to my life, but that would not help you. I've thought about it: what can help you, at least, what would console you a little, no matter how superficially. Well, what can help you is my life. Do with it what you wish. I can work for you, I can keep you company, I can protect you, I can play chess with you, I can cook for you, and I can do laundry. I am your servant. Use me, please. If you want to hurt me, take my life in your hands. If you say that I should end my life, I'll do it. Literally."

With closed eyes Joop shook his head.

"You're crazy. Godzilla, young man, you're raving. You don't know what you're saying."

"No sir, I've thought about this at length. I know what I'm doing. I always know what I'm doing."

"No, otherwise you wouldn't have taken my daughter with you last week."

"Sir, you're right."

"Are you married?"

"No, I'm unmarried. I'm twenty-eight; I have no children; I live in a penthouse in Ocean Views in Santa Monica, the one at the beginning; I've been world karate champion three times, and the day before yesterday I sold my health club. Got less for it than I wanted. But still seven hundred thousand dollars. Everything I have is for you."

"I want nothing from you!" Joop shouted bitterly. "I don't want you to make an attempt to buy off my daughter's death! If you want me to talk with you, then you shouldn't say such a thing!"

"I understand, sir, I don't want that. I don't want to buy off anything. I want to give. My life. Until I die. I want to take her place."

"Have you been suffering from these sorts of needs for a long time, Godzilla?"

"You are suggesting that I'm crazy, and I don't rule that out. Perhaps what I want to do is crazy. But I can't help it. I have to make good what I did wrong. I had that need already as a child, and I still do."

"You shouldn't have taken her along."

"I know that. But it was well-meant. There was an oil slick and we slipped."

That Friday afternoon an officer had explained the cause of the accident to him: a delivery truck with a defective oil pan had spilled oil, the motorcycle tires had lost their grip on the asphalt, and Miriam was flung off the pillion seat and was knocked under the wheels of an oncoming Ford Explorer. The helmet had not protected her. No one was to blame, except perhaps the driver of the delivery truck. A police cruiser had followed the oil spill and had traced the delivery truck; the driver didn't know that oil was leaking from the oil pan and collapsed when he heard of the accident. Yet Miriam would still be alive if Godzilla had made the ride alone, if Miriam had driven with Pat, or even with Caroline, if she could have driven herself...

"So I can have control of your life?" asked Joop.

"*Yes*, sir."

"Don't you think that's a bit...don't you think that you're appealing to something rather controversial?"

"I'm choosing. Freely," he said proudly.

"And then," said Joop, "what changes?"

"She is not coming back," answered the black man, "but there will again be someone who cares a lot about you."

Chapter thirteen

After he had written down the number and had put back the receiver, Joop stood still for a moment next to the espresso machine, staring at the empty kitchen in the empty house. Erroll Washington was a madman who acted like a saint. Or perhaps this was carelessly phrased: as a saint you were by definition insane. The saints in history were all possessed—they heard voices and experienced visions. But Erroll had been right when he said that Miriam was waiting for a ritual. Not a burial but a cremation. She had revealed it to him.

Joop lit one of his last cigarettes. Revelations are limited to movies, old-fashioned stories, and hysterical believers. Catholic wonders and revelations are investigated by Vatican specialists, and when they conclude that the phenomenon cannot be understood through reason, the church declares the incomprehensible to be an official miracle. Of course Miriam had not revealed anything. In the room with the machine that had kept her alive he had dreamed. Nothing more and nothing less. In the Torah, God spoke to his prophets when they slept. A dream with meaning was the domain of fortune-telling uroscopists and incense-burning palm readers. It was the pain of the moment that had disguised his dream as a revelation. He knew nothing about Miriam's ideas for her funeral. She had at times asked him about his ideas, but he had always avoided the question.

"I don't know and I don't want to know. It's too morbid to talk about."

"It's part of life, Dad."

"No, it's not part of life; therefore, I don't have to think about it. It's too soon. We'll talk about it later."

"Childish," she concluded.

He didn't know if she had ever thought about her own death and if she had a preference about the way that her next of kin would treat her body. Perhaps she had confided to a girlfriend. Perhaps Caroline knew.

He picked up the receiver again and dialed the voice mail access number. Thirty-six messages. Too many. Too tired. He hung up and lit a cigarette. Picked up the receiver again and called information. They connected him to Caroline Levi.

She picked up. Sleepy. Slow. It was still early and it was vacation.

"Caroline—this is Joop Koopman."

He sounded hoarse and weak. In a couple of days he had let a whole carton of cigarettes puff through his lungs.

"Mr. Koopm'n."

He heard her sit up.

"I'm glad that you're calling. The school, they want to organize a memorial assembly. We're all broken-up about it. It's so terrible. We've heard nothing about a funeral."

"No, she hasn't been buried yet. That's what I'm calling about, Caroline. I don't know exactly...by chance, has she ever talked to you about funerals?"

"Well..."

"Well?" he repeated.

"A few weeks ago, in class, we had a conversation about that sort of thing. That's when she said that she was for cremation. She thought that was better than a burial. But she said it more in general."

"Good," said Joop.

In his dream it wasn't only his desire, but also his intuition, that had taken shape. Cremation. Dissolve. Disappear.

"Do you know yet when it will take place?"

"No," he answered.

"If we can do something…"

"No, thank you."

He wanted no one there. "Oh yes, the cremation," he said, "that is…only for the family, you understand…"

"Oh. Yes. I understand. Of course. Take care."

"Yes, thank you."

He wanted to hang up, but she called out to him, "Mr. Koopm'n! One more thing…can we say good-bye to her somewhere?"

"You want to see her?"

"If it's possible, yes. She was my best friend—you know that."

He could hear her crying. And he didn't know where Miriam was. He had so little respect for the dead body of his daughter, the damaged body from which predators had cut her heart (Why had he agreed to that? What madness had possessed him?), that he didn't even know where she was. He knew quite well why he didn't know it—he didn't want to visualize her death—but it was a weakness that he was now ashamed of.

"Caroline, Jews don't do that. When someone has died, you don't bid farewell to the body."

"Yes, I know that, but…"

"Thank you, Caroline, I'll see what I can do."

He had to honor their friendship, he had no choice. He hung up, lit another cigarette, and called Erroll.

"Mr. Koopm'n," he heard him say.

"Where is she?" asked Joop.

"A funeral home on Beverly. Della Rosa. Italians."

Joop asked, "Can they have her cremated?"

"They can take care of all that."

"A girlfriend would still like to see her. I'll give you her number."

"And you, sir?"

"I don't want to."

"Do you want to have the urn put in a crypt, or do you want to have the urn at home?"

"I want to scatter her ashes. As soon as possible."

"I don't know if that's permitted in the city, sir."

"At sea. Near Catalina."

"So you'll need a boat?"

"Yes."

"I'll ask around, sir. I'll call back as soon as possible."

"Okay, till later," answered Joop.

An hour and a half later Erroll reported back. Joop had slept without dreaming. Everything hurt, even his bones were tired.

"Caroline Levi is going to take a look soon. Your daughter will be cremated later, at five o'clock. Tomorrow morning we get the urn, and the boat leaves at eleven o'clock."

"Thank you very much," said Joop matter-of-factly.

He was going to say good-bye forever to his little girl. Never again would she hang around here next to him at the kitchen counter, make a sandwich with sliced cucumber and peanut butter, stare together with him at the garden until the tea had steeped, gossip about the neighbors, grumble about the school schedule, stroke his shoulder when leaving to go back to her room—the empty, almost meaningless transition rituals between serious hours of work, concentration, and ambition that later are nothing more than the bookends of stories that have weathered time. Sometimes he watched her in the reflection of the kitchen windows, and if he concentrated he could perhaps see her image in the glass again, like before.

"Should I come for a moment?" he heard Erroll ask. "I would like to come and keep you company. I'll be with you in five seconds."

"Five seconds?" asked Joop, drying his face with his forearm.

"I'm standing in front of the door. May I come in? You should not be alone when you mourn."

Chapter fourteen

The temperature curve of the last day of the year 2000 displayed a fickle course. At seven thirty in the morning it was only forty-five degrees Fahrenheit, and the city lay under a thick fog that allowed a quarter mile visibility. After nine o'clock, the mercury began to rise quickly and visibility increased to almost five miles. At eleven o'clock, when they sailed, visibility was a little over six miles. After the quiet morning hours, the wind speed increased to nine point two miles per hour, a soft breeze that could not raise the waves. The air remained hazy. After they had sailed for half an hour, the outline of South Catalina Island appeared. Errol sat next to Joop on the U-shaped bench on the afterdeck, pressing the copper vase, closed with a lid decorated with rosettes, against his chest with both big hands.

The boat was a large pleasure yacht called *Ocean Blue*, with a crew of two: a helmsman and an assistant who, after casting off, had as his primary duty to supply the guests with drinks and snacks. Until this morning, Joop had worn the same clothes as on the day of the accident. He had let his body become dirty because he found it shameful to take care of himself, to clean his body, to use shampoo and deodorant, to shave and to sprinkle his cheeks, chin, and neck with aftershave (which he started using only a few years ago because Miriam had urged him to—it smelled nice and would make him attractive to women, she had predicted), or rather: celebrate the life of his body while his child's body was damaged forever. He could not present himself better than he felt. His own body no longer had any worth, but before they left for the boat, Errol had induced him to wash himself.

Without being invited, the big man had gone to her room that morning. Joop was in the kitchen and heard heavy footsteps in her room above him.

"What are you doing up there?" he roared. "Come downstairs! Don't touch anything! Keep your paws off her stuff, you hear!"

"Sir! I wouldn't even want to touch anything here!"

It remained quiet. Joop no longer heard anything, as if Erroll had lain down on the bed.

"Come downstairs!"

"If you come and get me!"

"Stop that silly game! I want you to come downstairs!"

"I'll come when you prove that you dare to come up here!"

"This is my house! I decide where I dare to go!"

"We both know why you sleep downstairs, why you don't put on clean clothes! Don't worry, you can come upstairs! It's an empty room, sir, very, very empty!"

It took Joop fifteen minutes to leave the kitchen. Five minutes or so in the hall in front of the staircase. And after the last step Erroll was waiting for him, screening the sight of her room with his large body. Because of Erroll's presence Joop dared to come that far.

"Why do you do all this, God? What do you want from me?"

"I do it because I'm guilty. And you are the only one who can forgive me."

"That I'll never do."

"I acknowledge that. I accept that punishment. What are you going to do with her things?"

"I don't want to think about that."

"You can leave the room intact. The organizer was her present that day?"

"Yes."

"That's terrible, sir. May I suggest something to you? You should use it yourself, that organizer. Every day you should touch it and open it, write something in it. She would have wanted it, I'm sure."

"You're sure about a lot."

"I'm sure about nothing. I doubt all day long. But I do know that you should dress properly. Out of respect for her."

Joop put on a white dress shirt and a dark suit.

Long Beach had disappeared behind fog. The sun was dimly visible but remained thin and did not break through. It was pleasant on the boat. The salty air skimmed along his temples and tempted Joop—for a few minutes—to accept life as it had happened to him: Ellen's leaving; the care for their child; the catastrophe of nine days ago. He slumped back with closed eyes and yielded to basking in the sun. But he couldn't indulge himself in this mood; it meant that he was betraying Miriam. He opened his eyes and sat up straight again.

Yesterday afternoon Erroll had gone to the mortuary of the funeral home in West Hollywood. On the way back he had stocked up on pizzas, pastas, and salads at the California Pizza Kitchen, had bought a new carton of Marlboros somewhere, and had kept Joop company until the early morning. They had mostly been silent. Erroll had tidied up, had driven once more to a supermarket on Lincoln to buy fresh milk, fruit juices, and bread, and after that he sat and watched Joop smoke his first two packs. In addition he offered him a light every time with a throw-away lighter, and after every cigarette he emptied the ashtray. Later he threw away the pizzas that had gotten cold. Between five and six in the afternoon her body was burned.

"You don't have to stay," Joop said halfway through the evening. They were sitting in the half-dark living room. At first Erroll had turned on all the lights, but Joop couldn't bear so much light.

"It's Saturday, go out, let yourself be admired by the ladies. I assume that they find you dangerous and attractive at the same time. You look like Mike Tyson, a mild-mannered version, insofar as such a thing is possible."

"I'm staying. Unless you send me away. But if you think that I'm mild-mannered—that's not so. I've destroyed people. In the ring.

Outside the ring. But there was always a justification. I meted out punishments. They had broken the rules. Insulted others. Insulted me. Then I teach them humility."

Twenty minutes and three cigarettes later Joop asked, "Where did you grow up?"

"South Central."

Errol had come a long way. From South Central in LA to Ocean Views in Santa Monica was the same as a trip to the moon.

They said nothing. Both listened in silence to the world outside the house: the passing cars; the helicopters on their way to nearby LAX which was almost four miles south of Venice; on Lincoln, the screaming of the ambulances, fire trucks, and police cars on their way to a catastrophe.

Half an hour later, Joop asked, "Since when have you been called Godzilla?"

"Not until I started fighting. That is, professionally. Until I was fifteen, I was a fearful fat boy. I was tall but not aggressive. All day long I ate chips and hamburgers and M&Ms. I read, I loved classical music. Those are unhealthy passions in South Central. To survive there you have to possess physical strength."

"What should I call you?"

"Most people call me God."

"Do you feel almighty because of that?"

"On the contrary. It makes you small."

"God's Gym—I remember, you caused a lot of hassle with that name."

"I didn't want to offend anyone. But it was short for Godzilla, not for God. It was meant ironically. You get a godlike body in our gym."

"Why did you sell the gym?"

"For the mausoleum."

"I don't believe a word of that."

"That suspicion is not necessary on my account, sir. I don't lie. As a matter of principle."

"Do you know that joke of Groucho Marx: these are my principles, and if you don't care for them then I have others for you."

"Witty but cynical," answered Erroll.

Around midnight Ellen had called from South Africa. She had listened to her answering machine. This moment had to come, the tragedy after the tragedy. He had to inform the woman who had borne her.

"An accident. She was sitting on the back of a motorcycle with someone. They lost their balance because of oil on the road. She was dragged by another car."

"Why did you let her get on a motorcycle!" screamed Ellen.

"I didn't let her. I didn't know."

"You are supposed to know something like that!"

Then she said softly, barely raising her voice above the noise of the line, "Usually I have premonitions. Not this time. We had a wonderful time here. I knew of nothing. I had no idea."

Ellen believed in iridology, aromatherapy, and horoscopes.

For the tenth time she asked, "When exactly did she die?"

"The twenty-third. Three thirty in the morning."

"Were you there?"

"Yes."

"Was she in pain?"

"No. She was not in pain."

"Of what exactly?"

"Brain damage. Cervical vertebrae. The doctors said that she felt nothing. She was immediately unconscious."

"Has she been buried?'

"She was cremated. I thought that she wanted that."

"Cremation is good, yes."

Again she was silent for a long time; he heard no breathing, nothing.

Then she said, "I've always thought that she wouldn't stay with us, you know. I never dared to tell you that, but…she was so beautiful, so clever; I was so afraid that she wasn't for us…she's gone now, right?"

"She's gone, Ellen."

"This can't be all! Joop! Say that it isn't true! You only want to…you want to punish me! Tell me the truth! You shouldn't make jokes about this!"

"She is no longer here," he said.

Ellen was silent, a minute, but he didn't hear her sob. Perhaps she had placed her hand on the receiver.

"I listened to the answering machine. If only I hadn't done it. Then none of it would be true."

She believed in magic, mythology, hidden signs.

"I didn't know how to reach you," he said.

"It was supposed to be that way," she said, "I wanted to be alone. I was with someone; we were very happy; and now this…" Then she started to cry. For two long hours she asked the same questions and he repeated his answers. He endured the lacerating anger that she screamed over the line—about the inadequacy of his care, about his failure as a father, about the tragedy that he had caused. She wanted to come to LA, but an hour later she called to say that she wasn't coming, she couldn't cope with it.

Joop fell asleep on the couch. When he opened his eyes, he watched how the big man woke up. Erroll was sitting in the large easy chair next to the television and came back from his sleep snorting and stretching his limbs.

"Good morning," he said when he noticed that Joop was looking at him.

"Good morning, God," answered Joop. "I don't know if I can manage all the God this and God that."

"You get used to anything. But call me what you wish. I am who I am, the name doesn't matter."

Subsequently Erroll went to West Hollywood to pick up the urn. Joop waited for him in the garden. The urn stood in an orange crate on the floor of the jeep, on the deep pile carpet in front of the leather backseat. The drive to Long Beach took less than twenty-five minutes on this quiet Sunday morning.

Catalina was not more than eighteen miles long and almost seven miles wide. The island consisted of two parts (the part on the right appeared to be a separate island) that were connected to each other by a narrow land bridge. An island with green hills, free-ranging buffaloes, and unspoiled small lakes.

Erroll clasped the urn as if it contained diamonds. He wore a polo shirt and a thin windbreaker whose sleeves stretched around his heavy muscles. His neck was wider than his head. He wore stretchy black jogging pants. The muscles of his thighs were as wide as a chair. He took up more space than any other human being that Joop knew.

"How do you do that in an airplane?" asked Joop.

"Business," answered Erroll. "Otherwise I don't go."

"Are you still asked a lot?"

"Yes, I still am."

"Competitions?"

"No longer, no. Demonstration matches. Always well paid. Beautiful island," he said. "I've never been here. When it's clear, I can see it from my apartment, but this is the first time that I see it from up close. Why here?"

"We were here together, last summer. She had dreams of later finding a small second house here."

"A second house? And the first one?"

"I don't know. I think that she didn't know herself either."

"Do you want music? They have a good stereo system on board and an extensive tape and CD library."

"No."

Errol gestured to the assistant. The latter went into the pilot house and evidently asked the helmsman to slow down, for the engine speed slowed down and the boat turned.

"This is how they turn into the wind," Erroll explained the boat's turning.

"Have you thought of everything?"

"I've done my best. That's the least I can do."

Joop remained seated and looked with open mouth, breathing deeply, at the mist above him, as if he could suck courage from the sky.

"Give it, please," he said.

"Just lean out," Erroll suggested, "then I'll hand you the urn."

Joop kneeled on the bench and leaned over the back of the seat. Below him was the water, lapping against the white side of the ship. The urn, which he had not yet touched, was held above the water by Errol, ready for Joop's hands.

The urn was no larger than a gallon carton of milk. That was all that remained of his child. Joop reached for the handles and Erroll handed it to him. The urn seemed empty.

"It doesn't weigh much," said Erroll. "Just say when the lid should come off."

Joop nodded. But he waited. Looked at the waves. At his hands. He had the feeling that he should say something, but he didn't know any prayers. He searched for ritual words, and from far away came sounds that he knew from the past.

"*Yit'gadal v'yit'kadash,*" he heard.

It was Erroll's voice.

"Would you like me to continue? It is the kaddish, I looked it up. I thought maybe you'd want to say the words. You can repeat them after me if you wish. Do you want something on your head? I understand that you have to cover your head with these words."

Joop nodded.

From his pants pockets Erroll pulled two baseball caps. He put one on his head and pushed the other one on Joop's head. The cap dropped halfway over his ears.

"Will you repeat after me? It's an old prayer. Thousands of years."

Erroll read the words from a piece of paper. Joop repeated after him. In a burst of love he tilted the urn so that the lid fell into the water. He saw her ashes. Slowly she drifted away in the wind, was taken along in gray, thin clouds until she became invisible. Erroll uttered sounds that Joop didn't understand but repeated anyway. He knew that there was no supreme being that would receive and console his daughter, and nevertheless he repeated the words—while the wind emptied the urn.

Chapter fifteen

It took days to thank the people who had called or written—her girlfriends, their parents, the neighbors, people with whom he had worked, even people in the Netherlands with whom he hadn't had contact in years and who had heard about Miriam's accident through an intangible information network, a few lawyers with thoughts about damages. He had thanked them with the mourning cards that Erroll had printed, adding a few words in his own writing. He had friends and acquaintances in this city, but the contacts were all based on common interests that grew out of projects, commissions, and rewrites that he had worked on. Some he had known since his arrival in LA, but he didn't have the strength to expose himself to their pity. They had called, often several times because he hadn't listened to his answering machine, and he sent them notes promising that he would get in touch with them as soon as he felt the need.

He received another letter from Linda, the wild seventeen-year-old of thirty years ago. He had not yet answered her first letter, but she didn't refer to that. She had spoken with Ellen, therefore knew about Miriam, and wished him strength and said that she would pray for her and for him. He sent a card.

At the start of the new semester, Miriam's school had held a memorial service; he had declined the invitation to speak. Caroline called to say that it had been beautiful and moving; everyone had cried and several students had played music, classmates had spoken, and a collection would be made for a plaque in the math classroom for the best math student that the school had ever had.

Human existence needed rituals—Erroll had made him understand that—and this meant that he was responsible especially now, after her death, for the maintenance of his memory. The rituals of the mind. There she still walked around, he could still listen to her, could still touch her as in the intense dreams that he had experienced during the past weeks. He still drank a lot, but without pills. Bathed in sweat, he woke in the morning from an intense world that was fortunately seldom recognizable as a dreamed reality, and several times he had woken in bed sobbing, returning lost in the house that had lost its heart. He took that last notion literally: they had informed him that her heart had been transplanted successfully. When he woke up crying, he could not bear to face the day. He would remain in bed for hours in a senseless attempt to return to the world that had just slipped from him, a dreamed world that, however fantastic and absurd, was dear to him because he could encounter Miriam in it. He lost a lot of weight.

"Mourning has its phases," Erroll had said, "I've seen that a lot. In a while the eating binges will come."

Joop could not work. Not only was the chance negligible that he would sell anything, but it was laughable to give himself over to his imagination while he had experienced something that had transformed his imagination into a boggy swamp. The source for the fictitious misery that he used to produce regularly in his scripts—murders, torture—was filled with real misery. Misery no longer had any amusement value for him. But he had to be distracted, according to Erroll. They took walks on the beach to the Santa Monica Pier, mostly in silence, drank something on the way, and walked back the same way. Erroll slept downstairs in a sleeping bag on the sofa, a large three-seater that was too short for his body, but he didn't complain. Every day he had to go to his gym for several hours to coach steady clients, and for the greatest part of the day he filled Joop's house with his noisy body. Erroll had asked permission to roam the Internet on Joop's computer, and sometimes he was immersed in faraway sites for hours on end. Or he read books that he had borrowed from the local library, popular science titles about geology, biblical scholarship, cosmology, physics. It was a mystery to Joop why he put up with the giant. He hated the man; at any rate, he felt that he should hate him, but his presence delivered him from the smarting silence that Miriam's departure had left behind. When Erroll had left for God's Gym, Joop looked forward to his return. When Erroll came home, his whole body, which breathed, wheezed, and rumbled disconcertingly and violently, seemed to warm the rooms.

The police had decided not to institute criminal proceedings, not against Erroll, nor against the driver of the panel truck that leaked oil, nor against the driver of the Explorer, but Joop was free to institute civil proceedings, said the policeman who informed him about it by telephone.

The days passed, days that brought the fatal moment to the horizon. Joop wanted to remain faithful to the emotion of that day, but it became increasingly hard to hold onto it in Erroll's presence. Erroll forced him to go into the street. When Joop trudged next to him on Broadway past sunglass stalls, tattoo salons, T-shirt sellers, hippies, drifters, dreamers, and exhibitionists, he was like a chronic invalid who bares his pale skin to the open air after a long time. But it distracted him, and he didn't know whether that was good or bad. At night in his dreams he went looking for his child. Blissfully he almost always encountered her somewhere, in a cave, on top of a mountain, in a city, in a ruin. When he looked in the mirror, he saw mourning as a shadow on his face, in the lines of his hands, and in the shape of his feet.

While Joop smoked silently, Erroll sat reading in the evening.
"Do you know this, *The Hidden Face of God*?"
"No," answered Joop.
"It's about the Bible. Why God has withdrawn from the world."
"Why are you reading it?" asked Joop.
"Because I want to know why God let this happen."

"Have you figured it out yet?"

"Not yet. But I'm on the track. Kabbalah, have you ever studied it?"

"No."

"Do you know that in it there is a description of the origin of the cosmos that corresponds to the big bang?"

"I didn't know."

"I want to get a broader picture of…of everything. That's why I'm reading this book. The man who wrote it lives in San Diego."

"Beautiful city," said Joop.

"The Kabbalah says that everything originated from one point through an explosion. And those Kabbalists have also described how matter originated, and it's remarkable: it looks exactly like what science thinks happened after the big bang. Interesting, don't you think, how mysticism and science come together?"

"Maybe," answered Joop.

Part two

Chapter sixteen

January passed. On February 11, 2001, it started to rain. On February fifteenth, the rain clouds lifted. The barometer started rising, and on February seventeenth, it was sixty-eight degrees around noon. Although it remained overcast all day, the temperature would reach a little over seventy degrees.

On Sunday, February eighteenth, Philip called. He was in the city and could be with Joop in an hour.

"I've thought of you a lot," said Philip. He placed a hand on Joop's shoulder. "Not that it does you a lot of good. No one can help for something like that."

"Help *with* something like that. Not *for*," said Joop.

Philip continued clasping his shoulder and said, "You know why I love to travel over six thousand miles? To have my Dutch corrected by you."

Since his return to Israel he had called a few times, but Joop had not answered. Danny, who remained outside waiting by the car, greeted him with a short, military wave.

"Danny can come in," said Joop.

"He's more useful outside. Do you have a moment?"

Joop walked ahead of him to the kitchen. "What can I pour for you?"

"A glass of water. Are you managing somewhat?" asked Philip.

"Manage—no idea."

When they entered the kitchen, Erroll stood up. He had been reading the fat Sunday edition of the *LA Times* at the table. Joop introduced them to each other and asked Erroll if he could continue his reading in the living room because he wanted to sit in the kitchen with his Dutch friend.

"Of course. I was just planning to go out. I'm going to get a few other papers. Can I bring back anything?"

"Not for me."

"Nice meeting you, sir," he said to Philip as he left the kitchen.

Philip nodded at him amiably. He had said nothing and waited until the front door closed: "The man with the motorcycle?"

"Yes. Strange story—I won't bother you with it."

"Do it anyway."

Joop poured him a glass of Evian. The water from the faucet was clean, but in this city you drank Evian, Perrier, Pellegrino. Every month he had bought several cases at a discount supermarket on Lincoln, and now that Miriam would no longer drink it he could save on the cost of water.

He described how Erroll had helped him the past weeks. "He wants to atone, make a sacrifice. He makes sure that the refrigerator remains filled, that everything is clean; he does the laundry, even does ironing, which we never did here at home because we sent everything to the cleaners…"

He heard himself start to ramble and left the rest of the sentence unfinished.

"A decent person," Joop continued. "A strange, intensely good man."

"If you'd meet him on the street at night…"

"…You wouldn't know how to get away fast enough. Appearances are deceiving."

Philip drank some water and said, "The strangest friendships can develop from this kind of tragedy." But surprise could be perceived in his voice.

Joop pulled a chair away from the table and sat down right in front of the kitchen counter. He lit a cigarette and said, "He's not a friend. No idea what he is. I trust him. Not in the beginning. He showed up here; I didn't know what to do about it. But now—I admit that I'm used to him. I'm glad that he's here."

"That's what counts," nodded Philip as he reached for the pack of Marlboros on the table. It was an empty remark.

"You've come just to keep me company," said Joop.

"Why do you never call back? There are people who sympathize with you, even if you don't think so."

"I really would have returned your call. But I wasn't up to it yet," said Joop.

"I also wanted to get back again to that Omar van Lieshout affair."

"I hadn't expected that," said Joop matter-of-factly. "I really thought that you came to keep me company."

"Why else would I come?"

"You think that I'm able to be of any value for you now? Philip, you point at me and I keel over. I see a broken branch and I start to blubber. I'm not capable of doing anything. Without...without Erroll I could not have managed."

"What would you have answered at the end of December?"

"NO. That would have been my answer. A daughter to take care of. Who could be in danger—"

"Danger, no, virtually out of the question," Philip interrupted him.

"I didn't want to end up in a difficult situation. And besides, I'm not a secret agent, or whatever that may be called! I'm an ordinary jerk from Holland who earns his living with ideas and insights. But I'm not—what you have become."

"I'm also a jerk from Holland."

"You are a professional spy from Israel. And you've been trained to lie and to deceive, and I assume to murder people."

With sarcasm in his voice Philip said, "Joop, you have no idea what we do. Not that."

"What do you do then?" asked Joop.

"What's the use of you knowing?"

"General edification."

"Read the paper."

"Why did you come, Philip?"

"To see how you were doing."

"Excellent, thank you."

"And to see if you'd be willing to do your best for the Jews in Israel."

"I can barely do my best for myself, how can I do my best for others?"

"Because life continues, Joop, because the world keeps turning. Because we must prevent the innocent from dying, because we must prevent the scum from ruling the world, and us from having to bury young people."

Joop got up and turned his back to Philip. The sun broke through the clouds and enveloped the garden in a warm glow. Hundreds of times he had eaten outside with Miriam. Just like all Americans, he had grilled hamburgers, chicken breasts, sausages, and they had drunk Coke and prepared salad with blue cheese or Thousand Island dressing from a plastic bottle. When she was little he had organized garden parties for her birthday, had set up jungle gyms, and had hired clowns. He had enjoyed all these moments; every moment had been precious; he had sanctified every moment the way that believers sanctify their statues, totems and temples. Daily happiness had casually danced around him.

He was furious. At the sun, these bushes, these trees. At this impossible impassiveness. At the warmth that dissolved the cold.

Chapter seventeen

On Pico Boulevard, in the Rancho Park district near the Fox studios, in a room behind a vacant store where the windows were covered with newspapers, Joop received instruction for a whole week.

"And I don't want what I'm going to do to be against the law here."

"You're not involved with anything that will endanger the security of America," said Philip. "On the contrary, you might even be promoting security. The only thing that you're doing is trying to get in touch with someone. Another Dutchman. The fact that you have a secret agenda is judicially completely irrelevant. You're not robbing him, you're not passing on state secrets. You want only one thing: to find out why Omar is hanging around LA. That can never be against any law whatsoever."

In the morning he was picked up by Danny. He was driven to the store, and until four o'clock he talked with Philip about the biography of Omar van Lieshout. They settled on procedures, the way they would communicate, and Philip agreed that Joop could stop at any time.

On the next-to-last day of his crash course, Joop heard

unfamiliar voices in the kitchen when he came home. From the hall he saw a man and a woman standing deep in conversation with Erroll. The man was Asian with a shaven head, dressed in a long orange robe that reached to right above his ankles, plastic sandals on his feet. He stood to the left of the Aquaviva, both hands around a cup of steaming tea. It was impossible to estimate his age or that of the woman. She was dressed in loose-fitting pants and an equally loose-fitting shirt, both made of soft red cotton that revealed little of the shape of her body. She was not shaven bald but her hair had been cropped, which caused a shadow of black bristle to lie on her beautifully shaped head. Around her neck, a wide chain. Two Buddhists, one Asian and one European. With her arms folded, the woman stood with her back against the kitchen counter, on the spot where Miriam had always stood, and smiling attentively she listened to Erroll whose voice resounded in the hall.

While Joop looked at her, it dawned on him who she was.

"Linda," he said.

She turned her eyes away from Erroll and looked into the hall inquiringly.

"Joop…"

She came toward him and the smile dissolved into serious-ness. Now he saw that she walked barefoot on the kitchen floor. The chain jingled.

"Joop," she repeated softly.

Big, clear blue eyes, no make-up, no lipstick. Around her eyes and her lips the first small lines showed, but the years had not marked her skin. From close-up she looked no older than forty, and the loose-fitting clothes could not hide the fact that she still had a beautiful body, just like the girl he had known.

When she stood in front of him, she said, "Hello, Joop."

Awkwardly they leaned toward each other and kissed each other on the cheek. She was much smaller than he remembered. He was moving away from her head when she wanted to give him a third kiss. They laughed shyly.

"Three times," Joop said cheerfully in order to mask their awk-wardness, "the Dutch way."

Shyly, she looked at him, uncertain about the words she should choose.

"Let me look at you," he said to break her silence. "When did we last see each other?"

In an attempt to ease her diffidence, he clasped her hands. Short bristly hair that accentuated the smooth form of her head, a well-proportioned face without make-up, a timid look that avoided his eyes and concentrated on a spot on the kitchen floor—she lived outside time, he thought.

"On March thirteenth, nineteen seventy-one, I was on a boat to Dover. So we saw each other that morning for the last time." A cautious voice, articulating carefully. Eyes like those of a watchful deer.

"Dover? I thought it was Harwich," said Joop.

"Dover. Saint Helena's in Bath. An exclusive girls' school…it's so good to see you," she said.

"Yes," he said, "it's strange to experience time like this, don't you think, when people meet each other again after so long."

He was sixteen. She had initiated him when she was no older than Miriam.

She turned to the man. "May I introduce you to Usso Apury? He has been one of my best friends for a very long time. He is considered a holy man by many."

The Asian man pressed his palms together, his fingertips right under his chin, and bowed slightly. An almost round head with a face frozen into a smile from which nothing could be read. His shaven head shone. Joop also bowed slightly as a greeting. A monk, lama, or priest, he thought. So she is something like that too. Iridology. Aromatherapy. Her gym shoes stood on the floor in front of a kitchen cabinet.

Erroll stood up. "I just came back from the supermarket and I thought they could wait inside for a moment. I hope that it's okay with you."

"Of course."

Linda was a year older than he, therefore forty-eight, but she looked ten years younger. In those days, when she came, she'd shiver pleasantly, like someone with cold limbs who got into a warm bath.

She smeared his semen on her nipples. The way she dressed now suggested that she had renounced the theater of the body—lingerie, make-up, fashionable clothes. The chain was probably an amulet. Against the evil eye or something like that.

"We were just talking about Tibet," said Erroll. "Mr. Apury comes from there. Whether the altitude, the mountains, and the air contribute to the feeling that there is more between heaven and earth. I am convinced that the holy places of humanity were not chosen at random. There must be something about those places. Jerusalem, Mecca, Delphi, just name it."

"It has to do with energy currents," said Linda, looking innocent.

"Unfortunately I know nothing about energy currents," said Joop.

"The earth is a living organism," she asserted without a shred of doubt.

"Living?"

"Living," she repeated decidedly, and she seemed to be slightly surprised by his opposition.

"A cooling planet," Joop insisted. Dreamer, he thought, a truth seeker. Formerly addicted to sex, now to higher spheres. But he should treat her with respect. She was sincere.

"A sphere, the perfect shape, on which beings can experience love, hope, understanding, liberation," she said.

"Yes. And also loss, hunger, want, fear," Joop added.

"Don't you believe that one is connected to the other?" she asked, surprised, as if he were the oddball and not she.

"I don't know what you mean by connected and by one and the other."

"That you experience what you prepared yourself for?"

"No. I was not prepared for what I've just experienced. My daughter was not prepared for what happened to her."

"Everything has a place in the cosmos," observed the monk with a deep resonant voice. His voice was even lower than Erroll's.

"There exist no places in the cosmos," said Joop, "the cosmos is chance."

Stooped slightly forward and looking at the ground—perhaps

a sign of respect—the monk asked, "But you won't deny that the cosmos is ordered?"

"The order of chance," said Joop. He wasn't going to let himself be argued down in his own house. And why had she taken off her shoes?

"In Buddhism, everything is connected to everything," said the monk, staring at Joop's knees. It must be deference that caused him to gaze down; it was a sign of good manners in Asia. "Sunyata, nothing is isolated, nothing is absolute."

"I respect your way of thinking," said Joop, "but those are abstractions that have no place in my life."

"What is abstract for you is concrete for me," answered the monk. "I sympathize with you, with the unexpected that has struck you. In the end, in everyone's life it is about overcoming suffering. And suffering and longing are one. It is our task to soar beyond it."

"If you succeed in that, I envy you."

"That's what I attempt," the monk bowed with self-conscious modesty. "You have to disappear in the essence of emptiness. And in that emptiness you will be able to unite with the essence."

Joop had nothing to say to that. The monk was still staring at his legs. Asking for support, Joop smiled at Linda. She saw that he didn't know what to do with this conversation.

"I believe that we are taking you by surprise with our teachings," she said apologetically. "I only came to say hello to you, see if I could do anything for you, to reminisce. For the rest, nothing special."

He could not send her away. They hadn't seen each other for thirty years.

"Would you stay for dinner?" asked Joop. "It's very nice of you to take the trouble to come by."

"We'd like to stay for dinner, wouldn't we?" she asked the monk.

"Gladly," the man bowed.

"But Usso is a strict vegetarian. I, somewhat less," explained Linda.

"We can do something about that," said Joop. "We have everything in the house. Shall we cook together for the gentlemen?"

For the first time she smiled, a wistful, disarming smile.

"That's a good idea," said Linda. "The two of us in the kitchen."

"Go and make yourselves comfortable in the living room," Joop said to Erroll and the monk, "we'll do the work."

He showed her the contents of the refrigerator and the pantry, and they chose rice with vegetables, and he was surprised at the quiet woman cloaked in loose-fitting clothing that she had become. He did not want to rake up their past. And while cutting vegetables and filling the pots they exchanged pleasantries; she praised the comfort of the kitchen, the view of the garden, asked about his neighbors. And when she appeared to be less tense, he asked what had brought her to LA. She was on a world tour with Usso Apury. Apury was a famous Tibetan monk, and with their trip they hoped to raise enough money to ensure the future of his monastery of Dharamsala in the north of India at the foot of the Himalayas. Did he know anything about the situation of the Tibetans? He confessed that he knew nothing about Tibet. In 1950, Tibet had been overpowered by the Chinese, and after nine years a popular uprising broke out in Lhasa, the capital. In March alone of that year, almost ninety thousand people were killed. Usso Apury, a seven-year-old child monk, fled from Tibet with thousands of other monks. Henceforth the center of Tibetan Buddhism was in Dharamsala, where the Dalai Lama settled too. That is where Linda had met her teacher Apury twelve years ago.

"When you arrive, the first thing you see is the lower town, and that is the true India," she said in a soft voice, and he went to stand next to her in order to hear her, "bustle, chaos, beggars. But the upper town is magical. There the Tibetans have settled in Macleodganj, their own quarter. Dharamsala used to be a vacation spot for the British in India, because the weather is delightfully mild in the summer, and in Macleodganj—you still feel the colonial atmosphere. You're at an altitude of almost five thousand feet, which the Tibetans find very low, of course. In the beginning they had adaptation problems, real physical problems, because they were used to living at close to ten thousand feet. And why is the upper town so beautiful? Because of the view: at one side the valley of Kangra, at the other side the granite rocks of the Dhauladhar range that rise from the earth like the towers of that church by Gaudí in Barcelona..."

"Sagrada Familia," Joop added, finishing her sentence.

"Yes," she said.

"What did you find there that you couldn't find elsewhere? You don't have to answer if you think that my question is intrusive."

"No, no." Reassuring, she nodded at him, but she spoke hesitantly, "I was sick a lot—something with my circulation. No one could tell me what it was. Not specialists. Then I got cardiac arrhythmias."

What had continued to function perfectly in his daughter after the death of her brain had started to falter in Linda. But she had made it, she now stood silently and breathing next to him, carefully cutting carrots into equal pieces, and waiting for the courage to continue talking. He searched for a question that could put an end to the report of her illness.

"I knew that it was not physical," she continued before he could say something. "Don't ask me how I knew. It was psychological. Something other than a breakdown in the mechanism of my body. I was living in New York—"

"New York?" asked Joop who immediately took advantage of the opportunity to change the subject. His mother had never told him what Linda had confided to her, just as you never offer a drink to an alcoholic. "Tell me what happened after…Bath, wasn't it?"

"Bath, yes," she said. "I went to school there after I…" Again she hesitated. "After I left Holland…"

"Were sent away," said Joop straightforwardly. He had contributed to her departure and still felt regret about it, even though the situation had demanded an urgent solution. Before they got into the bath where they were caught by his father, she had pushed him onto the hard tile floor of the bathroom. She had lifted her skirt elegantly and, without panties, sat down on his face. In the half-light under her skirt he held her by her buttocks, and small shivers traveled through her body when he did what she wanted. "If there is no penetration, then there is no screwing. Penetration is screwing, but we don't do that. We don't do that, do we, Joop?" He groaned with his mouth full. She leaned back and felt behind her with her hand. "Take it easy, pet, it will be your turn soon."

Absurd memories. He looked at her for a moment and searched

her face for traces of the wildcat she had been. He doubted that she still remembered. Perhaps he had become one of many. Or perhaps she had converted to an immaculate existence and was now living like a nun.

"I finished high school there and then went to America. Finished law school. I went to work at a law firm in New York. Until I left, and that was almost thirteen years ago, so I didn't do that for very long. Then I decided to travel and ended up in Dharamsala. Since that time I divide my life more or less in two. I work six or seven months consecutively in New York, and then I go back to India for a year."

"It seems like a huge distance, and not just literally."

"Yes, but I can't help it," she said, almost as if confessing a crime. "I have to earn money somewhere. I went to Dharamsala. And that's where I was healed."

He didn't know what he was stirring up, but he wanted to know. "Healed?"

"Yes. Through meditation," she answered, firmly convinced, with a look that left no room for doubt. "My heart is not only my heart. In Tibetan Buddhism, the heart stands for wisdom. In the Kabbalah, for beauty. In every ancient meditation tradition, the heart is a special organ. There is a connection between spirit and body, but it is so complex, and yet so intangible, that Western science still has no explanation for that connection. Therefore you can choose between two things: pretend as if it doesn't exist because you can't find an explanation or a verifiable theory, or start from the conclusion that something is going on and therefore deal realistically with the connection. Meditation has restored my heart rhythm. Without modern medicines or machinery." A serene smile crossed her face. "And you, how did things go for you at that time?"

During dinner Erroll asked one question after the other, almost possessed, about the ideas that guided the monk. The man ate with slow, almost ritual movements. Straight-backed, he sat on a small stool, picked at his food with sticks, and chewed slowly on tiny bites.

"In order to meditate you need the energy from your body," the monk explained to Erroll. "But conversely, a purification of your body takes place during meditation. Your body is charged by meditation.

Mind and body converge. There is no separation, as in the Western tradition, where there is tension between body and mind. For us there is no 'I think therefore I am' of Descartes. 'I am because I am' would suit us better. Or: 'I am when I disappear.' The variations are endless."

"Meditation and herbs have cured me," said Linda, "the sutra of the heart. Have you ever heard of that?"

"No," said Joop. He didn't know what a sutra was, but in spite of this he was convinced that he didn't want to hear a sutra, certainly not the one of the heart, but he didn't want to hurt her. The headstrong, physical girl she used to be had vanished and turned into a modest, almost ethereal woman who slightly got on his nerves.

"It is one of the most important sutras."

The monk said, "The sutras are original texts of the Buddha. About this sutra, the great teacher Tan Hsu says: 'The Sutra of the Heart is composed of parts of the Mahaprajnaparamita, texts and simple words were carefully used to convey deep meaning.'"

"What is in it?" asked Erroll.

Linda lowered her eyes and recited: "'There is no truth in suffering, in the cause of suffering, in the end of suffering, nor in the path. There is no wisdom, and there is no purpose.' Such things are in it. Words that leave you speechless."

When Linda left, she asked Joop if he had any time on Saturday. He gave her his telephone number. She annoyed him. And at the same time he realized that this annoyance was not justified. He resisted the confusing thought that he enjoyed her sudden presence.

Chapter eighteen

That night Joop didn't sleep. The monk had taught Linda to rid herself of touch and tastes, of music and mourning. "All suffering is caused by desire," the monk had said. Fine.

He still tried to fathom why he had in the hospital found certainty in a revelation about Miriam's cremation. He was level-headed enough to know that such experiences occurred only within the limits of a dream or a hallucination, and it was highly debatable that Buddhist, Jewish, or Freudian meanings could be attributed to it—the problem was that he could not get away from the intensity of that experience.

Halfway through the night, Joop got up, went to the kitchen, and drank a glass of wine. In the living room, Erroll rumbled sonorously in the rhythm of his deep breathing, the sleeping bag half open, his steel body almost invisible in the dark room. Joop pulled the band from the rustling cellophane of a fresh pack of cigarettes, turned the TV on softly so that he didn't wake Erroll, and tried to concentrate on a repeat of ABC News. Bush had officially become president. Joop hadn't noticed it at all. He smoked; he smoked day and night. It was laughable that he had stopped smoking because he wanted to grow old.

Linda had spoken about her heart, and even though he knew, even though he had accepted this thought much earlier, the full extent of the fact that the heart of his daughter was still beating—in another body—now registered. In the turmoil of the hospital he had given his consent—"What would your daughter have wanted, Mr. Koopm'n?"—and now somewhere someone was crapping on the john with a flushed face or was jerking off while the heart of his child was pumping blood to his prick. Why did he think that it was a man? Was it a scoundrel? A murderer? A monk? This was Joop's own sutra—whatever it might be—of the heart: the feeling of my child, the breath of my daughter, the place of her soul. Without a doubt it was totally different from what these old magic traditions made it appear, but the heart that that night was transplanted into another body by specialized hands and high-tech apparatus meant for him the incarnation of beauty and wisdom. Her heart. He wanted to know who had received her heart. Which body was enjoying her beauty.

Chapter nineteen

The empty store on Pico Boulevard was located in an unattractive row of businesses that seldom seemed to be visited by customers. Without paying attention, drivers passed the dusty shop windows; the parking lots were mostly deserted; the newspaper vending machines were still half-filled at the end of the afternoon.

Danny parked the car next to some large dumpsters, and Joop entered the store through the staff entrance. In the middle of the space, under three fittings with fluorescent tubes, stood a wooden table, four gray plastic chairs, an overhead projector, a laptop, and a thermos with coffee.

When Joop came in at nine o'clock, Philip was sitting in front of the laptop and greeted him with a growl without looking up from the screen.

"Had a good night?" mumbled Philip.

"Not bad."

After pouring a cup of coffee, Joop sat down across from Philip at the large square table and lit a cigarette. He said, "I'm not doing it."

"Not what?" asked Philip, obviously not listening.

"I'm not doing it," repeated Joop.

Now Philip looked up. "What are you not doing?"

"This. This crazy carnival. I think it was clever of you that you got me this far, but it's also irresponsible. On my part, and on yours. This is work for a professional. For a young, clever Jew. A guy like Danny. Someone who is knowingly willing to dupe someone. Philip, I'm a simple man. I always assume that people are well-disposed toward me, that the world is well-disposed toward me. You need a hardcore cynic. I have other things that preoccupy me; there is a lot that I need to sort out; I'm still raw inside, as if I've eaten glass. You're taking an unacceptable risk by wanting to take a chance with me."

"I want nothing. I have no choice," said Philip. "What happened yesterday evening?"

"Nothing special," Joop answered reluctantly.

"Tell me, why did you change your mind?"

"I can't keep my mind on it, that's all. I can't concentrate."

He had to find her heart. He had to devote himself completely to finding out where her heart was.

"And what about the last few days?"

"Superficially, yes." In reality he had absorbed everything attentively. It had distracted him, kept him busy, had given him ideas. "I'll make a mess of it. You shouldn't do that to yourself."

"You're getting a writing commission from us," said Philip.

"This is not a writing commission. This is something for experienced agents. Not for an amateur like me."

"You're getting a commission," said Philip. "We've arranged something with friends of ours. We've been busy working on it the past few days. You're getting an office on Sunset, on the Strip, and every day you'll lunch at Ristorante Primavera. Omar goes there several times a week. And the rest of the day you'll just work on a story. Of your own choice. The company pays."

"Which company?"

"Our friends."

"Who?"

"It's for Showcrime," said Philip.

Showcrime—a well-received series of made-for-TV films for a cable channel.

"Showcrime? Friends of yours?"

"Of ours. A real commission. If they check, they'll find the truth. That's how this game is played."

"You do go far, Philip."

"Joop—we have no choice. Without you we'll never get near him. We follow him, know where he hangs out, wiretap everything, but we can't really get close to him. A Dutchman has to do that. With Dutch words. With this kind of case you often have other ways to draw him out. Money, or women—often women, they remain number one. But language? Never. When you get home, there will be a letter from Showcrime asking you to write a script for them."

"How did you manage that?"

"They were going to ask you anyway. Do you know Jeff Silberman?"

"I've heard of him."

"He'll be your producer. He recommended you a few months ago. We didn't force them to do anything, we didn't ask them anything. We only made use of opportunities."

"Why don't I believe you?" Joop asked bitterly.

"Because you don't believe in yourself."

"That's a laugh."

"Call Silberman! Don't believe me, why should you? Ask Silberman, and you'll hear that you were really at the top of the list. You have a good track record."

"Nice to hear that from an expert."

"I know it from experts. Do you want some time today to think it over? I'm giving you time off," said Philip. He got up, walked around the table, placed his hands on Joop's shoulders amicably, and leaned forward. "Don't think that I'm asking you something you can't do."

Philip pulled a chair out from under the table and sat down next to Joop. "What we're asking of you is: go and have lunch at Primavera. You won't regret that. Many beautiful women come there, on the Strip. The food is first-rate. Listen to Omar. Tell us what he has said. That—is—all."

Joop stared straight ahead, surprised at how little remained of the resolve with which he had entered.

"I've got to…" He shook his head with a sigh. "We'll continue this discussion on Monday, okay?"

"Of course—listen, Joop, I've done this work for the past twenty years. I've been confronted with revolting facts. You don't become a philanthropist with this kind of work. I suddenly turn up in your life. At the wrong moment. But I know what can happen if we don't solve this. I know several Omars who were not handled well, and that led to disasters. And those Omars who were handled appropriately and in time—you have never read or heard about those. Sometimes we need people like you. Outsiders. Doctors, plumbers, teachers. We ask brave Jews to adopt their lives for some time—"

"Adapt."

"Adapt to prevent a tragedy."

"And to earn additional income."

"We reimburse their expenses."

"As regards that script—I have to think about it, I don't feel good about it."

"What happened last night? Did you meet a woman?"

"Yes." Perhaps Linda's visit had contributed to his realization that he had to break with Philip, but Miriam's heart was a decisive factor.

"That explains a lot."

"It explains nothing. Perhaps you still remember her. She lived in our house for a year. Linda de Vries. She came with us to the synagogue a few times." And gave him blowjobs in the ladies' bathroom. That was safe because the only regular woman at the Saturday morning service, Mrs. Kuilman, lived above the synagogue and always used her own toilet on the third floor.

"Do I still remember her? You bet. A pretty girl. For a while I was madly in love with her."

"She came by. After thirty years. For the first time since…since then, I felt…a little better."

"Why did she come by?"

"Because she is spying for the Palestinians! What do you think? She came by because she's in the city! Because she heard about Miriam!"

"I don't mean it like that," Philip apologized.

"I know that." Joop calmed down. He lit another cigarette. "I never knew that you were interested in her. I think that you received enough attention at school."

"Optical illusion. I prayed for the real thing when I jerked off," said Philip. "She lived with you, didn't she?"

"Yes."

Philip understood that he didn't want to divulge any details. "Do you know that building next to the Book Soup? Across from Tower Records? That's where Showcrime has a level. And an office for you."

"Philip—you're talking too much; you have to stop, otherwise I'll really quit."

"Sorry," said Philip, "you're right. Should Danny take you back?"

"Yes, please—no, I'd like to take a walk. I'll get a taxi somewhere. And in Dutch you say *floor*. They have a *floor*."

"Joop, don't quit, don't do that to me. Don't do it for the Jews, or for the Americans. Do it in the name of the purity of the Dutch language."

Joop felt duped and manipulated, but he couldn't suppress a smile. "Just give me a little time. If I do it, it's because I'm no match for you."

Chapter twenty

Buses and taxis passed him, but he continued walking. Except for joggers, who dressed up recognizably as joggers in Nikes, with sweatbands around their heads and heart meters around their wrists, no one in this part of the city would think of walking. Distances were bridged by cars. It had been one of the reasons to live on the coast. In Santa Monica and Venice you regularly encountered real hikers, and sometimes an eccentric who had gone shopping on foot and was carrying a filled shopping bag. No one wanted to be suspected of not being able to afford a car.

In the beginning he had bicycled with Ellen, which is possible in Hollywood if you avoid the hills. At that time, they lived in a dilapidated apartment complex on Franklin, between people on welfare, drunks, and young, self-assured writers, actors, directors, and other movie dreamers. No money, which was cool in the last phase right before the big breakthrough. Sometimes they ate in a diner on the corner of Argyle, a place that belonged to a hotel that also rented rooms by the hour. On Sunday morning the booths were filled with assertive, ambitious artists, all young people with aspirations and talent, all on their way to a killer entrance into the only industry that didn't need to be described any further. The psychological electricity hung above the Formica tables, and you got into conversations with people who, forced by the crowd, sat next to you or across from you on a bench, and you wondered whether you could compete with the intensity and single-mindedness of your unknown table-companion, whether you could find your place in a city that teemed with their talent. Joop had sold work, received commissions, and had not failed, as was the case for most of these seekers. But he knew that he hadn't really made it. A partial success. Good, but with bad luck. Only one script had made it onto the screen, a one-off opening performance. It was a MOW, a made for TV Movie of the Week with Tom Green, a young actor of Dutch origin who, after that, had been forgotten. Many hundreds wrote, just like Joop, one script after the other, were paid enough per year to survive, but seldom saw their idea develop into a movie.

In the beginning, after his first two sales, he experienced a period that in retrospect was his peak. He earned one hundred and fifty to two hundred thousand dollars per year. To be sure, he was divorced and had to take care of his baby daughter, but he had no lack of money and treated himself to a Jaguar, and a babysitter when that was needed. He didn't know yet that you could sell adequately but never see a film of your work. Consumed by jealousy and anger after Ellen's betrayal, with feelings of hate that bordered on murderousness, he wrote his scripts, on his way to recognition and acknowledgment, on his way to a beach house in Malibu and an apartment in the Hills.

Ellen went back to Holland, harassed him with lawyers, and for two years, out of revenge, he screwed everything that came along. Not at home, not near his child and the memories of Ellen, but chiefly in hotel rooms and once in a while in the women's homes. Women who worked at agencies or film production companies and urgently sought gratification. He did his best to consider sex as an independent urge, but in the end he admitted to himself that he was someone who looked for sex, love, and friendship all in one person, and he let the opportunities pass and slowly turned away from the singles scene. He was younger then, slim, looked good with the thick wavy hair and clear blue eyes of a Norwegian skating hero. One time, in the parking garage under the Century City Mall, he had contributed to the quality of life of a well-known movie maker in the back seat of her Rolls Silver Cloud II with a roof lower than he expected. With her skirt pulled up and her back bent, she crawled on top of him and rode him to a groan of satisfaction. Afterwards they had gone to get a drink in the bar at the Hilton across the street. A friendly kiss on his cheek at her hurried goodbye. When he encountered her a month later, he noticed no sign of recognition; he had been submerged into a sea of colleagues.

For years he hadn't thought of it, but the memory resurfaced because he walked past the mall. His memory was working overtime. Everything came back. Since Miriam's departure everything was there again. And nothing was allowed to get lost.

Even though it looked several times as though it was going to rain (it didn't happen until the following afternoon), it remained dry under heavy clouds. A walk of an hour and a half. The dark gray buildings of Cedars were in an area of overpriced restaurants, clothing and furniture stores. At the parking meters Bentleys, Ferraris, and the most expensive Cadillacs and Jaguars were waiting. The chilly terraces of restaurants and cafés were warmed by heaters, tall gas heaters that warmed the tables with a kind of heating umbrella. Skinny women, their faces behind sunglasses—the sun was of no importance—leaned toward one another with secrets, gossip, complaints.

Despite the cool air, Joop had warmed up. On Gracie Allen Drive he went up to the reception desk and asked for the transplant coordinator. Another building, another floor, other hours. He heard the echoes of the accident humming through the halls. The disappearance of his child was like a reflection in water, visible but intangible. He began to understand that people could continue to live after the departure of a loved one: it was habituation, nothing more than that. Habituation and exhaustion. But never acceptance. He would forget her more and more frequently, until one day he would realize that she had been out of his thoughts for more than a week. It wasn't until then that she would be dead.

At the appropriate desk he asked for the transplant coordinator. Debby Brown. Debby was outside the building in a conversation;

did he have an appointment? No. It was on the spur of the moment, his daughter, you see, during the night of December twenty-second to twenty-third of last year, just over two months ago, he had given his consent at the time, but he wanted to talk about it now. The woman at the desk nodded. Debby's beeper was off, but she would be talking to Debby within an hour; could she reach him? He gave his cell phone number.

He left the building via the Third Street exit. He walked around the building and followed San Vicente north, a twenty-five-minute walk under the same gray sky that had accompanied him all morning. It was twelve o'clock when he reached the Strip and walked past the dress shops and restaurants to Primavera. The restaurant was located on the north side of the Strip, diagonally across from Le Dome, one of the restaurants where top agents lunched with their top clients. Primavera was a small, Italian restaurant, dozens of authentic photos of Venice on the walls, oak paneling that reached just above the shoulder when you were sitting. The space measured at most twenty-six by twenty-six feet and was filled with tables covered with white tablecloths, most for two, and a few for four people. The majority of the chairs were occupied by carelessly dressed visitors like Joop, who listened intently to busily-talking, Pellegrino-drinking, junior agents; at least he assumed that they were agents because they looked like the agents he had encountered over the years: well-conditioned young men in Armani suits with snow-white dress shirts, shiny silk ties, large Rolexes, elaborately cut hair that stayed in perfect shape, gesturing in the highest state of agitation, playing with their Porsche keys, and always completely sure of themselves.

"Lunch?" asked a girl of about twenty, dark and beautiful, Mediterranean in appearance, and just as self-assured as her most important guests. She wore a low-cut, red sweater, too minimal for this cool day, but good for showing off her low neckline.

"Sure."

"How many?"

"One."

"Follow me, please."

She took a menu from a stack and slalomed ahead of him

between the tables. Her tight jeans clung to a beautiful ass, ideal for a waitress. She placed the menu on a table in the corner against the back wall. He was a stranger and alone, and therefore she didn't need to give him a central spot that brought him in direct eye-contact with those entering; these were the codes in this city. But the spot gave him an overview, and there was nothing that could escape his observation. He ordered a glass of Merlot, thereby revealing that he wasn't working today, because the code also said that a working lunch was consumed without alcohol. The menu offered traditional Italian dishes, rounded out by low-calorie Hollywood fare.

The beeps of the *Wilhelmus* melody sounded. An unknown number following the area code of this part of the city. He answered the call.

"Merchant. Koopman."

"Merchant?" he heard Linda ask. "A pseudonym?"

"Something like that, yes." A childlike joy on hearing her voice. Someone he knew from long ago. Familiar and unknown at the same time. With a shaven head.

She asked, girlishly, "Are you doing something nice?"

"I'm just going to eat something. You?"

"I'm going to have lunch with some money people in a minute. Bankers with a weakness for the Dalai Lama. And for the rest I'm calling for no reason. I wanted…I don't know why I'm calling—I just wanted to hear you."

"That's sweet," he said. Words that he hadn't spoken in a long time. His last girlfriend, a mistake that had lasted eight months, had turned down his services for good a year ago. It had been an awkward affair, for she was one of Miriam's teachers. She had sent him a condolence card. His restless right hand crumbled a piece of baguette.

Linda asked, "We'll see each other tomorrow, right?"

"That's what we agreed," he answered. "Do you want to eat something special?"

"Makes no difference. Everything is all right."

"Is your friend coming along?"

"He is on a retreat in the mountains this weekend. Giving a course. Big Bear. You probably know it."

"I've been there a few times, yes. There's a considerable amount of snow there right now."

"What do you think they have in Dharamsala in the winter?'

"Do those monks know how to ski?"

"They float over the snow. They have a gigantic quantity of words for snow and for all that we toss under that one little word 'white.'"

With a nod he thanked the waitress who put his glass of wine in front of him.

"Come with me to India some time," said Linda enthusiastically, "maybe it will give you ideas."

An intriguing thought that he couldn't suppress: had she shaved everywhere?

"I'm afraid that you are more sensitive to the void of meditation than I am," he said.

"When you write and are very concentrated, that's also meditation."

"Thank goodness. If we continue to think like this, then we can only establish that we have a lot in common."

He smiled, as he hoped she did.

"What does your friend do in such a course?" he asked.

"Meditation techniques. Of course you think that all you do is close your eyes and identify with your toes, but everything is very closely connected. Breathing, the steps in your concentration. I know that it all sounds vague and fuzzy, but the odd thing is that it's really about technique and precision."

"And what's the purpose?" asked Joop.

"The goal is to give up every goal."

"Does it work?"

She asked, "Why do you think that I'm calling you?"

"Because you're bored."

"A Buddhist is never bored. Someone's calling me. If there is anything, leave a message in the hotel. Carmel in Santa Monica."

"I'll do that," he said.

"Bye, dear Joop, till tomorrow."

He put down the telephone and brushed the breadcrumbs together. Was Linda able to drag him away from the rhythm of his mourning? Would he be capable of losing himself in the first woman who crossed his path after Miriam's departure? Or was it the memory of the past that stirred up illusions?

The waitress came back. She asked, "Have you made a choice?"

He said, "I haven't looked yet." And wondered why her words struck him so. He looked at her. A pretty young woman whom you'd like to come back for every day. Her work had taught her that she should be determined and careful, and that her youthful femininity was a means to get large tips if you showed some cleavage when serving.

"I'll be back in a minute," she said.

"You're speaking Dutch," he said before she moved away from his table.

"I am Dutch. I just heard you speak Dutch. It doesn't often happen here."

"I thought I heard something Italian in your accent."

"Spanish," she said, "a Spanish father, a Dutch mother, and working in an Italian restaurant in America."

"I'm Joop," he said.

She shook his hand. "Sandra."

"Have you been here long?"

"Two years. Have you decided yet?"

"Just give me a pasta," he said.

"From today's menu? Very good, *lekker.* Vongole today."

"That's good, yes."

"I always like to speak Dutch," she said, getting ready to greet newcomers. "Americans don't have a word like *lekker.* Thank you."

He handed the menu back to her, and she slalomed away. So, Omar didn't come only for the quality of the food. He could talk with her. Perhaps even flirt with her. A few minutes later she placed his order on the table. The telephone lay next to his glass.

"Refill?" she asked.

"Please do," he said.

He ate the pasta, wiped the left-over sauce from his plate with a piece of bread, drank an espresso, and the lunch went by without a message from the hospital.

While paying the bill, he asked, "Many Dutch in the neighborhood?"

"I know some people, yes," said Sandra. "I've never seen you before."

"I've just started working here," he said. "I'm trying out the restaurants in the neighborhood."

"Our ratio of price and quality is the best on the whole Strip."

He handed her the signed credit card slip.

"You'll go far," he said.

"I do my best," she said with a smile, "but the funny thing is that I don't doubt it. Come back soon, Joop wasn't it, not Job?"

"Joop," he repeated.

"I won't forget it," she said as she walked away with a professional smile, and by some means or other took into account the direction of his glance as soon as she turned her back to him.

Chapter twenty-one

Mr. Koopm'n? Debby Brown. I'm sorry I've made you wait. I don't have much time, but I heard that you'd like to speak with me, so I made some time. Would you please come with me?"

A blue silk dress with white polka dots, a belt of the same material, medium-high white platform heels. Her short hair, spherical and taut like a German steel helmet, was shiny with hairspray—Miriam would have described her in explosions of laughter. With resolute steps Debby walked ahead of him to an office that was no larger than a broom closet. She was small—petite, they called it here—with black hair and light brown skin, large brown eyes, Caribbean. In a waiting room that was used primarily by blacks and South Americans, he had leafed for half an hour through the unread newspaper sections that those who waited had dropped under their chairs: the economy, car ads, art and movie pages. After she closed the door behind him, she had to slide right past him in order to reach her swivel chair behind the desk.

"Do sit down," she said. Straight-backed, she remained seated on the edge of her chair and looked at a computer screen that divulged its information to her eyes only.

"I'll look it up. From the twenty-second to the twenty-third, isn't that right?"

"December," he said suddenly timid, afraid of the details in her computer. "The night from December twenty-second to the twenty-third, last year."

"We haven't met before, have we?"

"No," he said.

"I counsel the next of kin who want support. But you had indicated that you didn't want that."

He saw that her eyes quickly followed the lines on the screen.

"Yes," she said. "I don't know where the organ went; that's not in my computer; it's all centrally coordinated. We always talk about two parties, the donors and the recipients, and both parties have to agree. I don't know what the other party indicated. Was it pointed out to you at the time that there are excellent support groups for the family members of donors?"

"Perhaps," he said, "I didn't pay attention to it then."

"There are people who initially don't want anything at all because everyone is overcome by grief, but slowly on there is a need to talk about it. After all, it isn't exactly nothing that happened. Have you received all the brochures?"

"I believe so, yes."

"We can send them again, if you wish."

"I still have everything at home."

"So you want to get in touch?"

"I would like to know who has my daughter's heart."

"I understand that," she said with a nod, placing her hand under her chin, looking at him with heartfelt interest—learned during training.

She asked, sympathetically, "You're divorced, aren't you?"

"A long time ago."

"No relatives in the city?"

"No."

"Family is always the first line of support. If there is none, we often see that the survivors do need help. After a certain amount of time. There is a therapist in the city who is regularly brought in for such cases."

"I don't see myself as a case," said Joop.

"Who does?" she said with an impassive smile, avoiding any form of confrontation. "I just want to let you know about it."

With one middle finger she tapped the keyboard. Because her nails were an inch long, she kept her fingers spread out, as if the polish were still wet, and placed her fingers almost flat on the keys. In the course they had obviously not discussed nails.

"Have you yourself visited a doctor lately?" she asked.

"No."

"Do you dream about this problem?"

"Yes."

"Often?"

"Regularly, yes."

"You work?"

"I'm a writer. I don't always work."

"I mean: do you work regularly?"

"What do you want to know from me?" he asked grumpily.

"I just want to get an impression of you. When the family of the recipient, or the recipient him- or herself, receives the request, we would like to have a sense of the donor. Sometimes it's very moving, Mr. Koopm'n. Deep emotions surface. People who have lost a loved one come in touch with someone who is often—not always—a blissfully happy recipient. Through the organ of the loved one of others. That can lead to a severe reaction for the donors."

"I'm aware of that," said Joop, "for me it's exactly about meeting those blissfully happy people."

Debby let her chin rest on her hand again and said, "If you're open to that, it can be very comforting."

"What can you do for me?" asked Joop.

"I can get the process going. I don't know how long that will take. The recipients often want time to reflect. But sometimes not at all, and then we can set up something within a few days."

"It is my daughter's heart," Joop explained.

Chapter twenty-two

It cleared in the evening and the temperature fell to forty-eight degrees. Erroll had bought logs and was starting a fire. He had Joop sit down in one of the easy chairs by the fire and placed a pizza box on his lap. His care was touching.

"With little fishies," said Erroll, "exactly the way you like it. I think." He darkened the rest of the room so that only the glow of the wood fire lit their faces.

Joop opened the box. "This is a pizza for eight people."

"Eat what you can."

Joop didn't feel like having pizza. But he didn't want to offend Erroll. "God, I'm not very hungry, but I'll take a few bites to please you."

Erroll picked up a second pizza box and sat down on the floor next to the easy chair.

"Music?"

"No, nothing, it's fine like this."

Erroll took a slice. "A good pizza, man. Germans call such a joint a *geheimtip*, a not-yet-discovered place. Wafer-thin, crunchy crust, a nice amount of topping."

"God…"

"What is it, sir?"

Joop didn't doubt his intentions, but this scene made him uncomfortable: the big black man sitting cross-legged on the floor, the white one in the easy chair, the flickering wood fire in the dark room. Not only did he support Joop with his substantial presence and contrite humility, he also kept him imprisoned by it.

Joop said, "Shouldn't you start your life again?"

"This is my life."

"No. You're sacrificing yourself. You efface yourself. It's been enough. This whole situation is crazy. Why do you do this to yourself?"

"Do I really need to explain that?"

Bluntly, almost aggressively, Joop asked the question that had bothered him since that day: "Was there something between you and her?"

Errol seemed to wince with pain, which was a sorry sight for the big man. "No, sir. In the beginning she once asked if I ever played classical music in the gym; that beat drove her crazy. I said that I myself preferred listening to classical music, for it brought peace and quiet and concentration. That's how we got to talking. She was the pearl of the gym. She was athletic but above all she was very beautiful. And very intelligent. Did I know her? Yes, insofar as you get to know someone in these circumstances."

Joop couldn't keep it to himself, an unreasonable, rhetorical question, the complaint of a hysterical person: "How could you not have seen that oil slick?"

Erroll put the slice that he had started back into the box, and with his head down he placed his hands next to him on the floor. He squeezed his eyes shut and looked at the images on his retina.

"We were talking. I was paying attention to the road; I was absolutely paying attention to the road, but I was also paying attention to her words."

"When you sit on a motorcycle you should not talk! That's criminal recklessness!" Joop threw at him grimly.

"We had helmets with microphones and built-in headphones. It was not reckless, sir."

The specifications of modern helmets could not lessen his anger. He asked sternly, "What was it about?"

"She told me about school—that she should really work much harder."

"She worked hard," Joop defended her posthumously.

"She said that she actually wasted a lot of time and that she was going to work harder because she wanted to contribute to the number theory. She talked about a mathematician, a Hungarian…Paul…"

"Paul Erdös."

"Exactly. She said that he had devoted his whole life to his love of mathematics and she said that she should really do that as well. I always listened to her very carefully; it was obvious that she was very smart. And then—the oil on the road was greasy and thick. And then—my front wheel slid away. If your rear wheel slides away you can still catch yourself, foot off the gas, get your balance, but a front wheel is different, a front wheel is impossible. I immediately took my feet off the foot supports and tried to catch us. Everything went at lightning speed. The motorcycle flew from under me. I gripped the handlebars and slid onto the shoulder. Miriam was catapulted off. That is what happened. She shouldn't have been there. I should not have offered her that ride. That's why I'm doing this."

He saw how Erroll collapsed under his shame. Despite his dislike of the fire and the artificial sense of security that Erroll had wanted to create, Joop regretted that he had asked about that wretched day. But perhaps they could talk about nothing else but that day; it was the essence of their bizarre relationship.

Joop said, "Go on eating, your pizza is getting cold."

Erroll nodded, sat up straight, and took a bite.

"I'm figuring out something," he said as he chewed.

"What?"

"I want to understand the accident, really understand. There must be something to understand."

Visibly annoyed, Joop said, "The police have closed the investigation. There is nothing to understand."

"That oil slick, that I understand," said Erroll. "But: Why did the delivery truck leak oil? What had happened? And that Explorer which came by at that very moment? A second later or earlier—I want to know and understand more."

"What the hell are you trying to talk me into?" shouted Joop. "What is there to understand?"

"Mr. Koopm'n, I'm sorry that I'm upsetting you. I don't want to talk you into anything. With understanding, I mean above all insight. Deeper insight. I have the feeling that I still have to do something. After that you'll decide whether I'm still useful to you. I want to make sure that I get insight. And that you understand it."

"Don't bother."

"It has touched many people, Mr. Koopm'n. You above all, of course, it would be nonsense to think otherwise. But the woman in that Explorer—she has remained at home and has not gone back to work. The driver of the delivery truck, what do you think? So many people have been touched by it. Therefore I'm going to search for... for insight. And then you'll consider whether you still need me. Do you think that's a good proposal?"

"No. I think it's excessive. The way we're sitting here, that fire in this dark room..."

"Only because it's cold, that's all."

"Erroll, I think that this should stop. You are a...an extraordinary person. But it's going too far. I don't know what would have happened if you hadn't kept me company recently; I realize that, but it should stop now. I think you should go."

He saw Erroll stare at the fire, bite his lower lip, heard him sniff through his wide open nostrils.

"I understand—I'm rather present. I've tried to keep in the background, but with my stature that's rather difficult."

He placed the box next to him and stood up without using his hands to push up, as if gravity didn't matter.

"Mr. Koopm'n..."

He extended his arm and offered Joop his hand, a wide, invincible hand.

Joop clasped the hand and looked into the tear-filled eyes.

"I have brought about something bad in your life. I try to make amends for it."

"God…you don't have to leave the house right this minute."

"It seems better that I do…"

Suddenly Joop no longer knew why he wanted to get rid of this man. Three hundred pounds of tenderness.

"Stay for a moment to eat your pizza."

"I'll eat it at home. If you change your mind, you know where to find me. Take care."

"Thank you, God."

They held each other's hand for a few seconds, until Erroll turned around, picked up the pizza box, and left the room.

"When you have your insight," Joop said to the outline of Erroll's massive back in the doorway, "if you think that you've found something, do come by, all right?"

Erroll's face was barely visible in the distant reflection of the fire, but Joop knew that he cast him a sad look.

"Gladly."

Errol stopped, evidently searching for a suitable parting word. He said, "What I wanted to tell you—I've stopped by Chabad."

Chabad was the center for Lubavitch Jews who wanted to bring liberal Jews world-wide to the Orthodox path.

"Chabad? In Santa Monica?"

"Yes. I wanted to tell you: I'm going to study to become a Jew."

"You want to become a Jew?"

It was good that Erroll was leaving. He was sweet, but there was something pathological about his selflessness.

"God…why?"

"Because I believe in the coming of the Messiah. The Jewish Messiah. I want to study now, learn."

"Didn't they think it was odd, an Afro-American like you—your brothers are mostly becoming Muslims, not Jews."

"At Chabad they don't easily find something ridiculous, sir. Everyone is welcome."

"Good. Fine. God, success with it. Keep me informed."

"You bet.... Oh yes, the key is on the kitchen table."

Erroll walked away, the front door fell shut. Joop heard Erroll's footsteps on the paving stones of the path, and then the Jeep starting, the fading sound of the car driving away.

What sounds had died with Miriam? The click of the bathroom door lock, the rumbling of the pop music that she listened to in her room when she banned classical music for a while, the endless giggling when she was on the phone with a girlfriend, the opening of the refrigerator door, and the dull thud when she closed it too hard with her elbow, the small click when she pulled open a can.

Joop remained seated until the fire went out.

Chapter twenty-three

After a restless night and a walk on the cement strip as part of the procession of joggers, rollerbladers, speedwalkers, and bicyclists, Joop reached the Santa Monica Pier at ten thirty. In the drizzle he walked to the Carmel, the modest tourist hotel on Second Street. At the reception desk he stated her name, waited until the man called her room and handed him the receiver.

"Joop?" Linda asked sleepily.

"Did I wake you?"

"I was still dozing a little," she said so as not to put him off.

"I was in the area and I thought I'd come and see if you were there."

"Good idea," she said.

"Want to have some coffee?" he said. "Or breakfast. You haven't had breakfast yet, I assume."

"Yes. Fine," she said.

"Broadway Deli, on the corner of the Promenade."

"Okay. Give me fifteen minutes, all right?"

"Half an hour?"

"Yes, half an hour. Broadway Deli," she repeated in a sleepy voice.

The Deli is an institution in Santa Monica, a noisy, rectangular space with an open kitchen where dozens of Latinos, in front of ranges with tall flames, run back and forth in order to heap mountains of food on enormous plates. Half of the space is filled with austere booths and tables; the other half consists of a store where the local elite use hundred-dollar bills to purchase the expensive oven-fresh bread and the sausages and cheeses imported from Europe. In the store section there is also a snack bar with a wide table on tall legs. Sitting on a stool Joop waited and looked at the large TV screen above the bar that separated the store from the restaurant. All the tables were taken; dozens of people were in the store. Near the maître d', who had his own spot next to the bar from where he controlled the entrance to the restaurant, a small group of young couples and families with children were waiting. Joop had reserved on entering. Waiting time half an hour, the maître d' had warned. The memories were at the edge of his consciousness, but he was able to resist them.

Suddenly he heard Linda's voice. "Good idea, Joop."

She appeared next to him. Under the visor of a baseball cap he saw rested eyes, lips painted red. She kissed him on the cheek, pressing the visor against his ear. Perhaps she was uncomfortable when people stared at her because of her short hair.

"Am I too late?"

"No. We're on the list. I'll go and ask how long it will be."

"Wait a moment," she said, and with a casual intimacy brushed her thumb over his cheek.

Had she put on lipstick to please him? The lipstick accentuated her beautiful mouth. At one time he had been crazy about her tongue. He got up and caught the attention of the maître d'. The latter held up both hands and showed ten fingers. "Ten more minutes," he said when he stood next to her again. "Do you want something to drink?"

"Is this your coffee? I'll take a sip."

She wore a black skirt that came to her knees, a dark green wool sweater with a v-neck, a dark gray parka and running shoes. No symbols or leather clothing. No ritual orange clothes today.

She set down the mug and clasped his hand.

"Good of you," she repeated, delighted.

"I went for a walk, I thought..."

"This is wonderful weather for walking. I love to walk when it rains with these very small raindrops just like now. Do you have a lot to do today?"

"Nothing," he said.

"Me neither."

"Perhaps we can go somewhere later," he suggested, and he tried not to sound too pushy. "A movie or something."

"Always good."

"Tonight we're going to Spago in Beverly Hills. Star gazing, at least if you're in the mood for that. Lavish, a bit vulgar, but exciting." He had called yesterday, and to his surprise he'd gotten a table. "And the food is the best in the city."

"Stars and oysters," she said, squeezing his hand excitedly like a little girl, "sounds like a very nasty film. Bread with peanut butter is okay too, Joop."

"I know, but...we haven't seen each other in such a long time... something festive, I thought."

One time she had let him use a cucumber instead of the penetration for which he had begged for weeks. His father had been right. At school, on the street, and in bed he could think of nothing else. At dinner, the slices were used in the salad.

They got a booth in front of the window on the street side. Broadway on Saturday. SUVs, station wagons, and convertibles were waiting in double lines for the entrance to the parking garage. She kept the cap on her head but took off her jacket. The sweater stretched tightly around her breasts. The v-neck showed a part of her collarbone; the skin of her neck seemed just as smooth as three decades ago. She had obviously taken the trouble to keep her body youthful.

They ordered. Linda talked about the meetings she'd had the day before. About setting up meditation courses for managers. About her commitment to the cloister in Dharamsala. It escaped him why someone who was so sensual had arranged her life around attempts to elevate herself. When she asked if she should give him an introduction to meditation, he answered that he was too old for that.

"It seems to me that it's something like swimming," he said, "if you don't start in time, it will never work."

"You know nothing about it."

"Maybe not," he admitted," but I don't know if I'm supposed to understand what attracts you to Buddhism. I don't care for gods."

"Joop, Buddhism has no god," she said, forgiving.

"No god? What's the use of a religion without a god?"

"Everything," she answered, almost singing.

He lacked that faith. He envied her.

He asked, "Isn't there something like reincarnation in Buddhism?"

"Yes. But the goal is not to return. The ultimate goal is to stay away."

"In paradise?"

"Nirvana. But not in the Judeo-Christian way. In fact, there is no life after death."

"No god and no life after death—and you call that a religion?" He couldn't conceal his derision.

"I've heard—and read—that hundreds of times. Yet it is so. But you should see Buddhism as Walpola Rahula does—he is a great teacher—more as a therapy than as a philosophy. A therapy that constantly puts the facts of life in perspective."

"And that works for you?"

"Lately a bit less. When I was sick, yes. Buddhism has cured me of my heart ailment. But this last year was different. I have the feeling that I'm not far enough. And with that I mean that I don't possess the wisdom that would have enabled me to endure this last year."

"So you think that there is wisdom outside knowledge?"

Miriam would have laughed at him for that question.

"What does Buddhism teach? That life is synonymous with suffering. To be born is to suffer, to die is to suffer, everything is filled with suffering. And why? Because we desire. Physically as well as mentally. And the masters teach that you can free yourself from that. How? By the eightfold path."

She showed him her hands, and counted on her fingers: "Right understanding. Right thought. Right speech. Right action. Right livelihood. Right effort. Right mindfulness. Right concentration." And she held up eight fingers for him.

He shook his head, rejecting, leaned toward her and showed her his hands in turn. "But we have ten fingers, not eight. Linda, ten fingers! Why do you talk about eight paths? Why not ten or seven? It all sounds so arbitrary. And so abstract and timid. We have ten fingers. That's how it is."

"The way is eightfold, not ten," she said timidly, bewildered at the vehemence of his defense. "Why does a molecule have two hydrogen atoms and one oxygen atom?"

"What you say has nothing to do with chemistry."

"With the foundation of life," she said.

"I see that differently," he said in an attempt to avoid an escalation of their conflict. She was crazy.

She lowered her head, and the visor of her cap hid her eyes. "I'm not as strong as you."

"Me, strong?" he scoffed. "No. But evidently that meditation works for you. I can't make a judgment about it. That's your life."

"You are strong," she insisted again. She lifted her head and looked at him resolutely. "I can't survive without meditation."

A Latino appeared at their table with their plates. "Lox, right?"

"Right," said Joop.

Large plates with rich food. Fat slices of salmon. Thick slices of toast. Warm scrambled eggs.

"With meditation you learn to observe yourself," said Linda after the young man had slid the plates onto the table. "And you try to clean up the impurities. Like hate, desire, doubt, anger."

"So, everything that makes life and literature interesting."

"There are countless Buddhist writers!"

"But just imagine: a story without desire or hate or jealousy!"

"There can be a story about conquering these weaknesses."

"A fairy tale."

"Mankind can't do without fairy tales."

"Because life is hard and cruel."

"No, because they know deep down that there is a way out," she said with certainty. She stared at her plate. "In the Alagaddupama-sutra, the Buddha says the following—"

"Say that once more: Ala..."

"Alagaddupama. In this sutra the Buddha says: the theory of the soul would be acceptable if through it no sorrow, suffering, or pain would come about. But does such a theory exist? His answer is: 'No, I know no theory of the soul that would not cause sorrow or suffering or pain to come about.' But I've done nothing else this whole year. I no longer know if there is no soul. This past year I have experienced nothing but a world that is filled to bursting with souls."

"And that means?"

She looked into his eyes again, and he saw that she became uncertain. "That means that I've lain awake a lot—not last night—have difficulty concentrating—that I'm too preoccupied with the past."

"The past?"

Her parents had been killed in a traffic accident. She was sixteen. After she'd been in a home for several months, his parents had taken care of her. She was the only family member on his mother's side. Linda's grandfather and Joop's grandfather—both murdered in Poland—were brothers. When she was sixteen, unprotected, unprepared, she experienced what he had just experienced.

He said, "Your parents? You mean the accident?"

"It was suicide," she said matter-of-factly.

"I've always heard...," he whispered, bewildered.

"Should your parents have told you something else?" she asked, suddenly bitter. "My parents did away with themselves. I was saved because I had eaten candy right before. Stuffed myself with licorice. I had absorbed a lot, but it was not fatal. My parents had empty stomachs. It was in the soup. Poison in the soup."

"They told me, a car accident," he said. "And you were in a home...."

"First soup. Then the hospital. Three weeks. Then a children's home, under supervision of Child Welfare. And then with you."

He felt sorry for her and now understood why, thirty years ago, his mother had wanted to keep Linda in their home despite the fiasco.

They had been caught in the bathtub by his father and maintained that they hadn't done anything, but the shame was boundless. After initially taking the blame for it ("It was my idea; at first Linda didn't want to at all; we really did nothing!"), Joop had weakly submitted to his father's decision, and subsequently his mother gave in. In hindsight his father was right: if Linda had stayed, he would have wasted high school, and with that his future. What would he have done if he had caught Miriam in the bathroom with a boy?

He said, "An accident was bad enough, but—why did they do it?"

"I think—my father was a twin. He had a sister. She never returned. All that time he looked for her. But then, after all these years, he became certain. The Red Cross finally did find information about her. I think that he couldn't live with it. He had been very depressed for many years. And what's more: it was sixty-nine, and they really thought that the world could be destroyed at any moment by an atomic war. They talked about it often—they were pacifists, members of the Pacifist Socialist Party—about the threat, that things might get out of hand in Vietnam between America and China. They couldn't cope with the world. They were convinced that everything would fall apart. And then—then there was an additional thing, as if all of it wasn't enough: my mother found out that she had a tumor. They simply gave up. Last year I was just as old as my mother when they did it. Things came back. It was a sad year. I even wrote you, a few months ago."

"I know. I didn't answer. Sorry. Your letter lay ready to be answered—it still does."

"You did send me a card when I wrote about your daughter. It doesn't matter. You're the only relative I have; do you know that?"

"You have no children?"

"No. I couldn't. I mean physically yes, but—I was unfit for it."

"Never been married?"

"Several long-term relationships. But no marriage. I must say I never sought it."

"Yes, we are relatives," he said, surprised at the simple observation. He thought he was alone, but Linda possessed close genes.

"You know," he said softly, "I'm glad that you looked me up."

Across the table he clasped her hand and stroked her fingers as if they were lovers. He wanted to console her.

She smiled.

"Why are you alone?" she asked point-blank.

She moved her hand, and he thought that she wanted to struggle out of his grasp, but she twined her fingers around his.

He had no other answer but a counter-question: "I can ask you that same question."

"Until a year ago I was seldom alone. Then I no longer felt like it."

"Like what?" he asked.

"Like being with men. Everything came to a halt. Until the day before yesterday."

"What happened?" he asked businesslike.

She lifted his hand, leaned forward, and pressed it to her lips.

"You," she said softly.

Oh Miriam, he thought, will you forgive me? May I experience this? Forget your living heart for a moment?

She couldn't look at him for long, kept looking away at his hand. "When I saw you...I wasn't prepared for it, wasn't thinking about it. I thought it was natural to look you up. Certainly at this time, with the tragedy of...of what happened to you." She looked away. "I'm saying things that I shouldn't say. Don't pay too much attention to it, it's...I just woke up, I don't know what got into my head."

"Me neither," he said and wondered if he was falling in love. "You're saying terrible things."

"Yes, it's terrible, I know."

"You haven't eaten anything yet," he said.

She nodded, let go of his hand, and picked up the cutlery. She looked at him briefly with a guilty smile—or was it pity?—as she pricked her fork into the smoked salmon.

She asked what he was working on at the moment. It made him feel embarrassed, and he said that there were a couple of things he was checking out and that he had difficulty concentrating, but on Monday he would start on a project for Showcrime. Which wasn't exactly true. He wanted to know how she had managed to get his address. From Ellen. During her stay in Holland she had spoken with her. From a girlfriend in Den Bosch, she had heard to whom he had been married. She had called Ellen and had gotten his address from her.

"You still haven't answered me," she said. "Why did you stay alone? Did Miriam not accept your girlfriends?"

"Yes, but they remained at a distance. It wasn't my intention, nor was it Miriam's. It happened. The two of us could cope with the world."

"Wasn't it awkward when puberty began, a father and a daughter?"

"Yes, it was strange when she began to change into a woman. When she got her period, she needed Ellen. At that time they called each other regularly. One afternoon—I had a meeting in the city—Miriam was home alone and she called me. 'Dad, you have to do something for me.' 'What?' I asked. She said that she had called her girlfriends but no one was home and now there had been a disaster. A disaster. 'And what sort of disaster?' I, dense male, asked. 'Dad, I need something and I can't go out into the street.' Not into the street? Then it began to dawn. 'That bad?' I asked. 'Very bad, Dad,' she said, 'a deluge, Noah.' She liked to exaggerate. 'What do you need?' 'Tampax, *heavy duty*,' she said. From that moment on, it was something that she could complain about boldly, which became part of our lives and which didn't embarrass her. Not that she involved me in all the gory details, but she announced it when it would get that far. 'What all we have to go through for our ovules,' she'd say."

Like a beast of prey, mourning pounced on him. He let it maul him. He hid his face in his hands, pressed the palms of his hands against his eyes, and breathed in deeply several times.

"Nothing's the matter," sounded from his tight throat. "One second."

Suddenly he felt Linda slide next to him on the bench. She threw an arm around his neck, pulled his head toward her, and kissed him on the mouth, several times in a row as if she were exploring the terrain, and then opened her lips to give him her tongue.

Through the rain they hurried to her hotel, two hundred yards down the street, holding on to each other carefully, as if they were afraid that they would fall if they didn't lean on each other. They ran up the stairs to the fourth floor. The housekeeping cart stood a few rooms away in front of an open door. With trembling fingers Linda looked for her key, pulled him into the room which, because of the closed curtains, was still plunged in half-light, kicked the door closed with her foot, and threw her cap into a corner. She opened her mouth as though she were thirsty. While she kissed him, she tugged open his fly.

She took him with her to the unmade bed that was two steps from the door and fell with him on the sheets. She pushed off her shoes, pulled up her skirt, and kicked off her panties while Joop turned onto his back and stripped off his pants. She crawled on top of him, and strange to say, he thought of nothing. Just as formerly, not a single thought appeared during her embrace.

Chapter twenty-four

While Linda was in the bathroom, Joop called Philip. In the Broadway Deli he had told Linda that he was going to write a film for Showcrime. And therefore he had to call Philip if he wanted to prevent his comment about Showcrime from remaining an empty lie. He wanted to be strong; anyone who falls in love with a woman like Linda can also serve the rest of the Jewish people. In addition, there was the fact that he not only needed a new daily schedule—Erroll had left his house once and for all; Linda would be out with Usso during the day—but he also needed money. The high that had carried him through one whole night could not erase that truth. There were still a few thousand dollars in his account that could last him two months, if he was thrifty. But not if he was going to throw money around for a few weeks. At Spago they had eaten for more than two hundred dollars, tonight they would go to Il Cugini on Ocean Avenue, and they would probably eat out every evening. He was a traditional man who paid the restaurant bills. Without the prospect of a commission, he would be flat broke in a few weeks because of his increased expenses. Selling his mother's jewelry was inconceivable. His house was almost paid off and he could increase his mortgage, but

he wanted to prevent being unable to pay it off and having to give up
the house in order to provide for his daily costs. After breakfast at the
Broadway Deli, after Linda's hotel room, the walks in the rain on the
beach, the searches in bookstores on the Promenade, and the dinner
at Spago, he had again seen the shape of another, almost forgotten
life. Despite the empty organizer in Miriam's room.

He asked Philip, "Where is that office again?"

"On Sunset. You'll do it?"

"Yes." Even though there were countless solid reasons not to
do it. About which he kept silent.

"Thank you," said Philip.

"Wait just a little. You said that Showcrime would send a
contract."

"You'll get it tomorrow. When do you want to start?"

"Tomorrow."

"Tomorrow? With you it's all or nothing. But okay, tomorrow.
Can we still see each other today?"

"I'm busy all day, Philip." He was going to be with Linda.

"You have to get the key."

"Let Danny bring it by. At four o'clock I'll be home for a while.
Do you know what they offer?"

"A hundred."

"Good. I'll see it tomorrow."

In the afternoon he left Linda behind in the hotel, put on
clean clothes at home, and shaved. At exactly four o'clock Danny
rang the doorbell. Joop got the key to the office, the exact address,
instructions about the alarm system. And a new cell phone, the same
type of Motorola that he used.

"Put your SIM card in here," Danny explained. "And place the
telephone on the table when you two talk."

"What's in it?"

"Nothing special. If we want to, we can listen in, even when
you don't call."

"What's the name again of that inventor of weapons and gadgets
in the James Bond movies?"

"Cohen. Or Polak," answered Danny.

Chapter twenty-five

The Sunset Strip between Doheny and La Cienega was filled with small and large offices of lawyers, agencies, and film production companies. In the hotels and restaurants there was a continuous, tingling expectation that a star could enter, or a power agent, or the casting director who had everyone's number in his or her address book. Anyone who exchanged a simple study on Superba Avenue in Venice for a luxurious office suite on the Strip was ready for a Brioni suit, the newest Porsche Carrera, a Nokia with the latest gadgets, a Montblanc Meisterstück, and a gym in order to keep the hard-as-steel stomach muscles in shape. Joop couldn't afford all that.

His small office looked out on the slight curve that Sunset made halfway down the Strip to the northeast, at the busy intersection with Holloway Drive where the green median strip began that kept the streams of traffic separated at this part of the Strip. If Joop looked outside, he saw on his left the black building of Tower Records, and on his right the gray surfaces of the original postmodern establishment of Spago that had in the meantime been overshadowed in popularity by the new branch in Beverly Hills where he had eaten at a side table with Linda, the spot for the faceless and powerless. Across

Sunset, behind Tower and Spago, the hills sloped toward the crests of the Santa Monica Mountains, the name of the mountain ridge that included the Hollywood Hills. Every available spot had been built on.

His brand new office measured ten feet by ten feet. In it stood a table, two desk chairs, a couch, and a telephone. On the desktop lay the contract with Showcrime. With it a note from Jeff Silberman: "Dear Joe Merchant, we are happy that you are willing to write an episode for our network's Showcrime series."

A commission without the involvement of an agent seldom occurred. And signing a contract without the involvement of a lawyer did not occur very often either. But it was normal that writers were offered an office by those who commissioned them. The studios often housed their top writers in one of their office complexes on their own studio grounds or paid for the rent of an office—soon called a suite in LA—somewhere in the city.

Interrupted by a visit to Primavera (two hundred yards through the pouring rain where he encountered neither Sandra nor Omar), he spent the first day reading the one-inch-thick contract, made notes, and sent it back to Silberman. It rained all day, and on the way back he landed in an immovable traffic jam on the freeway between Robertson and the bend at the coast. Linda had notified the front desk that Joop was allowed to enter her room even if she wasn't there, and lying on her bed, he waited until she entered and jumped on top of him. "I've thought of you all day," she said, "and I have the feeling that you've thought of me all day." She stood up on the bed, pulled off her pants, lowered herself, and holding her breath dropped on top of him. Late in the evening they ate at Il Fornaio across from the Pier.

The next day, Tuesday, February twenty-seventh, Joop left the hotel in the morning, went to his house in Venice, put on clean clothes, drank a cappuccino, and read the *Times* in the kitchen until the traffic on the freeway had diminished.

Around nine thirty he left for the Strip, and forty minutes later he parked his old Jaguar in the parking garage under the building. At Book Soup, the bookstore next to his office, he bought newspapers and magazines, and he stared at the hills until it was one o'clock and he allowed himself to leave the building. At Primavera he was taken to his table by Sandra. "Hi, Joop, nice that you're here again. Same table?"

When the office buildings started to empty, he drove back to hotel Carmel in Santa Monica and waited until Linda appeared. Wednesday, February twenty-eighth, elapsed in the same way. It stayed cool, it drizzled, and once in a while the clouds tore open and the sun warmed the streets.

Chapter twenty-six

On Thursday, March first, Omar van Lieshout sat in the seat that Sandra had given Joop the past few days, at the table in the back corner. Over Sandra's shoulder Joop recognized him from the photos that Philip had shown him. An aristocratic looking North African with dark brown hair, striking blue, arrogant eyes, a feminine mouth, and an angular jaw; someone who was strong as well as clever and pleased with himself. Snow-white cuffs with gold cufflinks protruded from the sleeves of his expensive jacket. He sipped a glass of water, a strong, hairy hand.

"Hi, Joop. Alone again?" asked Sandra.

"Yes."

"Your place is gone. The table next to it is empty. Okay?"

"Excellent."

He followed her in between the tables, but suddenly he no longer felt like having lunch. Until now Omar had been a name, a face on photos. Joop now became aware that he had known intellectually what awaited him, but he had never realized that he would panic from one second to the next.

Having arrived at the table, he said, "I have to go to the men's room for a moment."

"Should I bring you something to drink?"

"Pellegrino."

In the bathroom Joop washed his hands frantically. You don't need to do anything, Philip had sworn to him, you go and have a nice lunch there every day, you wait and see, and the rest of the day you work on a script in your own office. Those were abstractions. Until now. A living man. A breathing, eating man. And what should Joop do if Omar started asking questions? Tell the truth, always tell the truth, Philip had emphasized, but never the whole truth. Joop knew that this undertaking would end in disaster. He wasn't made for this.

Someone rattled the door. Joop dried his hands and walked into the restaurant. He did not give in to the temptation to cast a glance at Omar, placed his cell phone—his old one, he refused to take along a James Bond device—on the table indicated by Sandra, and then took his seat in the narrow space between the table edge and his rear neighbor. If he raised his eyes, he could look straight at Omar. A small bottle of Pellegrino waited next to the menu. He tried to decipher the names of the dishes, but gave up trying to interpret the spots that were supposed to be letters when he realized that he had already studied the menu in detail in the past few days and now knew the menu by heart.

Sandra asked, "Want the special today?"

She stood next to him and he felt—it wasn't a feeling, somewhere on the periphery of his field of vision he saw it—that the Dutch words made Omar look up.

"Do you have vongole today?"

"No. But we do have a lovely mussel, crawfish, anchovy sauce. Really good."

"Okay. And also add a glass of Merlot."

"Good choice," she said before disappearing.

Joop gave her a forced smile and opened the *Hollywood Reporter.* Today at the newspaper stand of Book Soup, they had *De Telegraaf,* but he had decided that might arouse suspicion. Do nothing that you wouldn't usually do, Philip had advised; therefore, he had just now purchased one of the two daily trade journals and left behind *De Telegraaf,* even though his interest in news from the polder had never completely disappeared, and he had kept up—by now the last time was months ago—with the sites of Dutch newspapers.

News about successes and mega-deals filled the pages of the trade journals. His name was mentioned five times with a transaction; mention in the trade journals was important in this city. When the trades write about you, you're a player. But he had no agent, no publicity or business manager. In fact he was out of the action. In the months before Miriam's accident he had asked himself daily how he would be able to support them in the near future when their last reserve had dried up. Like many others, he had sunk the money that he possessed into an IT venture, and like many he had discovered too late that the results did not meet the expectations. Yet, if Miriam was still there, he would have disregarded Philip's offer. It was completely out of the question that he would expose his child to the slightest danger. Now the offer seemed to save him financially. He had ignored Erroll's offer because it went against all reason. The dark irony of fate.

The telephone beeped the first bars of the *Wilhelmus.* His eyes briefly crossed Omar's who looked at him, smiling. Joop answered with a brief nod.

"Hello?" he said.

"Mr. Koopm'n?" A woman's voice, but not Linda.

"Speaking."

"Debby Brown. Do you have a moment?"

During the past few days he had not once thought about the question that he had asked her. So this is what happened to faithfulness to your child when you went between the thighs of a woman. Miriam had not yet been gone for ten weeks, and now he was ready to allow something besides unadulterated mourning within himself.

He turned toward the wall and leaned forward as much as possible, withdrawing out of others' earshot.

"Yes, go ahead," he said, ashamed. It was an awkward moment, but he wanted to know what she was going to tell him.

"We set the process in motion, and the central office has

contacted the family of the recipient of your daughter's organ. But I have to inform you that the answer is negative."

"What do you mean, negative?"

"Negative means that the recipient does not care for direct communication."

"We don't have to communicate," he said grimly. "I just want to know things. Facts. And perhaps a conversation, once. I think that something like that...that it can have a positive effect."

"Mr. Koopm'n, I agree with you completely. But if the recipient wants nothing, then there is little to be done about it."

"It seems to me that the recipient is not in the position to want something or nothing. That should be reserved for the families of the donors," he answered indignantly.

"Perhaps you are right, but those are the rules. Communication must come from two sides. You can refuse, and so can they."

"Have they given a reason?"

"That's not necessary. There are recipients who like to have contact, for they know that they owe their life to the tragedy that has befallen others. But there are also recipients who for that very reason avoid any form of communication. It is too painful for them. You have bad luck."

"I find the term 'bad luck' rather offensive in these circumstances."

"I'm sorry."

"Can I appeal, or something of the kind?"

"No. What can be done, and that often happens in such cases, is that you try again in a year."

"Try again? This is not about tickets for a pop concert, Mrs. Brown."

"I'm sorry that it is like that, but it never stems from maliciousness, Mr. Koopm'n. People are afraid of the emotion, of the confrontation with the origin of the organ."

"The origin of the organ," he repeated. "How did you get this job? Is there training for it?"

"Of course one has to receive training."

"And what were you taught when you encounter people like me?"

She was quiet for a moment, searching for an answer that maintained her distance without offending him.

"Mr. Koopm'n, we don't think in cases or in generalizations. We think in individuals. We try to satisfy your wishes because we realize quite well how hard it is for you. Of course the problem is..."

"that there is another party too," he completed her sentence. "It's heartless. A rather appropriate term, don't you think?"

"I can't comment on that; I'm sorry. But if you want to, I'll really do my best to convince the central office to approach the recipient once more."

"Do they want money?"

"Money never plays a role in these things."

"I think that I have the right to know what has happened, don't you think?"

"Emotionally, certainly. But the system doesn't work like that."

"When will I hear from you again?"

"As soon as possible, Mr. Koopm'n. I'll call right now."

"Please."

"Take care, Mr. Koopm'n."

He broke off. This nightmare was only possible because science had developed knowledge and technique. A new heart offered a life expectancy of ten years. It had almost become a routine operation. The suppliers were primarily young people in car wrecks, and that night he had not been able to judge what the doctors told him. She had been declared brain dead; the computers showed no activity. How could he know whether those were definitive, irrevocable, and irreversible facts? Perhaps people returned from the void and opened their eyes a day later. He had read about coma patients who woke up after many years. They had explained to him that there were two teams working separately from each other so that no conflict of interest could be created. But that too was only a story—which he had not verified.

"Pasta di mare," said Sandra.

"Thank you," he said.

"Some Parmesan?"

"Please," he said mechanically. He wanted no cheese. No mussels or crawfish. He wanted to fast. Punish himself for the lack of concern for his child.

Sandra placed a small bowl of finely grated cheese in front of him. "Enjoy."

"Thank you," he said. "And don't forget the Merlot."

"Didn't I bring it? Oh, sorry, it's coming."

He placed his fork on a small fish and was disgusted with himself.

"Today's special. It's excellent," he heard.

A Dutch voice with a slight northern accent; he had grown up in Emmen. Joop raised his eyes and looked into Omar's face.

Joop nodded.

Omar was of secondary importance. Omar had met a professional Iraqi terrorist and therefore was a terrorist as well. Or a thief or a bandit—big deal. A scoundrel was much less terrifying than the question of whether your child would still be alive if you had kept your head. He had trusted the doctors. Nothing had moved him to observe the developments during that night with suspicion because everyone had been sincerely concerned. A team of fifteen people had fought for his daughter's life. That was the impression that he had, no, his firm conviction: with it he had endured the nightmare. The firm conviction that they had done everything in their power. And that was a lot. The most brilliant specialists had appeared at her bedside. Powerless. Wait and see. The coming hours. The catchphrase of that night.

Sandra placed the glass of Merlot in front of him.

"Sorry, I had forgotten it," she said.

"Thank you," he answered.

He took a gulp. A successful writer drinks no alcohol at lunch because a lot of writing has to be done in the afternoon.

"Visiting here?"

He looked up at Omar again. The man had well-cared-for hands with manicured nails. Intelligent eyes. The thick brown hair cut in stylish layers; Joop had had it done once when he could still spend sixty dollars on it; the anorexic hairdressers with silicone breasts in the hairdressing salons of Beverly Hills used a razorblade. Heavy gold cufflinks, and something gold also glistened under his shirt with the top two buttons casually open, giving a glimpse of his very hairy body. Omar looked like a successful film producer or musician, or like the owner of a restaurant. In this city restaurant owners could get the same reputation as film people since the management of a successful place to eat was considered as a very high form of entertainment. For the barbarians they were comparable to a director like Spielberg or a conductor like Zubin Mehta.

"I live here," said Joop.

"Well.... How long?"

"Since eighty-two."

"Still like it?"

"I never ask myself that," said Joop.

Omar chuckled. "Good attitude." And he gestured authoritatively at Joop's pasta, as if he were paying for it. "Enjoy it. Pasta cools quickly."

Joop nodded and took a bite. Looked at the *Reporter* without reading it. Turned the pages and read, even though the words seemed to have no meaning. He ate mechanically because he was observed by Omar. His eyes lingered on the real estate ads. Country estates in the Hills. Penthouses in Westwood.

When the busboy came by and asked if he had finished, he let the pasta be taken away even though he had eaten barely a fourth of it. That too was part of the rules. In Los Angeles you swallowed at top speed what you wanted to eat, and when you put your fork down that was the signal for the busboy—by definition a young Latino—to step in and clear the table. It had always annoyed Miriam. "I'll tell you when I'm finished, okay?" was always her reaction to the question: "Finished?" It was never said in a complete sentence. Only: "Finished?"

"Do you live here in the area?"

Omar wanted to talk. Philip was right. Omar was lonely.

"Venice. On the coast."

"Yes, I know it. It's nice there on the beach, the boardwalk."

"And you?" asked Joop. "Do you live in the area?"

"I don't live here. Just for a few months. Temporarily."

"For business?" asked Joop.

"Business," affirmed Omar. "What's your line of work?"

"I write, a writer."

"A writer?"

Omar nodded with a respectful expression and needed a few moments to process the import of the statement, as if Joop had told him that he was a Nobel Prize winner in chemistry.

"A special profession, seems to me. I admire people who can do that. What do you write about?"

"About...about things that interest me."

"Isn't it true that your publisher dictates what you should write about?"

A non-reader. Joop doubted whether Omar had ever seen a book up close.

"I write scripts. Movies. And long ago I wrote a book."

"Movies. Well. Of course you need writers for that. Stupid that it never occurs to you, isn't it?"

And he made a gesture with his finger; he pointed at the short distance from himself to Joop's table and asked, "Mind if I ...?"

"Be my guest," Joop invited him.

Omar slid out of his tight corner, bent to pick up something, and sat down across from him. He placed *De Telegraaf* on the table.

"I finished it. Take it with you if you wish."

"Great. Thank you."

In addition to Sandra, Omar had another reason to come here. Across the street he could buy a Dutch newspaper. Omar's nearness had nothing threatening. Other things were threatening, not this man.

"Can I offer you something?" asked Omar. His eyes had a lively, ironic sparkle.

"An espresso," said Joop.

"Sandra!"

She appeared promptly at their table.

"Espresso for us. Do you want anything with it? Grappa or something? I don't drink it, but they seem to have very good ones."

"No thank you, I still have to work."

"You hear that," he said to her. And again to Joop, "Writer, interesting profession. Did you study for it?"

Many thousands of writers lived in this city; except for a handful of stars, they were dogged working hacks who, like mine workers, brought the raw material of the industry to the surface. Their status wasn't much higher than that of camel drivers, but Joop's profession had impressed Omar.

"No. Not really."

"How do you start something like that? How old were you?"

"Sixteen, seventeen."

"One day you sat down and you thought: I'm going to be a writer?"

"Not quite like that, but it comes close."

"What do you write about? Do you get a commission or something?"

Omar was undeniably impressed by Joop's profession. Philip had struck Omar's weak point.

"No. Things that I make up."

"So just your imagination?"

"Yes."

Omar offered him his hand. "Omar van Lieshout."

"Joop Koopman."

They shook hands. The terrorist and the writer.

"I find it fascinating what you do, compose a story with your imagination. It seems to me that you need a lot of discipline and concentration for that...am I right?"

"You're right."

Sandra placed the two espresso cups on the table. "Biscotti?"

The small, rock-hard, Italian cookies were popular in this town. You dipped them in coffee to soften them a bit.

"Not for me," said Omar. "You?"

"I'm fine," said Joop, looking briefly at her almost black eyes.

When she walked away, Omar said, "A good-looking woman, don't you think?"

"She is beautiful, yes. And very young."

"Differences in age no longer count. How old are you if I may ask?"

"I'll turn forty-seven this year."

"I wouldn't have thought that. You could be her father. I'll be thirty-three in December. So you're in the movie industry?"

"I think so, yes." That question gave Joop the opportunity to be curious about him. "And you? What kind of business do you do?"

"IT."

Philip had already informed him about it. Omar was setting up a mail-order company for a website. Omar had answered honestly.

"IT? It must be a difficult time for you."

"Not simple, that's true. I should have done this a few years earlier."

"Are you in technology, in software?"

"Commercial. We offer things directly to the consumer on the Internet. Do you come here often?"

Omar didn't want to elaborate, which was understandable. If Joop were setting up a company, he wouldn't want to talk about it with a complete stranger either.

"Just since Monday," answered Joop. "I had never been here before. I got an office here; I'm working on a commission."

"You see—it is a commission!"

"That's right, in movies and television you get commissions."

"Then I did understand it correctly just now," smiled Omar.

It was clear that Omar attached importance to respect and was therefore continually concerned about the impression that he made. Vanity. Or an inferiority complex.

Omar said, "I come here regularly. The food is good, and the view of Sandra pleases me."

Joop smiled politely with him. Omar was not an impressive intellectual—which didn't mean that he was naïve. Omar had an intuitive intelligence. Perhaps that kind of intelligence was the most powerful. They both drank their espresso in one swallow.

"Good coffee," said Omar.

"But not as good as at Mirafiori in Amsterdam," answered Joop.

"You know Mirafiori?" asked Omar, surprised.

"When I'm in Amsterdam. Which doesn't happen often."

"It's my favorite Italian there," smiled Omar. "We may have been there at the same time."

"You can bet your boots on that," said Joop.

"And do you know l'Angoletto on Hemonylaan?" asked Omar with a big smile.

"Yes. I was there the last time I was in Amsterdam." Ellen had taken him and Miriam there. "A small neighborhood Italian restaurant. Also good."

"Mirafiori was closed last year," Omar reported. "A terrible shame."

"Mirafiori closed? Why? It's an Amsterdam institution."

"I don't know why. Perhaps no one to take over the place. Their pesto was delicious."

"And what about their preserved peppers and zucchini?"

Grinning, they looked at each other.

"When will you come here again?" Omar wanted to know.

"Tomorrow. Or Monday."

"Let's go over the fine points of the Amsterdam restaurants some time," said Omar. He pointed to Joop's empty espresso cup. "Another one?"

"Why not?"

"I'll tell Sandra." He got up and shook Joop's hand. "That coffee is on me. Nice to have met you, Joop. I'll be here again on Monday. I'll save a place for you if you're not here yet."

He walked away. A likeable terrorist.

Joop had agreed with Philip that he would report promptly when he had spoken with Omar—Philip kept emphasizing that communication was everything—but it seemed senseless to give an immediate account of the chit-chat. At the end of the day he drove to Santa Monica, and in the evening he walked with Linda on the Promenade, a part of Third Street that had been made into a pedestrian area, and resolved to inform Philip the next day. They sauntered amidst hundreds of tourists and evening strollers, past the stores and restaurants, past singers, guitarists, jugglers, dancers, and religious maniacs; they ate in an Asian restaurant across from Barnes & Noble and slept together in her hotel room.

Chapter twenty-seven

When Joop was at home, Miriam's absence reverberated between the walls. If this continued, he could do only one thing: sell the house. No. Not yet. Later perhaps. In a few months, or a year. He could smell Miriam here. Miriam had grown up in this house. Her organizer lay here. But as soon as he could, he got away from the furniture, the cutlery, the mugs, and the pans, and fled to Linda or to the Strip.

At ten o'clock on Friday, March second, when he had just entered his office on the Strip, the *Wilhelmus* sounded.

"Joop?" It was Linda.

"Hi," he said.

"I'm right near the Strip. I thought I'd come by."

"You're welcome. Do you know where it is?"

"Can't we go somewhere? Or just go for a ride? I have to talk to you."

"Where are you?"

"I'm in front of a bookstore here. Book Soup."

When he drove the Jaguar out of the parking garage, she was waiting in front of the entrance. She wore loose-fitting black pants, a loose-fitting black jacket, and a black beret, a dark variant of the Mao outfit. But she also carried a sophisticated small brown leather briefcase with a small label that said Marianelli. It was the first time that he saw her with a leather product.

He lowered the car window and looked up at her. "Where do you want to go?"

Leaning forward she stood next to the car, with one hand on the roof, and looked at him somberly. He should prepare himself for her telling him that she was going to end their relationship. Maybe that was for the best.

"Is something wrong?" he asked.

"You and I...that's what," she said seriously.

"What do you mean by that?"

"I mean...this wasn't supposed to happen. We have to talk. Not here."

"Let's drive around."

She walked around the car, and Joop leaned across the passenger seat to open the door. She got in. He drove the car up Holloway, the street that runs south of Sunset and becomes Santa Monica Boulevard after two-thirds of a mile. She placed a hand on his arm but was silent.

"Do you have a suggestion as to where you want to go?"

"I'd like to walk."

"Walking is a subversive activity in this city."

"Is there a park nearby?"

"Griffith Park. Hollywood. We'll go to the Observatory. All right?"

"Yes, fine."

All he needed to do now was to follow Santa Monica until Alexandria. A fifteen-minute drive.

He glanced at her; she was staring ahead nervously.

He asked, "Why do you look like that?"

"Like—what?"

"You know what I mean," he said. "What's eating you?"

"What's eating me?"

"You're very clear. That helps."

Conciliatory, she clasped his arm. "I don't mean it like that."

"You're married," he said. "Leave him, he's a jerk."

She chuckled. "No, I'm not married. If that were the case, I would have left him for you."

"Engaged?"

"Joop, who still gets engaged nowadays?"

"In this city? Everyone."

"No. It's not about that. It's about…it's so difficult to say it."

"Start at the beginning," he suggested.

"Okay. The beginning…that was…five years ago. In Dharamsala. That's where it started."

"There's something between you and Usso? I thought that these men lived as celibates!"

"No! That's not it! And I don't want to talk about it now. I'll talk about it when we're out of the car. But don't worry; it's not anything that needs to stand between us."

"Except: I have to share you with three others."

"Joop…it's about something that I should have told you right away. I have to remedy that. That's all. But in this case 'all'…is quite a lot."

"That's the nature of 'all,'" Joop remarked.

"Be serious," she said.

"I'm dead serious. I'm not crazy about revelations—this is a revelation, isn't it?" He looked at her briefly.

She stared ahead and nodded. "I think so, yes."

"Revelations have consequences."

"Not necessarily."

"We can go on like this forever," he concluded.

"I've neglected to tell you something," she said. "I have to remedy it. That's all."

"You just said that."

"Joop, don't be hostile. It's not like that."

"Then why are you acting so mysteriously?"

"I'm acting like that…because I know that what I'm going to tell you is beyond you."

"Beyond me? I'm starting to enjoy this. Do tell me about it."

"I want to, but you keep interrupting me!"

"I'll shut up. Go ahead."

"Good."

But she remained silent. He braked for a stoplight and looked at her. With clenched fists, she sat up straight in the low seat of the Jaguar. She noticed his worried glance and smiled at him nervously.

When he accelerated, she said, "Five years ago my life was a total mess. I'd had an affair with someone. In New York. He was married. The usual story, but I thought: He is different, he'll really do it, for me. But he stayed with his wife, two young children. She didn't know it, and...one day she suddenly stood in front of my door. She had discovered it. It was terrible. She was...a lovely, good person. I had created a situation there that had become untenable."

"He had caused it, it seems to me," said Joop.

"With my willing help. Anyway, then I went back to Dharamsala. I had to forget, empty my head and my heart. And there I met someone who told me about Usso Apury. I already knew him, from the beginning, but at a distance. He's a great teacher, specializing in care of the dying. If you can do that, you have a strong soul. An old soul that has suffered a lot, has experienced a lot. And there I heard about his dreams."

"Whose dreams?"

"Usso's dreams. Specific dreams. Dreams that came from another time. Memories of a previous life."

"Of a previous life," Joop repeated pointedly.

"That's exactly the tone I expected from you," she said, "That's why I find it so difficult to say this."

"Sorry—that was inappropriate. I'll shut up now. Go on."

"Good. But no more comments, really, okay?"

"Okay."

"Good. So I had just read the book by Rabbi Gershom, *Beyond the Ashes: Cases of Reincarnation from the Holocaust*. Do you know it?"

"No," he said.

"It's about people who have memories that they can't place. Memories of the camps, of the most terrible things. Gershom has researched them. Gershom is a kind of Hasid, an Orthodox rabbi, but he has also immersed himself in psychology and in sociology, and he is an expert in Jewish incarnation stories. The Jewish mystics were adherents of the idea of reincarnation, did you know that?"

"No," he said again, not yielding to his doubts.

"I also had dreams. Nightmares. That's why I read that book. My shrinks in New York said that they resulted from over-identification with my parents. But these dreams were always so…clear, that I often had the feeling that they were more than simply dreams. Well, in Dharamsala I heard about Usso. And in conversations he recounted his dreams. Those dreams—how can I say it?—those dreams were more than just aberrations of the brain caused by electrochemical waves. Usso's dreams were objectively identifiable. And everything fell into place. That's a strange experience: you feel that the life that you've led until then has consisted of fragments, and suddenly these fragments form a whole. You see form, color, direction, meaning. Order—perhaps that's the word. It was…atrociously touching. I cried for days. As if a dam had broken. As if I were cleansed."

She was silent for a moment. It became clear to him what she was going to tell him: that she had been Napoleon.

"I know that you think what I'm telling you is nonsense," she said, judging his expression, "but it's what happened there. I remembered things. From before the war. And Usso…and Usso has memories too. He had no doubt at all that his dreams had really happened, but he couldn't place them in context. But I could. It was unavoidable that we would get into a conversation one day. I knew where his dreams had originated. And once again, Joop, I understand if you think this sounds like poppycock. But I've come to know more aspects of reality than you can see in this part of the world. You have to open yourself to it. You, like most people here, don't do that. It doesn't occur to you that your experiences are limited by your senses, and that you would experience a lot more if you possessed more and different sensors. Buddhist meditation trains you in broadening and extending your senses—that's how it works, approximately—and through it you notice that there is something specific, something that exists outside of the physical and that characterizes you. I call that your soul. A certain essence. Every person has that. And experiences from former lives can therefore be a part of you too, because time doesn't exist for the essence. And my heart condition—it disappeared when I was in Dharamsala and meditated, but it didn't become clear to me until I met Usso that it had to do with something else. A former life. However crazy it may sound. All during my early childhood I dreamed that I was a six-year-old boy somewhere in Eastern Europe. In my dream, I sit alone under a table, and around me I hear screaming, outside something atrocious is happening that I can't see but can hear. Then I see boots in front of me, shiny black boots, and on the edge of the sole I see a thin line of mud. And a hand that drags me from under the table and holds me by my collar and lifts me. My collar strangles my throat; I'm almost unable to breathe. And I feel a stab go through my heart, a screaming pain that would awaken me every time. Years later I developed a cardiac arrhythmia. And through meditation with Usso, I learned to make the connection. It was psychosomatic. Caused by past experiences."

At that point Joop could not contain his disbelief.

"And who is sitting next to me now? How many people are you?"

"I knew beforehand that you wouldn't believe me. I don't know whether it makes sense to tell you the rest," she said, weary.

But he wanted no conflict with her. "Do continue. I want to know," he said. "If it's important to you, then I'll have to accept it. As a part of your existence."

"Then react a little more respectfully, please."

"I'm trying. Sorry."

Without looking at her, keeping an eye on the traffic, he placed his hand on her shoulder for just a moment as a gesture of peace. He felt that she pressed her cheek against it in a forgiving gesture.

"I don't know where my memories come from. I don't know the name of that little boy. I don't know where it took place. I know only that the images are more than random dreams. But Usso, initially he knew nothing either. Dreams that are disguised memories—of course he knew about that—but not anything more because he was not searching for reality. He accepted what he had to accept. Resistance means disruption, illness, suffering. I resisted and became ill. But

Usso, I heard about his dreams. And when I met him I didn't dare to start in about it. I didn't do that until later."

She straightened up again and breathed deeply. "Usso told me about his memories, and I knew about whom he was talking. He had heard names. Names that meant nothing to him but did to me. And which would have meant nothing to anyone except to me. I knew these names. And you. You know them too. He remembered things that…that he could never have imagined! Names and facts that were impossible for anyone to fabricate! That someone living in Dharamsala would never have been able to fake!"

Joop drove the car from Los Feliz to Fern Dell, the road that wound upward through Griffith Park to the Observatory. It was not yet the weekend, and it was cool and partly cloudy, but many cars were parked on the shoulder under the sycamores, the eucalyptus trees, and the conifers. The winding road required his attention, and they drove up the road, into the mountains. The bends in the road revealed a distant view of the far-away plain of Los Angeles, the downtown skyscrapers, the network of thousands of perfectly straight streets and boulevards.

After a few minutes, Linda said, "Usso remembers things about your grandfather, Herman de Vries. It's frightening, but if you don't resist, if you surrender to it, then it's so consoling, Joop. Then it's so beautiful and soothing. Do you understand?"

Joop understood nothing, drove the car up the mountain, and had no idea why Usso wanted to misappropriate his grandfather—murdered in a Polish camp. Or rather: why Linda believed that Usso knew facts of Herman's life. This was the dominion of psychos and new-age dreamers who refused to accept that life was absolutely finite for always and ever. The cosmos was the result of an explosion; if the sun was extinguished, there would in the whole universe no longer be any voice that would be able to pronounce the word "soul"; and when a person died, every identity, every memory, every vain attempt to escape the facts, vanished during the decomposition of the brain. It was a madness suffered by the believers, who—because of their naïve hope—nonetheless aroused a certain tenderness in Joop. But this went too far. Usso had at one time been Herman.

"You should explain it once more, I think," he said.

"There's not much to explain," said Linda. "In his dreams, Usso has seen things that you can see only if you can remember certain circumstances exactly—that is, if you've been someone else. And believe me, Joop, I'm not someone who goes along easily with that sort of thing. But it was so...overwhelming, and what happened with my own dreams, the way that my condition disappeared, those are all empirical facts. Rationally considered, they are impossible, and therefore my conclusion is that reason can take in only a certain part of total reality. Reason is not everything. For many things it is, of course. For the construction of this car, for the Observatory, but not for the essence of life and death."

Joop didn't want to think of his daughter, but in his thoughts she appeared—she was gone, lifeless, dissolved in dust, and the only place where she remained visible was in his memory. Except if you thought like Linda.

He stopped the car in the half-filled parking lot near the Observatory.

"Drink something first?" he asked.

"Please."

They walked to the cafeteria at the edge of the grounds, behind which towered the letters of the Hollywood sign.

Joop said, "So, if I understand you correctly—and don't get angry—Usso is related to us?"

Linda shook her head and wanted to express her disapproval, but she couldn't suppress a smile.

"Yes," she said. But she pulled herself together quickly. "When will you for once...react normally to what I tell you?"

"I react normally. These are normal reactions to such stories."

"Not in my world," said Linda. "In my world I find acknowledgment. And people feel liberated when there is so much insight."

"Linda, when someone comes and tells me that Herman de Vries has been succeeded by Usso—What's his last name again?"

"Apury."

"By Usso Apury, and that they have in fact the same soul or

something like that, then it seems only natural to me that I'm not immediately jumping with joy. Then it seems only natural to me that the messenger will encounter some…suspicion."

"There is no reason to treat something that I tell you with suspicion," Linda said sharply.

"It's not about you. It's about the…the way of thinking."

"My way of thinking."

Joop stopped and seized her hand. "Linda, my grandfather, there's nothing left of him, we know on which day he arrived in the camp and that, that very day, he was probably…and then it stops. Death makes everything stop. When the heart no longer pumps oxygen through the body, it stops."

She grabbed him by the shoulders. "No, Joop! No! That's not true! Our…our Western culture has reduced human life to only a physical life, and that is simply not true! Why would this world here have more insight into the truth of existence than that world there? There is *more*! For Herman, for you, for me, for Miriam!"

Fiercely she looked at him with devotion and with rock-solid certainty.

"Tell me more," he said, lonely in his disbelief, not because he was eager for more but rather to let her tell her story.

"You promised me something to drink," she said.

Joop ordered two Diet Cokes and sat down with her at one of the plastic tables. A busload of Japanese tourists lined up at the railing, smiling enthusiastically for a photo with the sign in the background.

"When did you discover this?"

"Five years ago."

"But you never thought: I'll surprise Joop?"

"Oh yes. Often. But at the same time it was too much of a good thing; I know how people react to this sort of thing. Until the end of last year."

"When you wrote me?" he asked.

"Yes. It was more than just: how are you, long time no see."

"So Usso is Herman. Then what, what does he know that I don't know?"

"Usso knows what happened that last day; Usso knows how

Herman died; Usso knows hundreds of facts from Herman's life. And Usso knows things about his brother, my grandfather. Joop, listen: down to the smallest detail."

Joop answered, "Sometimes strange things happen between heaven and earth."

With disgust Linda turned her face away from him, as if she suddenly realized how hideous he was.

"You don't take me seriously," she said. "That seems to me the least you could do. Even if you don't agree with me, you...you could at least hear me out before you start shooting from the hip!"

Wildly she stood up, and the chair legs scraped, squealing over the floor tiles. "I want to go back."

Joop got up. "Linda...don't let this get out of hand!"

"That's what you're doing! Take me back to the Strip, please." She looked at the parking lot and changed her mind. "Forget it. I'll take a taxi."

"I'll take you," said Joop.

But she was already walking to the parking lot, to one of the waiting taxis.

"Linda!"

Joop tried to grab her arm, but she shook him off.

"Linda, I think...that man is trying to con you. What you're telling me, it can't be...it has to be a scam, those things...they don't exist."

Suddenly she stopped and looked at him with fiery eyes. "Joop, you don't exist! You're a scam! Not Usso Apury! Usso is one of the greatest, most important, most profound priests of this time! Usso is a holy man! You're very badly mistaken, Joop." She swallowed and said softly and sorrowfully, "Sad to say you're very badly mistaken. I knew that this conversation would be terrible, but still...not this."

"I'll drive you back, Lin. What you're doing now is nonsense."

"Joop, I want to be alone for a bit. Let me, okay? We'll be in touch, all right?"

"Yes. We'll be in touch."

She gave him a quick kiss on the cheek and hurried to the taxi.

Chapter twenty-eight

Joop drove to Primavera, because he didn't want to go home where the distressing reminders of Miriam awaited him. Nor did he want to go to the office where a stack of white paper and a box of sharpened pencils were the evidence of a fraudulent writing commission.

He carried a notebook and a pencil with him. After submitting a synopsis, he would get paid the first installment. He had no synopsis. He had to write a crime story, but crimes no longer interested him, except for the crime of the big bang. For himself he could write a farce about a Tibetan monk who was the reincarnation of a Jew who died in the Holocaust. He felt revulsion at the grotesqueness of the thought, at the disdain suggested by the joke about the return of Herman de Vries.

"Joop?"

He looked up and saw Omar standing next to the table.

"Mind if I join you? It's awfully busy today."

"Go ahead."

Joop placed the *Calendar*, the entertainment supplement of the *Times*, under his chair and moved his glass to the side. Everything that he had imagined about contact with this man, the threat, the secrecy,

dissolved in the relaxation of ordinary reality. It was even pleasant
that Omar appeared suddenly. A conversation with someone else
was preferable to the conversation that he was having with himself.

"You came after all?" asked Joop.

"I was in the area. Nonsense not to eat here. You know what I
miss? Simple Dutch things."

"There's a Dutch store in the Valley," said Joop. "They have
everything, sweet Gouda waffles, Calvé peanut butter, things that
every Dutchman needs in a foreign country."

"I've got to have the address."

Today Omar was wearing a tight black sweater with a wide
neck that showed his chest hair and revealed a glimpse of his muscular
chest. There was no sun, but a pair of Ray-Ban sunglasses rested on his
head. His partly rolled-up sleeves showed hairy arms and a fat Rolex.
Omar was the picture of a trendy movie wheeler-dealer. Which he
was not. According to Philip, he was a former drug dealer who had
once had a meeting with an Iraqi terrorist leader. But Joop couldn't
rule out that Omar just wanted to convince the terrorist that a private
investment in a virtual mail-order business had a golden future. Why
would a terrorist leader not want to invest sensibly? At their first
meeting yesterday, Omar had not been vague about his origin. As
far as Joop knew, everything tallied with the facts. He had arranged
with Philip that he would call when he had made contact. He hadn't
done that because he had hurried to Linda's hotel room. He was not
allowed to use the telephone at home, nor the Motorola, but a pay
phone at the corner of Venice and Lincoln which had evidently been
secured against wiretapping by the Israelis. He hadn't called because
there had in fact been nothing to report, except that he and Omar
had exchanged a few words about restaurants in Amsterdam, and
according to Joop, that could wait. But he also felt a certain resistance
to Philip, to whom he didn't want to yield slavishly. First he wanted
to determine himself what plans Omar was going to use to threaten
the Jews in Israel before handing him over to Tel Aviv. Could someone
who liked Italian food be a terrorist? Yes, a Mafioso.

"It's often busy here on Friday," said Omar. "That's when the movie guys have their last-minute discussions. Of course you know all about that."

"No, nothing. The money guys yes, not the writers. We sit at home all alone, slaving away in a small room."

"Seems wonderful to me, slaving away by yourself at home," said Omar.

Sandra appeared. "I hope that you don't mind, Joop, that Omar is joining you?"

"Of course not."

She put down a napkin and cutlery for Omar. "The special today is swordfish. Joop has ordered it too. It's good, isn't it?"

"It's good," Joop said obligingly.

"Go ahead," said Omar. "And a Pellegrino."

"Exactly what I expected," Sandra flirted.

And when she walked away, she briefly put her hand on Omar's shoulder, actually stroking it briefly with her middle finger. It was a familiar, an almost intimate gesture with a strong erotic overtone, that middle finger on his shoulder. They slept together, Joop was convinced of it. And it was obvious what they saw in each other: two attractive young people from the same country, in a foreign city, with breathless expectations and warm nights in her room without air conditioning. Philip would be surprised at what he had discovered after just two encounters. Omar went to Primavera for the girl and for the newspaper stand across the street. This information would offer a lot of protection to Israel in the coming years.

"How is the writing going today?" asked Omar as he stuffed the napkin between his knees and the tabletop. When all the tables at the back wall were occupied, there remained no space to lean back or to drape a napkin comfortably across your lap.

"Nothing," answered Joop. "It hasn't been going well for a while. I can't concentrate."

"Seems tough, yes. It's all got to come out of you, of course you can't just look up in an instruction book what you should do. Or am I mistaken?"

"You're not mistaken."

Omar leaned with his elbows on the table. "And are you allowed to say what you're writing now? Or is that not allowed?"

"Most writers don't really like to say what they're doing. Except of course to your backer, the producer, the director, your agent, people with whom you are collaborating."

"I envy you, Joop. It's fantastic to have such a profession. Just quietly at home, lots of thinking, lots of reading. But I guess I should watch out what I tell you? Before I know it, I'll see myself in a movie."

"Yes, you should watch out with me," said Joop, aware of the ambiguity of his answer. There was a dubious pleasure in drawing out someone who had no suspicion about the intentions of the person he was talking to. He could imagine becoming hooked on it.

"I've tried it once or twice," Omar confessed with a smile. "For a while I felt the need to write about my youth, but I couldn't do that at all. I'm not a writer, and besides..." He hesitated and seemed to be looking for the right words and to wonder if there was anything damaging in his outpouring. Omar made a swatting gesture, as if he were rejecting an imaginary reservation.

"I'm dyslexic, have difficulty reading. It's all right if I concentrate, newspaper headlines and such, but reading dense texts—that remains difficult. When I was young, they thought I was stupid. It took me an eternity to read a book. In the end I lucked out, and at the moment it's no longer a problem for me, but when it really was important—then it was really shitty."

Joop wanted to keep him talking. "Where are you from?"

"Emmen. And after that Amsterdam, of course. But the last couple of years I've traveled a lot. I work with a group of investors from Saudi Arabia. I do a lot of things for them." Grinning, he pointed at Joop. "Perhaps they'd be interested in a movie; you never know."

Joop smiled politely. "And now here..."

"in the Valley. Even though I prefer coming to this side of the Hills. It's actually too respectable there for me. Some of my partners live there and eh...I rent an apartment, Oakwood Apartments; do you know the complex?"

"I've heard of it."

Because of the busy hour, the busboy was their server as well. Even though it was clear that Joop had a plate in front of him and that the order was for Omar, he still asked both of them foolishly: "Special?"

Omar pointed to the table in front of him. "I was here—for one hour—Pellegrino."

The server said, "Right away, sir."

Omar's English was not very impressive. But he was able to convey his wishes. Language was clearly an obstacle in his life.

Omar asked, "Where do you come from?" He took a bite, freeing a piece of fish from the fillet with his fork, not using the knife for the time being.

"Den Bosch, Brabant."

With a full mouth Omar said, "And then you came here?"

"Via Amsterdam, where I lived for nine years."

"Where you were a regular customer at Mirafiori."

They discussed restaurants they liked in Amsterdam, and Joop kept losing track of the fact that it was on Philip's orders that he had to strike up a conversation with this dangerous man. Omar was a guileless eater who polished off his meal with pleasure, gobbling down his food like Joop himself. His surrender to the food was disarming and childlike, a spectacle of high spirits that Joop had also been privileged to watch in Miriam before she entered puberty, and weight and shape became of cosmic importance. It was touching to watch Omar eat. Philip should have warned Joop about that. With his fork, Omar had cut the swordfish into bite-size chunks. His right hand lay protectively around the plate. His back vulnerable, he bent over his food, and while he was eating he was not conscious of any earthly danger. He wanted to know how Joop spent his weekends.

"The beach, reading, movies…the things you do in this city." Formerly, with Miriam, he did those things. Sometimes in the company of her girlfriends, acquaintances, people with whom he worked on scripts, the adored loved one of the moment. "And you?"

Looking at his plate, continuing to eat, smacking his lips, Omar said, "Often social obligations. If you move in Arab circles, you're often invited. A lot of eating, a lot of tea and coffee, a lot of sweets.

My weekends are completely filled. It's pleasant. But sometimes it's a bit much. Delicious fish. It must be wonderful to get a breath of fresh air on the beach. When I'm in the area, I always make a detour. The sauce is delicious too. Quickly out of the car. Shoes off and an hour on the beach."

"So you're often in this neighborhood?" It was an exemplary question, tying into his story, exactly as he had practiced with Philip.

"If at all possible." Omar's slight accent sounded like he came from the province of Drenthe. He said no more. With his right hand Omar picked up the glass and with a gulp of Pellegrino he washed down a bite, then with his left hand he eagerly took another bite. He wasn't only a fast eater, he was also in a hurry. And he knew that Joop noticed it.

"Actually I had no time for this, but I thought I'd come by for a moment. I have to go to Four Oaks now. A memorial service for the father of one of my partners. He just died. You're going back to your office after this?"

"I think I'll go home."

"I envy you, Joop. Your freedom—I'm not complaining!—you're not stuck in a certain pattern, you understand? I'm setting up our mail-order company, and after that I'll call it quits. I'll lead a life of leisure. I've always wanted that—stop working when I'm thirty, and then I'll have a life ahead of me. So now it won't be when I'm thirty, but five years later. Not bad either. So if I get to be...say seventy-five, that's manageable, don't you think; then I will have been able to enjoy the greatest part of my life. And for that you need dough. And that dough, that's what I'm working on. A simple plan. But it works."

He pulled his napkin from under the table and dabbed his lips. "I'm sorry that I have to be off so soon. An espresso, Joop?"

"Delicious."

"I'll tell Sandra. My treat. Can I have your number? Maybe we can drink a cup of coffee if my trip this weekend is suddenly canceled."

"You're going out of town?" Joop asked bluntly, as if he himself often went to Aspen for several days of skiing.

"San Francisco. A quick round trip."

Joop tore a page from his notebook and wrote his cell phone number on it.

"Great," said Omar as he accepted the piece of paper. "Joop, I'll see you next week at any rate."

He shook Joop's hand, a friendly tap on the shoulder. "Nice that I've met you here."

Omar walked away between the tables and disappeared behind dozens of guests, confidently feeling their glances, displaying the strength and the health of his body with his tight sweater and close-fitting jeans. And when he left the room and entered the hall where Sandra greeted her guests, he pushed the sunglasses from his head onto his nose in a gesture filled with enjoyment.

Chapter twenty-nine

In the car on the way home, the *Wilhelmus* sounded. Debby Brown.

"I have contacted headquarters, but I regret having to inform you that a specific period of time must pass before another request may be submitted to the recipient."

"These relations between donors and recipients—I see no balance, no justice," Joop answered, upset. "I really think that the donor's family has a greater right. They are coping with a loss. The others, at most with guilt feelings. There's something wrong with this deal."

"I understand your emotions, but unfortunately I can't do anything about it," said Debby. "You can try again in a few months."

"A few months is an eternity for people in my position," answered Joop before ending the conversation.

On a website, he had read an interview with a heart surgeon who had become religious through his work; according to the surgeon, knowledge about body and mind was still in an embryonic stage, and better insight into quantum mechanics might possibly contribute to the discovery that specific human energy survived in a certain way even after the death of the body, even though he didn't know yet to what extent, in what way, in what form. The specialist did not rule out that knowledge of life could be acquired in other ways than by Western methods. On this same website there were stories about changes in behavior that some recipients had undergone after a transplant. Recipients who had never drunk beer started drinking beer after the operation—their hearts had come from beer drinkers. Recipients who had never played chess began to play chess—just like their heart donors. In the world of heart transplants, stories circulated about the amazing ways that recipients had taken on certain character traits of their heart donors. Joop himself believed that Miriam's heart was more than a pump, and perhaps that was just as irrational as Linda's soul that remembered previous lives. And if the heart could take along and transmit certain character traits, then other organs could perhaps do that too. Had he reacted too brusquely to Linda's story? Perhaps his unyielding belief in reason was part of the tragic mistakes of Western culture; why did he torture himself with his superstition about the special place of the heart? If he couldn't rule out that there was something of her spirit in the heart that his daughter had left behind, then he shouldn't rule out either that the monk was his grandfather. No matter how ridiculous it sounded.

It was obvious how he had to lead his life: in her memory. That is what he owed Miriam; that was the sacrifice that he had to make. But he had clung to Linda like a drowning man clinging to a sinking raft. Oddly enough, it was at this sort of moment that he missed Erroll who had helped him daily through these fits of doubt, simply by his presence. He should call him and ask about his worries, but he left the phone untouched on the passenger seat.

He could not analyze in a rational way what he had experienced at Miriam's deathbed. Never would he talk about it with anyone; he could conjure it up in silence; he could warm himself on it or flee from it, but he denied himself the possibility of constructing any theory whatsoever about it. It was completely clear to him that belief and superstition, the longing for an existence separate from the physical, were the unavoidable consequences of the death of a loved one. Because that longing could nourish the hope that one day there would be a reunion. A reunion, that's what it was about. The embrace. The reversal of parting. He knew how that hope felt.

That night he did not fall asleep until two o'clock. Almost immediately he was in a dream that was so clear and specific that when he woke perspiring, it made him think of the experience in the hospital.

The dream had seamlessly followed his waking: he lay in bed, unable to close off the day, too tired to let go of the images in his head. Linda. Omar. And suddenly the door of his bedroom opened and Miriam appeared on the threshold. She was nude, her hands protectively in front of her breasts, her belly curving to the narrow vertical line of pubic hair.

"I'm so cold, Dad," she said.

"Come here quickly," he answered.

Inviting, he pushed aside the comforter and saw her coming toward him with quick, short steps. To his right she lowered herself onto the mattress. Her buttocks, the line of her spine, her loose hair. He pulled the comforter over her shoulders, and lying on her side she rubbed herself against him, with her back toward him searching the warmth of his body. She was still alive. Finally he had awoken from the nightmare. The sorrow, the despair, everything dissolved in the delight that he now experienced. She was again lying next to him the way she used to lie next to him, safely and innocently, as a small child, during warm summer nights. Under the comforter he placed an arm around her. Suddenly his hand encircled one of her breasts. A full woman's breast. He realized that he violated a taboo, but he wanted there to exist no distance at all between them and every pore of his body to be filled with her nearness. But he knew: this is not right, this is not good.

He let go of her and turned away.

"What's the matter, Dad?" he heard her whisper.

"This is not done, sweetheart."

"Why not?"

"Because. The rules of civilization. Children are inviolable. Sacred," he said. "By all that is holy, keep your distance."

"But it's okay with me."

"Not with me."

She threw off the comforter and said, "Look at me, Dad. Don't you think I'm beautiful?"

He leaned on his elbows and saw her body.

"Dearest, you're dazzling."

"I'm your flesh and blood. Therefore, yours."

"No longer. Since you...since you've become a woman. I have no rights."

"Here," she said. She took his hand and placed it between the curves of her breasts.

"Do you feel it?"

Her felt her heart beat quickly.

Then she moved his hand to her belly.

He woke up. Sat up with a start and looked at the place where she had lain. His heart pounded in his throat. He had an erection. He was disgusted with himself. Of the filth in his head. He turned on the light, went downstairs, and drank a glass of wine. On TV he watched the repeat of a late-hour news broadcast.

Chapter thirty

It was three thirty in the morning when Joop went outside. Exactly ten weeks ago she had been declared brain dead. The street was lit by ornamental lights that the inhabitants had placed along their garden paths. He walked past the endearingly well-kept gardens, past the dark houses that protected the sleeping, past their means of transport that waited faithfully along the sidewalks, and he walked silently under the black clouds on the cement strip of the beach. Catalina Island could not be seen at all. On the beach lay the homeless, motionless in a sleeping bag or only a heavy coat, sometimes next to a supermarket cart stacked full, mostly next to a shabby bag or an old plastic bag with belongings. After an hour he reached the Santa Monica Pier, left the beach, and for a moment considered going to Linda's hotel. But he knew that he couldn't bear a conversation about incarnation right now and continued on his way to the Ocean Views which stood at the beginning of Ocean Avenue, two towers with exclusive apartments, situated in the curve of the bay that connected Santa Monica to Malibu. The Pacific Coast Highway was stuck between the sea and Ocean Avenue, which was on a plateau situated sixty-five feet above the beach.

At five thirty Joop reached the residential towers. On the freeway below, the traffic transmitted a moderate noise which would increase to a gray rumble within half an hour.

The lobby of Ocean Views was a vast marble entry with sitting areas and planters, situated centrally between the wide halls to the towers. It smelled of cleaning products. Two night watchmen sat behind a black reception desk at the rear of the lobby; by pressing a button they opened the locked glass door and kept an eye on Joop as he approached them across the shiny, polished floor.

One of them, a tall blond man in his early twenties, stood up and greeted him: "Can we help you?"

"Erroll Washington."

"Do you know the apartment number?"

"No."

"Is he expecting you?"

"Yes." For he assumed that Erroll expected him at any moment.

The other night watchman asked, "Mr. Erroll Washington, the karate champion?" He remained seated, a short, broad Latino whose tightly stretched shirt revealed that he did body-building.

"Yes."

"Mr. Washington left two days ago."

"Left? Do you know where to?"

"Yes. A short way back. He's living in his jeep in the parking lot."

"What do you mean?'

"He lived in the last apartment that had to be renovated. The whole building was done this past year."

"And he spends the night in his car?" Joop asked, surprised.

"I saw him sitting in his car last night. If it's not him, then it looks an awful lot like him."

"No kidding," said the colleague.

"Haven't you heard it yet?"

"You're joking," said the colleague.

"No. Mr. Washington sits in his Jeep at night."

"Where exactly?" asked Joop, worried.

"Here, on Ocean, in the parking lot a hundred and fifty yards down the road. There are a number of people sleeping in cars there."

Joop walked back through the lobby, waited for the buzz before pulling open the door, and stepped back out into the morning air. He had just come past the parking lot but hadn't bothered to look at the cars. Why would he? Many thousands of people in Los Angeles lived in their cars, mostly driving wrecks that were crammed full with the possessions of the occupants, people who could not afford rental housing. But God had money. The sale of his gym had netted him seven hundred thousand dollars—he claimed.

When Joop reached the parking lot, he immediately recognized the new Jeep, the only new car in a row of old model Fords, Buicks, Chevrolets with ruined paint that had faded under the burning sun. The windows were screened off by cardboard, just as in the other cars. Joop tapped on the back window.

"Stop that!" came from the car.

Joop moved his face very near to the window. "God, it's me, Joop."

"Mr. Koopm'n!"

The piece of cardboard moved, and Erroll's broadly smiling face appeared.

"How did you know I was here?"

"Were you awake?"

"Yes, I just woke up. I was just lying here, thinking."

"I was at your old address."

"One moment."

The door swung open, and Joop looked into the back of the jeep. The back seat had been pulled down flat, as was the passenger's seat, and Erroll sat on his knees on a thin mattress. He wore light blue pajamas of a shiny material. Against the side stood a weekend bag, a thick plastic bag, and a stack of books. The title of the top book was: *Hyperspace, the Amazing New Theories about our Origin.*

"What a surprise," said Erroll.

"Do you spend the night here?"

"Yes, I sleep here. I barely fit, but I manage. I can only offer you some water. What time is it?"

"A quarter to six."

"Starbucks isn't open yet. But I know a twenty-four-hour diner on Wilshire; it's not far. May I offer you a cup of coffee there?"

"Why didn't you rent something else until your apartment is ready?"

"The apartment belongs to someone else. There are no rental apartments in Ocean Views, and…last week things didn't go at all as I expected."

"What did you expect?"

"I didn't expect the IRS to come around."

The IRS, the American tax authorities, a state within a state.

"And what does that mean, the IRS came around?"

"I hadn't really kept the bookkeeping up to date the last few years. There was a lot of undeclared income. For everyone in the gym. They discovered that when I had money left after the sale—it's gone. Confiscated."

"And now?"

"Wait for better times, I think. I didn't want to tell you. Actually, it's your money because my life belongs to you."

"Stop that nonsense. So you have nothing left?"

"A few hundred dollars. Yesterday I paid the architect who worked on the mausoleum—it was canceled but I had to pay him anyway—I have three hundred twenty-six dollars to be exact. I counted it before I went to sleep. But I have a lawyer and have lodged an appeal."

"Is it safe here?"

"Everything is safe for me, Mr. Koopm'n. Gee, it's wonderful that you've come."

"Let's go to the diner. Can we walk?"

"We'll drive."

He crawled out of the car and walked barefoot around the car to the passenger door. "I'll pull up the seat and then we'll go."

"Shouldn't you get dressed?"

"I'll just put on a coat."

"And shoes," said Joop. Errol was disoriented.

"Of course, shoes," said Erroll.

"So you can keep your car?"

"It's leased. Until the end of the month."

"And then?"

"It doesn't matter. I can sleep anywhere. Every night here on the boulevard, at least five hundred people sleep outside, maybe more."

Joop sat down on the black leather and waited until Erroll put on his shoes and sat down next to him.

"An unexpected pleasure," said Erroll.

"That's the least you can say. And it's mutual."

Erroll drove the car out of the parking area. The first daylight appeared over the eastern part of the city.

He said, "You're up early."

"I barely slept last night."

"Me neither," Erroll admitted.

"I had an...unpleasant dream," Joop confessed.

Erroll glanced at him. "About...?"

"Yes," said Joop. "That dream—I think—we haven't buried her completely."

"That can last a lifetime."

"I don't mean that. Something else that I didn't tell you. About Miriam."

"I believe I don't understand what you mean."

"At the time I gave permission for a transplant. An organ was removed."

Erroll shifted uneasily back and forth behind the wheel. "An organ? Like a kidney?"

"Her heart."

"Her heart? Oh, sir, her heart...so her heart is still beating?"

"Yes."

"Oh...that is...that is very strange, sir. That her heart still beats, that is..."

Erroll swallowed. His eyes filled with tears.

"But I don't know in whose body."

"You don't know who received her heart?"

"No. I regret it. As if she was wronged. It's not right."

"So, if I understand it correctly—she donated her heart to someone."

"I gave it away. I didn't know what she wanted."

Erroll dried his eyes with the back of his hand. "People who have died—I don't know exactly what the rabbis say about it. When someone has died, the body must be buried as soon as possible. Cremation is actually not allowed, but we didn't know that at the time. The body rises again, according to the rabbis."

"When the Messiah comes, but I don't count on that for the time being."

"I do. I'm reading a lot about it. I recommend it."

"I'm not in the mood for it."

"Her heart," repeated Erroll.

"The people who received it, they don't want me to know their names and what the effect of Miriam's heart is."

"Effect?"

"I don't know," Joop said bluntly, aware of the absurdity of his remark. "There are stories about people who receive another heart and are changed by it—taking on something from the person whose heart it was. It sounds absurd, and it is. It's nonsense, but I can't get it out of my mind."

"Now I understand what you mean. Something of her is still alive, in a certain way. And a heart, that isn't just a thing. A heart is something like the place of the soul."

"I don't know beans about souls. I'm talking gibberish. It's that dream…that's why I'm going on."

"No, no, what you're saying is important. What are you going to do about it?"

"I can't do anything. Where a heart goes is completely shielded."

"And you thought…can I help? What can I do for you?"

"I thought nothing. I wanted out of the house, clear my head."

"Mr. Koopm'n, I'll do anything you want me to—sometimes it helps when people know who I am. If I go with you to that organization—people are suddenly very different when they see me."

"No," said Joop. He didn't want people to feel threatened.

"What can I do then?"

"Nothing. Have a cup of coffee with me."

"I have to watch the time. I have to go to shul soon."

"Shul? The synagogue?"

"Yes. I'm only an auditor; I can't participate yet because it's a long course of study. It'll take three years at least. My teacher, Rabbi Mayer, is Dutch; do you know him?"

"No."

"Rabbi Mayer was first a Reform rabbi in New York. Then in Suriname. He has become Orthodox."

"I'm really happy for him," said Joop.

Erroll stopped the car alongside the sidewalk, behind a police car.

"You're not permitted to drive on Saturday."

"I know, but I'm still in training."

Errol turned around and pulled a parka from his belongings.

The diner was a classic American café with leatherette booths, plastic paneling, and tabletops with imitation wood grain. Under the fluorescent lights two policemen looked up from their coffee when Erroll, whose parka couldn't hide the fact that he was wearing pajamas, entered the place.

From a waitress who was eagerly awaiting the morning shift, they ordered coffee and fried eggs, with bacon for Joop.

"I no longer eat pork," declared Erroll. "I'm preparing. Did they keep kosher in your home?"

"No. We ate no pork, but we didn't keep kosher."

"But you did have a bar mitzvah?"

"Yes. My mother wanted to hold onto that. Sentimentality. A feeling that she had to continue things that she herself had experienced in her youth."

"Is your mother still alive?"

"No. She died six years ago."

"Sorry."

"She was quite old."

And it wasn't until then that Joop realized that she had been spared this. She had called every week, had always asked to talk to Miriam, and had shown more interest in her development than Ellen did.

"What are you going to do about the heart?" asked Erroll.

"I can't do anything. At the time, I signed papers before I was able to think about it carefully. Or perhaps I did. A heart like that, it can stay alive outside the body for only four hours. It has to be put into another body within that time."

"Can you find out who is in that organization? Through my work I've become acquainted with people who admire me. I know people all over the country. If you can find one name—and of course I still know guys from the hood."

"The hood? The neighborhood?"

"South Central. Where I come from. I was fifteen when I met Jews for the first time."

"In South Central?"

"No. Maybe Jews live there, but that's not where I met them. Do you know the neighborhood?"

"No."

"One of the most violent areas in the country, a war zone."

Joop made a decision: He had almost paid off his small mortgage, but he was going to increase it now. With the money that he would get that way, he could support himself and engage a good detective agency to look for Miriam's heart. The payments from Showcrime could lower the mortgage again.

"I can lend you money."

"Out of the question," said Erroll, shaking his head.

"I'll lend it to you. You can't live like this. I'll make an arrangement with the bank. Then you'll have a buffer to build up something new."

Erroll was determined. "Mr. Koopm'n, this is not good. I'm here for you, not the other way around."

"God, I can't stand those statements any longer. It's the last time that you say something like that. It was an accident, but you were there for me at…at a time that I needed you. I'll lend you the money."

"But what if I can't pay it back?"

"We'll worry about it then."

Erroll smiled. "If it's not possible. Miriam told me about *The Merchant of Venice*. Koopm'n means Merchant, doesn't it?"

Joop nodded.

"I read it, that play. It's offensive to Jews. But…I'll give you a pound of my flesh if I can't pay it back."

"Are you out of your mind?"

"You'll get a pound of my flesh. I have enough pounds."

Erroll grinned. And Joop couldn't suppress a smile either.

"No. Dear God, *no*."

"Then it won't happen," said Erroll.

"Come to my house later on. You can stay with me until you have something else."

"Are you sure?"

"Accept before I change my mind."

Chapter thirty-one

The maximum temperature on this day, Saturday, March third, would almost reach sixty-three degrees Fahrenheit, and it would stay dry, except for some drizzle.

In Joop's house in Venice, Erroll took a shower, then put on a suit and left for the synagogue. He would spend the rest of the day with Lubavitchers and would not return until sundown, the end of the Sabbath. Joop gave him the key to the front door.

With the unread *Times* on his lap Joop fell asleep, half slumped back in his chair—chin on his chest, his open hands next to him on the pillows as if he had to catch something that could fall from the sky at any moment—and dreamed dreams that did not reverberate, transparent images and moods that lingered for a moment and dissolved in oceans and landscapes.

The *Wilhelmus* woke him. He sat up, which made the sections of the newspaper slide onto the floor, and pulled the telephone from his pants pocket. He sat bent forward, his hand under his chin, his elbow on a knee, like Rodin's Thinker after a nervous breakdown.

"Hello," he said, his mouth dry.

"It's Philip," he heard.

"Hello…"

Joop didn't know what to say. He should have informed Philip, should have driven to the telephone booth on the corner of Venice and Lincoln to report about his adventures with Omar.

He said, "Er…I was planning to call you. I've met him a few times."

He was supposed to report immediately about each contact. Philip had hammered that into him.

Philip asked, "Could we see each other for a moment?"

"Of course."

"Your bicycle is still here in storage. Can you come here? I have the same room."

"Yes, yes…but I can't take it back in the trunk of the Jag. Er…"

"Take a taxi. Get a receipt, I'll reimburse you."

"Okay…good…er, half an hour, okay?"

His tone was that of an inept schoolboy, caught red-handed; he had not lived up to expectations.

Philip asked, "Do you still remember where it is?"

"Yes. See you soon."

Twenty minutes later he was sitting in a yellow cab. They had agreed on specific rules about the way that Philip would be informed: call immediately after the first meeting with Omar and pass on the most important message, then write a report and subsequently wait for instructions for the next meeting. For hours they had practiced conversation techniques. Which questions were good, which not; how do you put someone at ease, how do you build toward personal confidences? He wasn't sure if he had employed the techniques and doubted whether it had done him any good. Communication, Philip had emphasized several times, contact between you and us, that's what it's all about in this sort of operation. But once Joop was face to face with Omar, he had immediately neglected to follow through.

It bordered on recklessness for Philip to ask him for this work. Omar had met an Iraqi who was in league with the enemy, and there was a suspicion that this person was in contact with bombers. Philip himself had to stay out of the picture because Omar was possibly linked to groups that could trace his background. He had explained that half the world thought that Israel's Mossad had many thousands of employees, but the total work force, including the whole logistical staff, consisted of fifteen hundred people. And of those there were only close to fifty *katsa*, case officers who led operations. Philip was the only Dutch-speaking *katsa*. And therefore in this case he had to rely on the help of a Dutch *sayan*, a Jew who was willing to lend a helping hand to support the beleaguered Jewish state. Better an amateur than no one at all. Joop, the hero.

Katsa, sayan—those were terms that Joop had never heard before. Philip had explained that in most countries they could call on the help of a few local Jews with guts. Mostly it only involved renting a car for a *katsa* or making a house available for a few days—small things that involved no danger and that even with a possible complication could not cause any consequences for the helper. The motivation of the helpers was clear, and that was also why they were asked: their loyalty to Israel. For many Jews, Israel was a country where close or distant relatives lived and whose creation, irrespective of anyone's opinion about the present policy, was regarded as a miracle. Joop had no relatives there; he had no relatives anywhere. Except for Linda, and a reincarnated monk who claimed that he was his grandfather. Yet, Joop had a sentimental bond with that country. But that was not the reason why he joined Philip's lunacy. Money. It was indicative of Philip's power that an American company like Showcrime engaged the writer designated by Philip at the designated moment. Of course he had access to an executive who could pull strings. "Ask no questions, just engage Joe Merchant." "Joe who?" "A writer." "Never heard of him." "Good. Make sure that he starts working for you." "Why?" "Didn't I say no questions?" That's how the conversation had gone. Humiliating. He got money in order to draw someone out. Without the pressure of financial problems he would never have done it. Or perhaps he would have, for it was bizarre, and when it was all over he could write about it.

The driver gave him a receipt, and Joop walked up the outside staircase to the upper level of the motel. Apparently Philip had seen

him coming, for the door opened and Philip waited for him in front
of his room.

"Hey, man, how are you?"

Philip hugged him briefly and patted him on the back.

"Let's go and sit inside."

The bed, the chair, the expensive suitcase, as if it were still that
day in December.

"Take the chair," said Philip.

Joop sat down.

"Are you writing yet?"

"Some notes," Joop lied, "nothing special."

"But you have an idea by now?"

"The start of an idea."

"Good," said Philip. He offered Joop a cigarette, a light, and sat
down on the corner of the bed. For several puffs they remained silent.

Without looking at him, Philip said, "We're worried. We've
had experience with this kind of guy, and the fact that he's here,
with money that he's apparently spending in great quantities, means
something, but we have no idea what." It was a flanking move. He
was in no position to call Joop names.

"He told me what you already told me. A virtual mail-order
company."

"Backers?"

"He says Saudis."

"Any names?"

"No."

Philip leaned toward him. "Why didn't you report immediately?"

This was the question that Joop had not wanted to hear.
Philip was capable of controlling his exasperation and now acted as
a concerned uncle.

"I didn't think of it. Forgot."

"Joop, I know that you're doing your best. But it's difficult
to work with someone who doesn't stick to the rules." Still very
understanding.

"It didn't occur to me how important this reporting is for you,"
Joop tried.

"Nonsense," Philip interrupted him. He abandoned the gentle approach. He knew exactly how all this should be carried out. "We talked about it at length! You're a small cog in this operation, but at this moment a damn important one! You're our link with the subject; without you we can't get near him!" Conciliatory, he tapped Joop's knee.

"I know," said Joop, avoiding any conflict.

He had to twist and turn in order to keep his job as informer. If he wanted to look for Miriam's heart, he needed money. He wanted to engage a good private detective and give him a budget. But for some reason or another, he had not allowed himself to reveal immediately what Omar had told him, as if he weren't taking the situation too seriously, or to prove that he himself would decide when and what he would report to Philip. His laxness had a childish edge, a juvenile rebellion against the man on whom he depended financially.

"I think that you actually don't know," answered Philip. "I'm afraid that I made a mistake."

"You haven't made a mistake. But let's be clear, this is not my work. I'm a writer, not a spy."

"You have to draw him out at your ease when you're having lunch."

"Drawing someone out is a strange occupation for someone who hasn't trained for it," Joop defended himself. And he concealed the impression that he had of Omar.

"You could have refused."

"You knew that I needed money. That's why I accepted."

"Money seems a strong incentive to me."

"Always. But...I have to get used to it. You need a certain attitude for it. You have to be determined, self-assured, experienced."

Philip did not let the opportunity pass. "If you're no longer certain, then just stop." He gave Joop an encouraging nod. "No hard feelings. We tried it, but it doesn't work. Another time, gladly. If it's not possible, then we shouldn't force it."

"And Showcrime?" asked Joop, lost.

"Yes, how that will go...I'm afraid that that will be canceled."

"You're really asking too much of me!" Joop shouted, annoyed and suddenly completely disgusted with Philip's manipulations. "You're asking something of an outsider who doesn't know a damn thing about…about your tricks and stupid rules! For someone like me it's pretty crazy to become involved in this! Perhaps you thought that you were bringing in a sports star, but instead you took in a man with a paralyzed leg!" He calmed down a little, still trying to prevent an escalation. He had other interests at hand. "You make demands that I can't meet. Or perhaps I can, but I have to get used to it. I've never given any thought to the things that you do. Your world is foreign to me. It demands someone with nerves of steel, which right now is a difficult thing for me."

"I know that," said Philip, whose eyes seemed to understand everything.

"That's all I have."

"When I came to you…I knew that I was asking too much. We discussed it for a long time internally—can we do this, a man without training, a father?—and we decided that we had to try it, because the Iraqi with whom we encountered the subject is a man who directs operations. We took a chance with you. Fully aware of the risk. I knew you, there was a bond. With a stranger we would never have risked it. But it's better to stop when it's still possible."

"You have no one else."

"I'll have to go in myself."

"You said yourself that it was dangerous!" Joop reacted with Philip's own argument. "That through him others will know that you…are you!"

"If I had wanted peace and quiet, I should have become a dentist."

"Recently a dentist in my neighborhood committed suicide."

"No profession is perfect," answered Philip.

Joop's cigarette had burned down to the filter. He got up and reached for the box that lay on the bed next to Philip. Philip handed it to him.

"We're stopping," decided Joop while he remained standing and lit the cigarette. No Showcrime. He was broke. He would have to pay for a private detective in another way. He had to think of something.

But anything was better than this circus. It distracted him too much from his task: finding her heart. He was going to sell his house.

Philip nodded. "Yes." But Joop had the impression that he hadn't expected this.

"Your battle is not mine," said Joop.

"If you think that you can avoid the dangers that these people create for us, then you're mistaken." It was an attempt to restart the conversation.

"Everyone has the right to his own weaknesses."

"Don't push a wedge between us."

"It's *drive*. The wedge is there already, Philip. You've gone a long way. A lot must have happened in your life."

"Any image that you have of it is inadequate."

"I'm starting to understand that. Okay, Philip, I'm going."

"Yes."

"You shouldn't have called me," said Joop. "That day started wrong, with you."

Philip got up too. "That's a crazy thought."

"Since that moment a lot has gone wrong."

Philip no longer resisted. "I shouldn't have called. You're right."

They stood silently facing each other, looking at the lines in their faces, the furrows, the wrinkles.

Looking sorrowful, Philip said, "Maybe I shouldn't have contacted you. Shake my hand."

He showed Joop his strong fingers, the broad, tanned palm which had held the heavy butt of weapons. And which had also wiped the sweat from his head and had offered candy to his children. Did Philip actually have children?

Joop bicycled like a madman. Back home. It seemed to be March third, but it was actually December twenty-third. Nothing had happened. A flash in the infinite time-space continuum of the cosmos. A few hours ago he had bicycled to the motel and now he returned. If he concentrated, if he exerted every nerve in his body and could crush the unbearable images in his head, then everything had been nothing but a painful illusion, an exercise in masochism, a self-imposed test to experience the limits of his imagination. Miriam sat next to Caroline in the Porsche. He had forbidden it, but he had little confidence that she still listened to him. But anything was better than the pillion seat of a motorcycle. He pedaled so hard that he no longer felt the pain in his lungs, and for a moment it seemed that his consciousness dissolved and that he was nothing more than a raging muscle, a burning body that coincided with the revolutions of the pedals, the breath through his throat, the rhythm of his head moving above the handlebars, the foam on his lips. He flew past the long lines of cars at the traffic lights, plunged like a brick down the slope to the beach, and shot over the cement strip past rollerbladers and runners. For a moment he had no memories, no thoughts, no past.

Chapter thirty-two

At one o'clock Omar called.

"How nice that you're calling," said Joop.

Omar said, "I'm in Santa Monica, so I thought I'd call you."

"Good idea."

But was it a good idea? At Philip's request he had become involved with Omar from Drenthe, and since this morning there was no longer any reason to get into a conversation with the dyslexic Internet entrepreneur.

"Feel like having a cup of coffee?" asked Omar.

"Coffee?"

"I want to discuss something with you. I have a proposal."

Not only the Philips, but also the Omars of this world were making proposals. They decided to meet at a Starbucks on Main Street.

When Joop was back on his bike, he wondered whether the appointment with Omar could lead to a renewed contact with Philip. Joop had decided that he no longer wanted anything to do with Philip, but he realized that he was capable of going back to him and of reporting again for the task. He was going to work for him once more, even though Philip didn't know it yet. Other things were more important than the loss of Philip's respect. He needed money if he wanted to find Miriam's heart.

Evidently Omar had an extensive wardrobe. Today he wore cream-colored trousers, a dark blue sweater with a v-neck, and expensive calfskin loafers without socks. Again, carefully dressed like a successful entertainment executive. He was sitting at a table with a tall Starbucks cup in front of him.

"Hey, Joop." He stood up to shake Joop's hand. "What would you like?"

"A large cappuccino. And a muffin or something."

Omar joined the long Saturday line for the coffee machines. Most of the customers, in carefully chosen casual leisure wear, waited politely for their ritual cup of Starbucks coffee. Joop grabbed one of the newspaper sections that lay on the table, the first news section of the *Times*. An announcement on the front page: "Fiber-optic Adventure Fails." And below it the beginning of the story, continued in detail on one of the inside pages. The article described the ruin of Globsol. Yesterday the company had asked for a postponement of payment, the first step toward a bankruptcy, after it had been popular for years with large individual investors, among whom were politicians, which had then caused a run on its shares. Joop had been one of the breathless small investors and had put his money in the company. When Joop bought, on March 16, 2000, the price was at sixty-three dollars. Yesterday, at eleven cents. He had lost everything. Before the shares crashed, the chairman of the board had, thanks to the sale of shares, personally been able to cash in almost four hundred million dollars. If Globsol went under once and for all, the man would not have to plea for a pension.

The article quoted a shareholder who expressed his surprise that the company bosses had been able to fill their pockets while the ordinary investor had lost everything. Globsol had invested billions in the installation of cable networks and in the takeover of existing networks, based on the expectation that an enormous demand for broadband transfer would be created. But that failed to occur. Globsol was in negotiations with several banks in order to purge its debts, which was only possible if the networks were sold. The investors would get their turn after the banks, and it was clear that the kitty would then be empty.

For years he had carefully invested his mother's inheritance, upwards of two hundred and fifty thousand guilders, and during the bull market he had managed to get a twenty percent yearly return. With that he could pay their low fixed costs. Then he had sold everything and at the price of sixty-three dollars had bought exactly 2222 shares of Globsol. He calculated quickly: the 2222 shares were now worth two hundred and forty-four dollars and forty-two cents. A dinner for two at Spago. That was left of the small fortune for which his parents had saved all their lives. Greed, unrestrainedly reinforced by the fury that raced through the market, had tempted him into buying. Just like many others, he had thought that it was possible to double the value of his investments in a few months. Become rich without working. That's what the stock market promised. Two hundred and forty-four dollars and forty-two cents.

His house was worth five and a half to six hundred thousand dollars, perhaps even more, and only sixty thousand was left on the mortgage. He would have to sell it. He would make half a million dollars on the sale, and with that he could hire a legion of detectives. Miriam's room would be rearranged by another family as another girl's room. With other flower-patterned wallpaper, another fairy-tale bedspread, other stuffed animals, other toe-shoes for ballet lessons. The thought was unbearable.

Omar placed the coffee cup and the muffin on the table.

"Low fat, sugar free," he announced about the muffin. "I figured you were one of those."

"Exactly," Joop said helplessly. "Thank you very much." He put the newspaper aside.

"Do you bike a lot?" asked Omar.

"Not much. Not actually. Today, by coincidence." He thought: this morning my bicycle was standing in the motel, where the man who is pursuing you is staying. Philip had taught him about the danger of these mental impulses; never get in conversation with them in your mind, refrain from imaginary commentary, stay on the subject—that is the reality of the moment.

"Actually, I've always hated it," said Omar. "As a child I pedaled in the rain endlessly."

"Today is perfect bicycling weather," said Joop.

"Today is okay. Did you know that LA and Casablanca lie at the same latitude?"

"You don't say," said Joop as he freed the muffin from the cellophane.

"Almost the same climate too. At the coast, many west winds. But much more irrigation here. Therefore greener. Have you ever been in Morocco?"

"No." Joop pulled the lid off the cup and used a small wooden stirrer to blend the thick collar of foam.

"Beautiful land. Lots of poverty. If you've grown up in Holland, then you can't ever fit in there."

Joop could not know that Omar had a Moroccan father, and therefore he had to try to find out the reason for his remarks about Morocco: "Do you have relatives there?"

"My father was a guest worker. Moroccan."

"But your name is Van Lieshout."

"My mother's name. They're divorced."

Another question showing that he had no background information: "Do you visit him often?"

"He's dead. But I have half-sisters there. I visit them sometimes. Do you go back often?"

"Not a lot. The last time was a few years ago." Philip had taught him: don't lie about the facts.

"You're different from me. I've been here a few months, but I'm already homesick. Even though I hate Holland. Joop, be glad that you're no longer there. Holland is a hypocritical, corrupt little country. And at the same time a holy little country of pastors. They always know things better over there." Omar showed his index finger and waved it. "Always the raised index finger. But the things that I know, the corruption with drugs, the 'narco' Netherlands, you've heard that term, haven't you?"

"I keep up with the Dutch newspapers, yes."

"Guys I've worked with are in prison for murder. A few others are dead, liquidation, and about ten are in for drugs. Coke. But most of them walk around free."

Now things were getting serious. Omar was starting to take him into his confidence. Or acted as if. Joop asked, "And this was your...milieu?"

"My milieu, yes...criminal milieu."

"But you've managed."

You'll see, Philip had predicted, if it goes well you have to do almost nothing. Keep feeding, and the subject will just keep talking.

"I managed, yes."

"Omar...why are you telling me this?"

"Why do you think?" He smiled.

"I don't know," answered Joop, also smiling, although he felt the adrenaline rush through his body. He brushed the crumbs of the muffin from the corners of his mouth.

Omar said, "For you—a story."

"For me?" He could become Omar's biographer. "But Omar, what story?"

"The story of what I have experienced."

"Why do you want to tell that?"

"Because...because of, let's say, the truth. So that everyone will get to know the hypocrites. Because that is Holland." He smiled. "Well, what do you think?"

Joop didn't want to say what he thought. He would ask Philip for a bonus. As if he were highly doubtful, he asked, "You want your story to become known?"

"Yes. I want it to become clear, yes, that people find out what was going on. And what is still going on."

"What do you want me to do?"

"Write a movie. How long do you think it will take us? A few weeks, a month?"

"First we'll have to talk at length. I want to know what you know. It will be months before we've gone over all that. And the writing itself—again months. Count on at least half a year. Probably longer."

"That long?"

"And then there's the financing. It can take years. Unless it's really explosive…"

"It is."

"Financing always remains a problem that you can't estimate."

"I know people with money. Sometimes they want to get rid of it. In a certain way, of course."

"Have you also thought about a book?"

"Whatever you want," Omar said obligingly.

"Half a year's work, I've got to make time for that, put aside other things," Joop tried. "Do you think it's crazy if I say that I have to consider it?"

"Yes, I think that's crazy," said Omar, smiling. "But I understand that it's necessary."

Joop took a swallow of the lukewarm cappuccino. Now he could go back to Philip and write Omar's story for Showcrime and in that way prevent the sale of his house. The *Wilhelmus* sounded.

"You have to tell me where I can find that tune," said Omar.

Joop pressed the answer button. "Hello?"

"It's Linda," he heard.

"Hey, Linda," he said, surprised, curious about the reason for her call.

He motioned to Omar that the conversation wouldn't take long. Omar nodded patiently.

Linda said, "I'm leaving for San Francisco shortly, and I thought, I feel really horrible about what happened between us."

"The beginning or the end?"

"The end, of course."

She wanted to get rid of the chill between them. He was still annoyed when he thought of her remarks about his grandfather, but over the past week he had pursued her like an eager dog.

"I don't really like it either," he answered.

"I thought, why don't you come along? Or tomorrow? We really can't leave things like this, Joop."

"No," he said.

"I have to be there for a few days—we can talk. And there

is...I want you to talk with Usso, and with someone else who is in San Francisco."

"Who?"

"I'll tell you when you're there."

He wasn't in the mood for Usso or other reincarnated people. But he longed for her.

"When do you want me to come?"

"Come tonight, or tomorrow. When it suits you. I'm staying at the Fairmont Hotel."

Joop knew it. In that hotel his marriage had broken down. "Elegant place."

"We get it courtesy of the organization."

"Who is the organization?"

"People who are concerned about the fate of the Tibetans. I'll ask if they will pay for a room for you. If you want to sleep by yourself."

He made sure that she heard the irony in his voice. "I like to sleep alone. Can I call you in a few minutes?"

"In a few minutes I'll be in the air. But you can call me in the hotel at the end of the afternoon. I don't have the number handy."

"I'll find it."

"I miss you," she said, and she hung up.

"Sorry," he said to Omar as he put away the phone. A trip to San Francisco. A few nights in the Fairmont. It was surprising that he actually looked forward to something.

"Good news?" asked Omar.

"I'm going to San Francisco very soon."

A day before departure usually meant the highest price. A few hundred dollars. More than the value of his shares.

"Consider it," repeated Omar. "If you're looking for a story—you probably hear this often—but still, if you want to hear a story then we should sit down. I'm younger than you, but I have experienced an incredible amount. I'm not proud of all of it. Things that happened and that I have to live with—that's how it is. But maybe it's something that a writer can use."

"I'm always looking for material. That's what it's called here: material, just as a builder needs stones."

"If you need stones, I know where there are a few," said Omar.

"Are they memoirs or is there a plot?"

"You mean with all sorts of surprises?"

Joop nodded.

Omar looked at him sardonically. "I have a plot. The best plot: that of reality."

"That beats any fantasy," agreed Joop.

They looked at each other with mutual sympathy, but not without mutual mistrust. In an unusual way they were well matched.

Omar seemed to be making a decision. He said, "I also have to go to San Francisco very soon. With the car. I had hoped that I wouldn't have to; but if you want to ride with me, then we can talk a bit. It's a lot nicer than driving by yourself."

Chapter thirty-three

After packing a weekend bag, Joop waited at the window. Even though he had given Omar his address, he didn't want to let him inside. Distance had to be maintained. Omar dressed as a brash millionaire and acted as a widely traveled freethinker; the face behind it remained unknown. He claimed that he had been a successful criminal entrepreneur, and Joop needed little imagination to imagine the ruthlessness of such an entrepreneur's business methods. It was unwise to assume that Omar had become a different person. Yet, Joop had never once felt threatened in Omar's presence; on the contrary, he felt less tense with him than in the company of Philip, whose machinations were not obvious to him. Omar gave the impression that he did not need secret agendas; he seemed to be clever yet simple, a man who was honest as long as he was treated honestly. A gentleman gangster. But despite Omar's rather unthreatening demeanor, Joop did not want to ignore the risk of falling into a trap with open eyes. It was best to take everything that Omar told him with a grain of salt. Listen without showing skepticism. Joop was now going to sit in a car with him for at least seven hours, and he should assume that he was going to hear lies for seven hours. Should he inform Philip? It was obvious that he should, but he decided not to dial Philip's number until he had a sensational report. Now that Philip no longer took him seriously, he wanted to surprise him even though that might carry a risk.

On the kitchen table he left a letter for Erroll, explaining that he had left for San Francisco unexpectedly and could be reached on his cell phone. He slipped three twenty-dollar bills under the letter, sufficient for several days' shopping. After looking up the number of the Fairmont, he called the hotel and left a message for Linda. "I'm arriving late tonight."

Joop didn't know what he had expected, but at any rate not that Omar would climb out of a GMC delivery van owned by U-Haul, the largest American truck rental company where every private mover arranges his transportation. Even before Omar reached the garden path, Joop closed the door behind him and walked to the GMC.

Omar stopped at the gate when he saw Joop.

"Got your driver's license?" asked Omar.

"Yes."

"Shall I drive the first leg?" Omar suggested.

"If you wish."

"Nice place you've got here."

Joop opened the passenger door of the GMC, a large white van decorated with a red lightning stripe that ran the whole length of the van. The roomy interior showed the consequences of intensive use—worn seats, damaged dashboard—but was clean and smelled of an aromatic cleaning compound. The two wide front seats, separated by a middle console, were screened from the deep back by a partition. An opening in the middle of the partition offered a view for the rearview mirror.

"I'll put your bag in the back," said Omar.

Joop handed him the bag, climbed into the car, and sat down. The van, higher than an SUV like Erroll's Jeep, was heavy and wide like a truck, but also fast and comfortable. He threw a glance over his shoulder when Omar opened the back door and placed his bag in the cargo space. In it stood cardboard boxes without lettering.

On the dashboard Joop discovered a small, flat, black plastic box, fastened with suction cups and connected to the lighter with a cable. A radar detector.

Omar opened the driver's door and sat down behind the wheel.

With a glance at the radar detector, Joop said, "That's forbidden here."

"This one is invisible. The very latest system."

Omar started the motor and used the steering column gearshift to start moving the car.

"Shall we take the PCH for a while?"

Joop still hadn't been back there and wanted to avoid that road. "Saturday afternoon—it's always busy there. Let's take the 405, it's quiet now."

"You're right."

Omar drove the car out of the street and turned left in the direction of Venice Boulevard, the wide artery that connects Venice with the rest of Los Angeles. He asked, "Do you know yet when you go back?"

"No idea. I think I'll stay three days or so. And you?"

"Something like that. If we keep in touch, you can ride back with me."

"Gladly."

Omar asked if he knew San Francisco well, and Joop told him that he went there regularly ten years ago. For three years he had worked with a producer who lived there, on a script about Joseph Strauss, the chief designer of the Golden Gate Bridge. Omar had been there for the first time a month ago.

"Nice city. Very different from LA. A real city, not a large area without a heart, which is what LA is."

Without a heart—Joop couldn't do anything but think of his child. And, as if he had to defend her even though they were speaking of LA, he said, "Yet I'd rather live here."

"Yes, I feel that also," said Omar. "Is it a woman?"

"What do you mean?"

"Well—the telephone call that you got."

"Yes, it's a woman."

"Your girlfriend?"

Joop hadn't as yet given a name to his relationship with Linda.

"My girlfriend, I think so, yes."

"You say that very carefully."

"It's still very young."

"Is she young?"

"No, I mean: what we have is young. I know her from before. From my youth. We had a relationship then. And suddenly I see her again here. And...we fall for each other again."

To fall for each other. A simple, raw physical reaction. But he shared more with her. A distant past. A mood.

"You're a romantic," Omar looked at him with a smile.

"Well, I doubt that."

"Never been married?"

"Divorced. And you?" asked Joop.

"No. I first want to be...free for a while. You know what I mean. I can always marry."

The 405 is an eight-lane freeway that cuts straight across the western part of Los Angeles. To the north of the city, the 405 becomes Highway 5, the traffic artery that runs from the Mexican to the Canadian border. For hours on end they would drive on a straight road that runs through the middle of the San Joaquin Valley, the long and narrow fertile valley with vineyards, orange groves, vast farmland. On the left, the mountain ranges that separate the coast from the valley, and in clear weather the snowcapped tops of the Sierra Nevada on the right.

During the first part of the trip they exchanged short remarks about the traffic, the landscape, the houses. They drove through the San Fernando Valley, the flat, suburban part of LA that lies on the north side of the Santa Monica Mountains and is surrounded by steep mountainsides. Without delay they drove over the mountain pass that connects West Los Angeles with the Valley, a busy freeway that becomes a thick, roasting ribbon of tin on weekdays but usually has no traffic jams on weekends. It remained overcast, not a day for a massive trek to the beach.

On leaving the Valley, Omar asked, "Have you considered?"

"Yes," said Joop. "Of course I'm curious about what you're going to tell me. But I can't judge yet what we can do with it. For that I need to know more."

"I understand," nodded Omar. "Do you think that we should put something on paper?"

"A contract, you mean?"

"Yes, something like that," said Omar.

"Can't do any harm." But Joop realized that a contract could have legal consequences. If he were sworn to silence and informed Philip nonetheless, then he would be committing a formal breach of contract. "I can write up a piece of paper with agreements." He would have to phrase them in such a way that he would cause no problems when he informed Philip.

"Yes, please," said Omar.

"I'll do it when I'm back home."

"Fine. But it's more important that we trust each other."

"Of course," said Joop. He was deceiving Omar.

Omar's right hand left the steering wheel and suddenly hovered above the middle console.

"Shake on it," said Omar.

Joop turned halfway toward him and shook Omar's hand to seal their agreement. He was going to hand this man over to the Mossad. He prayed that Philip had not made a mistake.

"Word of honor," said Omar. He sat up straight and looked ahead, satisfied. "I'll begin at the beginning. Is that okay?"

He told Joop what the latter had already heard from Philip: his father, the guest worker; his mother, the daughter of a Beverwijk street cleaner; the cultural differences; his mother's flight; and his father's accident and return to Morocco.

Joop wondered what Omar's intentions were, for it was nonsense that he wanted to show the whole world that the Dutch constitutional state was built on a foundation of drugs and corruption. Philip would also ask himself that question. It was unthinkable that Omar knew that he had been sent by Philip, but he shouldn't exclude anything and should try to set aside the sympathy that he felt for

Omar. Like a robot. How did those *katsa*s do that? They probably hated their subjects or looked down on them. Joop couldn't do that.

"I was scum, Joop. Screwed-up. That's the word. Screwed-up. Actually that didn't go away until I started to believe in God. God cured me of that. But I was an animal until I was twenty-two. I don't have another word for it. Always with a knife at someone's throat. Fights. Hold-ups. But…when I went to the mosque for the first time…that's when I was really born, I swear. But it's difficult to explain when you haven't experienced it yourself."

"When did you become religious?"

"Actually, after I'd been in Morocco. My life consists of—three parts actually. First: my childhood. Then: after Morocco. And after that: when I stopped the import and the trade."

"And with import and trade you mean…?"

"Exactly what you think."

"What was it that you did when you were still scum?" A question in the form that Philip had taught him.

"Muggings. Break-ins. Armed robberies. I was fifteen, sixteen. At seventeen I was a big dealer. In Emmen, a nothing town, but there I was someone. When I went to Groningen, I had enough dough to buy a business. A store with living quarters above it. A kebab and pita shop—ideal money laundering place. We bought legally and made incredible profits. More than ninety percent was fake, a little nothing store that was a goldmine on paper. Supposedly thousands of servings of pita and kebab every week. We simply dumped the meat and the pitas if they'd been in the refrigerator for too long. I let my profits from drugs flow in, handed over tax money properly, and had legal money left over. Joop, there's nothing better than legal money—paying sixty percent taxes is worth it. When I was twenty, I was swimming in money. Bought clothes—only designer stuff—the most expensive boots, silk shirts, and I drove a big, fat BMW. When I was twenty-one, I had half a million cash. In the bank. Completely legal. Me! A fucking Moroccan!"

Omar shook his head, amazed, astonished, but also proud.

"And your parents?"

"My father had returned to Morocco. I had no contact with

him. I gave my mother money for a jewelry store in Emmen. She'd always wanted to do that. It was an attempt to make it up to her. I didn't make life much fun for her when I was young."

"Is she still alive?"

"Yes. Still in Emmen. With her little store which makes a small profit. I send her some money every month."

"And when did your father die?"

"Right after my first trip to Morocco. I had gone because I'd heard that he was doing poorly. I wanted to see him before he died. Actually, to give him hell. To make him pay for what he'd done to my mother. He was a traditional Moroccan man. The wife has to be obedient. She became Muslim, but not in her heart. So when I went to Morocco—I was pretty worked up. I was twenty-two, I had dough, and I drove my shiny BMW to Morocco. I wanted to show it to my old man, show him that I had it made, and that I had done it without him, and that he could croak as far as I was concerned. These are harsh words, and that's how I was then. So I get there, a dump in the Rif Mountains, just like the Middle Ages; you have no idea, Joop, what it looks like there—to this day nothing has changed since the fourteen hundreds. So I arrive there and I meet a sweet old man and I *know* that he's just like I am, that I have his blood dammit, and I *know* that I would have behaved the same way as he did. Because actually I did the same; I was just as aggressive, just as… just as cruel and…and bitter as he was. But I had turned my anger into concrete action and he had been eating his heart out in an iron foundry. I had managed to turn my anger into dough, and he…he'd actually been lucky with that accident…"

He was silent, and Joop asked, "And then?"

Respond to the mood, Philip had said, show empathy when the subject threatens to go back into his shell (he had said "push back" and Joop had corrected him), and if it goes well, then all you have to do is roll with the waves like a surfer.

"And then, in the village, I arrived in the village over dusty dirt roads, so my car wasn't shiny at all anymore, and there I saw my uncles and aunts, and everyone was really welcoming. And my father was ill. I knew that, but he was visibly ill, a skeleton, and I knew that I had no more time to get to know him, to really get to know him. I had intended to tell him the truth about what he had done to my mother, but people change. That was the first lesson of the visit. People who have done something bad can also do something good. And he had. In the village. With his small pension—for us peanuts, but for them over there a fortune—he'd helped families that really needed it. And I met his new wife, my five half sisters, and I turned out to be his only son. Whatever has happened, people should always get a second chance because they can see the light—I experienced that. I came home, to a place that I didn't know. It was obvious that my father did not have long. I talked with him. Suddenly I saw…isn't it called the big picture? Everything that happened to him and my mother was the consequence of poverty, injustice, ignorance. Suddenly it all became less the consequence of fate or something like that. It could be understood. A victim of circumstances. But circumstances that came from somewhere, and that you could change."

Omar was silent for a moment. Suddenly he grinned. "Are you going to remember it all?"

"I'd like to take notes," said Joop.

"Go ahead."

"My pen and paper are in my bag. Do you have anything to write with?"

Omar drove the car to an exit off Highway 5, to a mall that was situated along the road in an apparently unspoiled green landscape that revealed not a single residence. Before the car had completely stopped in the parking space, Joop opened his door.

He walked to the back of the van, opened the door, and pulled his weekend bag toward him. He zipped it open, and between his clothes he looked for the small notebook that he had taken along for this purpose. Between square cardboard boxes—there were five—lay a plastic bag from Barnes & Noble. The driving had caused the three books to slide half out of the bag. Three books, all three about the Golden Gate Bridge. On top was *The Gate* by Brian van der Molen, with the rust-colored bridge on the cover. Joop knew the book. He had read it when he was working with Robbie Fray, the producer, on the script about Joseph Strauss, and it was strange that Omar had said nothing about buying the books. Evidently there was something between Omar and the bridge, but he didn't want Joop to know it. Was this one of Philip's "significant" details?

"Is the door really closed?" asked Omar when Joop sat next to him again.

"Yes."

In his mind Joop went over the conversation once again, noting down keywords, and looked in vain for the answer to Omar's need to share his life's story with him. In silence the car zoomed over the freeway, which after the Valley, was used by less and less traffic. A calm Saturday in the first week of March. The road ran through an immensely large nature reserve. Signs alongside it pointed to lakes, campgrounds, and rest areas. The landscape lay brazenly massive under thick, white cumulus clouds that at various places left space for the sun and strengthened the solitary play of green and gray mountains with large patches of shade. If Joop had taken the airplane, he would already be in San Francisco, but this drive, past mountains, valleys, and rivers, offered glorious views.

Once he had taken Miriam to Big Bear, a vacation spot situated high in the mountains in one of the foothills of this gigantic scenic area east of LA. It was a few months after she'd had her period for the first time, a spring day after the last snow had melted. Nature was beginning to awaken just as the femininity in his daughter was awakening. She asked a question that had obviously been bothering her for some time: "Dad, when did you have sex for the first time?"

They were sitting on the afterdeck of the half-filled tourist boat that sailed across Big Bear Lake, a reservoir between slopes densely covered with conifers. Expensive country houses, hidden behind trees and bushes, stood on the waterfront. A guide explained the origin of the lake.

"When I...? That's a...serious question."

"Do you think that I shouldn't know that?"

"Aren't you too young for it?"

"In a while it won't matter anymore."

"Why not?'

"Well, I mean, in a few years I'll be ready for it myself."

"What age did you have in mind?"

"Well, I thought sixteen, when I have a driver's license."

"Sweetheart, sex is different from driving a car."

"Most people have sex for the first time in a car, Daddy. That's why I say that."

"How do you know that?"

"From school."

"I don't want you to start driving at sixteen."

"What!?"

"You hear me—no driver's license on your sixteenth."

"Why not?"

"I don't think it's right that in this country they give young people the opportunity to operate a big machine like a car on their sixteenth. On your sixteenth your senses are not sufficiently developed. You have too little experience. Why do you think that young people in particular are involved in accidents just after getting their driver's licenses?"

"Then when?"

"Your eighteenth. Not before."

"Dad, you're making me into a pariah."

"No, I don't want you to take risks with such things. And not with sex either."

"Do you want me to stay a virgin until marriage?"

"That you have to decide yourself. But at the moment it seems wise to postpone your first introduction for several years."

"Until when?"

"Until your eighteenth. It seems a good idea to couple the driver's license to a sex license."

"Bullshit," she said. "You just said the opposite. You're beating around the bush. How old were you?"

"I'm a guy. That's different."

"Dad, you're bullshitting. It makes no difference whether you're a girl or a guy."

"With sex it makes a big difference."

"I mean: age makes no difference."

"Eighteen," he said, which was a lie. But a lie out of love. "I was eighteen."

"With whom?"

"A girl."

"Daaad—" A half-chanted exhortation to get him to be explicit.

"She was a year older."

"Did you think it was scary?"

"Yes, it was scary." And after the lie he wanted to be honest: "But it was also beautiful."

"What did you think of her? Did you think she was a dirty slut?"

"No, why should I?"

"Well, because she did it with you just like that."

"She didn't do it just like that."

"What was her name?"

"Linda," he said.

"Did you ever see her again?"

"No. Never again."

"Were you in love with her?"

"Yes. I was madly in love."

"And she with you?"

"I think so, yes."

She rested her head against his shoulder and he wrapped his arm around her. He felt her hair against his cheek. One day she would love someone. She would sit like this with someone else. Inevitable. Irreversible.

"Eighteen...Jesus..."

"That seems long, doesn't it?"

"Awfully."

"But tomorrow you'll reach that point."

"Tomorrow?"

"Tomorrow, just wait and see."

"I always want to be sitting like this, Dad, right next to you."

He pressed her against him for a moment; a small, gentle movement of his arm sufficed to tell her what he felt. The sun reflected on the water and the hills slowly glided past. It was his task to save these moments; he realized that even then.

"I was sixteen," he said.

A small movement of her head, a tightening of the muscles in her body. He didn't need to look to know that she had opened her eyes and stared pensively at the shore.

"Sixteen," she repeated.

"I was too young. I didn't want to say it. Sorry."

From the way she breathed, he felt that she was searching for an answer. Then she relaxed and without resistance she entrusted herself again to his arm.

"Eighteen," she said.

Chapter thirty-four

Joop opened his eyes. Outside it was getting dark. Omar had turned on the headlights.

"Slept well?" Omar asked in his Drenthe accent.

"Yes."

Joop looked at his watch. An hour had passed. In his hand he was holding his notebook. He sat up straight and said, "Just say when I should take over."

"I can still manage," said Omar.

"Where are we?"

"We're already past Bakersfield."

"How fast are you driving?"

"Eighty, ninety."

"If they catch you, you'll get slapped with a thousand-dollar fine."

"They can't see this detector yet. I want to be there on time."

"Are you going for business?"

"I have to speak to some people about my project."

Joop wanted to hear names. Perhaps Philip would find it useful.

"Investors?"

"Yes, that kind of people. And people who design websites.

233

Internet freaks. I don't understand a damn thing about that technology, but I do know what I want. I know the Muslims' taste."

"So you have financial backers, people who are working on it?"

"We've prepared everything. But it isn't simple. We are now working on a program that can be understood by illiterate women; many of our customers can't read. Simple icons, everything geared to people who have no experience with computers. And here in America I've found the right kind of computers for our purpose. Machines that can do only one thing: connect to the Internet. So everything is ready—now it's a question of time. Build it up steadily. Our sites need to have much more gold and glitter than sites for Dutch Calvinists."

"And those two tastes, the Islamic and the Dutch, do they battle in your soul?" Soul. He had no better word at his disposal.

"No longer. That's past. I'm a Muslim. With a Dutch exterior."

Omar recounted how he was picked up from the street by the police one day. In the northeast of the Netherlands, Omar was a criminal celebrity. Four policemen took him in a delivery van to the police station in Emmen. They were looking for an informant who knew the Moroccan underworld. Someone with the kind of past that no one would suspect worked for the police.

"They were from a special team. Took me to a small room in the basement. It was the first time that I saw my man."

"Who is 'my man'?"

"I'll call him A, okay? A is in charge of an investigation into the import of heavy stuff. The kind of stuff that I earned my money with. He had a long story about my eh…activities, but it was obvious that they had nothing. This was supposed to make an impression, but they hadn't officially arrested me; they had nothing on me. First A ranted and raved for about an hour, but I knew he'd have to let me go soon. And then he came with a proposal. If I cooperated they'd make a deal with me: no charge, not in the future either, if I would give them names. So I made a deal."

Philip had said: We always have a background story ready that's a complete pack of lies, and why shouldn't a subject have one? The greatest danger is to underestimate the subject. Always assume that the subject is at least as intelligent as you.

"Omar, you're going too fast—what you're telling me is a bit much."

Never be directly critical, never cast doubt on the integrity of the statements of the subject. Do it indirectly. Say that you don't understand it, that it's too much or too difficult to follow, or that you need a little time to digest his story. Remain on his side. Don't let the two of you drift apart.

"Yes, it's a lot," Omar chuckled.

Philip would undoubtedly resist the publication of Omar's story because it was not in his interest for Joop to draw attention to Omar. If he wanted to write a screenplay or a book, then it was more sensible not to inform Philip anymore about his contact with Omar. He would have to try and find a publisher in the Netherlands and engage a researcher to check on the facts. At the same time he should not lose track of the fact that Omar's story could be a complete fabrication. For Joop could still not understand why Omar wanted to tell the world about his experiences. Omar had more to lose than to gain. Maybe this wish for disclosure was a symptom and every word was fabricated and the product of a pathological liar. No, it was nonsense to deny what he was doing in this van: he was here to satisfy Philip's curiosity, to justify the Showcrime commission, and to demonstrate his solidarity with Israel. And suddenly he wondered whether they were being followed. Philip had said that they were keeping an eye on Omar, and perhaps they had shadowed Omar when he rented a U-Haul van and drove to Superba Avenue in Venice.

Omar's confession continued. He recounted—fabricated or the truth—how he came to an agreement with A and a public prosecutor, whom he called B. He was going to import drugs under police supervision. That gave A and B the opportunity to figure out the routes and possibly track down the groups that smuggled bulk shipments into the country.

"At a certain moment I started recording my conversations with A and B with a pocket recorder. I thought: I need to have something as security. Something so that they wouldn't dare to touch me if it ever gets to that. Joop—a shoebox filled with cassette tapes! I left three sets with three different notaries. I went crazy copying. If something happens to me, they'll send these tapes to the newspapers. Five newspapers and four weeklies. I'll destroy half the police departments in Holland."

Joop stared at him. An attractive man. A handsome body. With beautiful skin, almost feminine lips, gentle looking eyes, graceful piano fingers. Why did he want to risk his existence, the creation of a company in California, his wardrobe purchased at Armani Exchange, and the chance to screw women like Sandra by disclosing his criminal past? Omar was a liar—his story couldn't be true.

"I have to note this down," said Joop.

He needed the help of an expert. If they were going to make a stop, he would immediately call Philip from a toilet and ask him for advice. Omar was manipulating him, even though Joop could not imagine his motives. Perhaps Omar had discovered that he had been sent by Philip, and to mislead him, Joop was now being stuffed with false information. Or Omar derived a curious form of satisfaction from his lies. Or he was telling the truth. Philip knew the facts and Joop wanted to know what Philip had kept from him. He had to call. If this was true, they would have a blackmail weapon in their hands that could be used to put pressure on Omar.

And maybe Joop had now stumbled across a motive: Did Omar want to take the men he called A and B for a ride? Did he tell his story because he wanted vengeance?

"You're blowing up the police department," Joop recapped, the way Philip had taught him. In the semidarkness he jotted down Omar's words.

"So to speak. The reputation. The prestige. For that matter, one time we actually did blow up something."

"You really blew up something?"

Philip had said nothing and clearly didn't know about it. But if it had actually happened, then it could be checked out. If Omar had blown up something or someone, then the press would probably have reported it. Joop could look it up on the Internet, or Philip could verify it on their computers. It could mean that Omar knew how to handle explosives. Who had taught him that? Joop wanted to find out: "Do you want to tell me?"

Omar nodded. He changed position, moving as far back as possible in his seat. "It was careless—shortsighted—someone who had nothing to do with it died because of it. It did produce the effect that we wanted."

"What effect?"

"B—the man I call B, the public prosecutor—was at one point himself suspected by a colleague, C. This C started asking questions, stirring things up. C had the reputation that he would never buckle under for money. A spotless guy. That is commendable. But he was a danger. Together with A and B we then decided that C should keep his mouth shut. Punctured the tires of his car. Then a fire in his home. Then we agreed that he should really be silent. I got the stuff from A."

"The policeman?"

"Yes. He taught me how to assemble a bomb. Then I myself drove to C. He had a second house in the south of France. Then, in a small town where they went shopping and where they sometimes went out to eat, I placed the bomb under the car. It was one o'clock in the afternoon. They were sitting in a restaurant. A guy drives up. First he enters their restaurant, stays inside for a few minutes, and then comes back outside. But the jerk doesn't walk back to his own car—no, he goes to C's car. I think: What's that asshole doing? He has the keys! He sits down in the car—and *boom*! He blows himself up! Shit! Half the street buried under rubble, windows shattered. There was nothing left of that guy. A, the fool, had let me make a bomb that was much too strong, as if we had to blow up a bunker. And then we lucked out."

"Hold on…who was that man?"

"A garage owner. He came to pick up C's car because the gears were slipping. He had driven to them with a loaner so that they wouldn't be without a car that day. Bad timing. Shitty timing."

"And you lucked out?"

"They were unable to close the investigation. The police there thought that it had to do with ETA. Do you know why?"

"Well?"

"That garage man was a Spaniard. A Basque. He had in the past been a bomber himself but had fled from it. Wanted to stop doing it. So the police thought it was payback. They thought it was strange that he had been blown up in the car of a Dutchman. But they were never able to find anything."

"And C?"

"C was no fool. Several months later I stuck a note, a yellow Post-it, on the steering wheel of his new car, with the urgent request not to start the car. C took early retirement."

"And when was all this?"

"Ten years ago. This year…exactly ten years ago."

"How old were you then?"

"Twenty-two."

"And how old were you when you found your…your roots?"

"I didn't find my roots. I found God. It was in the same year. That bomb was…a few months after my trip to Morocco."

"And how can you let that—this murder and your faith—exist side by side?"

"Joop, that's an interesting question. We'll have to discuss that some more." A sparkle in his eyes. Sarcasm in his voice. As if implying how much fun he had playing a dirty trick on Joop.

"I don't understand it…at all," said Joop.

"If you were me, you would. God gives you the chance to protect yourself."

"God allows such a man to die?"

"That man was a murderer! An ETA man! That was the hand of God! It can't be otherwise. I blew up a murderer! Then I knew that God really existed. Even at such a moment, in such a situation—when you think that you've killed an innocent person and you discover that you've bombed a bomber, then you know that chance doesn't exist. Joop, everything has a meaning! Even the fact that you went to eat in Primavera! That we now sit together in this car! We don't know the meaning yet! But one day everything will become clear. Maybe that happens late, at the moment that you die, or when you have to give an account of yourself to God. But one day everything will become clear. I know that for sure. Absolutely, solemnly, sure—and you?"

"I know nothing for sure," mumbled Joop. "Nothing at all."

"Perhaps that's why you've met me…to get certainty," answered Omar. "And I'm thirsty and would like something to eat. You too?"

Chapter thirty-five

Omar took the next exit off the freeway. Night had fallen. Colored neon advertising signs blazed in the dark landscape. Two gas stations, a couple of fast-food restaurants, and a video store alongside a long and narrow parking lot that was filled with cars of Saturday evening guests from the surrounding area. They chose Mexican food. Joop's cell phone gave three beeps to indicate that there was a message. Obviously someone had called while they were driving through an area with weak reception. In the busy diner they joined the line in front of the counter, and Joop entered his voicemail number. It was Erroll. He had received the note and wished him a good trip. No message from Linda.

Both ordered vegetarian enchiladas that were paid for by Omar; he insisted. They waited in the restaurant until a table became available and emptied their cardboard plates in ten minutes. "Pretty good," decided Omar. Again he sat like a child bent over his food, filled with innocent pleasure.

When Joop got up to go to the men's room, Omar said that he'd go with him. Separated from each other by a thin synthetic partition, they unzipped their flies next to each other, heard their urine splatter in the urinals. Omar was still standing in front of the urinal when Joop went to wash his hands.

"I had to go for hours," Omar explained, chuckling, as he walked to the sink.

They changed seats. Joop took over the steering wheel and Omar sprawled in his seat, leaning back languidly. On an unlit road Joop drove the car back to Highway 5. He hadn't had the chance to call Philip. Was all of it true? Or a chain of lies? Omar couldn't have knowledge of his link with Philip and therefore was not driven by motives that were connected to it—or did he know about Philip? Why did he divulge all this? Overconfidence, innocence? Or a colossal hate whose contours Joop could barely discern? Had A screwed him, and did he now hate him so intensely that he was going to crucify A? He seemed to be hiding nothing from Joop's ears. Maybe the simple key to Omar's need to share his experiences with him was the desire for a confessor. Omar was more Catholic than he himself knew. Finally a chance to bring his transgressions and his victories to the attention of a listener, a stranger. It was unlikely.

"So you've known that woman for a long time?" asked Omar.

"Which woman?"

"The one you're going to see."

Joop didn't want to name names either. "Yes. I was sixteen. I hadn't seen her in thirty years."

"Marriage plans?"

"No. That's no longer necessary."

That was a clumsy answer, for it gave Omar the chance to "feed" him in turn. Tell the truth. As much as possible. But *never* the whole truth.

"Were you married for a long time?"

"A year and a half."

"Children?"

"No," said Joop.

Shameful. He denied the existence of his daughter. He most certainly had a child. She had died, but still his child.

"A year and a half—short," fed Omar.

"We came to America together, but…she went back to Holland."

"You never thought about going back?"

"No. I found my place. My wife didn't."

"That's why I'm not getting married," said Omar. "I hate mistakes."

Joop asked, "Are you busy the next few days?" Away from Ellen. From questions that he didn't want to answer.

"You're going for pleasure, I for my project. Life's not fair."

"Do you have many appointments?"

"Not too bad. They seem to be wild guys, the ones I'm going to see."

"Wild guys?"

"Hackers."

"Hackers—what do you need with hackers?"

Omar sat up straight. "I'll tell you, but this is not allowed in the book. And nowhere. Confidential, okay?"

"Is it about something that…that is not according to the rules?"

"I'm not a respectable gentleman, I warned you."

Joop hadn't the faintest idea what Omar wanted with hackers, but it couldn't be legal. He said, "I know that by now."

"Is it safe with you?"

"Everything is safe with me," Joop lied. It was bad, but he couldn't go back on his word.

"Word of honor," Omar said again.

"Out with your secret," said Joop.

"If this becomes known I'll lose my business, and the consequences…Joop, I really think you're a great guy, but you should know what you'll mess up if this gets out."

"I'm silent," said Joop. And wondered if he would be considered an accessory if he were informed about a crime still to be committed.

"Those hackers," said Omar, slumping back again, "they're going to get files for me. At any rate they'll try. Maybe it won't work. These files are invaluable. Names of Muslims who are already on the Internet. People with an Internet connection. We need them for our project. It will give us a base so that we can get a running start. There is a company that has those files; they sit on them. Don't want to sell them. So I'll get them in another way. If those files were in the possession of Muslims, I wouldn't touch them. But they are Americans. Jews. I have no pity for them. Anyway, isn't the film world packed with Jews? Are you bothered by them?"

"It has never come up," answered Joop.

At last, clarity about Omar. A fanatic. Joop wanted to stop the car by the side of the road and escape. Inconceivable. As soon as he was alone, he would call Philip and report everything. Not yield to panic. Keep a cool head. Not reveal any of his agitation. He changed position and clenched the steering wheel. And there, in the chaos of his head, suddenly appeared a thought that made Omar's words harmless—no, a thought that took the danger out of Omar's words and swept away his resolve to call Philip.

He had to make a choice. Now. Fully aware, he would make an agreement with Omar, and that meant that he would offer trust and would receive trust. The book no longer interested him. And the Jews in Israel had atom bombs at their disposal and could save themselves. He should not contact Philip anymore. If the story about the hackers was true. He should take Omar, a stupid Jew-hater from Emmen, in his confidence about his daughter. About her heart. And he should ask him if the hackers could help him.

Five minutes later Joop looked next to him. Omar was asleep. The car sped through one of the most fertile areas of North America. In the darkness nothing could be seen, but Joop knew the landscape. Sixteen years ago he had driven here with Miriam.

Chapter thirty-six

The first three months after she gave birth, Ellen had stayed home and had breastfed; afterwards Joop, who had fixed up a study at home, had taken over the care and fed Miriam concoctions from jars and cans. Ellen wanted to get back to work. But that no longer seemed available, as if her clients were under the impression that her pregnancy had taken away her talent. Suddenly Ellen's career as art director seemed to have foundered, an intangible, fatal phenomenon that often happened in this city and especially hit crewmembers who were so successful that clients thought that they were too expensive or overbooked, even though in reality they sat at home, waiting nervously next to the telephone.

Out of necessity Ellen worked in wardrobe again. She started to complain about the lack of opportunities and recognition and about the mistake she had made in staying at home for almost half a year. In hindsight it became clear that she suffered from postpartum depression, but at that moment she blamed her worries entirely on her career. She felt downgraded.

While Ellen walked around with clothes on a location or in a studio and Joop was writing at home in his study, Miriam lay in her cradle next to his desk, seldom crying, often babbling and gurgling, mostly sleeping. Her presence, even when she crawled through the room and under his table, did not detract from his ability to concentrate and to follow his work schedule.

It took half a year before Ellen could get back to work again as an art director. During the week of her birthday she was asked to go and work on three Dutch commercials that were produced in San Francisco. She wanted to take Miriam along—the production would pay for babysitting—but three days before her departure the pediatrician determined that Miriam's continuous crying was caused by an ear infection.

Ellen considered calling off her job in San Francisco, but Joop insisted that she go; it was important for her to build up new credits as art director with these ads and to show the city that she was available. They could get along without her for two weeks. She went.

The antibiotics worked. After a few days the doctor gave the go-ahead, and at seven o'clock in the morning they drove off in order to surprise Ellen with their arrival. The ride would take them most of the day. Miriam, ten months old, sat in a car seat on the narrow backseat of his brand-new dark blue Jaguar xjs, the visible proof of his success. His former buddy Bert Hulscher was directing the commercials, and Joop couldn't conceal that he looked forward to driving up with the elegant car. Miriam slept for most of the trip. He stopped a few times to change her, to give her baby food, and he enjoyed the first long trip with the car. At the end of the afternoon they reached San Francisco, and he drove the car to Nob Hill. In front of the entrance of the Fairmont two valets appeared next to his car. They lifted his suitcase and Miriam's portable cradle from the trunk, and with Miriam on his arm he entered between the pillars the grand lobby of the hotel. At the brown marble desk he explained that he was the husband of Ellen Koopman, that this was a surprise, and they kindly let him into her room. Heavy, classic furniture, a deep-pile carpet, night stands with salmon-colored lampshades on copper feet, mirrors in gilded frames, a marble bathroom. While Miriam explored the room, cooing, he set up her cradle. At eight o'clock Ellen had not yet appeared, which was not unusual; crews often had long days. He put Miriam in bed and waited for Ellen's arrival while watching television without sound. An hour later he called the number of the production office, but there was no answer. At two o'clock he called the reception and asked in a whisper if any Dutch people were staying in the hotel. The reception couldn't answer that. He spelled Bert's name. He was indeed in the hotel. Was he in his room? His key was gone, so it could be assumed that he was in his room. Should he put the call through? No, said Joop, but he did want to have the room number. One floor lower, six rooms down. They had no night shoot—he had seen the shooting schedule, and a form of insanity took hold of him. He couldn't remain sitting, paced nervously back and forth through the room, trying feverishly to control the nightmare in his imagination, sometimes stared for minutes on end at his daughter, and prayed—Joop had no idea to whom—that his wife's absence could be explained in a simple way. After he had at length practiced a few sentences with a disguised voice, he picked up the telephone at three thirty, draped the corner of a towel over the mouthpiece, and entered the number of Bert's room. The telephone rang five times.

"Yes?" Bert. An annoyed voice.

Joop was overwhelmed with disgust by his own lunacy, but now he went through with it. With a high-pitched voice he said: "Reception. We have an urgent message for Mrs. Koopm'n. She's not in her room, and since you are part of her group, we thought, maybe you might know how to reach her."

Bert was quiet for a moment in order to let the meaning of the message penetrate. "Yes—okay—wait a moment."

Joop heard him talk with someone, but it was not clear who this person was. Two seconds later it became clear.

"Hello?"

Now he had to play out his role. He concentrated on the squeaky voice and his accent. And oddly enough, he was suddenly completely calm. His suspicion had been confirmed.

"Sorry to disturb you. Urgent message. Mr. Koopm'n called. Everything okay with Miriam. Please call tomorrow."

She asked, "That's all?"

"Yes ma'am."

"You're waking me up because of this?"

"It's marked urgent, ma'am."

"Ridiculous. Okay—thanks."

"Sorry, ma'am. Good night."

He hung up immediately. Had she recognized his voice? No, then she wouldn't have entered into a discussion with him. Now she was talking with Bert about the goofiness of the receptionist. And Bert would caress her and would seize the telephone incident to do something else. While she squeezed his hand between her thighs, she would laugh and cram her tongue into his throat. He was disgusted. Why did he play this out? Why hadn't he called her a traitor? Because he now had power? The stupid power of the betrayed?

Resigned, he packed his stuff and left the hotel half an hour later. He had carefully put Miriam in the car seat without waking her. Seven hours later he reached Venice. He could not explain Ellen's behavior. He thought that she was happy. He had been happy—Ellen obviously not. He had overlooked something crucial, but even after seven hours of contemplative silence facing the walnut dashboard, in the fragrant, leather-upholstered interior of the Jaguar, his child sleeping or talking baby-talk behind his right arm, he could find no reason. That's how she was. Ellen was a stranger. Someone who could never be trusted.

In the evening she called. Eight thirty. Miriam was asleep in the cradle next to his work table.

"Hi! How are things?" Natural. Affectionate.

"Everything is fine," he said.

"I just heard that you called yesterday. I went to bed early and had turned off the phone."

"Where were you last night?" he asked.

"What do you mean?"

"Am I speaking in riddles? A simple question: where were you?"

"In my room, as I just said!"

"You were not there."

"Joop, I unplugged it!"

"I don't believe you."

"Joop, don't make a fool of yourself. We worked until ten o'clock, and I was so tired that I went to bed immediately. What are you imagining?"

For a moment it went through his head that everything could be a misunderstanding. No, absurd, he had waited in her room, in the dead of night he had heard her voice, after Hulscher's.

"Why are you lying, Ellen?"

"Joop...I'm not lying."

"You're lying."

"Shall I call back in a while? You won't listen to reason."

"I was in your room. Yesterday we drove to...to your hotel. From around six o'clock we waited for you. In your room. And... halfway through the night I called the room of your lover. With a message."

Ellen remained silent for a few seconds.

"You drove to San Francisco?"

"Yes."

"With Miriam? She's sick!"

"The doctor said it was okay."

"You're not in your right mind to put her in a car for hours!"

He asked, "Why are you doing this?"

She paid no attention to his question. "How can you do that to Miriam?" She went on the attack in an attempt to weaken his. He was guilty, not she.

"Everything is fine with her! She's glowing with health! But you! Why...why someone else?"

"Why do you want to hear that?" she asked softly.

"Because I'm your husband."

Again she was silent. Then she said something that he didn't understand.

"What?" he asked.

"I've fallen in love," he now heard.

"Why?!" he roared.

"Why? Because...because here I'm special again! You give me no space! That's why! Because everything has started to be about you! Your successes, your ridiculous car! Do you still remember why we moved here? That was because of me! But I've become a dumb, passive little mother—and I can't stand that! The past couple of days I've…I've found myself again!"

Joop slammed down the phone. Miriam was frightened by the crash and started to cry. But now he shouldn't lift her out of her cradle to comfort her, because he had to protect her from the hate in his hands. He went outside, wandered dazed through the garden, circled the house while Miriam was shrieking inside. The phone rang continuously. It was a warm evening in October. The crickets buzzed. The stars twinkled in the night.

After half an hour he went inside. Miriam had fallen asleep, three feet from the telephone which kept ringing without stopping. He answered.

"I want Miriam," he heard her say.

"Never," he answered and broke off the connection.

Sixteen years ago. If their child had been awarded to her, Miriam would have grown up in the Netherlands. And she would probably still be alive. But he had fought Ellen's claims, and two years later as the betrayed party, he was awarded custody by the court. Sometimes Ellen didn't keep in touch for months, and then there would be periods when she called every day. It wasn't until Miriam got her period and needed the voice of a woman that relations thawed out somewhat. Would Miriam have survived in the Netherlands?

In the silence of the fast-moving GMC van, next to a soundly sleeping Omar, who sometimes snored with his mouth open for minutes on end, he let such pointless thoughts and memories enter his mind.

Chapter thirty-seven

His message had reached Linda, for he got the key to her room without any problem. When he opened the door to her room, she yelled from the bathroom, "I would appreciate it if the staff of this hotel knocked before disturbing the privacy of the guests!"

Wearing a heavy bathrobe that she held closed with one hand as if she was cold, Linda stormed angrily out of the bathroom in order to put the hotel worker in his place—and when she saw Joop, she smiled broadly. She let go of the bathrobe and wrapped her arms around him. She was naked; her skin was still warm from the shower. Holding on to his neck, she jumped athletically up against him with legs spread, and he caught her by her buttocks and carried her to bed while she squeezed her thighs around his hips.

He called room service. With a few quick movements two waiters expanded the serving cart on the spot into a round table.

Linda said, "Would you be willing to speak with Usso some time?"

"No. My grandfather has been dead for a very long time."

"In a certain sense, yes."

"No, not in a certain sense. In no matter what sense. I wonder if I should punch him in his face or laugh at him."

"I think that you'll behave. When you hear what he has to tell you."

It was annoying that she insisted. The monk was a charlatan. But Joop didn't want to provoke another conflict about this with her. Or did she provoke it?

"Linda, I've come here for you. Not for him."

"I've made an appointment for you. The day after tomorrow. In the city. With him and someone else."

"My grandmother?"

"No."

"What do you want from me anyway?"

"What I wanted…when I wrote you the first time, I wanted to inform you about something. I didn't know that this would happen. That was not the intention. But it has happened. But that first thing remains: the reason why I wrote you. That's still there. And it's something good."

Perhaps she meant that she had indications that Joop had been a saint in a previous life.

"Can you be more precise?"

"No. I want you to hear it from others. Not from me. And: come with me. The worst thing that can happen is that you're bored for half an hour. Okay?"

She took his hand. Starched table linen, heavy silver-plated cutlery, gold-edged plates. Sixteen years ago he had also called room service and had left the food untouched in Ellen's room. At his departure he had rolled the serving cart to the hall in order to erase the traces of his presence.

"I have to think about it," Joop said, "but don't expect anything from me."

"I'm free today," she said, "we can walk through the city, take the cable car, go down to Fisherman's Wharf, the regular tourist route, what do you think?"

"Good. But—I may get a telephone call, and then I'll have to be off for a couple of hours."

On Sunday it was damp as well. A third of an inch of rain. Not cold, but there was a stiff wind. They visited the Museum of Modern Art, lunched at one of the fish restaurants on the Wharf. No phone call from Omar. Joop was confused about all the things he wanted to reflect on in peace, but he was distracted by her magnificent body and sometimes by her bizarre discourses that filled him with loathing as well as fascination. She was a believer who knew the quotations of the Buddhists by heart.

" 'The whole cosmos can be found in one flower. We cannot say that the flower is less than this or more than that. If we let go of our ideas about more or less, being and not-being, we reach what is called nirvana in Buddhism: the destruction of all ideas and conceptions.' This is what Thich Nhat Hanh, a Zen monk, has said. He demonstrates that a Western conception of God can be combined with a Buddhist worldview."

"I'm lost," Joop interrupted. "Buddhists don't believe in a God, do they?"

"The Buddha gives no formula. He offers ideas to everyone. But when you make an absolute of something, you no longer think according to his spirit."

Joop had made an absolute of his memories. The memory of his daughter. The Buddha felt that you had to give that up too. But if he did that, she would die once again.

Omar did not get in touch.

Chapter thirty-eight

On Monday, March fifth, the highest temperature in San Francisco reached fifty-seven degrees Fahrenheit; the average temperature remained four degrees lower. It rained and was windy—gusts with speeds measuring up to thirty-nine miles per hour—and there was a quarter inch of precipitation although it remained damp all day.

At ten o'clock in the morning, Linda had a taxi stop in front of a tall office building near Union Square, the square that is the heart of the city. When Joop worked for Robbie Fray on the script about Joseph Strauss, he had stayed in the St. Francis Hotel a few times, two streets from the office building.

A medium-sized box, austere, like a Mies van der Rohe. A nondescript large office building. A revolving door opened into a hall with a marble floor and a black counter. Behind the counter, on the wall, hung a black marbled board that displayed in gold letters the list of tenants for each floor.

"Eighth and ninth," said Linda.

Joop read the name: Schweizerische Handelsbank.

He asked, "What's that?"

"A bank."

"I can see that. What are we doing at a bank?"

"We have an appointment with someone. May I use your phone for a moment?"

She entered a number and waited.

"Hello? Mr. Hürlimann? Linda de Vries. We're downstairs. Should we come to the eighth or the ninth floor?" She listened and nodded. "What is the name of that place?" Again she nodded. "Good. We'll go there. Can we order something for you in the meantime? I'll do that. See you shortly." She gave the phone back to Joop. "He's coming down. The conference room is in use. We'll go to a diner across the street."

They went back to the revolving door. This was not to his liking. It was about more than a reincarnation.

"Hürlimann...a Swiss?"

"Yes."

"That's the man I was supposed to meet?"

"Yes."

"Also a Buddhist?"

"I think a true-blue Calvinist."

"What does he want from me?"

"Be patient."

"What do you want from me?"

"Once again: patience."

In the drizzle they waited until the traffic came to a stop, then ran across the wet street. The diner was located across from the building, on the ground floor of another office complex. Linda chose a booth in front of the window.

"Is the monk coming too?"

"Yes. Usso is already with him."

"For what? Do they want me to write a screenplay?"

"That depends on you. But it does seem suitable for a movie."

"Do you think it's odd that I find all this...awkward?"

"No. Everything will become clear very soon. Relax! It's something good. Something marvelous."

"I have little faith in marvels."

"Joop, it's time that you start thinking differently about that."

Across the street he saw the monk leaving the office building, a long nylon jacket over his orange robe. Next to him walked a man in a beige trench coat, an attaché case in his hand, who tried clumsily to open an umbrella. The monk gestured to him that he didn't need protection against the rain, and they crossed the street quickly.

Joop's telephone beeped the *Wilhelmus*, and he leaned to the side to squeeze a hand into his pants pocket.

Omar's voice in his ear: "Those guys—I was just with them—they started on it this morning."

The hackers. Miriam's heart. They had agreed not to mention the word "hacker."

"Good. Will they call when they have it?"

"Right away," said Omar. "And Joop, they're doing it for free. They understand what it's about. These guys have hearts of gold."

Clearly Omar had done his best to hide his Drenthe accent during their first conversations, for now you could hear in every word where he had learned to speak.

"No need to do it for nothing. I'm happy to pay for it."

"They don't want that. Everything all right with you?"

"Yes, of course. Do you know yet when you're going back?"

"I'll know soon. I'll call you." He looked at the screen of his cell phone, read Omar's number, and broke off the connection.

In life there was a hierarchy. He said to Linda, "I may have to leave for a moment in a little while."

"First you have to listen for a moment, all right?"

"I'm listening," he said.

Linda stood up when they entered the diner. Smiling, the man raised his hand, causing him to swing the umbrella dangerously close to the face of the monk. Followed by the monk, he came to their table.

"Mrs. De Vries, nice to see you again."

He spoke English with a heavy German accent. He was thirty-five, tall and slim, with an attractive face with regular, boyish features, someone who gave the impression that he was never bothered by misfortune. No, it was worse: he couldn't even spell the word "misfortune." Light blond hair, clear blue eyes, and tanned as if he had just been on a ski vacation for weeks in the Gstaad sun.

"Mr. Hürlimann, this is Joop Koopman."

"Mr. Koopman, nice to meet you. You've already met Mr. Apury."

Joop shook his hand, "Certainly."

The monk folded his hands, bowed, and Joop imitated the greeting.

"Sit down," said Linda, "we have just ordered coffee. For you too, Mr. Hürlimann. And tea for the master."

The monk nodded. He slid onto the bench next to Hürlimann.

"Good that you could come," said Hürlimann. Seated, he extricated himself from his coat, and he pulled a business card from the breast pocket of his dark blue blazer. A wide, dark red silk necktie, a stylish white shirt with French cuffs closed with silver cufflinks.

"Here you are."

Joop accepted the business card. Under the name of the bank he read: Dr. Christian Hürlimann, Vice President. With an address in Basel, Switzerland.

"Good that you could take the time. You arrived this morning?"

"The day before yesterday."

"Good. Has Mrs. De Vries told you anything yet?"

"No. Nothing. I'm a total blank. But I always like to meet bankers."

"I don't often experience that," answered Hürlimann. "Shall I tell you something about myself?"

"Please."

"I work for the Schweizerische Handelsbank. For five years, five and a half to be exact. I'm secretary of the executive board of the bank. And the board has asked me to handle this matter."

"What matter?" asked Joop. He flatly refused to listen to another reincarnation story. Was the Swiss guy Linda's grandfather Moses, Herman's brother?

"The De Vries matter. The matter of your grandfather."

"My grandfather?" Joop repeated with reluctance.

"I think I'll take over," Linda said, soothing.

"Please," said Joop. She knew how he thought about this matter. If it continued in this way, he would soon be rude and walk out.

A waitress brought their order. They waited in silence and avoided each other's eyes until the woman had placed their cups on the table.

Joop leaned toward Linda and said softly in Dutch, "Linda, you're not going to play a trick on me, are you?"

Gently she placed her hand on his arm. "No. What do you think?" Then she continued in English and addressed Hürlimann, "I haven't informed Joop yet. I wanted to wait with that until you were present."

The banker nodded understandingly.

She turned again back to Joop. "What I'm going to say is at odds with everything that you believe in. Or rather, that you don't believe in. It has to do with what the master has told me. I know your skepticism. But Mr. Hürlimann is the proof. He *has* the proof. Joop—try to open yourself for a moment. What I am going to tell you will change your life. And that's no overstatement. Will you promise me?"

Uneasily he shifted back and forth on the bench. Five minutes, he thought, I give the Swiss guy five minutes.

"I'll do my best," he said.

Linda looked at the monk. "Usso?"

Not the banker but the monk would familiarize him with the glorious dimension of reincarnation. This bald-shaven Asian man, a perfect stranger, was his grandfather.

The man sat straight-backed on the bench, completely relaxed and serene. He said, "Mr. Koopman, I know the limits of Western culture. I know how people in your culture generally think about reincarnation. I have grown up in other surroundings. For us reincarnation is a fact. For us life consists of one long chain of efforts to reach eternity. During each human life we have to perfect ourselves. That is the goal of life. And when we reach the perfect life, a presence awaits us. Timeless. Without matter. A presence that we have difficulty imagining but which is reality for us. Nirvana. But we haven't reached that state yet, none of us—otherwise we wouldn't be here."

The monk held the cup of tea in both hands and carefully took a sip. With considered, purposeful movement. He slurped loudly.

That was probably permitted in Tibet, thought Joop. His grandfather probably used to slurp too.

The monk set down his cup and said, "The Buddha teaches us that there are five *shandha*s that determine our life: body, emotions, observations, awareness, and states of mind. These *shandha*s, aspects, are always in motion. For us incarnation is a true rebirth. When you are born, you come into being from nothingness. When you die, you disappear into nothingness. But nothing comes into being from nothing. Before a flower becomes a flower, it already exists—in the sun, in the earth, in the seed. The aspects change continually, sometimes coming together in a flower, then again in another form. Nirvana is the end of all words, of all ideas. There the elements stop existing. One time a Zen teacher and his student had a conversation. The student asked: 'Where is the world of no birth and no death?' And the teacher said: 'It is in the midst of the world of birth and death.' Why do I mention this? To make the interconnectedness of everything clear to you. And to explain my memories."

He was silent and stared at his tea. There was no visible movement, as if his heart had stopped beating too. Joop looked at the banker for a moment and tried to determine what he thought of it. The banker leaned on the table and listened, evidently interested, to the monk who suddenly started to speak again.

"Since my appearance on earth, I have remembered things. Even as a child. I remember streets that I could not see in Tibet. I remember that I had a daughter. I remember my occupation. I remember trips to Istanbul. I remember a life. With the pain of the end. I remember fears and joy. I remember sickness and health. I remember a complete earthly life. And I remember names. Those of my parents, my wife, my child, my brother. For you all this is incomprehensible. For me, a fact."

What this man was saying was madness. This grown man claimed that he had memories from before the beginning of his life.

Peacefully the monk stared into his tea. Perhaps monks read the future in it.

"I came into the world as Herman de Vries. I was born on April third of the year eighteen hundred and ninety of your era. On June fifteenth of the year nineteen hundred and fifteen I married Esther Eijsman. Ten months later we had a child, our only one, Johanna Miriam, whom we called Anneke. I left this earth on April thirty-first, nineteen forty-three. That is what I remember."

With burning eyes Joop stared at the man. With a throat that was dry as dust. The names tallied. As did the facts. Apury had gotten them from Linda or had looked them up somewhere. That wasn't easy, but someone who was persistent could gather the data. Maybe he had worked on it for years. A master crook.

"I feel your skepticism," said the monk. "I would have that too. If I had grown up in your culture, I would accept nothing from a man like me who suddenly appears in your life and seems to ruin your certainties. Are there objective proofs, you will ask. Except for my memories—no. And then I met your second cousin Linda in Dharamsala. And she contacted the bank in Switzerland. And then she received a letter from Mr. Hürlimann."

Joop looked at the Swiss banker. The latter turned to Joop, and in his glazed eyes Joop recognized the same dizzying suspicion that he felt. He was afraid he was going to throw up.

"I er…think I understand what is going through your mind," said Hürlimann. "Believe me, I didn't know what to make of this. I checked what I had to check, and one day I had to admit that the words of Master Apury tallied on at least one point. An important point. I accept Master Apury's words insofar as I could verify them. And I have to ask for your discretion. You have to sign for this; my bank doesn't want this to become generally known—in a moment you'll understand why. But thanks to Master Apury, I have at any rate been able to identify one anonymous account that without a rightful claimant, we would otherwise have had to close."

Joop could no longer collect his thoughts, let alone formulate them. He looked outside for a moment, at the gray sky above the high buildings, the red logo of the Swiss bank on the façade, the intertwined letters SHB, and decided that he had nothing to lose. Joop had once read that if you let a monkey type long enough on a laptop—thousands or millions of years—he would one day spontaneously type *The Merchant of Venice*. He should look at this in the same way. He should make no attempt to understand it. The Swiss had obviously given in. He was a banker—therefore it was about money. But if it was legal and he could make money on it, then he would play along.

"Can you be more specific?" he asked Hürlimann.

"Do you want to tell it, or should I?" the latter asked Usso Apury. The monk bowed modestly. "With your approval, I would like to tell it."

Hürlimann made an accommodating gesture. "As you wish."

The monk thanked him with a nod. "Herman de Vries made regular trips to Istanbul. He traded in tea. In Istanbul he did business with a Sephardic family, originally from Greece. Thanks to these contacts he was able to amass a sizeable fortune that he kept in a bank in Istanbul. In December nineteen thirty-nine, he took that sum out in hard cash and took it with him in a suitcase. In January nineteen forty, he obtained a visa for Switzerland and deposited the money in an account at the Basler Getreidebank. Herman de Vries remembers the code number. And the password."

The monk bowed again, to conclude the story.

So it was about his grandfather's fortune. His mother had told him that it had disappeared during the war. But it was inconceivable that the monk had discovered what had since that time remained hidden from his mother (and from his father who had also tried to retrieve it).

Hürlimann took over from the monk. "Ultimately Linda de Vries ended up in my office when she discovered that the Basler Getreidebank no longer existed. In nineteen fifty-nine the SHB took over the Basler. Initially our client department had some difficulty—with her request for information. It goes without saying that the Swiss had overlooked matters of reincarnation in setting up banking rules. It took some time before her letters were sent to higher powers."

"You can safely say half a year," Linda interrupted him.

"That's true, but what is on the table here is indeed exceptional. Very exceptional. Perhaps even unique."

"I knew immediately that the master's story was correct," said

Linda. "Every detail. And if that was so, then the story about the trip to Basel would also have to be correct."

Joop had to pay close attention. He cleared his throat. "And that number...and the password...they were correct?"

"Your grandfather had opened a numbered account. An account without a name. A password goes with it—yes, both were correct," Hürlimann responded.

"What kind of money is it?"

"Apparently money that your grandfather earned with his business. As you know, we in Switzerland are involved in an extensive investigation into the so-called 'Jewish claims.' This coded account was also on the list, but it could not be traced back to the names of persons. Normally that is the advantage of such accounts, but if something happens to the account holder, then it's practically impossible to discover the rightful claimant of the account."

Joop looked at the motionless monk staring into his tea. Joop could not look inside his head. The world was filled to the rafters with irrationality. "And so I am...I am Mr. Apury's heir?"

Hürlimann nodded. "Yes, but it is also rather complex. Mr. Usso Apury is your grandfather, at least that's what he says. So in fact he is here to withdraw the money from the account. But..." Mr. Hürlimann gestured excitedly, "rules for this still have to be invented; we have no idea how we could justify it legally. Therefore the money is yours. As legal claimant."

"As legal claimant," repeated Joop, unable to place the situation within a rationally ordered reality. But hadn't his world been turned upside down since December twenty-second? Hadn't everything that he had trusted with reason slipped out of his hands?

"And what do you want?" asked Joop, turning to the monk.

The monk said, "I am your grandfather, but at the same time I'm not. In a certain way I am his continuation, but also my own beginning. I have no right to that fortune."

At his wit's end Joop looked at Linda. And he asked in Dutch, "What do I do with this, Lin?"

She smiled affectionately. "Whatever you want. Accept it. Don't think about it anymore. It's a miracle. I would love it if from now on you would listen to me with less skepticism, but it's your money. Your right."

"Do you understand it?" he pleaded.

"No. And that's not necessary. I believe it. Leave understanding alone for a while."

His ears ringing, Joop nodded. "And what now?"

Hürlimann said, "I have papers with me. If you sign them, the money is yours."

Joop nodded. And again turned to Linda in Dutch, "Is this a joke, Linda? Something with a hidden camera?"

"The world is full of hidden cameras," said Linda. "But all this is real."

Hürlimann said, "I have to ask you to sign a non-disclosure agreement. The general management is cooperating on the basis of discretion. They absolutely don't want this to be known by the press. The consequences would be immense. Within no time we would have to handle thousands of reincarnation cases. I'm afraid I have to ask you to sign this agreement."

"All right," Joop said. What did he have to lose? His grandfather's vanished money.

"Signing will take ten minutes," said Hürlimann. "Or I can send the papers with you, as you wish."

"How much money are we talking about?" Joop managed to say, looking desperately for guidelines for this new life.

"In nineteen forty, when your grandfather was in Basel, he deposited a sum of one hundred and fifty thousand dollars, when converted."

"That much?" said Joop, his voice breaking.

"That much," repeated Hürlimann. "And in the course of sixty years it has increased to a fortune of a little over two million dollars."

Joop looked at Linda. "Please let me pass by you, Lin."

She had expected an outburst of joy, for she looked at him with a delighted expression, but he was incapable of reacting right then and got up. Across the bench he slipped out of the booth. Took big steps past other tables and booths to the bathroom in the back of the diner. Pushed with his shoulder against the swinging door and pulled open the door of one of the toilet stalls. Leaned over the toilet and vomited. From deep in his intestines he expelled his breakfast, felt the sour slime in his esophagus and in his throat, saw how badly he had chewed this morning, chunks of bread and smoked salmon spattered undigested to the bottom of the bowl, and something in his body enjoyed this discharge which also seemed to clear his head—a purification, a deliverance.

He washed his hands, wiped his mouth clean with a paper towel, and returned to the booth with a calm head. But it was the calm in the eye of a hurricane. His hands and legs trembled.

Linda got up when he walked toward her.

"You look white as a sheet."

"I didn't feel well for a moment. I'm better now."

"I'll ask for some water."

"Yes, please."

She went up to a waitress. When Joop sat down, he noticed that the monk had left his seat.

The banker said, "Mr. Apury begged to be excused. He has left."

Linda sat back down on the bench next to Joop.

With a nod to the place where the monk had been sitting, Joop asked her, "He left?"

"He was…he saw that you had trouble with this. He regretted that he caused all of this."

"Regretted? No reason to have regrets. What should I give him, Linda?"

"Joop, that's not my responsibility."

"Ten percent? A kind of finder's fee? Which it isn't, of course. It's his own money—sort of. Or should I give him everything?"

"Think about it a while; you don't have decide anything now."

Hürlimann placed some papers on the table. On the top page the red logo was displayed above a typed text. He pointed at it, turned over three pages. Under a dotted line, where his handwritten signature still needed to be added, Joop's name had already been entered.

"This is the document that indicates that we accept your identity—do you by chance have your ID on hand?"

"My driver's license."

Hürlimann pushed aside the set of documents and pointed to a second set. "With this you open a new account at our bank." He pushed aside this set as well. "This is your approval for the transfer of the balance of your grandfather's account to your new account. This is the non-disclosure. And the last document—it indicates that we recognize your rights to your grandfather's account."

Joop asked, "What was the password?"

"Miriam," said Hürlimann. "I understand that it was your mother's name."

"Her middle name," muttered Joop, "of course—Miriam."

Nothing of the world that he used to live in was accessible and understandable to him. He had become lost in Linda's world. Iridology. Aromatherapy. He had always talked about it with passionate aversion. Everything was different now.

"May I see your driver's license?"

Silently Joop handed it to him. Hürlimann took down the number.

Joop leaned over to Linda. "And you, Linda? I want to give you something too."

She shook her head. "I want nothing. If you want to do something, give something for the monastery."

"Do you really mean that?"

"Sweetheart," she said tenderly, with eyes that radiated love and care, and caressed his cheek with the back of her hand.

His telephone rang again.

"Yes?"

A strange voice: "Mr. Koopm'n?"

"Yes. With whom am I speaking?"

"I'm Samir. Omar asked me to look up a name for you. We have it." He spoke with an accent.

"You have it? Really?"

A nervous look at Linda, who looked at him questioning.

"Really. We have all the information, Mr. Koopm'n. Will you stop by, or shall I tell you now?"

"Tell me—one second," said Joop. He sat up straight. He had to be decisive now. Strong. And he made an impatient gesture at Hürlimann: "A piece of paper, please. And a pen."

The man opened his attaché case and placed a pen and paper in front of Joop. A blank piece of bank stationery.

"Yes, go ahead."

"That night, there was only one such operation. So it was simple. Besides, their firewalls didn't amount to anything."

Joop could place the accent: the Middle-East, Arabic or Persian. A bunch of young Arab hackers. Immigrants. Or perhaps Palestinian young people. He had heard that they worked the Internet actively.

"The operation was in Atlanta. At seven thirty in the morning. A girl received the heart. Nineteen. Alia Abbasi."

"Repeat that," said Joop.

"Alia...Abbasi."

Joop wrote down the name. "What kind of name is that?"

"Alia is Arabic, I know that. Abbasi—no idea. Also sounds Arabic."

"Do you have an address?"

"She lives in Paris. France."

"Paris, France?"

"Yes."

They had airlifted her. At night, across the ocean. To the operating room in Atlanta because it was within the radius where the heart could be transported. A girl from France. An Arab girl from Paris. He knew someone who had been in Paris recently, but he no longer remembered who.

"Do you have the exact address?"

"I have it, yes. Three, three...rue, with an e...Rabelais." He distorted the pronunciation. "Should I spell it?"

"No, I've got it. I repeat, 33, rue Rabelais."

"That's right. Zip code?"

"Go ahead."

"75008 Paris, France."

"I've got it—Samir, I'd like to pay you."

"No need. We're doing it for nothing. All for a good cause. Mr. Koopm'n, we earn enough."

"Samir—and where's your name from?"

"Arabic. We're Palestinians. We came from Lebanon six years ago. We were lucky."

"Thank you very much. Samir—thank you very much."

"You're welcome."

The young man hung up. Joop had the name. Alia. The girl with Miriam's heart. And he knew where she lived. Alia. He would call Air France and book the first flight to Paris, even though he had no idea what he was going to do there, but he had to go there. Suddenly he was also able to financially. He was a wealthy man, just as Herman de Vries had been.

Apologetically, Joop looked at Linda and the Swiss.

"It was important. Sorry. What should I do now? Sign?"

"If you wish," said Hürlimann.

He leafed through the sets of documents, showed Joop where he had to sign, and Joop blindly set down his meandering signature six times.

After the last one, Hürlimann said, "Fine. May I congratulate you?"

Elated, Linda grabbed his arm with both hands. "Joop! Joop! Didn't I tell you that it would be something good? Didn't I tell you that something nice was about to happen?"

He nodded. Hürlimann opened his attaché case and put the documents in it.

Joop looked up and saw Philip standing at the entrance of the diner, looking at him. The madness of this moment ended in a hallucination. Immediately Joop lowered his eyes and heard Hürlimann explain the procedure: The money would be transferred to Joop's account in Basel; it would be sensible to take a little time and then decide whether the money should be sent to America.

Joop looked at the door again. Philip was still standing there. He wore jeans, a worn brown bomber jacket on which raindrops were visible. Laced shoes polished to a shine. Philip couldn't be here. Philip didn't know where he was. Joop was prey to delusions.

Philip moved his head in the direction of the bathroom and walked to the back of the restaurant.

Joop said, "Linda, can you please let me get out?"

She got up and made room for him. Philip opened the door to the bathroom.

Linda asked, "You aren't leaving, are you?"

"Just to the bathroom," he answered.

Bewildered, he hurried past the tables. They had followed him. That was the only explanation. They had kept an eye on him from the beginning. Philip was washing his hands and looked up when Joop entered.

Philip said, "Go and wash your hands too."

Joop did what he was instructed to do and stationed himself in front of the other sink, opened the faucet, and asked, "How did you know where I was?"

"Surely you know that we're following him? We saw you step into the subject's car. Panic. We've had to assign extra people to keep an eye on you during your ridiculous adventure. Then we thought: you never know how a hare catches a tortoise..."

"The reverse: how a tortoise catches a hare."

"Joop, you're playing with fire. You have no idea what's going on."

Philip pressed the button of the hot-air blower and held his hands under it. The machine made a roaring sound. Philip had to raise his voice. "In a minute, when I leave, you'll wait ten seconds—and don't leave the bathroom until then. In fifteen minutes I'll see you in room 730 in the St. Francis. Knock three times. But don't walk there directly. You'll go through the door here and you turn right. First you walk all the way around the block until you end up here in front of the diner. Only then do you come to me."

Intimidated, suspicious, Joop asked, "What do you know about me?"

"Too little. Till shortly."

Chapter thirty-nine

Joop said goodbye to the banker, kissed Linda, said that he would be at the hotel in an hour—perhaps have lunch together; he turned to the Swiss banker, you're welcome too, but the man declined—and started the rainy lap around the block.

How many absurdities could a person stand in an hour? His grandfather's fortune had been returned, and he had traced Miriam's heart. Linda was right. A miracle. But miracles frightened him.

When he came around the last corner, he caught a glimpse of Linda and the Swiss getting into a taxi. Then he walked to the St. Francis, an impressive building from 1904, a grand hotel with more than a thousand rooms on the corner of Union Square and Powell Street. Without checking in at the reception, Joop took the elevator to the seventh floor. He knocked three times and Philip opened. He had taken off his jacket and now wore a checked shirt over a white T-shirt, the top of which was visible under the open shirt collar.

The room was just as luxurious as the one in the Fairmont. On the table lay a packet of Marlboros, in the ashtray a crushed butt next to a broken-off filter.

"You've got some explaining to do," said Joop.

Philip sat down. "You too."

"No. No joking around. You screwed me."

"And you took incredible risks. Are you out of your mind?"

Joop lowered himself onto the other chair. "You're the last person who can say something like that to me. Risks? You talk about risks? That you encouraged me to take? You're a bastard!"

"Keep your voice down, please. They can hear you in the hall."

"So you followed me?"

"Yes. It was interesting that you set out with him, yes."

"I didn't set out with him. He offered me a ride. That's all."

"Nothing is ever all. I put all my cards on the table with you. From the beginning. As long as you played according to the rules, nothing was the matter. Unless you start playing the hero on your own. Then it becomes risky."

"You're wrong. Your subject is not an average citizen, but he's no bastard." Omar had blown up someone. In spite of that Joop wanted to defend him. Thanks to him, he now possessed the name of the girl who was living with Miriam's heart.

Looking intently at Joop, Philip said, "Alia Abbasi."

"Alia Abbasi?" repeated Joop.

Did Philip know her? While continuing to watch Joop, Philip leaned toward the pack of cigarettes, pushed one out, and broke off the filter.

"You wiretapped me," Joop concluded.

"When we noticed that you didn't use our telephone, we fixed your telephone."

"How, when?"

"Doesn't matter. We heard your conversations just now. You've gone too far. Joop, you're releasing forces about which you have no idea."

He kept looking at Joop. "Who called you?" he asked after lighting the cigarette.

It made no sense for Joop to resist, for without Philip's cooperation he could never approach her. The man could block or clear the way for everything. He had power.

"A couple of Internet freaks. Hackers. They hacked the computers. The organization didn't want to give me her name."

Philip looked away, took in the room as if he had been asked to get its measurements.

He said, "I should have told you, about her. But I was in the impression—"

"Under the impression," Joop interrupted.

"Under the impression that you didn't want to hear any name. I know her, Joop."

"Philip, what do you know? In God's name, what happened that day?"

Philip sat up straight and looked at him again, but now with a pained expression. "That day—that afternoon, when it became clear that it was hopeless, I went and called. I knew someone who was waiting for this. The daughter of…of a person with whom I work. I told him about your daughter. That's when it was arranged. Should I have told you right away? Yes. Now, yes. Now I know that you apparently wanted it. I didn't know that. I wanted to help that person. Help his child. I'm sorry." He leaned forward. "Joop, I'm really sorry. If I had known that you had exchanged your mind—"

"Changed your mind."

"Then I wouldn't have done it. My apologies."

"You should have told me. Right away, on that day."

"I know. But there were other considerations."

"There are no other considerations except human ones!" roared Joop.

He sank back into the chair. Exhausted. Stinking rich but at the same time down and out.

Philip leaned with a hand on the small table and said, "When we just heard you, when we caught her name…all the lights flashed red. Her heart was a…we promised her father to help him in finding a donor. And we would pay for the transplant. Her father is important, and therefore she is too."

"Where does she live?"

"In Maine. On the east coast."

Did it matter now that Philip had withheld her name? He should have said it sooner, but Joop had never told him that he wanted to find the heart.

"Philip, I want to see her."

"Why?"

"Because I want to! It's my privilege not to talk about it!"

Philip nodded, swallowed. "I'll see what I can do."

"And what you just said about Maine: you're lying. You don't want to help me. The only thing that counts for you are your paranoid ideas."

"Joop, she's in Maine."

"Your lies no longer work. She's in Paris."

"No."

"The computer says Paris."

"The computer can say anything—I say that that's wrong, Joop."

"33, rue Rabelais."

"I know that, yes."

"So you do know it?"

"I know that that address is registered. But she doesn't live there. Not at that address."

"And what is there?"

"A safe house. A house that we use. Our embassy is at number three."

Philip was lying. And Joop had the proof. He remembered that Danny had bought a carton of duty-free Marlboros at De Gaulle Airport. In the motel. During their first conversation, Philip had asked for it, and Danny had brought the carton in the plastic bag of the airport store to his motel room. It was the first time that he met Danny. Danny had been wearing a track suit. Dark green. Adidas. It was out of the question that Philip had by coincidence flown via Paris because other flights had been fully booked; in his world nothing was coincidence.

"Why were you in Paris?"

"When?" asked Philip.

"When I saw you—the first time. Danny brought you a carton of cigarettes. In a plastic bag from the Paris airport."

Philip chuckled. "Maybe I was right about you after all. You're a born agent. But your conclusion is wrong. I almost always fly through Paris. She's not there, Joop, believe me, she's someplace else."

"Where is she then?"

Philip whispered, as if the room was full of people. "This is a state secret. I'll tell it to you. But with a serious warning. If this becomes known by anyone else, you will be punished. The penalty for that is heavy. Do you understand?"

"What are you trying to put over on me?"

"Abbasi is a cover name. Her name is Nuri, Alia Nuri. Her father is Hussein Nuri."

He kept looking intently at Joop.

"So what? Who is Hussein Nuri?"

"An Iranian. He worked with the contact group of the secret service there. Maintained contact with Hezbollah, our Islamic northern neighbors in Lebanon. We're afraid that Hezbollah will in the long run become the greatest threat to us. The Iranians have already brought thousands of short range missiles into Lebanon that they can use to hit the entire northern part of our country. They are busy infiltrating Syria, even though everyone thinks that they are being reined in by the Syrians; and we're doing everything to collect data about them. Then we succeeded in getting Nuri to defect. With his family. We have given him a new identity. And the promise that we would help his daughter. Do you understand it now?"

"No, I understand nothing. What do you have to do with Miriam's death?"

"Have you gone crazy? The very question—Joop, don't become paranoid!"

"Why were you in the hospital that day?"

"Jesus! Because I was with you! To support you! Not to murder your daughter because we wanted to have her heart! We're capable of a lot, but not of such monstrosities!"

Joop believed him. He wanted to believe him. He had no choice but to believe him.

Philip said, "I telephoned when it was completely certain that she could no longer be saved—and because she had blood group AB. I managed to get Nuri's daughter placed at the top of the list. She was immediately transferred to Atlanta."

"Where does she live?" asked Joop.

"Maine. Portland, Maine. Joop, what do you want from her?"

Joop didn't know what he wanted. He wanted to see her. A girl. A living girl.

"Is she nineteen? Is that correct?"

"Yes."

"How is she? Do you know her?"

"I know her, yes. She is…has a life ahead of her. Don't destroy it, Joop."

Joop shook his head. He didn't want to destroy anything. The only thing he wanted was…he wanted to see her breathe. He wanted to hear her heart beat, even though that was impossible; he would have to take her pulse for that, place a hand on the scar on her chest. No, that was not possible. He only wanted to look at her. Actually, that was all.

"Tell me about the subject," said Philip.

"I don't know anything. He told me about his youth."

"Please tell me more. Do you have an hour for me? I would like you to remember as much as possible. The exact phrases. And that van…why a van? When you went to eat something in the Mexican restaurant, we quickly checked in the back. But we had no time—and we thought it was too risky—to open the door. Boxes. Five boxes. What was in them, do you know?"

"No. No idea. He had bought books. That's all I know."

"What books?"

"About the bridge. The Golden Gate. Three books."

"Three books? About the Golden Gate?"

"Yes. Why are you looking like that?"

Philip moved forward, leaned as close as possible to him, concentrated, completely absorbed in thoughts that Joop couldn't guess at.

"Did he say anything about it?"

"No. Why should he?" asked Joop agitated.

"Do you still remember the titles?"

"One at any rate. I knew that book. Do you think that…Philip, it was innocent! A man has bought a couple of books about the Golden Gate. I did the same years ago!"

"Joop, he can barely read."

"He's a nice man. Rough, but not malicious."

Even sweet, the way Omar had, silent and moved, listened to Joop's story. Joop had continued looking at him in the reflection of the soft green dashboard light. The patches of light that their car threw on the straight, unlit highway. The red taillights of the cars ahead of them. The bright headlights on the other side of the divided highway. Joop had told him everything about Miriam.

Omar had asked, "So these hackers should break into their computers?"

"Yes. I'd gladly pay five thousand dollars for that." He didn't have it at the time. Now he did.

"Those guys seem to be able to do everything," Omar had revealed. "They break in everywhere. At the Pentagon, you name it. But it is against the law, Joop. A respectable man like you should know that."

"I understand that, yes."

"And what will you do when you get the information?"

"Nothing. I only want to hear a name."

"You aren't going to do anything foolish, are you?" Omar had asked.

"What should I do? Get back the heart? No…I only want to… perhaps talk with the person who…feels my daughter's heart beat."

"Strange, yes. That never occurred to me," Omar had said.

Philip got up, followed by Joop who grabbed him by an arm.

"What are you going to do with him?" asked Joop.

"I don't know. But as soon as you know something, you're responsible. I know, and therefore I have to do something now."

"What are you going to do? Philip, he helped me! With compassion!"

"Those Internet boys of his, those are the hackers?"

"Yes."

"Joop, you're not very clever, are you?"

"What?" Joop reacted, confused, wondering what he was missing now.

"Those hackers. They found a house on the rue Rabelais as the address of Abbasi. The street of our embassy. There is a link between you, that girl, and us. Do you understand?"

"So…what now?"

Finally he let go of Philip, waking up to the risk that he had taken.

"Philip, what are you going to do with Omar?"

"I'm afraid that you won't hear much from Mr. Van Lieshout anymore."

Joop did not want to know what these words meant. He asked, "May I see her? Philip, can you arrange that?"

Part three

Chapter forty

Well over forty-eight hours later, Joop was dropped off at home by a taxi. The afternoon flight from Portland, Maine, via New York to LA had taken more than seven hours, and because of the time difference he could put his weekend bag in the unlit hall by as early as seven o'clock. The only light burning was in the kitchen.

Smiling, Erroll appeared in the doorway of the kitchen.

"Mr. Koopm'n! Welcome home! Did you have a good trip?"

"Yes. It was…it was good, yes."

"Did it go well in San Francisco?"

Erroll didn't know that he had been in Portland, and Joop answered, "Everything went well."

"Can I pour you something? A cup of tea?"

Joop was tired and could do without a conversation, but he was happy that someone was at home.

"A cup of tea, yes."

"Sit down. I've saved the papers."

"Great."

Joop followed him into the kitchen. A spotless counter, neatly stacked newspapers on the table.

"Did you manage to have a good time, sir?"

"No," Joop answered curtly.

"No? That's too bad. I've worked hard—did a lot of research. I think I figured it out."

"Figured what out?"

With his back toward him, Erroll filled a kettle with water. "Figured out...don't get angry; I really think that I've discovered more...about Miriam."

Joop felt an uncontrollable repugnance rise up, a suffocating anger at Erroll's obsession.

"I don't want to hear anything!" he exploded. "I never want to talk about it again! You hear that? It's been enough. No understanding! No fussing around! No discoveries! Lay off!"

Erroll turned around, holding the kettle, and stared at him, startled.

"Mr. Koopm'n, sorry, I want...I only want to help. Things that I know now, that I didn't know at first. I don't want to cause you distress. I've only...I've gone deeply into things. That's all. I'm sorry."

He lowered his head, and Joop immediately regretted his outburst.

"God, I shouldn't have reacted like that. I'm tired...I'm exhausted...If you really want to—is it something that I really should hear?"

Erroll turned to the counter. "Not if you don't want to."

"I don't know if I want to."

"I accept that. Maybe later. When you're ready for it. In a year or so."

"What did you discover?" Joop asked calmly.

"I've researched things."

"Researched? What things?"

"Things about the world. About how the world works."

"Did you learn these things from the Jews?"

"No," answered Erroll over his shoulder, "this is different. I've read. I started talking with everyone, those...involved. Circumstances. I've been to the library. I've researched it."

"Circumstances?" repeated Joop.

"A confluence of circumstances, sir."

"And you can report about that?"

"That I can. But I've written it all down. You can read it if you want."

Chapter forty-one

It was ten o'clock at night when Joop and Erroll left the house. Silently they walked down Superba and took the shortest way to the beach. It was dry, the temperature mild.

A handful of fearless joggers and bicyclists followed the dark concrete path. The thousands of lights of the city promised warmth, intense discussions, filled restaurants, living rooms full of security, laughter in movie theaters, but on the silent beach the only thing that could be heard was the deep black ocean which lay almost sleeping behind the sand. Joop had taken the pink backpack from the coat hook to carry his wallet, telephone, and notebook. It had not been hard for him. The little backpack offered him safety, like a suit of armor.

After fifteen minutes, Erroll broke the silence. "Everything fine with your friend Linda?"

"No, God."

"That's a disappointment, sir. I...I thought she was a nice woman."

"Me too, but...I was mistaken."

"Mistaken? That's terrible."

On the sand, the homeless were getting ready for the night. Rags were used to make the climbing frames on the children's playground into an improvised tent.

Joop listened to the languid rhythm of the waves in which her remains were dissolved.

"Linda had discovered something," he said, "no, someone in Switzerland had discovered something. A banker. Money of my grandfather's. But this Swiss banker—I think that he was initially planning nothing malicious—he was looking for a family member of my grandfather. And because I was no longer registered in the Netherlands, he found only…he found Linda. Then they concocted a plan. A clever plan. Her plan, I think. I'll write about it. They swindled me. Robbed me. They had my grandfather's money transferred to the Antilles, and from there to other banks. Of course, stealing is technically speaking not correct."

"But she was…she seemed an honest person. And does that priest know about it?"

"God, that man was probably not real. Tibetan monks are not called Usso Apury. I think that it was a made-up name."

"All that seems against the law."

"Maybe so, yes. I think that she has hated me all these years."

"Why would she hate you?"

"She was sent away from the Netherlands by my parents. And she knew that I didn't defend her. Out of self-protection. It was also better for her—I thought at the time. But maybe she was right."

"She was very fond of you."

"Really? I no longer know. I'm confused, I think."

"Was it a lot of money?"

"A lot of money."

"And you discovered all that in San Francisco?"

"I found out early this morning. Yesterday she suddenly disappeared. From the hotel where she was staying. Without leaving any message. I started to…to feel something then. A friend of mine from Israel has reconstructed all this for me. It took him no more than half an hour. A couple of telephone calls, and he figured it out. The Swiss man was no longer a banker. He suddenly quit a month ago. I think that they had an affair. They had me sign papers that I shouldn't have signed. Real documents in which I relinquished the money. I'll write about it; that I promise you. It was good for something."

"The monk said wise things."

"Yes? Perhaps he was real. But in the airplane I played around a little with the letters of his name. Usso Apury—I think that it's an anagram."

"An anagram? Of what, sir?"

"Up your ass."

Erroll chuckled. "Sorry."

"Actually you're right," said Joop, and he grinned with him. "And I've started to write again, God."

"I'm very glad to hear that, sir. I empathize with you. People exist by the grace of stories. May I hold your hand?"

"Yes, God."

Joop felt Erroll's strong fingers protectively holding his searching hand.

"Where are you actually from, God?"

"You know that, don't you? South Central LA."

"How did you become who you are?"

"Every sociologist and psychologist knows that, don't they? An unmarried mother, three children from three different fathers. Drugs at every street corner and quick and easy money. Elliott, my oldest brother—at ten he did his first burglary, at twelve his first armed robbery. But I didn't belong there. I don't know why, a birth defect. I loved to read. I went to the library and devoured Henry James, Faulkner, Poe. On the radio I listened to Mozart, Bach, Schubert. Until I was fifteen, I could retreat from everything. Then we were assaulted at home. A drive-by shooting. We were sitting on the porch outside. Elliott was the target. He caught seven bullets in his body and bled to death. I had three hits. I passed out when the paramedics arrived. Hitting the mark is not so difficult with my size. I was in the hospital for two months, and that was paid for by a Jewish charity; my mother couldn't pay for health insurance. I had to do physical therapy, and then I began to realize that I had to use my body for my future. I had almost let it be shot to bits. At seventeen I was youth karate champion of California. I read Bellow and Roth and Singer. I earned money with advertising work and show performances, and then it just continued. Up to and including God's Gym."

"And now?"

"Now I'm going to work on my body again. Take care that I can make a come-back. I have until my thirtieth with karate. You can't keep it up for long when you're in your thirties."

"You shouldn't have sold your gym. It was your life."

"Until December twenty-second. Then everything changed. For you. For me."

"I don't believe your story at all, God."

"No?"

"No."

"Then what do you want to hear, sir?"

"The truth."

"There is no truth in suffering, in the cause of suffering, in the end of suffering, nor in the path. There is no wisdom, and there is no purpose."

And so they continued their walk.

Chapter forty-two

When the windshield threatened to become covered by snow, Danny turned on the windshield wipers and made sure that Joop had an unobstructed view of the school complex. Lights were on behind all the windows.

They had flown via New York and had reached Portland late in the evening in heavy snow. Joop was not dressed for snow and freezing cold, nor was Danny. Until he fell asleep in the Holiday Inn, he had leafed through the magazines and colored folders about Maine that lay in his room. A state of lobsters, moose, thousands of islands, and zillions of mosquitoes. It was still snowing when he woke up. On the cleared streets they drove in a rental car to her school. Danny continued to be cold, even though he turned the heater to its highest setting. The wipers squeaked across the glass and pushed the snow to the corners of the windshield. A couple of times Joop rubbed the misted-over side window with his arm. They avoided the center—a real downtown with a few skyscrapers—and under a sky filled with snow they drove to one of the suburbs situated on the hills. The rest of the city lay under a thick white blanket. Both of them smoked.

Twenty minutes before the start of classes Danny parked the

car across from the school, a three-story brick building next to snow-covered basketball courts and athletic fields. These were separated from the street by a wire-mesh fence to which the snow was sticking. A northern suburb. Wide streets with detached houses. Snowmen. Smoking chimneys. Mountain ranges of pushed-away snow edged the sidewalks.

The school was on a small shopping street with a couple of fast food restaurants, a supermarket, a laundromat, a small bookstore. In an uninterrupted stream, SUVs and station wagons stopped in front of the entrance of the school. Kids of all ages got out of the cars with big bags or backpacks and, slipping and sliding, hurried into the building. A white Mercury station wagon approached.

"There she is," said Danny.

Joop got out, suddenly his legs were weak.

"Don't do anything foolish, Mr. Koopman," said Danny.

Joop didn't answer. Quickly he started to cross the street. He watched the Mercury which stopped in front of the school. After one or two steps, his thin summer shoes, which offered enough protection in California, became drenched with the brown mud on the road. When he reached the sidewalk in front of the school, the moisture had penetrated his shoes and he felt that his socks were sopping wet. He trembled with cold. The back door swung open. Two girls got out. The first one was around fourteen, a red cap on her head, a thick scarf, mittens, and red rubber boots on her feet. She walked straight to the entrance. Then an older girl got out.

Joop walked toward her. She leaned inside for a moment and said something to the driver, a woman of around forty, a dark, good-looking woman who looked over her shoulder at the girl and spoke with her for a moment. The girl nodded and slammed the door shut. She remained standing and waved when the Mercury accelerated.

Joop reached her before she could walk away. Maybe she would recognize him, maybe something in her heart said that she knew him. So this was what had driven him all that time: the chance of recognition by her heart.

"Sorry," he said. His lower jaw trembled and he hoped that she didn't feel threatened. "I have a silly question. I have an appointment with the director. But I've lost his name. Something like Gelson."

He had clenched his fists, held them in front of his mouth, and blew warmth into them. In her eyes he searched for a sparkle, a moment of reunion. A heart transplant took three hours, an operation that had become almost routine and could be compared to placing a new motor in a car: tighten screws, connect tubes and wires, give it the spark of life with the starter.

"Garrison," she said suspiciously. Her hand slipped into her jacket. Every family member carried a beeper that could warn one of the two American security officers, who were living in a house near her home.

She was smaller than Miriam. Large, pitch-black eyes. A narrow, pointed nose. Thin lips, a small vulnerable face. She wore a bulky nylon jacket, a scarf that was wrapped around her neck once or twice, and gloves, but she left her hair uncovered. Black hair that tumbled onto the scarf and the shoulders of the jacket. Snowflakes fell on her head and on her face. She had innocent eyes. Expectant eyes. Confidence-inspiring eyes. Eyes that had forgotten the pain in her chest. Eyes that didn't know him.

With the back of her glove she wiped her cheek. Breath steamed from her mouth.

He tried to inhale it.

"I'm visiting some schools in the area because we're going to live here. Do you think it's a good school?"

She stamped on the ground a couple of times, keeping her feet warm. Her heart pumped warm blood to her ankles. She wanted to go inside and replied in order to get rid of him.

"Yes," she said.

"Garrison," repeated Joop. "Thanks."

She nodded with a standoffish smile and moved cautiously to the door, placing her feet carefully, balancing herself with her heavy book bag. She wore calf-length suede boots, fur-trimmed, with thick soles. Because of the bulky coat he couldn't judge how she was built, but she seemed slight, almost fragile. Very carefully, as if she was afraid to harm her vulnerable body, she inched away from him. She would probably report about him later.

The condensation now steamed over her shoulder, toward him; and he knew why she could walk, why she could talk and go to classes and could giggle with her girlfriends in a Burger King during recess and during weekends and could dream about love at night.

Joop turned back, staggered across the street. He knew that they could mislead him. He hadn't asked her for her name, and perhaps she had been born with a strong heart, but he had made his peace with her. Whoever she was. For him she was Alia. When he made a move to get into the warm car, Danny said: "Go back. You have an appointment with the principal."

"Do I really have to?"

"Do it. We mustn't arouse suspicion."

Joop crossed the street again. His toes were cold and wet. In the hall he checked in with a teacher. He was directed to an office. Subsequently he lied to a nice fat man with a childish face. He was coming to live here, was looking for a school for his children. He received a brochure with information about the school.

At one o'clock Joop and Danny were back at the school. Alia came out without her younger sister and got into the white Mercury next to her mother. The car started up with half-skidding tires on the slippery road and slowly drove past them through the thick snowflakes. Joop turned around and watched the car, the stream of exhaust gases, and the red taillights. Through the rear window of the Mercury he could see the increasingly vague outline of her head, half above the seat back, until the snow on the rear window of the car in which he was sitting blocked his view.

In silence they drove back to the hotel. He would ask Philip if he could give her an organizer, under the pretext of a present from the Mossad. Of course she had one, but it was doubtful that she had a Kate Spade organizer. Alia would fill the days that Miriam could no longer experience.

In his room he took off his shoes, rubbed his feet warm, and called the Fairmont. Longing for her voice, for insight, for tenderness, he asked for Linda.

She had left the hotel.

Without leaving a message, she had checked out.

Chapter forty-three

In the evening, in the hotel in Portland, Joop found some blank sheets of paper in a desk drawer next to the TV and a hotel pen on the nightstand. He sat down and wrote.

"Miriam admired the Hungarian mathematician Paul Erdös, who had arranged his whole existence around his search for the only true form of knowledge in the cosmos. He devoted his life to mathematics and had no house, no children, no wife, no possessions. Only an old suitcase and a worn orange plastic bag from a Hungarian department store. Erdös was her hero. When she was haunted by the fear that she would never be capable of rivaling Erdös's extreme discipline and way of life—because she wanted to go out, flirt, love—then I would say that one day she would know how she should lead her life. Because what is not of value disappears with time.

She was thirteen when, in imitation of her mother, she called me *The Merchant of Venice*. My name in full is Joop Herman Koopman ('merchant' in English), I am forty-seven years old, live in Venice, California, and am a screenwriter by profession. We had a fight about raising her allowance—she thought I was stingy—and suddenly she knew what she would call me. I burst out laughing, and her angry face showed surprise, followed by satisfaction, and then she joined in the laughter.

On December 22, 2000, she turned seventeen.

The average temperature on that day was 52 degrees Fahrenheit. The high was 62 and the low 46. Average wind speed was 5.3 miles per hour. The highest wind speed was 10.25. There were fog banks. Visibility varied from 1.75 to 4 miles an hour. No precipitation."

Epilogue

Continuation of the confluence of circumstances

Notes by God for Mr. Koopman

Elaine Jacobs

Like most of the over four hundred theoretical physicists in the world who explore the boundaries of the fundamental knowledge of matter, Elaine Jacobs wrestled with gravity.

Between the two central paradigms of physics—the quantum theory and the theory of relativity—there used to be a wide gap without hope of reconciliation. Until the string theory was formulated. Ultimately, the string theory seemed to reconcile quantum mechanics, the theory that describes everything that is known about matter, that is to say elementary particles and their interaction, with the general theory of relativity, the theory of space and time which among other things describes the evolution of the cosmos. This reconciliation did not come without a cost. Because string theory asserted the following: in addition to the familiar four dimensions of space-time (height, width, depth, time), there exist six other spatial dimensions. But these extra dimensions could not be determined experimentally. Most physicists assumed that this would never be possible because the size of these dimensions was much too small to ever be observed, with no matter what machine. To find out what exactly was going on at small-scale distances, physicists built ever larger particle accelerators, a kind of super microscope that enabled physicists to discern a billionth of a billionth of a centimeter and to discover quarks as the smallest building stones of matter. But that was by no means sufficient to show the strings themselves, or these internal dimensions—they were a millionth of a billionth smaller. To penetrate so inconceivably deeply into matter, accelerators would have to be built with the diameter of the solar system, a disillusioning prospect which caused these physicists to begin to fear that the string theory would be eternally doomed to being considered as metaphysical hot air. String theory was, to be sure, a brilliant construct of the human mind, but it was not a reliable, empirically based theory—not in the twentieth century and not in the thirtieth either. Moreover, there were countless phenomena for which the strings could not give an explanation, while they should be able to do just that. Granted, both the theory of relativity and the standard model of elementary particles seemed to be covered by string theory, but the gigantic difference in strength between gravity and the other fundamental forces (electromagnetic, strong and weak) remained a mystery.

Elaine lived with her husband Fred Jacobs and their black Labrador Albert—after Einstein—in a spacious apartment on the PCH. Through the enormous window of her study she could see the waves of the Pacific hit the beach under the building. The four fundamental forces had originated in the Big Bang itself, when the whole universe observed by men was an inconceivably small cup with inconceivably hot quark and gluon soup. And everything that was now present in the cosmos—the sea, Albert, her desk, and her own body—was constructed according to a master plan out of the building blocks that had originated through cooling, right after the Big Bang. Order from chaos—that could be understood scientifically, but why was gravity so much weaker than the other three? Why did the parameters in these beautiful theories have the exact values they had: coincidence?

Newton's law of gravity explained perfectly the attraction and the movement of large objects like the sun, the moon, the earth, an apple that falls from a tree, but how did gravity work at extremely small distances? Calculations pointed out that gravity does get as strong as the other forces at ten to the minus thirty-fifth meter, a length that can't be tested. Elaine was searching for a theoretical model that would be able to explain this unmanageable hierarchy between the strengths of the different forces, and with this she hoped to be able to unlock the path to the "theory of everything." She wouldn't find God with it, but instead the certainty that the cosmos is built according to the rules of a unique, knowable theory, and she realized that many people would call that theory God. Not she. For her, God was at most a mathematical equation.

As early as the nineteen-twenties, the Polish/German mathematician Kaluza and the Swedish physicist Klein had developed a theory about the unification of gravity and electromagnetism that used an extra dimension. Their theory was expanded to at least nine spatial dimensions by modern string theory. The six extra dimensions are, as it were, rolled up into very compact circles and spheres the size of ten to the minus thirty-fifth meter—a phenomenon that can be calculated by a cosmologist or a physicist—and are therefore invisible to human perception until the end of time. In conventional string theory, ten to the minus thirty-fifth is also—coincidentally?—the typical length of a string, the most fundamental physical object, a tiny, unique, very energetic rubber band that vibrates like a small string.

On December 22, 2000, at exactly twenty-five minutes past twelve, Elaine Jacobs closed the door of her apartment. Albert barked, but she couldn't take him along on her hunt for Christmas presents. As she walked to the elevator, Albert's pleading bark became weaker. He stayed behind, alone in the apartment, waiting desperately for her return, without the expectation that she would return, even though she always did return. While the elevator door closed, she still heard him softly calling her, imprisoned in his world. And during the elevator's descent, a movement that was impossible without gravity, she wondered if it was perhaps possible that three of the four fundamental interactions would be limited to the familiar three dimensions and that only gravity would be active in the six extra spatial dimensions, just as Albert's barking was audible inside the elevator, but the photons that could make his image appear on her retina were held back by the walls of the building.

Sound and light, two wave phenomena, but with totally different properties on the face of it; sound went around corners, crawled underneath doors, went effortlessly through walls. And light: straight against the wall where it was absorbed without seemingly leaving behind a trace. Noise could simply go into more directions than light. Essentially the same, but at the same time totally different under everyday, ordinary circumstances. Something just like these fundamental forces, that immensely relative weakness of gravity? Electromagnetism exists in three dimensions, but gravity in all ten—would that be it, she wondered.

A simple thought that made her almost sick to her stomach with fascination from one moment to the next. And she realized that she didn't actually know for sure whether gravity manifested itself at distances of a thousandth of a millimeter in the same way as at greater distances, since that had never been measured—why not? Why did we accept this without questioning? A thousandth of a millimeter was measurable; you could investigate that.

While she waited in the Explorer for a chance to drive away, the thought of a special, extra-dimensional action of gravity became increasingly strong. She swallowed, could barely manage to remain sitting still in her seat and felt a tingle go through her limbs that she recognized immediately as a sign that her work would take a liberating turn. The nervousness of a dog that smells a scent but is still on the leash. Albert was never on a leash. But he had barked at the right moment.

She found it a very strange coincidence that this idea had come to her in the elevator. Hadn't Einstein's central idea of the general theory of relativity come to him in an elevator? Elaine had gone over it a number of times with students at the university. The idea was simple: If you went in the elevator at a constant speed, you felt nothing special; all the experiments that you did in the elevator would be exactly the same as when you stood still. But at the moment that the elevator accelerated it would be different, you felt that immediately—you became heavy when going up and light when going down. If you cut the elevator cable, you would be weightless, and things that you dropped would not fall out of your hands. Free fall is a condition in which gravity is not operative. The best part was that the understanding of this very simple connection between relative movement and the force of gravity was the nucleus of the revolution in our thinking about space, time, and gravity that Einstein ultimately brought about.

Elaine could not rule out that she was on the track of the mysterious properties of gravity, and she quickly made some notes on the notepad that hung on the dashboard with a suction cup. At twenty-nine minutes to one she drove away, with trembling hands, a ringing head filled with breathtaking ideas.

(Dr. Jacobs revealed her new theory at the end of February in *The Archives,* an Internet site that has in the meantime become the most important cutting edge publication of theoretical physics.)

Frank Miller

Frank Miller waited for the medicines for Margaret. He had handed over the prescription and shuffled past the racks with knickknacks that were offered for sale in the drugstore. It was obviously the intention that those waiting would make impulse purchases, but that stuff was wasted on him. He possessed everything that he had ever wanted. They had had a good life, but he noticed that the warm glow of the past offered no consolation for what was awaiting Margaret and him in the near future. Fortunately they had already found God many years ago. Brian, who was nineteen minutes older than his brother Bill, had contracted bacterial meningitis at the age of sixteen and had almost died. But their prayers had been granted. Margaret and Frank had taken turns at the bedside in the hospital and on the bench at the Presbyterian church, and after an extremely high fever Brian recovered. Later, the doctors declared that the chance for recovery had been minimal, and Frank and Margaret were convinced that God had intervened. They remained thankful to Him for the rest of their lives. They led a careful, caring existence without great words or gestures, raised the twins to become serious, sound people, and supported each other and the people around them.

Frank failed to understand why God had decided to strike

Margaret. Maybe He wanted to tell them that they should prepare for the end of their life on earth. That is what they did. But they didn't want to take leave of their sons yet and accepted the medicines and Margaret's weaknesses in the bargain. Did God want to test whether they loved their children more than Him? Frank didn't know if he could give an answer to that. The eternal hereafter was probably not dearer to him than a day with his children. He suppressed such thoughts with the realization that nothing was hidden from Him.

"Mr. Miller?" he heard behind his back.

Frank turned around and looked into the face of a stout, dark man with graying sideburns. The man wore an expensive silk shirt and had sunglasses in his hand. Large, lively eyes. And Frank still remembered his name.

"Mr. Banelli," he said.

Banelli grinned and shook his hand at length.

"Mr. Miller, it's been a long time! When did you retire?"

"Eleven years ago."

"Every time that I enter the bank, I think of you. I'll never forget what you've done for me."

Frank had given him a loan for his travel agency, even though Banelli did not completely meet all the requirements and had in fact hardly any collateral—he was an enthusiastic young businessman with a detailed business plan, and Frank knew that he would put his heart and soul into his business. He had convinced the credit committee that Banelli would fulfill his obligations.

"Mr. Miller, we have just opened our one hundred and sixtieth branch. When I came to you the first time, I had made the rounds of quite a few banks, but you were the only one who believed in me. And the stupid thing is…I've thought about it for a long time…I want to do something in return. I couldn't do that when you were still with the bank—there are rules against that. But now, Mr. Miller, I want to offer you a trip—for two. By the way, how are you?"

"I'm all right," said Frank. He didn't want to say that his wife had had a serious stroke. Her face was crooked, but she could again think reasonably well, and sometimes she could even stand and take a few steps.

"May I offer you a trip? I'm serious, Mr. Miller. You can go to any spot on the planet. Europe, Africa, it makes no difference. I want to thank you. Better late than never. This is the moment. Good that I met you here. Where would you like to go, Mr. Miller?"

Frank knew, but he doubted that he could talk about it. Lately the memories were more intense, which had happened because he had seen *The Thin Red Line,* the film by Terrence Malick about the fighting on Guadalcanal where Frank had fought in 1942. He had shown courage there and received a decoration. He would like to go and look around there, but the question was whether Margaret would be allowed to travel or could be transported there.

A car horn sounded outside, and for a moment he knew that it was meant for him because he had parked his car in front of an exit.

"You're taking me by surprise with this," said Frank.

"I should have contacted you much sooner. I'm bad at this sort of thing; I forget birthdays and presents for my wife. But I'm not letting you go now. You have to give me your address; I'll give you my business card."

Banelli pulled his wallet from his back pocket and took out his business card. "AFI—Affordable Flights International," Frank read. Outside, the car horn kept screaming for attention.

"I really want you to accept this, Mr. Miller. You'd be doing me a big favor. If I hadn't run into you, I wouldn't have had this chance. Will you think about it?"

Over the years Frank had put aside enough money to be able to finance the trip himself, but he had never really considered it. And oddly enough, at his age almost every expenditure—even for personal purchases like clothing and food—became a wasteful act. They had never thrown money around, but with advancing years they had become thrifty in order to leave their children, both doctors with ample incomes, as much as possible. Strange how, as you became older, you slowly wi hdrew from the world.

"Yes, it's an unbelievably wonderful offer," answered Frank, bewildered by the thought that he wanted to go to Guadalcanal. Until a minute ago it hadn't been clear at all that this wish had been dormant in the back of his mind for several years. Starting on

October 7, 1942, he had fought as a member of the First Battalion Seventh Marines under the legendary Colonel "Chesty" Puller on Edson's Ridge and had participated in the battle during the night of October twenty-fourth. While the rain came down in buckets, the battalion, which had drawn up an almost one mile long defense line in the jungle to protect the vital Henderson airfield, had held out for three hours against a superior number of Japanese. Frank belonged to the squad that operated one of the sixty mortar batteries. "Chesty" repeatedly turned up at different places behind his men and spurred them on, seemingly fearless, not afraid of the thousands of Japanese or of death. While firing mortars, Frank had prayed. He caused death because he valued life.

"I have to discuss it with my wife, may I call you tomorrow?"

The car horn now had a rhythmic sound. Maybe Frank's car was in the way. But he wanted to know whether Banelli made an empty promise out of politeness or sincerely wanted to give him a present.

(Until now there has been no contact between Frank Miller and Leo Banelli).

Jeremy Swindon

It was love at first sight. Jeremy Swindon had never believed in it, an illusion of young girls, old women, and scriptwriters who delivered stories as fairy tales for the studios. It took months before he dared to admit it. He had been convinced that he was incapable of love. Until he met Jonathan Golding. Jeremy had already produced three films when he entered Jonathan's room at an agency in a pre-war building on Wilshire Boulevard whose art deco style features had survived the demolition of the sixties. It was three o'clock in the afternoon, and the bright California September sun was kept out of the room by green Venetian blinds. Jeremy was taken to Jonathan's room by a secretary, and as he entered, Jonathan stood up behind his desk, a tall, slim, dark-haired man just like he, and the same age. His black jacket hung around the back of his leather desk chair; he wore a white shirt, a soft yellow necktie, dark gray suspenders, and they looked at each other surprised, struck by something that Jeremy could not describe. He had come to discuss the casting of a new film with Jonathan, but the conversation went beyond the names of actors and actresses and their market value, salaries and conditions. After only ten minutes they told each other about their families, their ambitions, their doubts—strangers who did not want to make a secret of anything from each other. After forty-five minutes, Jonathan canceled the later meetings of that day, and they continued talking until late in the evening.

Jeremy had never attributed the cause of his failed loves to a possible homosexual inclination. Initially he told himself that his friendship with Jonathan, which developed in a conventional male manner (going together to basketball games, to special film screenings, jogging in Santa Monica, sweating in the gym), differed in no way from his other relationships with men. But his longing for Jonathan's glance, for a touch of his hand, for a sign of affection, penetrated his daydreams and caused a kind of despair that he had not known before. Jonathan too had initially had a depressing string of affairs with women, but he'd had to conclude that he was denying something that had waited for acceptance since his adolescence.

After months of almost daily contact, Jeremy decided that the strange inclinations that trapped him in despair and didn't allow for a second's concentration on his work, encroached too much on his life. He feigned work and trips to other parts of the country and tried to rid himself of the sick pain in his stomach.

After three weeks his doorbell rang one evening. The blurry video image from the security camera at the front door showed Jonathan standing outside. Champagne, red roses—desperate, touching symbols that had to express the unutterable with clichés. Jonathan stood there like a man courting a woman. Jeremy opened the door. Unsmiling, trembling nervously, Jonathan presented his offerings. Silently, Jeremy accepted the bottle and the flowers. He placed the bottle on the table in the living room and felt Jonathan standing very close behind him. Then felt Jonathan throw his arms around him and put his head on his shoulder. And it was ridiculous that both of them started to sob like schoolgirls—until they were overcome by hilarity and through their tears got the giggles for minutes on end. When he recovered, gasping and with wet cheeks, Jeremy no longer gave a damn what he should call his feelings for Jonathan and how the world would react. He threw his arms around Jonathan and kissed him the way he used to kiss women. He had come home.

It was December 22, 1979, thirteen minutes past nine in the evening. A year later they bought a house in Malibu together; they started to produce movies as a twosome and were as successful as their sense of quality allowed.

Jonathan had caught his illness during one of the wild parties that they had given in the eighties. They were faithful to each other, but once or twice a year they were not monogamous. Jeremy, his life partner, was not affected by the disease; this occurred from time to time—a medical mystery which, according to the doctors, could probably be explained by genetic resistance and chance. The symptoms of the illness failed to appear for such a long time that they produced the illusion that the illness would pass Jonathan by. But one day they appeared, many years after the first diagnosis. Jeremy did not leave his side and took care of him, cherished him when the fear became too great to be laughed off, searched for the newest medicines and the most modern therapies, and saw him through his final hour.

He had not needed to use six of the filled morphine ampules. Together with hypodermic syringes they lay in a leather case between condoms, cufflinks, watches, and rings in a drawer in their vast walk-in closet where sixty suits, two hundred shirts, and sixty pairs of shoes waited. After Jonathan's death he had not disposed of anything.

At the approach of Jeremy's sixty-fifth birthday on December 28, 2000, he realized that he had spent his previous birthday alone and in mourning and that he did not have the strength to grow old by himself. At Jonathan's side he had discovered his qualities and weaknesses but had also realized that without him he had arms without hands. When he called Kelly Hendel, his decision had been made. The celebration of his last birthday would take place on December twenty-second, exactly twenty-one years after their first kiss, and at nine o'clock in the evening he would inject the morphine ampules into his blood just as he had done for Jonathan.

Kelly doubted that they would get much of a response to the invitation to a pre-Christmas party because there would be lots of cocktail parties on the twenty-second, but Jeremy was adamant about a lunch event. In addition, he insisted that everything be cleaned up by seven o'clock. He wrote his testament and had it delivered to his attorney in a closed envelope—on which he wrote a melodramatic "To be opened after my death."

Although he had been agnostic all of his life, the expectation that he would reunite with Jonathan became stronger as the date neared. The most beautiful part of his life would then become a circle, and he was convinced that in this way he would pay tribute to Jonathan.

In complete peace he watched how a team of Latinos prepared the party under Kelly's direction that morning. As always no detail escaped her; she reprimanded the staff; she called late caterers to order; she alerted a waiter to a spot on his shirt, and checked whether the tables stood perfectly level on the grass. Jeremy took a bite from all the colorful salads, quiches, and cakes and remembered—sad and yearning at the same time—the meals that he had enjoyed with Jonathan in Kyoto, Florence, Paris, Buenos Aires. And soon again. Soon, forever.

(On the morning of December twenty-eighth, Jeremy Swindon was found dead by Kelly Hendel, who had wanted to review the party with him but had no answer to her telephone calls.)

Juan Armillo

When Juan had the early shift, he had to report at four o'clock in the morning; but he could combine the late shift, which started at ten o'clock, with an evening's work as valet at one of the many upscale restaurants that offered their guests the convenience of a friendly Latino.

The restaurant theatrics started outside on the street. After stopping his car and having the car door opened by a quick hand, the guest casually placed the key in the opened hand of the faceless valet and then strode inside commandingly. Evenings around the holidays, during the weekend, and in the summer when the German and Japanese tourists drove up in their rental cars, Juan could earn a hundred dollars. A quiet, chilly Thursday evening right before Christmas brought in little. Yet, after walking into his one-room apartment on Melrose at eleven thirty, he counted twenty thousand dollars in one-hundred-dollar bills. The proceeds of one evening's parking and pulling up cars at Le Ciel on Robertson.

It was robbery. Just like the other valets, he sometimes looked inside the glove compartment. Sometimes you'd find a weapon, a dildo, condoms, drugs that made for tall tales as they waited outside. At nine thirty an old model Mercedes drove up. Juan opened the door, let the driver get out—a man of sixty, perhaps sixty-five, who looked like a doctor or an accountant and was accompanied by an equally old woman—and drove the car to the parking lot. The corner of a beige envelope stuck out of the glove compartment. A thick envelope with a lot of hundred-dollar bills. He didn't dare to count them, suddenly looked around him, afraid and sick with desire, and decided to take the envelope with him and hide it in his own old Corolla.

Discovery was unavoidable. Who leaves behind so much money in a car? Was it drug money? Illegal income? Or was he now being filmed by a hidden camera for a TV program about valets stealing? When the people got into their car later on, they would see right away what had happened. And maybe the man was no doctor but instead a professional criminal, and Juan had just signed his own death warrant.

A few minutes later he brought back a Cadillac for departing guests. With a screwdriver he forced the lock of one of the back doors of the Mercedes. When he was again waiting in front of the restaurant, the tension was almost unbearable and he paced back and forth, smoking continuously. Fredo, his colleague who was in charge that evening, asked him why he was so restless, and Juan answered that his stomach was bothering him. Many Latinos had upset stomachs. They ate too much and their food was too greasy. Fredo said that he could go home if he wanted; this evening they could easily handle things with just two of them. Drifting on the road, as if he were drunk, Juan drove his Corolla to the poor part of Melrose where he lived.

He hadn't touched a drop but was dizzy with fear and excitement. If he were stopped, they would find the money.

Around midnight he decided to pack a bag and flee, but he didn't know to where. He had stolen a lot of money, but it was a fraction of what he needed for a carefree future. Half an hour later he started to realize that he could live on this money for at most a year and that what he had done was sheer madness. There was no proof that he was the thief, and messing with the lock of the back door had been a smart move that he could use to ward off any accusation. At around four o'clock in the morning he thought that he should go to the police to report the money as found—discovered by chance in the parking lot—for this sum was not worth so much uncertainty.

At six o'clock in the morning he was so exhausted that he fell asleep. At nine thirty he was woken up by the telephone. His boss Michel from Progress Bakery. No police. No Fredo. No mafia boss demanding his money. Michel was a young Frenchman, a nice guy who was easy-going in dealing with Latinos and showed patience and understanding. Juan had never been late, and he knew that Michel would forgive him. Come quickly, said Michel calmly, when you get here we'll be half an hour behind schedule.

Juan hurried to the bakery. He had hidden the money in a plastic bag in the toilet tank, just as he had sometimes seen in movies. It was a mystery why people left twenty thousand dollars in their car, and it was a mystery that he was still alive. Maybe these people had themselves stolen the money somewhere and were happy to be rid of it. Just as he would be happy when he was rid of it. Maybe he should throw it away or burn it. He had the feeling that the plastic bag in the toilet tank didn't contain banknotes but a bomb, and it was completely clear to him that he was not a born thief. When he drove off in the truck and encountered a badly parked car, he hit the horn furiously in anger and regret.

(Of course I have imagined the above, but I went to him because I wanted to know how he was doing. When I arrived at the building where he lives, he was just getting into a used Chevrolet Camaro in excellent condition, a fast red convertible with a wide white racing stripe that he purchased six weeks after the accident. He really can't afford such a car on his salary at Progress Bakery. The young woman with him was a pretty Latina with thick black hair that shone almost blue in the sun. It was a beautiful, warm day. She wore a light blue silk dress with short, puffed sleeves, a petticoat that let the seams of her dress dance around her legs as she walked, a flower in her hair, dressed up as women from the South do for a party. He opened the door for her and waited until she was seated. She grabbed his shoulder when he pressed on the gas pedal and drove away with screeching tires, her hair blown about.

Perhaps they'll get married. Perhaps they'll have children. And perhaps they'll grow very old together. Perhaps there's a good story in it for you about hope and happiness, Mr. Koopman.)

About the Author

Leon de Winter is a prize-winning Dutch novelist, born in 1954. He is also an internationally recognized film writer and director. This is his second book to be translated into English. His first, *Hoffman's Hunger*, is also available from *The* Toby Press.

The fonts used in this book are from the Garamond family

Other works by Leon de Winter
available from *The* Toby Press
Hoffman's Hunger

The Toby Press publishes fine writing, available at
bookstores everywhere. For more information,
please visit www.tobypress.com